I0708319

VILNIUS
UNDER FOUR FLAGS

VILNIUS

UNDER FOUR FLAGS

A Novel by

GRACE AUSTIN

HIPPOCLIDES PRESS

180 East Pearson Street
Suite 3506
Chicago, Illinois 60611
hippoclidespress.com

BOOKS TO CHALLENGE THE COMPLACENT

ISBN: Hard Cover: 979-8-9865594-3-8
ISBN: eBook   987-8-9865594-4-5

Region Map Image Credit: Peter Hermes Furian

Printed in the United States of America

VILNIUS, LITHUANIA
BALTIC SEA REGION

LITHUANIA TERRITORY 1939-1940

From Wikimedia Commons

Timeline

1918	February 16, Lithuanian Independence from Russia declared
1920	Treaty of Versailles: Klaipeda under French mandate Peace treaties signed with Russia and Poland
1922	Vilnius annexed by Poland: Kaunas temporary capital
1923	Lithuanian army took back Klaipeda
1926	President Smetona was elected and served until 1940
1936	Depression in Lithuania
1939	March, Germany occupied Klaipeda
1939	August, German-Russian non-aggression pact
1939	September, USSR occupied Vilnius after invading Poland
1939	October, USSR ceded Vilnius to Lithuania
1940	June, USSR occupied Lithuania
1941	January, Germany sold part of Lithuania to USSR
1941	June, USSR mass deportations of Lithuanians into Siberia
1941	June, Nazi occupation of Lithuania
1944	Red Army reoccupied Lithuania
1944	Lithuania under USSR occupation
1990	Declaration of the restoration of Lithuanian independence
1991	January, attack on the Vilnius TV tower
1991	September, USSR Supreme Soviet voted to recognize the restoration of Lithuanian independence

CONTENTS

PROLOGUE

Vilnius is a city born of a dream. King Gediminas, asleep after a hunt, had a vision of an iron wolf howling on top of a hill. Was it a howl of victory or a howl of pain? This legend, instructing Gediminas to build a fortress on the hill, made Vilnius the capital of Lithuania. The name is a multifaceted mirror reflecting its inhabitants: the Lithuanian Vilnius, the Polish Wilno, the Jewish Vilne, the Russian Vilna, and the German Wilna. At the crossroads of Europe, Vilnius is surrounded by endless forests, winding rivers, and swampy marshes where pagan people worshiped nature—the sun, snakes, thunder, and stars.

Vilnius lives in the heart of Lithuania, a country in existence since AD 1000 but officially united in response to invaders who were determined to convert its pagans to Christianity. The following two centuries were marked by continual wars between the Crusaders and the Lithuanians. Mindaugas, the grand duke, converted to Christianity in 1251 so the Teutonic Knights would leave Lithuania in peace, but he renounced the Catholic faith after two years.

One hundred years later, King Gediminas, the last remaining pagan ruler in Europe (but also a broad-minded man), gave freedom of worship to all religions. The quest of the Catholic Church to baptize him was met with his answer: "Let the devil himself baptize me!" The pagan elite finally accepted the Catholic faith in 1387 after a marriage between his grandson Jagiello and the Polish princess Jadvyga. This union produced the Lithuanian-Polish Commonwealth.

Victory was proclaimed in 1410 at the First Battle of Tannenberg when the Polish and Lithuanian forces led by Gediminas's grandsons, Vytautas (grand duke of Lithuania) and Jagiello (king of Poland), defeated the Teutonic Order. The combined forces made Lithuania the most powerful and largest country in Europe, stretching from the Baltic to the Black Sea.

Due to constant warfare and its agrarian economy, prosperity eluded Lithuania. Grand Duke Vytautas accepted all religions in his realm and granted special concessions to the Germans and Jews, the most astute promoters of trade and commerce. Vilnius became the noted Jewish center of all of Europe, even called the second Jerusalem.

Lithuania has the earliest recorded history of elected rulers in Europe. The strong Lithuanian-Polish Commonwealth succumbed to intrigues, intermarriages, and murders. After the death of Grand Duke Vytautas, Poland's continual interference in Lithuanian affairs led to a gradual disintegration of Lithuanian culture.

In the sixteenth century, Lithuania defeated Moscow but was invaded by the Swedes. The next invasion by Russia enslaved Lithuania for 120 years. An unsuccessful uprising led by Tadeusz Kosciuszko against both Prussia and Russia divided the Lithuanian-Polish Commonwealth in 1792. The Tsars prevailed and replaced all upper echelon officials with Russians. The peasants, particularly the serfs, were in dire straits with higher taxes and mobilization into the Russian Army.

Napoleon and his 600,000-strong army invaded Lithuania on the way to Moscow in 1812. In Vilnius, Napoleon expressed a desire to take the beautiful Gothic church, St. Anne's, back to Paris with him in the palm of his hand. At the retreat from Russia, the French army was a shell of its former self, famished and frozen. Eighty thousand French soldiers lay buried in Lithuania. The Russians, again, became the occupying force.

In 1864, the Russians issued an edict prohibiting the use of the Latin alphabet and burned all books printed in Lithuanian. The language only survived by speaking it secretly at home. Catholicism was persecuted in an attempt to introduce the Orthodox rites. To escape, mass emigration to the United States began in 1861 after serfdom in Russia was abolished.

Lithuanians considered Vilnius their historic capital, but in the second half of the nineteenth century, the number of Lithuanians in the city was small. The Polish-Lithuanian conflict ensued since Poles saw Vilnius as a Polish city.

As World War I began, Russian and German armies sawed back and forth, cutting through the country. The nightmare ended with President Wilson's Proclamation of the Fourteen Points that gave self-determination to all nations. On February 16, 1918, Vilnius became the capital of an independent Lithuania. After two hundred years of a union with Poland and more than a hundred years of Russian rule, Lithuania was free.

In 1922, General Pilsudski of Poland invaded Lithuania, resurrecting the idea of a Polish-Lithuanian union. The League of Nations entered the litigation, but Vilnius was held captive by Poland from 1922 to 1939. The title of Temporary Lithuanian Capital was given to Kaunas.

In 1939, the Russians gave Vilnius back to Lithuania. The joy was only fool's gold since, in return, twenty thousand Russian soldiers were stationed in Lithuania. Hitler confiscated the country's only seaport, Klaipeda, and renamed it the German Memel. Meetings between Molotov and Ribbentrop in August of 1939 divided their spheres of influence: Russia took Finland, Estonia, Latvia, and Eastern Poland, and Germany received Western Poland and Lithuania. The German invasion of Poland in September of 1939 began World War II.

In June of 1940, the Soviets occupied Lithuania, arrested more than 40,000 Lithuanians, and deported them to Siberia. In June of 1941, the Germans arrived to occupy the country until 1944. Many citizens rejoiced at the German occupation, signifying liberation from the Soviets, but there was only sorrow for the 42,000 Lithuanian Jews who were executed by the Nazis and their collaborators. The German occupation for most Lithuanians was not as harsh as the Soviet occupation. Under the Germans, an attempt was made at restoring a provisional Lithuanian government.

Near the end of the war, on July 13, 1944, Lithuanians experienced their greatest panic as the Red Army was advancing and sure to impose an even more brutal occupation. Eighty thousand Lithuanians fled west to escape and seek protection from the Allied forces. Many citizens who remained were arrested, tortured, and deported to Siberia. This period lasted for five decades and was most brutal during Stalin's lifetime.

In 1945, more than 100,000 Poles left for Poland to be supplanted by Lithuanians from the other cities and farms of Lithuania. Lithuanians finally reached a majority in Vilnius.

Lithuanian partisan fighters conducted guerrilla warfare in the forests to protect civilians from a hostile occupier, but they also subsisted from the population and put it at risk for reprisals. There were Jewish partisans fighting the Germans, preferring the Russian occupation, but the majority of Lithuanian fighters, called the Forest Brothers, were against the Soviets. The movement started in 1944 but continued until 1953, with 30,000 partisans and their supporters killed.

The fight for independence in the face of a disintegrating Soviet Empire started in 1988, and on March 11, 1990, Lithuania's independence was declared. Vilnius saw fourteen Lithuanians killed at a TV tower by Soviet bullets and tanks. This sacrifice provided the first signal for the final fall of the Soviet Union. In 2004, Lithuania, with Vilnius as its capital, joined the European Union.

CAST OF CHARACTERS

POLISH	
Casimir Kataski	railroad worker
Paulina Kataski	maid for the Eimontas family
Stefan Kataski / Katas	son working in Memel
Valeria Kataski / Katas	daughter in Memel, marries Obermeyer
Pranas Kataski	son who becomes a communist
Jan Kataski	son studying to be a priest
Anna Kataski	schoolgirl
General Kuzas	mayor of Vilnius under Lithuanian rule
Nina Kuzas	wife of the mayor of Vilnius
JEWISH	
Abraham Bernstein	fur shop owner in Vilnius
Sarah Bernstein	wife of Abraham
Daniel Bernstein	Bernstein son, furrier
Jacob Bernstein	Bernstein son, communist, Father Vebra
Rachel Bernstein	Bernstein daughter
Beata Rosenfelt	friend of Katerina Eimontas
LITHUANIAN	
Baron Algirdas Eimontas	Lithuanian nobleman
Baroness Maria Eimontas	wife of Algirdas
Baron Vytautas "Vytas" Eimontas	Lithuanian leader
Jadvyga Eimontas	Polish first wife of Vytautas
Antanas Eimontas	son of Vytautas and Jadvyga
Katerina Eimontas	second wife of Vytautas, a physician
Astrid Eimontas	daughter of Vytautas and Katerina
Dalia Eimontas	sister of Vytautas
Zygmond Dielka	Rector of University and leading intellectual
Elena Dielka	wife of Zygmond

Bishop Venclovas	Catholic bishop of Vilnius
Jonas Saulis	patriot and partisan fighter
Aunt Teresa	cousin of Katerina
Joseph Rudis	medical intern
GERMAN	
Count Doban	Nazi in Memel
Countess Gretchen Doban	wife of Count Doban
General Helmut Obermeyer	husband of Valeria Kataski
Gebietskommissar Hans Heinz	mayor of Vilnius under German occupation
Monica Faust	wife of Stefan Kataski
RUSSIAN	
Yuri Sabanov	mayor of Vilnius under USSR occupation
Georgi Norgolov	Soviet colonel
Professor Victor Kuznetsov	communist economist
Svetlana	Daniel Bernstein's lover
General Bulgarin	Soviet general

CHAPTER 1
JUNE 1939

The Lady of the Gate of Dawn, a symbol of the city, hovered over Vilnius, accepting desperate pleadings and dispensing fate in the face of poverty, war, and suffering. The icon, in a chapel enclosed in the arch of the medieval gates of Vilnius, was visible at the end of the Gate of Dawn, a cobblestone lane that echoed the prayers of generations. Centuries of smoke from beseeching lighted candles had darkened the face of the Mother of God to mahogany. Garbed in her golden robes, crowned with rays of the sun and the moon at her feet, she glistened with heavenly splendor in the afternoon sun.

Paulina Kataski, draped in a shapeless gray dress, weary of her day's labor, lacked the energy to climb the thirty-nine steps to the chapel. The sole supplicant at this sunset hour, kneeling on the cobblestones, Paulina transported her soul upward to the exposed icon and prayed for her husband, Casimir, and their five children, pleading for food, work, and shelter. The thought of Christ's love for the poor infused her heart with solace and love. Paulina's lumpy body, weighed down by pendulous breasts, was not redeemed by her face, which was devoid of beauty: blonde eyebrows and eyelashes and a small mouth melted into a sea of pasty white skin. Her thin brown hair hid under a kerchief. Her hands clasped in prayer were calloused and rough from constant scrubbing and cleaning. Small bright blue eyes provided the only distinctive feature.

Glancing to the right to avoid the sun's direct rays, she saw Antanas Eimontas, her employer's handsome son, exiting an adjacent apartment building and stopping to passionately kiss a woman. Paulina recognized the disheveled woman as the mayor's wife. The mayor's car pulled up, but by then, the door had closed, and Antanas had sauntered away. Paulina, face burning, added a prayer, "Dear God, forgive Antanas for his immoral life. He is the luckiest man in Vilnius but is in danger of losing his soul."

As Paulina finished her prayers, she made the sign of the cross, hauled herself up, and ambled along Pilsudski Street, the main city street of Vilnius with a plethora of expensive apartments and elegant shops.

Passing Bernstein's Furs' windows, she felt no desire for these luxury items, as out of reach as a royal crown. Hurrying, she almost collided with a young, tall man with a yarmulke exiting the store. She gasped at her close confrontation when she saw his facial deformity. A beautiful woman with raven hair followed. He apologized to Paulina and turned to the woman and said, "I'll lock up, Mother." Paulina recognized the woman as the owner's wife, Sarah Bernstein.

Further, Paulina entered the crowded Jewish neighborhood with pervasive aromas of pickles and herring, a foreign enclave of people in black clothes, beards, hats, and shawls speaking a strange language. Finally, she reached her Polish neighborhood of tenements and noisy children. She greeted her neighbors and lumbered up the steps to the third floor, where aromas of fried meats and cabbage permeated the crumbling corridors.

Opening the door, she stepped into their family's communal life—a stove, a sofa covered with a blanket, a wooden dining table with six mismatched chairs, and a small ledge below a window with a few books. A cross hung on the wall, as well as a photograph of the President of Poland, Jozef Pilsudski. The sun revealed a slight layer of dust, so Paulina picked up a rag from a pail by the stove and polished the table. She used soap and water to rise above her neighbors; cleanliness was her passport to status.

She moved to the bedroom she shared with her two daughters, Valeria and little Anna, and found it needed no attention. Under the thumb of deprivation, the girls tried to ease their mother's burden by almost saintly obedience to her standards of cleanliness. Paulina brushed the covers of the girls' shared bed as if to confirm its perfection. In Paulina's view, Valeria's goodness translated into beauty, and her best features were her clear translucent skin and perfect white teeth. However, her brown hair was always in a humble bun, and she chose black and gray dresses to blend her pudgy body into a colorless background.

A rubber-draped corner contained a toilet and a primitive shower. As Paulina scrubbed the space, she smiled at the luxury of indoor plumbing after a lifetime of using an outdoor outhouse and washing in an ice-cold stream. Life on her parents' farm amid her nine brothers and sisters was an existence marked by dirt floors, darkness, freezing winters, and constant hunger. Brief happiness came only in the summers bathed with warmth and light, followed by autumn harvests with songs and dances.

The last room, now inhabited by her husband, Casimir, and sons, Jan and Pranas, confronted her with unmade beds and scattered clothes. Only her son Jan's corner, graced with a large crucifix, had a semblance of order. She made the four beds, two of which were occupied by Pranas, who used Stefan's bed as a jumbled repository for books. Under Casimir's bed, she found a silver-colored button and remembered how upset Stefan had been when he could not find it. She wished she could give him the button now and watch his blue eyes sparkle. She found her eyes misting since, unreasonably, her heart loved her oldest child best. Paulina had wanted Stefan to continue in school, but he found books boring. Casimir never believed in education, and the family needed money, so the tall, blonde, quiet sixteen-year-old youth looked for work. The best pay was in Klaipeda, a bustling Lithuanian seaport with a large German population, so Stefan had moved there to work as a longshoreman on the docks. He sent his pay home with an occasional note consisting of a few words: "Health good, hello to all." Nazis had just occupied the city, but Stefan, now twenty-one, spoke German and had a steady job, so he remained, unlike many Lithuanians who left the city in fear of the Nazis. In compliance with the times, his boss advised him to change his name to the Lithuanian Katas, more acceptable to Nazi ideology.

Valeria and Anna, back from school, ran up to hug their mother as she rinsed out her cleaning rags. Valeria sang out, "Mother, a letter from Stefan was in our mailbox!" Paulina's face lit up but changed into a look of concern as she heard a pitiful cry.

Anna, the little five-year-old, tearfully complained, "Mama, I lost one of my ribbons today." She had two blonde braids but only one blue ribbon bow.

"There, there, we'll get other ribbons, prettier ones," soothed Paulina, hugging the distraught little girl. "Valeria, there are some zloty in my bedroom drawer. Count out a few." As soon as Anna heard the reprieve, she lit up a sudden smile as if the sun had burst forth from the clouds. Little Anna radiated warmth and sincere pleasure in living—an optimistic, cheerful child, not yet aware of the hard realities ahead.

Valeria hugged Anna and twirled her around. "We will go tomorrow to buy you the prettiest ribbons in all of Vilnius." Valeria, at seventeen, protected her little sister from the sad family dynamics and was torn between her father's and her mother's view of the future. Her father, Casimir, distant and illiterate, worked for the railroad with only mere survival and bread on the table as a goal. Her mother, Paulina, good-hearted and religious, worked as a maid in the home of Baron Eimontas. Observing life in the rich household, she aspired to a better life for her children. Valeria lived for Paulina's stories of life at the baron's home—the food, the dresses, and the parties. She dreamed of a charmed life but woke up to a different reality.

With Anna's crisis solved, Paulina said, "Please, read Stefan's letter," as she opened the envelope and, putting the money on the table, handed the letter over to Valeria, who still bristled at the name change to Katas.

Valeria translated the German text with ease:

Dear Mother, Father, Pranas, Jan, Valeria, and Anna,
Our future is with Germany, so Valeria, teach German to all.
Work is paying well. Health is good, greetings to all.

Stefan

"The Germans took over Klaipeda, but we live in Poland, in Vilnius. What can he mean, our future is with Germany?" Paulina commented in Polish.

"Is the reason he wants us to learn German is because he wants to marry a German girl there?" Valeria asked, her attention focused on romance.

"Better a German than a Lithuanian girl," Paulina answered with an instinctive dislike of Lithuanians, who always caused problems for her hero, Pilsudski. The only tolerable Lithuanians were her employers, the Baron Eimontas family. Paulina mused, "Who knows the ways of love? I only hope the girl Stefan finds will be as beautiful as you are, Valeria. It's only by the grace of God you don't resemble me," she blurted out, covering her mouth with her rough hands to hide her missing front teeth.

"Mama, don't say these things. You're the beautiful one. Look at your hands. They speak of your hard work for us. What could be more convincing of your love for us?"

Valeria then finished setting the table and started supervising Anna's homework. "I will teach you a few words in German," she said. "Say, 'Danke.' It means thanks." Anna giggled.

After a day of cooking for her employers, Paulina examined her primitive kitchen for the makings of supper. She found black bread, potatoes, onions, and mushrooms the family collected in a forest. She uncovered a bowl with sour cream left over from Sunday and started her mushroom stew. "If only I had some pork from the roast I made for the baron's family," sighed Paulina. "But they gave the little end piece to their dog, Sabaka."

The front door banged open, and Casimir, her husband, marched in, holding a newspaper. A tall and hefty man, muscular from years of physical labor, displayed a vigorous mustache and beard in compensation for his bald head. Paulina grimaced at his soiled railroad worker's uniform. "Paulina, there's news of an impending catastrophe!" shouted Casimir, his eyes dark with fury, while waving the newspaper. "Vilnius is to be given to the Lithuanians! The Russians will be making a deal with Lithuania to give them Vilnius. Would you please read it for me?"

Paulina banged down her bowl and asked, "Where did you get this crazy idea? How can Russia give away a Polish city to Lithuania?" She picked up the paper with a heavy heart that Casimir was illiterate.

Casimir, to assert his superiority, announced, "The Russian bear does whatever he wants. He squatted here for one hundred twenty years."

Paulina glanced at the paper, "There's nothing in this paper about any Russian deal. Where did you hear this?"

Casimir, untying his work boots, said, "I overheard two Russian officers talking while I was cleaning out their compartment. They said if the Lithuanians take over the city, the Polish would be driven out."

"They must've been drunk. That was vodka talking," said Paulina with a frown, superior to Casimir in common sense.

"The older officer talked about the Lithuanian Polish Commonwealth," Casimir countered with the little knowledge he had to impress his wife.

"We know the history. The Lithuanians always claimed Vilnius as their ancient capital, although Vilnius has been a part of Poland since 1922. The few Lithuanians in Vilnius would not be able to take this Polish city." Paulina's face, etched in deep worry lines, collapsed further as she contemplated the future if there were any truth to this rumor. Coming from the countryside to Vilnius for a better future, it had taken them ten years to eke out even a simple subsistence. Where would they go, and what would they do? Paulina made the decisions in the family. Casimir was a good man and not an alcoholic but with a scant ability to cope with radical change.

They first met at a farm festival where Casimir won the competition for breeding the best calf. Paulina had the honor of presenting him with the prize, a basket of her baked goods. He saw in her a good cook and honest woman, and Paulina saw him as a healthy, strong worker. Basking in her happiness at the first man to ever show any interest in her, she overlooked the shortcomings of his mind. Aware of her plainness, she had lost any hope of marriage, so Casimir's romantic interest was welcome. Their country marriage led to five children and a difficult life.

The door opened quietly, and her youngest son, Jan, entered and gave her a kiss on the cheek. His thin blond hair always fell on his forehead, and flicking it back had become a habit. He was the only gentle and affectionate male in the household. Casimir observed this greeting with a sneer since he considered his son Jan to be effeminate.

Pranas, eighteen, a tall, muscular, self-confidant, and boisterous young man, arrived last. He dismissed his only imperfection—missing much of his left ear, which had occurred in a game with a boy who had a real gun as a toy. While playing, Pranas was shot. The doctor said Pranas was lucky he lost only his ear, two more millimeters, and he would have lost his life. The rich father sent money but no apology and laughingly said Pranas owed his life to his son's excellent marksmanship. Each time he saw his left ear, he heard the man's laughter and vowed revenge on the rich.

Pranas worked at the library as a stock boy at Stefan Batory University, where he saw the students, heard their conversations, and envied their lives. Attending this prestigious, ancient university was out of the question. In the school library, he read books omnivorously. Exploding with information, he wanted to discuss and argue his newfound knowledge with the students, but he did not belong to their league. They wore uniforms with hats and sashes to proclaim their fraternities or sororities, and being without these symbols made him an outsider. Burning ambition heated to hatred at his exclusion. He hated the injustice of poverty.

Dinner started with a lengthy prayer by sixteen-year-old Jan, who had expressed a desire to enter the priesthood. A quiet, introspective boy with the pale skin and slender body of one more spiritual than physical, he planned to go to the Jesuit Seminary. Paulina thanked God for this blessing. Her spiritual and temporal status would increase by having a priest in her own family.

Casimir, taking a drink of homemade beer, looked over at Pranas. "Are you working hard at the university? If you get a good recommendation, I will try to get you to work with me on the railroad."

"Papa, I don't want to work on the railroad. I want to be a professor at the university, lecturing students, not cleaning out railroad cars." Pranas resented his parents for their inferior status. Their lack of education distanced him from them, and he did not respect them.

"Your high and mighty dreams will do nothing for you. You need reality to put food on this table," Casimir said as he cut a hunk of bread.

The rough black bread absorbed the last dregs of the mushroom stew on their plates when Pranas spoke, "Mama, at school today, I saw Astrid Eimontas. She dropped a book in the library, and I picked it up for her, but she just passed by as if I did not exist, not a word of thanks. With all the university boys swarming about her, I guess she can afford to be impolite to a library worker." Astrid's insult rankled deeply, and their inequality of status gnawed at him. He swore that someday when he would move beyond being the son of a household maid, he would have proud Astrid at his feet.

Paulina, surprised at Pranas's interest in her employer's daughter, answered in annoyance, "You've work to do. Don't waste your time thinking about your betters." At work, Paulina chafed under the girl's inconsiderateness and haughty demands.

Pranas looked over at his mother and noticed the deep dark circles under her eyes. "You look so tired today." He bristled at the thought of his mother on her knees, scrubbing the baron's floors.

"We are very busy with spring cleaning. I had to wash all the windows and take the baroness's fur coats to Bernstein's for storage. I had to stand a long time at the fur store since so many maids were in line to turn in their employers' coats. Bernstein's made a fortune today."

"The business for the Jews of Vilnius is excellent. They call it the little Jerusalem," said Pranas, envious of anyone's success.

Paulina, oblivious of his comment, continued, "Then I had to bake a baumkuchen standing for hours over a fire."

Little Anna said, "I know that tree cake. Mama brought me a little piece in a napkin once. She told me how she makes it. The dough is spread over a log set on iron bars, and as the log turns over the fire, the drippings form spikes. When it comes off the log, it looks just like a tree." Anna clapped her hands in glee at the end of her recital, eliciting a smile from everyone.

"They're lucky to have you make the baumkuchen. I agree with Anna, I had a small piece once, and it smelled of vanilla and honey and tasted like heaven," Casimir proudly proclaimed.

"The ingredients of sixty eggs and five pounds of butter are useless ostentation. But the baron's family has the means." Paulina shrugged her shoulders, accepting the inevitable contrast between her mushroom stew and the baron's extravagance.

Valeria started taking away the dishes and blurted out, "It would be so nice to have some sausages sometimes instead of mushrooms."

Paulina, with eyes misting, looked at Valeria. "We should all be grateful for this meal. I received a letter from my friend Ilona, who described the starvation in Ukraine. All farmers have strict government grain quotas set by Stalin, and people not complying are shot to death. In order to meet the required quotas, they often give up their own food. Ilona wrote of her baby and her mother, who both died of starvation. I'd just read Ilona's letter, and using all those rich ingredients for the baumkuchen brought me to tears at the unfairness of life."

When the meal ended, Jan bowed his head in prayer. "Great God of the universe, thank you for our food, especially in the face of mass starvation next door in Ukraine. Let us not envy, for it is the serpent of life poisoning our happiness. Give health to our parents who work so hard for our well-being, and protect Stefan so far away."

Casimir patted Jan's shoulder. "Stalin's rule is brutal. Thank God we are free."

"The baron and his family will have their turn to suffer," said Pranas with a sneer, thinking of Astrid eating pork roast and baumkuchen.

CHAPTER 2
JULY 1939

After several days of humid heat in Vilnius, the sky thundered open to a summer storm. Raindrops pelted the crystal windows of Bernstein's, the most elegant shop on Pilsudski Avenue of Vilnius. People holding their umbrellas hurried by the store displays on this main boulevard but not without a sigh of longing for the style and beauty of the curly black Persian lamb jackets, long shiny mink and sable coats, glistening lynx and ermine stoles. In winter, these fashionable pelts would be the most sought-after item akin to diamonds and gold.

Abraham Bernstein, a furrier on the main street of Vilnius, imported the best animal pelts from Siberia and, with the help of his five workers, transformed them into custom furs, according to the latest Parisian fashion. His family had been in the fur trade for generations, but he was the first to set up a shop. His wife, Sarah, and his son Daniel were integral to the running of the store. His younger son Jacob and his daughter Rachel were still students, but Abraham's dream was to have the whole family working for the success of Bernstein's.

Vilnius, with its large Jewish population, prospered with four synagogues, many rabbis, and opportunities for commercial activity. With the rise of anti-Semitism evident in Germany and Russia, Jews considered the city a safe, welcoming place.

Sarah, Abraham's petite wife, with glossy, black, abundant hair and classic features, wearing fashionable sable coats and sauntering along Pilsudski Avenue, proclaimed the success of Bernstein's Furs. Sarah, the only daughter of a rabbi, had been raised in a conservative household, so when she expressed a desire to be an artist, her ambition met the cutting edge of reality. She demurred to her family's wishes and relinquished her dream.

The only acceptable career for a Jewish woman was a suitable marriage into a known family. According to her parents, Sarah's arranged betrothal at fifteen to the rich and gentle Abraham was a gift from heaven. The whole community celebrated the wedding in jubilant rejoicing.

Abraham, a wise man and good husband, aware of his fortune in obtaining a lovelier woman than he had ever dreamed of, tried to please her. He understood Sarah's unrequited artistic ambition and assumed the role of guide and protector. He instructed her in the field of fashion design. Thereby, she fulfilled some of her creative dreams and talents yet functioned in the commerce of furs. She enjoyed fashioning the different animal pelts into outerwear to suit rich customers from far and wide. Three children—Daniel, Jacob, and Rachel—completed her family. Blessed with a content nature, she never considered alternate ways of life.

The rain continued into the early evening. Locking the door of their shop and opening an umbrella, Sarah commented, "Business is so slow. People have no interest in our furs in this warm, humid weather."

"Things will pick up in September," said Abraham, giving his wife a pat on the shoulder as they walked home to the Jewish quarter. Abraham, a short, thin man with deep-set, brown, kindly eyes, chewed his very fleshy lips when making complex decisions. A large black beard hid his narrow face, and a yarmulke covered his balding head; nothing hid his very prominent nose. His perception of himself as an ugly man made him inwardly rejoice every time he looked at beautiful Sarah—a good, modest woman besides.

Abraham's veins pulsed with practical blood. His business acumen allowed him to outperform all the other furriers in the city by undercutting their prices. Once he gained victory over a rival and drove them out of business, he returned prices to normal. Since furs were not an everyday purchase, no one but his vanquished competitors was aware of his strategy. Over the years, he had invested in the safest of commodities, gold and diamonds, which he kept hidden in a secret place.

The Jewish quarter of Vilnius was a crowded area of apartment buildings where Jews self-segregated by adhering to their religion, rituals, and customs. Fierce competition existed for larger living quarters. One of the largest apartments, inherited from a rich childless uncle, belonged to Abraham, who considered the legacy a miracle from God since he came from a poor family: his second miracle was the love of Sarah.

Abraham and Sarah entered their home. Furniture, paintings, antiques, and symbols of their Jewish heritage crowded their first-floor apartment. Treasures from past generations collected by his uncle, Jakob, included many silver menorahs. Books, a testament to Jakob's voracious reading habits, lined the walls. A grand piano, embellished by an embroidered throw and pushed into a corner, displayed photographs of ancestors.

Sarah looked around at the dark carved wood and said, "Abraham, the furniture, so dark and heavy, is especially depressing on this rainy day. Your uncle bought it at a sale from a mansion for a song, but it seems out of place in this apartment. Please let me redecorate in a different style."

"My love, you may buy anything you want, but to dispose of Jakob's items is sacrilege," said Abraham as judge and jury of the family.

Their oldest son, Daniel, walked in with a stooped posture and a downward-facing gaze. He was much taller than his father with the dark eyes and large nose of a classic Semitic face. A poorly corrected harelip, not even concealed by the facial hair, which refused to grow on the scar tissue, condemned him to a life of shame and introversion. To ingratiate himself, he always strived for service to his family, even to the point of obsequiousness. He ran up to his father, saying, "Father, let me take your coat. It seems damp from the rain."

Abraham averted his eyes as Daniel approached and removed his damp raincoat. Abraham remembered the disappointment of seeing the infant Daniel for the first time. Sarah presented their son with downcast eyes, "I'm sorry, there seems to have been a problem." Abraham had pulled down the blanket from the little face and experienced horror at the birth defect, a huge void in his lip and mouth. He had tried to hide his feelings in front of Sarah, heartbroken at the malformation of her firstborn son.

When Abraham's mother had arrived from their backward village, she looked at Daniel and pronounced, "Beware! He has the mark of the devil." Daniel had been branded by his grandmother's curse, and Abraham could not erase his unease with his son. A series of painful, unsuccessful surgeries followed with minimal resolution but maximal scarring.

Daniel had just returned from Irkutsk in Russia with a new shipment of sable pelts and now opened his valise on the dining room table, revealing a treasure trove of furs. Sarah kissed Daniel, stroked his fur bounty, and said, "Son, you outdid yourself. I have never seen lovelier pelts."

He showed them to his father with pride and said, "I found a new source of sable pelts. I want to tell you how it came about."

As Abraham looked at the furs, as always, he faced away from Daniel's gruesome harelip. Abraham, acutely aware of his own poor appearance, honed by comments from family and taunted by schoolmates, could not overcome his revulsion as Daniel mirrored the physical inferiority that he despised in himself. He evinced discomfort in loving Daniel by avoidance.

"Yes, the furs are of a good quality," Abraham reluctantly admitted. He had overcome his background of poor fur traders by employing a quick mind and razor-sharp business instincts but was blind to the same character traits in his son Daniel.

Daniel, elated by a rare comment of praise from his father, beamed and said, "Father, no one could get anything better at a lower price in all of Siberia." Daniel wanted his business acumen to prove his worth and somewhat ameliorate the physical deformity he inflicted on his parents.

Daniel could not miss the light in his father's eyes upon seeing Jacob, his younger brother—handsome, confident, and without defect—as he lounged on the sofa. Without much more than a mumbled "Well done," his father walked toward Jacob.

Observing this scene pained Sarah, who believed parents owe equal love to all their children. But Abraham could not conceal his preference for Jacob; he avoided looking directly at Daniel. Her heart ached for Daniel, seeing his crestfallen face and misting eyes.

Jacob smiled at Abraham. "Father, what's this about our neighbors, the Goldsteins, wanting to immigrate to Palestine? Isn't being here in Vilnius the best possible life for us?" Jacob asked as Abraham sat down by his side on the blue velvet sofa and patted him affectionately on the shoulder.

Abraham frowned and, after a moment of silence, answered, "Vilnius is our Jerusalem. We practice our religion and customs here and run almost all the business in the city. Thousands of Jewish refugees are moving here to Vilnius, fleeing persecution in Germany. Of course, life here is much better for them than Germany, but Palestine is our home promised by God."

Unconvinced, Jacob retorted, "How can you compare life here to life in Palestine? A life among uncivilized Arabs in the middle of the desert? Here we have everything. Vilnius has always been a good place for us to do business because commerce is beneath the natives as a trade."

Jacob, at eighteen, two years younger than Daniel and a shorter man, had the self-confident swagger of a winner. Fine-boned but muscular, he took after his mother in his facial features, his prominent nose being the only genetic contribution from his father. Being known as a handsome, smart member of a rich family within the community added to his allure. He was a student of the Torah, intending to become a rabbi.

Abraham looked at Jacob with arched eyebrows. "Jacob, the Jews have been persecuted all over the world. Do you suppose it can't happen here? Palestine is the only place where we could be permanently safe."

"I think we would be safer under communism. Many of my friends are joining the communist party in reaction to the fascists in Germany," Jacob stated with an air of superiority. "I have read *Das Capital* by Marx, and it seems to answer the world's problems."

Daniel, completely ignored, leaped into the conversation. "Jacob, your knowledge is all from books. Let me tell you facts. Coming home from Siberia, I met many Jews who spoke about what is happening in Germany. But the idea that communists are more benevolent toward the Jews is crazy. Don't you know Stalin is exiling Jews to Siberia? To Siberia! What is their chance of survival in a place like that?"

"I'm sure Stalin has his reasons for sending some Jews to Siberia, but our life would be better under communism," Jacob countered.

"You're dreaming! If communism took over, we would lose our business! The communists believe everything is owned by the state," Daniel argued.

With no respect for his brother's opinion, Jacob suddenly looked away in boredom, shaking his head as if confronted by a dunce.

Abraham had the final say in the discussion: "Palestine is our only safety."

In the silence that followed, Daniel paused, before again launching with pride, "Getting back to business. I want to tell you in detail how I negotiated for these sable pelts in Irkutsk."

"Yes, Daniel, we want to hear about your business triumph," Sarah said, realizing all the focus had again shifted. Her feelings for Daniel consisted of guilt at his birth defect, empathy with his poor looks, and sorrow at the burden of not being accepted by his father. She felt for him the same acute pain as she did once upon seeing a small bird struggling with a broken wing. She wanted to help but did not know how.

Daniel, realizing his business triumph had no interest to anyone except his mother, packed up the furs, closed the valise, and asked with a sneer, "Tell us more about Marx, Jacob. Perhaps I missed something important."

The whirling, laughing presence of Rachel entering the room halted any further discussion. With flashing brown eyes and dark curls flying, she made a deep bow. Her birth was the apex of Sarah's desires, a little girl to love. Now she was a lovely young lady, taller and thinner than her mother.

Rachel sang out, "Applause, please! You are seeing the winner of the Vilnius Violin Competition. I played Curlonis, a Lithuanian composer. I did not tell you I entered because I had no idea I could win. I cannot imagine being happier than with a life of music. When I finish at the Conservatory, I will go on to Paris or Berlin to work with famous composers."

"Why, darling, how wonderful!" said Sarah beaming with pride. "I'm sure you'll be a famous violinist, but you must go to medical school first for your livelihood." Rachel was a copy of Sarah in looks and grace but had a strong streak of independence. Sarah tried to dampen the unrealistic longing in her daughter, the same artistic streak denied to her in her youth.

"Mama, I don't want to follow your practical life. Let me be free." Rachel had heard her mother's quiet stories of unrealized dreams and vowed never to follow in her footsteps. Why did her mother spend her days working with drawings and pelts and seamstresses when her fate should be expressing idealized visions of the world? She saw her mother in Paris in a light-filled studio painting masterpieces.

Daniel was again pushed into the background; his accomplishments diminished as if poisoned by his birth defect. He had no friends, and the thought of a woman or love exceeded all his expectations. He had looked at a young girl at a family party once, but she returned his gaze in disgust. As the oldest son, he had tried to please his father, but the love he expected flowed without effort to Jacob and Rachel.

Rachel went around the room, planting a kiss on her mother, father, Jacob, and Daniel. Daniel, touching his kissed cheek, had the sad realization that no one in his whole life had kissed him but his mother and Rachel.

Cooking aromas called them to the Friday evening meal prepared by the Polish cook who understood kosher requirements. The Shabbat meal was to be eaten at sunset. Candles were to be lit, and the braided bread, challah, and wine were to be blessed. Sarah said, "Come, we have a special dinner to celebrate Daniel's return and Rachel's musical triumph."

A massive table covered by an embroidered tablecloth replete with candles anchored the family as they said, "Shabbat shalom," to one another.

Abraham looked at his fifteen-year-old daughter and sighed. He wondered if the state of the world would allow for the fruition of her dreams. He didn't want to alarm them, but the rise of the Nazis frightened him. The possibility of communism was also alien. He saw his beautiful Sarah and Rachel and his proud son Jacob and tried to avoid the downcast deformed face of forever-sad Daniel.

Jacob pondered Daniel's statements of Russians mistreating the Jews and asked, "Daniel, the Russians have many communist Jews in the government. After all, Karl Marx was a Jew. What could their justification be for pogroms against the Jews?"

Daniel, taking a piece of challah bread, surprised at being asked, answered his brother, "The communists have some Jews in the government, but we all know the Russians have despised us for centuries as killers of Jesus, and it's not easy to change the attitudes of centuries of prejudice."

Abraham drank a sip of kosher wine, looked around the table, and said, "For now, we have been left in peace. We must stay to ourselves and not get involved in politics, mind our business and our profits, and we will do well. Let's not worry about something that may never happen in Vilnius."

Nazis and communists were all but forgotten as they ate their meal of a matzos ball soup and chicken with kugel. Changes, invasion, and exile did not intrude on their happiness in being together. They were the Bernsteins.

CHAPTER 3
AUGUST 1939

After preparing a breakfast of bread, farmer's cheese, and honey for her family, Paulina rushed off to work in the early morning heat. She passed the Jewish section and crossed the Neris River by the Zoo Bridge. After a few miles, she entered the exclusive neighborhood of the Zoo, the ancient hunting grounds of the aristocracy. Large mansions surrounded by towering trees and manicured greenery dominated the hillsides. The most impressive structure was the city dwelling of her employer, Baron Vytautas Eimontas, a Lithuanian, the scion of a family with Prussian roots and a vast country estate, Erelis.

Paulina, running late and breathing heavily, hauled her heavy body up the backdoor steps. Entering the hot, bustling kitchen, she encountered the four live hens to be butchered for lunch. She carried the cage and an ax to the yard. She dreaded chopping off their heads and seeing them run around with blood spurting from their necks. "Please, St. Francis," she prayed, "give them a quick and painless death."

Returning from the bloody duty, Paulina met the parlor maid, Nina, bringing in the dishes from breakfast. Nina said with a huff, "Well, you certainly took your time this morning. There is so much to do today, and Kascia is sick, so you will also have to help with serving." With a sigh, Paulina went to the pantry and put on a black dress, a white apron, and a cap.

"I think the guest of honor is a count from Klaipeda and his new wife," said Nina, looking with derision at disheveled Paulina, and continued, "Look sharp, these are important guests. Count Doban has been here before. Give him big helpings. You'll know him by his big belly and a fringe of white hair on his baldhead. People say he met his new young love even before his wife was cool in the grave."

"Stop gossiping!" Katerina Eimontas, the baron's second wife, said as she entered the kitchen, reading the menu. Paulina examined Katerina's green crepe dress with a multitude of tucks and the puffed sleeves of the latest Parisian fashion. Paulina admired Katerina, who used her assets of a slender figure, lively green eyes, perfect manners, and melodious, soft voice to become the baroness in spite of her humble background.

"Baroness," Paulina hesitantly addressed her mistress, "it'll be too hot today for the ox-tail soup. Perhaps you will let me change the menu to cold beet soup."

Katerina, also studying the guest seating chart, looked up as if she were seeing Paulina for the first time. "Yes, that will be fine."

"No!" shouted Astrid, the baron's seventeen-year-old daughter, sprinting into the kitchen. "No, beet soup is for peasants. The ox-tail soup recipe is straight from Paris, and we want to be sophisticated." Paulina turned to the imperious blonde young girl in her simple shift with its pink sash, observing her beauty was at odds with her arrogant disposition.

"Astrid, Paulina is right. It is too hot for ox-tail soup. Make sure your brother is dressed." Katerina left the kitchen in an envelope of fine French perfume.

Astrid ran upstairs to Antanas's room, where he was adjusting his tie, a cigarette in his mouth. The walls were covered with trophies for swimming, tennis, and sailing. "Mother wanted me to check if you are finished dressing," Astrid said, observing the tall, perfectly sculpted man as he threw back his shoulders and flashed a smile with even, white teeth.

Antanas, twenty-five, a child from the baron's first marriage, was reputed to be the handsomest man in Vilnius and suspected of an embarrassing number of amorous affairs. He had an academic appointment at Stefan Batory University, where he had studied history and economics. The complexity of politics interested him as a means to be exceptional. Everyone agreed he was born under a lucky star.

"Yes, Astrid, I'm coming. Just seeing which cravat is more attractive. I hear the Countess Doban has quite a reputation." He smiled at the mirror, reflecting his handsome, chiseled features and light brown hair.

Astrid grimaced at the thought of her brother's attention diverted by yet another woman who was sure to be seduced by his charms.

Guests started arriving in the early afternoon. The rector of Stefan Batory University, Zygmond Dielka, and his wife, Elena, arrived first. Elena, clad in a black silk dress, whose severity was relieved by gleaming antique gold jewelry, epitomized elegance. Elena, not born a beauty, transformed into a very attractive woman due to intelligence and discipline. With her imperious posture and impeccable style, she was a formidable social arbiter. This slender, dark-haired woman, a good friend and mentor of Katerina, instructed her in the customs, manners, and social protocol of life in Vilnius. Elena, in greeting, air-kissed Katerina's cheeks.

"Darling, how lovely you look in green. Your home is heaven in this heat." Elena looked around at the gleaming silver and profusion of flowers and selected a chair next to the breeze of an open window.

The rector, Dielka, a thin, tall man of rapid movements, quick bright eyes, a high forehead, and bushy eyebrows, followed his wife. He was the premier intellectual of Vilnius, and he kissed Katerina's hand in greeting. "Katerina, the only invitation more welcome today would be a picnic by the river, preferably in Siberia."

"A picnic would be cooler, but it would not honor our guest, the count. And I would prefer any heat to even a thought of Siberia." Katerina smiled and escorted Dielka to her husband standing in front of a painting of the Battle of Tannenberg in 1410, a massive depiction of the horrors of war.

Baron Eimontas, with graying hair and piercing brown eyes, had the comfortable body of a bear. Chewing on his ever-present pipe, he greeted the rector and commented, "I am sure, with the presence of Count Doban, the expansion of Germany will be a topic."

Next to arrive was the bishop of Vilnius, Venclovas. He was an austere, tall, humorless man, always seemingly prepared for Judgment Day. "Baroness, your invitation was a blessing to this old priest. I have been looking forward to your bountiful table. My mind will be sated as well by the joy of interesting conversation."

Count Doban entered last, following the countess, wiping the perspiration from his face. "Baron, you and your wife do me the great honor of being our hosts. It's my first visit to Vilnius after the border adjustment of Memel, and I'm anxious to hear political opinions." He accepted a glass of champagne, set it down, took a piece of toast from a maid's proffered tray, and piled upon it a mountain of caviar.

His bride of only a few months, the Countess Doban, a vivacious redhead, was a child of eighteen. Befitting an occasion in their honor, she wore a tight, low-cut red dress. "Katerina, hello," she stated, her curls bouncing as she entered the reception room.

Katerina cut her with a glance judging this woman has no manners, calling Katerina by her first name when they had not even been introduced. The countess's excellent figure and revealing dress detracted from her piggy face of small eyes in a round puffy face. Her smile revealed very small teeth with a huge expanse of pink gum. Katerina then remembered herself as a hostess and said, "Countess Doban, welcome."

After partaking of champagne and caviar in the portrait-filled salon, they moved to the dining room, where a prayer by the bishop started the dinner. Lavish food and drink established status and hospitality, so Paulina had prepared the various courses of fish in aspic, chicken with mushrooms, and ham with all the varying accompaniments. Gold-rimmed china and heavy silverware graced the table surrounded by multitudes of fragrant flowers in crystal vases. A weak breeze from the open windows moved the gossamer curtains but did not dispel the extreme August heat.

Paulina hovered by the door, listening to the conversation in Polish, but when the count would revert to German, she did not understand a word.

The count continued in Polish with a flourish of his wine glass. "After the German takeover, the Germans have been kind to the native population who welcomed them and have left things alone with the exception of high government posts."

Hearing this, Paulina breathed a sigh of relief, realizing her son Stefan would not lose his job to the Germans. She observed Astrid leaving most of her food due to her mother's influence on constant dieting.

The baron interjected, "Lithuania lost much of its foreign trade since Germany occupied its only port and access to the sea."

Count Doban dismissed his comment and continued, "I was there on March 23 in a group to meet Hitler when he drove through our city. He had arrived in grand style on a battleship, the *Deutschland*. Hitler aims to reunite all German-speaking people back to the Fatherland. An excellent move." The count gulped his wine, and Paulina refilled his glass as the rest of the party sat in uncomfortable silence.

With a look of severe distress, the bishop rubbed his hands together. "Dear Count, it cannot be a good day to have Hitler's Nazis being welcomed into our Baltic area. Are you aware of what Nazis did to the Jewish population in Germany? Last November, there were killings and arrests during Kristallnacht. This is blasphemy on Christian principles!"

The count, taken aback, said in a trembling voice, "Bishop, with all respect to your religious feelings, the people were only expressing their outrage over the murder in Paris of our German diplomat by a Jew." With no response, the count took another huge helping of chicken and continued, "The golden age of history comes to Germany. The German expansion into Czechoslovakia was a God-given right because she has a right to rule her German natives."

"Will all peoples with German blood fall into the coming German empire?" asked Katerina.

"God willing, German blood will prevail," the count said, raising his glass.

The Countess Doban started to yawn, but as her eyes lit on Antanas, she covered her mouth. Her eyes absorbed this specimen of a man with his handsome face and sublime figure, and her contemplation aroused warmth in her lower reaches. She wondered if he was attracted to her. She dropped her hand to her bosom, and when she caught Antanas's eyes, she opened her hand as if to reveal her breasts to him. He did not miss the gesture or its implication.

"Paulina, bring the dessert!" Katerina said as she observed Paulina languishing by the door. Paulina rushed to bring in a cranberry pudding and her two-foot-high masterpiece, her beautiful tree cake, baumkuchen.

Katerina responded to the appreciative smiles of her guests, "Perhaps this will sweeten our conversation." Katerina knew of the bitter differences of opinion on German rights and did not want a political argument to spoil her dinner.

"What do you think of the chances of war? The rise of Germany will surely put Russia on the defensive," the worried bishop addressed the count.

The count, taking a noble portion of the baumkuchen, said with a smile, "Oh no, nothing to worry about. There's recognition of equal strength between Hitler and Stalin. They will be at peace. None of this will affect us."

"Nonsense!" said the rector, hitting the table with emphasis. "But of course, this will affect us. Stalin and Hitler will probably divide Eastern Europe between themselves to avoid fighting over the territories."

"The Western democracies would not stand for this. Just an agreement between two men and free states fall under their dominion?" The shocked baron asked, his face pale as he pushed away his empty plate. "Where in God's name did you get this idea?"

"A Lithuanian military conference had a speaker, Professor Ridikas, a historian, who posited that when powers of equal strength collide, either there is a war or a partition of the spoils."

"Fiction! I refuse to listen to academic speculation," the red-faced count replied as he took a gulp of wine and motioned for another glass.

The baron shifted in his chair and turned toward the count. "I am afraid I don't trust the Russians. Wilson's Fourteen Points gave us our freedom, but it may be temporary."

Antanas took a glass of honey liquor. "There is a rumor Vilnius is to revert to Lithuania. Poor Vilnius has been a contested bride for so long. This city is sixty percent Polish, thirty percent Jewish, and perhaps three percent Lithuanian. What claim could the Lithuanians have?"

The baron, Lithuanian at heart, could trace his aristocratic lineage to the grand duke of Lithuania, Vytautas. Upon hearing this opinion from his son, he felt a stirring in his heart, "Antanas, what is this insanity? Of course, the Lithuanians want their ancient capital back." He looked over at Katerina, a passionate Lithuanian, who was smiling at him.

To quell the heated discussion, Bishop Venclovas, pushing away his chair, leaned forward and icily interjected, "The nationalistic Lithuanians desperately want Vilnius back, but the horse is out of the barn. It has not had a Lithuanian majority population for hundreds of years."

Antanas stated with authority, "The great powers always treat Lithuania and Poland like chess pieces, and being small, we move according to their whims. If we are occupied, it will be a disaster."

The countess, glowing with sexual energy, looked at Antanas with admiration and bobbed her red-gold curls in agreement. "But when the Germans took over Klaipeda, nothing bad happened to us, so don't be concerned if Lithuania takes over Vilnius." A deep blush covered her face as her husband flashed a poisonous look.

"Dear Countess, I beg to disagree. The forced takeover of Klaipeda culminated in ten thousand Lithuanian refugees who wanted to live in their own independent country and not under fascist rule," the baron stated. Of course, the count and countess welcomed the Germans, being German.

The bishop interjected, "The Klaipeda Nazi trials of 1934 in Kaunas were the first time Nazis were tried outside of Germany, and they were punished severely. They came back with a vengeance and annexed all of Klaipeda, changing its name to Memel."

The count said, "Of course, justice! Memel was a part of Germany that they were robbed of by the Versailles Treaty after the Great War."

Astrid, playing with her cranberry pudding, found this conversation boring, and only when Antanas asked her what she thought did she blurt out, "Lithuania is a land of illiterate farmers and peasants. How could they dream of taking over our city? For centuries, the Poles have been cultured, educated, and in charge. Many speak French, and all our fashions are straight from Paris. I know our name and family come from the Lithuanian side of the Polish-Lithuanian Commonwealth, but most of my friends are willing to overlook that fact and accept me into their circle."

Baron Eimontas looked over at Astrid. "Dear girl, how can you be so ignorant of your heritage?"

Astrid rolled her eyes and said in a singsong voice, "I know my history. In 1245 Mindaugas became the first King of Lithuania." Astrid sighed and continued, "Later, to ensure peace, Grand Duke Gediminas formed a union with Poland. Russia took over both countries, and Poland and Lithuania became independent again only after the Great War."

"Excellent, Astrid," said the proud baron. "So you see, there was a combined history from the beginning."

Katerina Eimontas corrected her husband: "No, not combined. We should not be ashamed of Lithuanian superiority. Vytautas the Great extended the borders of Lithuania from the Baltic to the Black Sea, making it the largest country in Europe in the fifteenth century."

Count Doban almost rose from his chair in protest at this show of Lithuanian chauvinism. Hah! This Lithuanian mouse was ancient history, not realizing the great lion of Germany was afoot.

Nodding to Paulina and Nina to clear the table, Katerina continued, "The government under the Lithuanian President is stable, and commerce is improving. But because it's a small country between aggressive neighbors, the Lithuanians are powerless over the theft of Klaipeda."

Count Doban's face was turning a deeper red, but with the aristocratic instinct of not insulting his hostess, he closed his mouth on yet another large piece of baumkuchen.

The Rector Dielka observed the age-old superiority question being played out, "I agree with Astrid. Poland has been the dominating force for a long time."

Astrid sighed at this intellectual reprieve. She took a small sliver of baumkuchen and said, "Lithuania is definitely an inferior nation."

Hearing this from her daughter, Katerina rose from her chair and, with burning cheeks, proclaimed, "Lithuania is superior to have survived both the Polish and over a hundred years of Russian domination! Shame, Astrid! Learn more about your heritage."

Astrid's eyes started to tear at this reprimand, and Katerina quickly said, "Coffee in the drawing room. Astrid can take some air in the garden. Antanas, keep your sister company."

As they moved into the drawing room, Antanas realized, much to his disappointment, the young countess had to remain with her husband. He rushed to the antique gilt-edged desk, wrote a note, folded it into a small square, and pressed it into the Countess Doban's soft, warm hand as he kissed it, saying goodnight.

The countess excused herself to powder her nose and read the note: "You are a beautiful woman. My heart pounds so loudly when I look at you everyone must hear it. Please come to the garden at midnight so I may see you for one minute." She hid the note in her cosmetics case. She knew his desire for her was not her beauty, but it proved she provoked his lust.

After long hours of kitchen labor, Paulina finished cleaning and left for home along the garden path. She confronted the scene of the German countess in a sheer gown, her breasts exposed, embracing Antanas in the shadows under a birch tree. Paulina blessed herself and exited at the back gate. The audacity of this mortal sin of adultery made her shudder.

Paulina rushed home through the deserted cobblestone streets, erasing the outrage. She beamed with happiness because Doctor Katerina, pleased with the dinner, gave her the leftover ham bone and some chicken. As a special favor, she even got a piece of the baumkuchen.

She groaned from her painful joints as she lumbered up the three stories to their apartment. Her hands were red and swollen from scrubbing the pots as she inserted the key. The Kataski household was quiet; all were asleep except Pranas, who had his head buried in a book. Paulina displayed the treats. "Pranas, it's one o'clock. Look what I brought home! Have a snack." Paulina looked at the book Pranas was reading: Karl Marx.

"No, I don't want anything from them. They treat you like a dog, and you are happy about it. We are all equal, and the rich should share all their wealth, not only their leftovers!" In spite of his communist fervor, the aroma of the chicken and ham won out, and he had a hearty helping before he went to bed. Sated, he dreamed of stripping Astrid of her wealth and her pride.

Katerina and Vytas went upstairs after a long night of entertaining. In her bedroom filled with dark antique furniture, Katerina sat by her vanity and brushed her long light brown hair. Her reflection showed her eyes sparkle with happiness at her successful dinner. Her husband came in and kissed the nape of her neck. She looked up at Vytas and thought he appeared tired, noting his slight stoop and graying hair.

At their first meeting almost twenty years ago, he was a vigorous, black-haired man with a gleam in his eyes and the posture of a leader. His many responsibilities had aged him. Even his voice, once so firm, was now mellow as he addressed her, "Darling, perhaps you should be more careful in expressing your Lithuanian patriotism in front of guests. Count Doban was taken aback by your intensity. You should apologize."

"I will not apologize for expressing my feelings. Vytas, I know you feel as I do about our heritage, but you are so correct and polite it extinguishes all your passion!" Katerina blurted out.

Vytas recoiled as if he had been struck. His brown eyes clouded over at this rebuke from his wife. He lit his pipe and turned as if to say something but left the room, closing the door.

Katerina knew Vytas's expertise in controlling his emotions and felt denied the emotional release of having an argument. She regretted this insult to her husband, but she could not forget her patriotic cause or the contrasting passion of love so many years ago.

The thoughts of her first love gushed forth in a torrent of memories to the past, to Palanga, a resort on the Baltic Sea. Katerina, then a seventeen-year-old student, attended a political conference where she first encountered Jonas Saulis, a featured presenter at the meeting. She had been struck by this tall, slender, blond-haired man, speaking with conviction about patriotism. His booming voice, charged with excitement, mesmerized his audience with his prophecy of danger. She sat spellbound listening to his lecture:

"Lithuanians must understand their role in history and fight and sacrifice for freedom. The repressive tsarist policies could not extinguish Lithuania. We fought for a century against Russification to keep our language, our religion, and our culture! We smuggled books into Lithuania written in Latin characters from the printing presses in Prussia under pain of imprisonment. Our churches survived the Orthodox onslaught. Neither Russia nor Germany nor Poland has the right to impose their values and their rules on us as a sovereign people!"

His words mirrored her thoughts and fired her imagination. When it was time for questions, he called on her raised hand. She introduced herself as a medical student. "How could I personally help Lithuania?"

Jonas answered her with a litany of patriotic activities: volunteer for causes, write letters, instruct the young on the history of the country. "These are good activities for a young woman student. I am pleased to find students who are eager to participate." Heated discussions as to the best ways and means ensued by all the attendees. At the end of the program, as everyone was leaving, Saulis followed her out of the lecture hall. "Thank you for your question. It led to an interesting discussion."

They walked toward the seashore. "So, how far would you go in promoting your ideas?" Katerina asked, eyes downcast, afraid to look into his aquamarine eyes directly for fear they would pierce her heart. Her heart pounded with excitement as she observed his profile, and they sat down on a wooden bench facing the sea.

"As an attorney, I'm doing all I can to legally challenge any impositions on Lithuanian sovereignty, but if occupation comes, which it will, according to history, I would fight physically to my last breath." He turned and smiled.

She looked up at him, feeling the current of electricity passing between them. "How could you fight Germany or Russia? We are free now, but Lithuania is so small with no powerful friends." The setting sun glistened on the waves, and the sea murmured in the background.

"Katerina, I would fight a guerrilla war as a partisan. You know the damage Lawrence of Arabia inflicted on the Ottoman armies with only a band of Arabs in the Great War. He is my hero, and I would do the same with a few patriots hiding in the forests."

She laughed but noticed him wince, so she caught his arm and said, "I'm so sorry. You don't seem to be a typical guerrilla fighter. Please, let's get a beer so I can apologize." With his arm around her, they walked to a small restaurant by the sea where all was forgiven over beer and fried smelt.

For a month, dinners and evening walks in brilliant sunsets along the sand dunes of the Baltic beaches with never-ending conversations exhilarated her. Each time they were together, the connection grew deeper, even discovering their families were from the same village. She drowned in the pleasure of looking at him and hearing him: he was her hero. He satisfied her intellectual thirst and her romantic longings, but her strict morals and religious beliefs would not allow any expression of the physical attraction.

She had found a kindred soul since they shared common interests, opinions, pleasures, and even foods. She was seventeen and in love for the first time. Her only disappointment was that Jonas did not attend Mass with her, but most men were not as religious as women, and she knew he was a Catholic. Her daydreams of marriage and children played out in her fantasy world that summer. She could see their home, their three sons, and their patriotic activities in tangible reality.

One Sunday, at Mass, her good friend Alicia, a rotund chatterbox, burst her bubble, "Jonas is a married man. I found out he has a sick wife in a sanatorium in Germany. I'm telling you this for your own good. I can't believe he had not told you."

Thinking this a lie, born of envy, she stared at Alicia with disbelief. "No! He never spoke of this. Of course, we haven't been intimate and have never discussed any future plans." Katerina said while blushing at the thought of their prolonged lustful kisses.

"Now that you know, I think you should never see him again because a future with him is impossible," hissed Alicia. "Divorce is a great stigma, and you would experience complete social ostracism. Your morals would never allow you to live in sin, and if you marry, you would be excommunicated by the Church."

"If you are right, Alicia, of course, I would never consent to marry a man who is still married in the eyes of the Church," Katerina concluded.

The next day a storm was brewing in nature and in her heart. In the pouring rain, she met Jonas at the doorway of their favorite café. Overcome by sadness, contemplating her loss, Katerina confronted Jonas, "Why did you deceive me? You know I am in love with you. You are married." She broke down in a torrent of tears.

Jonas, taken aback at the desolation in her eyes, took her in his arms and kissed her wet cheeks. "Let's sit down. I will explain." They sat at a small table where Katerina wiped her eyes. "Katerina, I am divorced. I married very young, and within a few months, Lina's behavior became bizarre. She disappeared for days at a time and saw non-existent beings. She became paranoid and then turned violent. As a last resort, I had her hospitalized at the best institute in Germany, and only after many years with no hope of recovery, I divorced her. I love you, and we should seize our happiness."

"There can be no happiness for us in the ashes of your broken vows. I can never see you again." Katerina trembled on actually voicing these words out loud to him. She stood up and wrenched herself away from all the joy she had known. She left the café and her hopes for the future.

Pain invaded her heart and numbed her to all other influences. Work and religion became her salvation. She never saw him again but remembered him in all that was good and beautiful when unbidden, acute feelings returned to her, and she remembered the aquamarine eyes.

Two years later, she met and married Vytas, and she loved him with a love of safety and home. For over twenty years, she had been a good and faithful wife. She finished brushing her hair, part of her bedtime ritual, and slipped into bed as tears flooded her eyes. The attraction to Jonas burned in her mind and body and the intervening years did nothing to ease the pain of longing. A firm belief in her moral superiority constituted her compensation. By doing the right thing, she had not betrayed her religion or her principles. At times, it seemed an empty victory.

Chapter 4
September 1939

The first day of September streamed seamlessly from the days of summer with no hint, no sign, and no portent that life would drastically change forever. Katerina smiled at her sleeping husband, Vytas, as she woke early for a surgical case. She longed to kiss him but did not want to wake him.

Katerina washed, dressed, had breakfast, and set out on a brisk walk to the clinic. Passing a still-closed newsstand, she glimpsed yesterday's headline: Germany claims attack by Polish troops. There were always skirmishes at the border.

While Katerina was taking a shortcut through the park in the crisp morning air, the aroma of pine trees evoked the memory of her first meeting with Vytas. Over twenty-five years ago, Katerina, a twenty-year-old medical student, attended a conference in Berlin to present her research on trachoma, an eye disease. Vytas, a thirty-five-year-old professor at the Stefan Batory University in Vilnius, gave a lecture on surgery. Impressed by the lecture, especially by a Lithuanian professor, she introduced herself to Professor Eimontas, propelled by a force she later credited to destiny.

"Professor, your brilliant lecture should be presented in Kaunas at our university," Katerina said, clutching her hands to dissipate her shyness.

"Young lady, you certainly know how to flatter me, but Poland and Lithuania do not enjoy diplomatic relations, and any cooperation between medical schools in Kaunas and Vilnius would be very difficult." He lit a fragrant pipe as he observed her blushing face with amusement.

Katerina, looking into his intense brown eyes, sensed the elusive chemistry of attraction. She smiled again. "Yes, Poland and Lithuania are not friends, but perhaps you could at least comment on my trachoma research."

As they walked out of the lecture hall together, she slipped on the highly polished wood floor, twisting off and losing her right high-heeled shoe. Professor Eimontas held out his arms, preventing her fall. His nearness made her aware of his strong arms and the fragrance of pine trees.

"My new shoes, the new leather soles . . ." she murmured in embarrassment. Vytas picked up the errant shoe and, bending over, slipped it on Katerina's foot as she leaned on his shoulder.

"Thank you so much," Katerina said, blushing.

"Were I the Prince and you Cinderella, this would be my occasion to claim you," Vytas said with a laugh. "Unfortunately, I am only a baron." Sensing her discomfort, he continued, "Perhaps we could prevent further mishaps and improve international relations by having some coffee." The professor took Katerina's elbow and, walking in the sunlit September afternoon, steered her toward a nearby coffeehouse. "What intrigued you about trachoma?"

They sat at a corner table, and Katerina explained, "I studied microbiology, and there has been considerable progress identifying the bacteria causing syphilis. Paul Erlich already has done so much work in this field, and I believe even more medicines will be developed to kill bacteria."

He looked with admiration at her slim figure in her clinging sky-blue silk dress and the small gold cross above her high breasts. She tossed her long light-brown hair in a flirtatious gesture, and the sun backlit her hair in a golden haze, making her appear as an angel with a halo.

Across from her, Vytas, a distinguished older man with thick black hair and piercing brown eyes, twinkled with amusement at the young girl's desperation to impress him with her knowledge.

Katerina ordered coffee and hazelnut cake. "I want to study these microscopic enemies that cause so much suffering. Trachoma causes blindness in the poorest regions of the world. Spread by flies and unhygienic conditions, this gruesome disease could be eliminated with the new antibacterial medicine. My research would document all the laboratory studies on this medicine and the prevalence of trachoma in countries around the world."

"You have a very ambitious agenda," concluded Vytas. "I think it is a noble cause you aspire to. But as to your research, I do have some advice on your statistical analysis." They spent the next few hours speaking as if connected by a magnetic force. They discussed statistics, politics, language, medicine, and history. They shared a common Lithuanian identity; fate bestowed upon them the joy of instant familiarity.

"Please send me those articles on statistics," Katerina said as they exchanged addresses, confirming the beginning of their relationship. Her heart leaped at the possibility of a more personal friendship with the renowned professor. Back at school, Katerina spent endless hours on research papers to send to him for his review.

The voluminous professional correspondence became personal after a few months:

Katerina,

I am a recent widower with a young son, Antanas. I met my wife, Jadvyga, the daughter of our Polish neighbors, in childhood. Jadvyga wanted to be an artist, an abstract painter, and was studying art in Paris when I pursued and married her. My parents initially objected to the marriage because she was Polish but finally accepted her because of her noble blood. I loved her and cared for her for two years before she succumbed to cancer.

Vytas

Reading this letter, Katerina sensed the impossibility of a romantic relationship with Vytas. He must have loved Jadvyga passionately to defy his parents and marry her. How could she, Katerina, compete with his past? Their difference in status was a chasm difficult to breach. She was a poor student in Lithuania, whereas he was a rich aristocrat living in Poland with a previous marriage, a son, and life. Katerina decided to reveal her personal life to Vytas. She wanted him to know of the difficulties she had overcome and what was most important in her life.

Dear Vytas,

You have questioned me about my strong religious and patriotic convictions. I became an orphan at an early age when both my parents succumbed in their early thirties to bacterial diseases. I was raised on a farm by my Aunt Teresa. It was only through the influence of a Catholic priest that I pursued my studies. Free state-sponsored education made medical school a possibility. I consider the Catholic Church and Lithuania my real family.

Katerina

After the lengthy correspondence of winter, Vytas realized the depth of her convictions. He found her to be beautiful, intelligent, and moral—a magnificent soul and a woman to be cherished. He only hoped the Lithuanian-Polish question of living in Vilnius would not be a problem since she seemed quite inflexible.

> *Darling Katerina,*
> *Since we met in Berlin this year, we revealed so much of ourselves in our letters. Our goals are the same—to help people with their physical suffering and to be true to the principles of the Catholic Church. I have your face before me at all times and wait for your letters impatiently. My diplomatic friends will obtain your visa to come to Vilnius. Please make arrangements to be my guest. Springtime in Vilnius is beautiful. My mother will write you a formal invitation.*
>
> *Vytas*

Katerina loved her work, her friends, and her lively social life as a medical intern in Kaunas. She kept her meeting and correspondence with Vytas a secret since a future seemed impossible. She did not want to subject herself to another failed infatuation as she had experienced with the unavailable Jonas. Thoughts of Jonas still scoured her heart.

On a student trip to Paris to attend a medical conference with her friend Alicia, Katerina was overjoyed to discover the beautiful, sophisticated city. They roamed the streets of Paris and studied all the boutique windows with seriousness—the cloche hats, high-heeled boots, silk stockings, fox pelts, and figure-skimming dresses. "Alicia, let's buy some silk and have the fashions copied in Vilnius." Katerina, at last, confessed her secret about Vytas and his invitation. "Alicia, my heart tells me a trip to Vytas's house in Vilnius will be a turning point in my life."

"I thought you would never get over Jonas, your great love," Alicia answered in surprise. Hearing Vytas's background, Alicia held little hope for a happy ending since Katerina was obviously not in his league. Alicia, a plain, pudgy young woman, could not help but feel envy but enjoyed living vicariously through Katerina.

"He is not Jonas, but Vytas is a good man, and I could be a wife and mother with a settled future," said Katerina with unwavering belief.

Returning to Kaunas, determined to be trim, they ate only rare, expensive oranges for weeks. The seamstress fashioned three dresses in the latest Parisian style. As Katerina modeled her new wardrobe, she asked Alicia, "Which of my new dresses is the most attractive?"

Alice said, laughing, "Well, your dark-green crepe is the most flattering for your audition as baroness."

On the train from Kaunas to Vilnius, after inspection of visas and stamps, Katerina mentally reviewed her wardrobe and imagined what the baron's house would be like. Could she ever belong there? If they marry, could she ever fulfill the role of baroness?

On the foggy May afternoon of Katerina's arrival, Vytas met her at the train station laden with a plethora of red roses and a beaming smile. A waiting black car took them to the imposing stone mansion on the hill. During the trip, he held her cold, clammy hand, and his assurance let her begin to relax. He described the passing sites, but all she could hear was the pounding of her heart.

Her trepidation dissipated at the entry hall when the Eimontas family—Vytas's parents and his sister Dalia—warmly welcomed her. As the old baroness took Katerina's hand, she said, "My dear, it is a pleasure to meet the woman who has given such joy to my son."

The books, the gleaming silver, the paintings of ancestors, the Persian carpets, the numerous servants, and the grand luxury of the baron's lifestyle overwhelmed her.

Katerina went to unpack and freshen up in the large pink-and-yellow guest room. Large windows overlooked acres of budding fruit trees. Her bed had a quilted satin coverlet and a chaise longue where she reclined and imagined her life as a baroness. Coming downstairs later, she encountered an eight-year-old boy in a suit and tie who eyed her suspiciously. "Katerina, I would like you to meet Antanas, my son," Vytas said.

"Hello, Antanas, it's wonderful to meet you. Your father is very proud of you. I hope we can become friends." Katerina bent over to shake his hand.

Ignoring Katerina's hand, he pointed to a painting on the wall, a large portrait of a dark, imperious beauty titled *Baroness Eimontas* in gold letters on the ornate wooden frame. Antanas said, "That's my mother. You can never be my mother. She died, but you are not as beautiful as she was."

The distraught baron, sensing his son's hostility, said, "Antanas, apologize and go to your room." The boy mumbled an apology, broke into tears, and fled to his room. Vytas took Katerina's hand and said, "I'm sorry for my son's behavior, but it's no secret in this household I'm planning to ask you to be my wife." Katerina's heart leaped with joy.

Weeks of meeting relatives, shopping, and long romantic dinners with Vytas constituted a whirlwind of happiness for Katerina. After a heartfelt discussion of their future, Vytas turned to her and said, "Are you sure you know what you're doing? I'm older than you, have a child, and this is not your country."

"I've found my home in you. My mind, heart, and soul are all willing to share the rest of my time on earth with you," she replied softly.

Simplicity marked the June wedding since Katerina insisted on a Lithuanian Catholic ceremony and there was only one Lithuanian church, St. Nicholas, in Vilnius. The other two hundred churches were Polish, Orthodox, or Protestant. The elegant reception in the baron's mansion was a small affair—as required by etiquette—since it was the baron's second marriage. Katerina's only guest, Alicia, arrived from Kaunas.

"I think you are the luckiest person alive to have avoided Jonas. Here, you will live like a queen," said Alicia while inspecting the magnificence of the baron's home.

Katerina and Vytas started their honeymoon in the Carpathian Mountains of Poland, in a resort called Zakopane. Vytas rented a villa high in the mountains. Hiking the trails covered in a profusion of wildflowers were occasions for Katerina to sing her favorite Lithuanian songs to an audience of one. They picked wild blueberries and strawberries on the sun-filled July days. In winter, these mountains would be covered with snow, and Katerina suggested, "Darling, let's come back here in winter to ski!"

"I'm too old to break my neck," Vytas replied with a kiss.

Good wine and delicious food enhanced their joyful evenings full of laughter. As night fell, Katerina experienced the thrill of sexual union. She was a virgin, and her expectations were simple. The closeness and gentleness of Vytas's body uniting with hers resonated in her body and soul. She had found home and safety.

The honeymoon continued in Paris, where the Seine glistened against the magnificent architecture. The exclusive shops, famous restaurants, and opera formed the sophisticated part of their honeymoon, and Vytas spared no expense on his young bride. Memories of her student trip with Alicia marked the difference in status. Before, as a student, she was counting every franc; now, as a baroness, she experienced a different Paris, sophisticated and exclusive. She returned to Vilnius a month later with suitcases full of Parisian luxuries and a mind full of priceless memories. Astrid, their daughter, was born a year later, and their marriage became a perfect partnership of medicine and family life.

Lost in thought, she almost passed the hospital entrance. Looking at her watch, she shook her head in disbelief at the time spent in reverie and ran up the back steps to the ophthalmology clinic. She donned her white clinic jacket and entered her office. Her first patient was waiting. After reviewing his chart, she administered anesthetic eye drops. Suddenly the door swung open, and Joseph Rudis, an intern, shouted, "Germany invaded Poland. The war has begun! I just heard it on the radio."

Startled, Katerina dropped the vial of eye medicine, alarmed by Joseph's news.

The patient bent over, picked up the vial, and said, "Sorry, Doctor Eimontas, but if this is true, I must get home as soon as possible," and left.

"Katerina, you are trembling. Perhaps it's not true or just a border incident," Joseph said. Rudis attended her lectures and had an unabashed crush on her. She sometimes stopped at a local bar with her colleagues to drink beer and eat dried salted peas, and Joseph always insinuated himself into her company.

"I know it's true. Hitler took Klaipeda, and now he will take Vilnius. The approach of war is a thought straight from hell." Her eyes filled with tears as Joseph, trying to comfort her, took her in his arms.

She raised her eyes to meet his and saw two blue eyes in a face that evoked a familiarity and attraction. His eyes reminded her of Jonas, and she could drown in those blue pools. "Please leave immediately. I must go see my next patient." Joseph, chastened, head bent, shuffled out the door.

As Katerina ran to the nurses' station, a cacophony of sound accosted her as everyone discussed the news of war. Seeing Beata, her best friend since the start of medical school, she ran toward her. "Did you hear?"

Beata picked up a newspaper on the counter. WAR DECLARED! GERMANY INVADES POLAND screamed the headlines. "Tragedy! Tragedy of the worst kind! This means an initiation of the same Nazi policies against Jews that exist in Germany. Poland will suffer the horror of occupation.

My husband and I will be identified as Jews and persecuted. Katerina, always be my friend. I'm so afraid."

"Of course, Beata. We vowed in medical school to always stand by one another. I'll always be your friend and help you. But you are a psychiatrist. Be rational. It may not be a permanent occupation. It may not affect us since, as doctors, we will always be needed in wartime, and our professions will protect us." Beata calmed down and hugged Katerina.

A mood of suspenseful dread covered Vilnius over the next few weeks. People went about their business in an eerie calm. No invading armies changed their lives. Only the constant monitoring of the news indicated impending disaster.

Baron Eimontas, in constant contact with his friends in the government, again heard the rumor that Germany and Russia would broker a deal and split Poland. He wanted to discuss the situation further with the rector of the university. "Katerina, could you please call Elena Dielka and see if they could join us at Metropole Café tomorrow at five? I would like to discuss events with Dielka."

Katerina loved to go to fashionable cafés for the "five o'clock" tradition. In Vilnius, the main meal of the day, dinner, was served in the early afternoon at one or two o'clock. People would then meet at cafés, which had small orchestras for dancing, at five in the afternoon to have coffee, pastries, and liquors. Supper was a simple meal at home at seven or eight. Katerina loved the music-and-dance-filled cafés with well-dressed people in deep discussions interspersed with raucous laughter. She enjoyed wearing her new dresses with pride before a crowd envious of her looks and status.

Katerina dressed with care, pulling up the sides of her shiny brown hair with combs and inspecting the straightness of her stocking seams. She put on her high-heeled shoes and twirled before a mirror. The large sapphire necklace Vytas gave her upon the birth of Astrid enhanced the new light-blue georgette dress. She threw the two fox pelts over her shoulder as she preened before a mirror and met Vytas's appreciative look.

Astrid, reading, looked up and said, "You will be the most elegant couple at the Metropole." They kissed her and departed.

At the Metropole Café, Katerina greeted the rector and his wife, Elena, who had already arrived and had been joined by the Polish General Kuzas. They ordered coffee, pastries, and cognac. The conversation turned to the current political situation. The general whispered, "Polish intelligence has uncovered that Lithuania will regain Vilnius." They had all been aware of the rumors, but here was official confirmation. Katerina, devouring the news, flushed with happiness. At long last—justice! She wanted to shout with joy but remained quiet and composed in this Polish city.

Noise levels increased to a crescendo in the crowded café. Waiters wheeled around a cart of chocolate-covered cream-filled pastries, raspberry bars, hazelnut torte, rushing to get coffee and cognac to their clientele. The small orchestra started playing *Jealousy*, the new tango rage, and the general asked Katerina to dance. Gliding on the crowded dance floor, Katerina found this short, plump man agile and rhythmic. The general led Katerina back to the table, thanking her, and lit a cigarette. She mused how the nicotine failed to stain his luxuriant snow-white mustache.

The door of the café crashed open, and a harried young man shouted in anguish, "Vilnius has been invaded by the Red Army! Tanks and troops are entering the city!" Stunned people ran to peer out the windows, and indeed, soldiers were marching, waving the red flag, followed by motorcycle troops. The radio blaring news of the arrival of the Red Army also announced a forthcoming statement by the president of Lithuania.

Immediately everything stopped: all the tension, discussions, and speculation about the future ended. The orchestra stopped playing, took their instruments, and fled. Curses of disbelief and anger punctuated the sounds of people rushing out as waiters cleared the room.

Rector Dielka was the first to speak: "Life as we know it is over. We are under occupation." Katerina noticed Elena holding her husband's hand so tightly that both hands appeared together as a white marble tableau.

"No," the general countered, "this is not a permanent occupation. The troops are here only to officially give Vilnius back to Lithuania."

Katerina, shocked by General Kuzas's assurance, murmured, "This can't be. Why are Soviet troops entering if Lithuania is to occupy Vilnius?"

Vytas said, "Perhaps the USSR wants to be perceived as a generous patron giving the gift of an ancient capital back to its rightful owners. By giving Vilnius to Lithuania, they are courting good world opinion."

The general spoke, "This is not a free gift. The USSR will station troops here in exchange for giving them Vilnius." He continued in a soft, sad voice, "But in essence, it will be the occupation of all of Lithuania since the entire Lithuanian army will not equal twenty thousand Soviet troops." In silence, the couples and the general wished each other a good night and went their separate ways.

The news of the arrival of the Soviets reached the seminary, where Jan Kataski was at an all-day retreat led by Bishop Venclovas. High Mass with Latin chanting and incense preceded the lectures, which were interspersed by prayer and contemplation.

The bishop, informed of events, had knowledge of history, and the presence of the Red Army confirmed his greatest fears of an eventual takeover. After concentrated prayer, he rewrote his closing lecture. The usually pale bishop appeared specter-like in his long black robe before the students.

"A martyr of the Church is one whose life is taken away because of his faith. Martyrdom is pictured as a dramatic and sudden death, but it is also suffering for your faith in a slow and agonizing death by torture or prison. Today, the Soviets invaded our city, and the first sign of a communist takeover is persecution of the Church. Communists consider religion to be an opiate of the people to be extinguished at all costs. Knowing their methods, I can assure you we will suffer. The religious will be hunted down and considered enemies of the state."

"Are they not here only to give Vilnius back to Lithuania?" asked a student.

"Vilnius will be given to Lithuania, but in turn, Lithuania will be given to the USSR," the bishop prognosticated. "Students, maintain your faith and pray we survive this onslaught with the help of God."

Jan inwardly felt calm in the midst of his panicked classmates. His relationship to God could withstand any suffering. If his time on earth were a test for eternal life, he would welcome this challenge to his faith.

Running home to the Polish section, Jan burst forth to his mother, "Do you know today's news? Russian troops have entered Vilnius. The bishop said we are temporarily excused from our studies."

Paulina dropped her laundry basket and collapsed into the nearest kitchen chair. "Mother of God, I know the godless Asiatics have seized our city." She clutched at her heart. "Jan, take off your uniform. I don't know what will happen, but it will be all bad."

Casimir returned from work and heard the news about Jan. "Good! Let Jan leave the seminary and start to work with me. It will be better for us than his constant praying and monitoring us for church attendance and adherence to their thousands of rules. The communists will make life better for us."

"Life better?" Paulina asked. "Already Albert at our grocery store could not sell me anything since they got a big order from the Russian Army. He laughed when I said his business should be great. He replied, 'I don't think so, since they don't pay!'"

After dinner, Paulina grabbed Valeria and Anna and ran to the Gates of Dawn, where a large crowd had gathered, singing hymns in Latin to the Mother of God, the Protector of the City. The young and old, the rich and poor, cohered into one moving terrified organism in the grasp of a great enemy. Falling on her knees on the cobblestones, Paulina prayed for the safety of her family and the deliverance of her city: it was the only thing she could do, her only source of help.

As news of the Red Army's arrival reached the Jewish Quarter, Jacob was beaming. "The best news ever! We are saved from the Nazis." He was to meet with his communist friends to welcome the Red Army into Vilnius. He saw Daniel downcast. "What's wrong? You should be overjoyed."

Daniel, worried, said, "Communism doesn't allow private enterprise. This will be the death of our business." Abraham, chewing on his lower lip, nodded in agreement, thoughts of his savings and Palestine swirling in his head.

Sarah, in the midst of these discussions, said, "Nothing has happened yet. Let's wait, and it may all come to nothing, only the great powers playing games with each other. Abraham, we must go to the store."

The news and turmoil also excited Rachel. But the thought of the communists coming did not disturb her; her mind was focused on an encounter she had a week ago when, on the way to school, her bicycle had a flat tire on a deserted street. A young man walking on the opposite side of the street saw the situation and approached. "Do you need any help?"

"You are Pranas, the boy who works in the library." Rachel said with relief, seeing a familiar face made unique by his missing left ear.

Pranas recognized Rachel as a Jewish student at the university, always in the library with her bountiful dark curls falling into some heavy textbook on music. He thought, a beautiful girl—a shame she was Jewish. He took the tire off and examined it. "Wait, I'll run home and get a patch to fix it."

He soon returned with a patch and pump. "You are very kind, Pranas, to help me. I know I'm not from your neighborhood."

"Well, my people believe in helping each other," said Pranas to indicate his superior Christianity.

"We Jews help one another, too," Rachel said, observing him kneel to remove the flat tire. He sat on the curb, placing the patch, and filled the tire with air. "I think all religions are good," Rachel concluded as she inspected Pranas. She thought him good-looking but for the missing ear.

Pranas examined the tire and said to the grateful Rachel, "I don't believe in religion. My parents are hard-working, but they will never be rewarded no matter how much my mother prays to God. She works for a baron and slaves for a pittance while his lands build up his wealth. There is no justice! The communists have the right idea—from each according to his ability, to each according to his needs. Is that not a better way of life?"

"I know nothing about communism. I only know Nazis hate the Jews," said Rachel, peering at him from under her long lashes, smiling.

"Here, I'll give you a book. Promise to give it back," said Pranas, handing over the *Communist Manifesto* and her bicycle.

Rachel spent the next few days reading the book, and a light went off in her head. Marx's genius solved all the world's problems and changed life into a paradise of equality. What was wrong with this world? Some people suffered to enrich other people. Religion separated people and only strived to have riches and power. In a romantic reverie, she wanted to impress her friend Pranas with her newfound conversion.

Jacob came into her room a few days later as she was finishing a chapter, and after a friendly tousle, he grabbed the book. "So this is what you are reading! I thought it would be some love story. I know this book, and there are some good points in it. It's certainly more acceptable than the Nazi ideology of racial superiority." Rachel blushed a bright red. "Your ears are on fire. Certainly, an economic theory can't have you so entranced. Who is he?" asked Jacob.

Today, her family's discussion of the occupation and the constant drone of the plight of the Jews bored Rachel; her mind was on Pranas. To escape, she decided to ride her bicycle and practice her violin. Immersed in thought at her professor's interpretation of Beethoven's Violin Concerto, Rachel rapidly pedaled her bicycle to the Music Institute.

"Rachel!" came a cry from the other side of the street. It was Pranas.

"Wait a moment, I'll run home, and I'll return your book," answered Rachel.

"The Red Army has entered Vilnius!" shouted Pranas, eyes blazing with excitement, as he ran up to her. "Let's greet them!"

"I'll go with you, but wait until I get your book." Rachel spun her bicycle home through the cool autumn afternoon and passed many people from the Jewish quarter, laughing and smiling on their way to the town square. The festive atmosphere was contagious.

Entering her house, she grabbed her book, and as she turned to leave, Jacob stopped her. "Rachel, you told me how impressed you were by Marx's theories. Come, let's go welcome the Red Army. There's no way the fascists would dare to come now."

Daniel stood at the door, observing. "Both of you are idiots, especially you, Jacob, a student of the Torah. The communists are trying to eliminate God. Both national socialism and communism are against our people. Democracy is the only solution for us where we will be equal and free to practice our religion and our trade."

"Is that all you care about, Daniel, trade?" countered Jacob. "Don't you ever think of justice? Our country's pro-Nazi nationalists limit access of Jews to the government. And the Nazis don't even consider the Jews human. Only the Soviets will give us equality."

Rachel and Jacob sneered at Daniel and left. Outside the ghetto, they ran into Pranas, waiting for Rachel. She gave the book back to Pranas, introducing him to her brother. They ran along the street to the town square and merged with a multitude cheering, carrying flowers, and waving pieces of red fabric to symbolize the Red Army. "Welcome, brothers! Comrades forever!"

Streams of Soviet soldiers pounded the streets, carrying rifles gleaming in the sun, interspersed by massive tanks. They marched in unison as red flags emblazoned with the hammer and sickle waved in the breeze. A young, blonde woman ran up to a soldier and planted a kiss on his cheek to the cheers of the crowd. The soldiers marched by, smiling quizzically at this enthusiastic yet unexpected welcome.

Citizens of Vilnius peered through the windows in horror to see some of their own people welcoming the dreaded Soviet occupying forces. Older people on Pilsudski Street trembled with tears remembering the brutality of Russian rule. Comments buzzed in the crowd: "Who are these people welcoming the Soviet plague?" "I recognize the Bernstein children. Look, there's Jacob, and there is Rachel." "The Jews were never patriotic to Vilnius." "My god, isn't that the Kataski boy Pranas? His parents must be horrified. It must be breaking Paulina's heart."

Antanas Eimontas finished his lecture in economics and hurried to a faculty meeting at the university. The aroma of exotic heavy perfume and a feminine hand halted him in the corridor. The Countess Doban, dressed in a tight black suit with décolletage revealing her assets, appeared licking her full lips in a provocative smile.

"Countess, what a pleasant surprise," Antanas said in a hoarse voice.

"Please call me Gretchen. My husband is with government officials and will not return until late tonight. I'm staying at the Astoria Hotel. Come to me in about an hour," she purred, her face flushed with anticipation. She put a key to her hotel room in his pocket as she pressed her body against his. The curves of her body melting into his commandeered his senses, leaving him helpless and compliant. He went into the washroom to douse his face with cold water before going to the faculty meeting.

Two hours later, at the Astoria Hotel, the luxurious suite appeared empty as he unlocked the door and entered. He walked to the bedroom, where Gretchen lay naked on the bed with the flaming-red hair of her head echoing on her pubis. In a fury of lust, he stripped and, without a word, fell upon her. Her wildness almost drove him into exhaustion.

No conversation was necessary, although she did refer to dissatisfaction with Count Doban as a lover. Antanas tried to remedy the situation by caressing the full high breasts, the firm melons of her backside, and the long shapely legs under the slim waist. Her skin shimmered with a slight sheen of sweat. Only her face lacked perfection, but he was not concentrating on that area. After three hours, she jumped up.

"It's late! You must come with me. I must buy something to show my husband since I said I would be shopping." With this, she started dressing in a provocative way, exciting Antanas and leading to some delay in plans. Finally dressed, she went out, meeting him a few minutes later in the lobby.

They entered the damp cold wind of the late autumn afternoon. "What I need—a new fur coat. The best furrier is Bernstein's. Let's go."

Entering the mirrored Bernstein showroom, they were seated and offered coffee by a young man. The back door opened, and Sarah entered, a diminutive woman enhanced with regal bearing and posture of a prima ballerina. She did not walk; she glided as if skating on ice. A pale, oval, porcelain face outlined by black brows and huge brown eyes flecked with gold hovered above her sensual and plump red lips. Her glossy black hair was piled on her head. The minute Antanas encountered her, he was mesmerized and imagined softly biting her moist lips and freeing the lustrous hair. If only he could graft Sarah's face on Gretchen's body!

They introduced themselves as Countess Doban and Mr. Eimontas. Sarah recognized both names.

The stench of sweat and ammonia, the unmistakable reek of recent sex on their bodies, took Sarah aback. She observed the flushed face and sparkling eyes of the buxom countess as she said, "Countess Doban, may I show you our most recent acquisition of sable pelts with a hint of gold and red that would be magnificent with your hair? I can sketch the design and provide you with a muslin pattern."

Sarah continued, "I see you live in Memel, and it would be impossible for me to deliver the coat to you, but perhaps you could impose on this gentleman to be the currier." Sarah looked directly at Antanas.

Petting the pelts, Gretchen decided it would be a perfect excuse to see Antanas again. "Yes, show me your sketches."

Antanas stepped aside to let Sarah pass and was struck by the aroma of eucalyptus, a smell so fresh and inviting he found himself saying, "I need a fur cap. Would you be able to help me?"

"Of course, Mr. Eimontas, with pleasure," Sarah said with a flirtatious smile, pleased at a large sale so early in the season.

"I will return with my specifications later so your entire time could be devoted to the countess." Antanas grinned at the prospect.

Antanas and Gretchen left Bernstein's and parted at the hotel entrance. Gretchen brazenly kissed him in public view. "We will meet again," she promised. "We are meant for each other." Antanas nodded as he thought, *Each woman thinks of herself as unique to my life as the Holy Grail, but they are as interchangeable for me as my neckties.*

Gretchen returned to her rooms where the angry count met her at the door. "Where were you?"

"Darling, I had such a long day shopping for a new fur coat for winter. I must return tomorrow to approve the design."

"Have you not heard Vilnius is under Russian occupation? What sort of bubble have you been in today? We are leaving immediately for Memel!" The count, flushing a deep red, threw their belongings into suitcases.

Antanas showered and dressed in his uniform. Sated physically by Gretchen and beguiled by Sarah, he sauntered down Pilsudski Street in the sunshine when a friend, a fellow officer, rushed up to him. "Officer Eimontas, we have been looking for you. You should immediately go to army headquarters. A state of emergency has been declared."

"What happened?" Antanas asked. "I have been at the university."

"The Russians are coming. We are burning sensitive government documents," the pale, sweating fellow officer blurted out.

Panicking at his ignorance, he rushed to report at headquarters. Heading toward the main square of the city, Antanas saw the large jubilant crowd, mostly dressed in Jewish garb, welcoming the Red Army into Vilnius. They stood on both sides of the street, yelling, "Welcome, freedom fighters!" "Glory to the revolution!" "Power to the proletariat!" People waved red flags or even pieces of red flannel on sticks and threw flowers at the Soviet soldiers whose boots hammered the cobblestones. The drumming sounds of the occupation were at odds with the joyous cries.

A young woman approached a soldier and crowned his rifle with a wreath of flowers. A young man with a yarmulke hoisted a red flag and screamed, "Liberation at last!" Antanas saw the soldiers marching, stomping their boots in unison, and almost vomited in disgust. An occupier of his city being welcomed! He approached the young man with clenched fists. "Why are you celebrating? Don't you understand our city is being raped by the Russians?" Antanas asked with resentment.

Surprised at the question, the man lowered the red flag and answered, "The arrival of the Red Army means Hitler will not come here. I escaped from Munich, and there, life for a Jew like me is a disaster under Hitler."

"A Soviet occupation for us is as bad as Hitler is for you. This is your city too! Don't you care that it's now under the control of foreigners?" Antanas asked while shaking his fist, feeling a hot surge of anger. "Wait until Stalin puts you in a concentration camp!" Antanas, in bitter rage, thought, *Now I know the collaborators—the communist Jews.* To think they had been sheltering the enemy in their midst! At least the enemy has been identified.

Arriving at the army headquarters, he wanted to issue a condemnation of the people who welcomed the Russians. "Not so fast," said General Kuzas. "Do you want them to arrest you? The communist sympathizers are now protected by the occupiers, and to be against them would bring severe punishment." Antanas felt the dread of restraint. His frustration grew with the despair of being powerless.

The Russian occupation of Vilnius threw the city into turmoil. The officials claimed the Russians had come to liberate Vilnius and return it to its rightful owners, but confusion reigned. The expectation that the city would immediately revert to Lithuania faded. Were the Russians to fight the Germans for the city? Who was in charge of this city? Was an occupation by Lithuania imminent?

The facts were clear: The great powers put Vilnius in play, and the city would not be a part of poor, abused Poland. People overloaded the telephone lines with speculation and met in the streets to discuss their future. Chasms were opening in society; the occupation was a tragedy for the Poles, joy for the Jews, and uncertainty for the Lithuanians.

Antanas had studied history and was aware of the consequences of regime change. His family, rich and aristocratic, and his father, a leading intellectual, were in more danger than the average inhabitant of Vilnius. They fulfilled the criteria for elimination under communist doctrine. Cleverness, courage, and luck were vital to survive in this scenario.

However, if the occupation dissipated and Vilnius indeed reverted to Lithuania, supreme joy would reign. The transition would require energy and inventiveness to subdue the Poles and Jews, who outnumbered the Lithuanians. Antanas saw the turmoil, but in all this tragedy, he saw the opportunity of a crisis when new leaders would emerge, dogma would be revised, and history would be written.

CHAPTER 5
OCTOBER 1939

For the next month, Vilnius chafed under Soviet control. In its gray, silent streets, the Russian presence made everyday life bitter. Food, formerly plentiful, was now requisitioned to feed the occupiers, and this led to shortages. The Red Army officers were well behaved and paid for their supplies. However, the soldiers, especially the Asian Soviets, robbed what they could from the shop owners. Unease and fear spread among the local population. When general looting began in earnest, there was no place to lodge a complaint. Who was in charge?

However, in other respects, life went on almost uninterrupted. Wealth, position, and influence enabled people to circumvent many inconveniences. To them, the changing times were primarily a subject of conversation.

Antanas burst in on Katerina at the clinic. "Mother, I've been blessed by lady luck! I've been asked to go to Moscow with the Foreign Minister of Lithuania to a meeting with Russian officials. They need someone with Russian language skills to take notes. Rector Dielka recommended me."

"Darling, what a great honor!" Katerina hugged Antanas and patted his cheek as a patient quizzically observed this scene. "But it's not only luck—you've been working day and night as a translator. Be sure to do the job well, and don't forget the interests of Lithuania." But luck was a gift of the gods, mused Katerina and, although certainly arbitrary, was the most precious gift bestowed.

On October 3, Antanas Eimontas flew to Moscow with the Lithuanian Foreign Minister's delegation. At the airport, resplendent with Lithuanian and Soviet flags, a Soviet delegation welcomed them before they were driven to a hotel. They spent the next few days in lower-level meetings discussing the welfare of Russian troops stationed in Lithuania.

One evening, the Lithuanian delegation received a summons at about eleven, got into two black cars, and entered the Kremlin gates. The USSR Commissar for Foreign Affairs greeted them and led them to an office to sit at a highly polished conference table with Molotov. Before long, Stalin appeared in the doorway: medium height, burly frame, graying, thick hair combed upward, luxuriant mustache, piercing black eyes, sand-colored jacket, peasant trousers stuffed into soft low black boots. A closer inspection revealed that these ordinary clothes and shoes were of exceptional quality, fabric, and workmanship. The power of the man filled the room.

As two sovereign nations, each enjoying equal rights, they began negotiations. Their friendly relations were based on signed accords still in effect. Stalin spoke and stated bluntly that the Soviet Union had made a pact with Germany on August 23. Placing a map of Eastern Europe on the table, he pointed to the line demarcating the Soviet and German domains. "You must sign two treaties: one, dealing with the return of Vilnius, and the other, regarding the mutual assistance of Russia and Lithuania," he said softly in heavily Georgian-accented Russian.

"What mutual assistance?" the foreign minister of Lithuania asked.

"You must agree to the permanent placement on Lithuanian territory of up to fifty thousand Soviet troops." Stalin rose and walked toward Molotov sitting in the back. Molotov, with pale yellow waxy skin, seemed unwell.

"But this is the occupation of Lithuania! The entire Lithuanian army has only twenty thousand troops," retorted the angered Lithuanian foreign minister. Antanas saw his hand was shaking as he took down these words and realized the dawn of occupation waiting in the wings.

Stalin and Molotov both smiled. "I realize Lithuania is not armed," Stalin said as he stopped smiling. "This is your protection from the fascists."

"If the Lithuanian government would agree to any Soviet troops at all, could they not be based solely in the newly re-acquired territory of Vilnius?" the foreign minister pleaded.

"No. The army must be stationed throughout the entire country," asserted Stalin as he pulled out a newspaper and shoved it in the direction of the Lithuanian delegation. The Moscow newspaper, *Pravda*, of October 4 had printed an article, together with pictures, of celebratory demonstrations in Vilnius. Stalin boasted, "You see how your people welcome our regime."

Stalin poured Antanas a glassful of vodka. "Drink. You are young and must have faith in the glorious USSR. Drink! Drink! Come, come. A Russian likes to drink," Stalin insisted.

Antanas lifted the glass and drained it in a gulp. Stalin offered the Lithuanian delegation a lavish buffet—blini with caviar, bouillon with piroshki, herring with onions and sour cream, red beet salad, pickles, black bread, smoked salmon, and cold beef. All these delicacies were accompanied by a river of vodka. After much prodding, the Lithuanians consumed polite quantities of food and drink and sat awhile in silence. It appeared time to leave, so they rose to thank their host.

"No, no, sit down! We are going to the cinema," Stalin insisted. After one film, the American movie *Tarzan*, the Lithuanians again began to rise. Stalin ordered another film, the American movie *Boys Town*. As it ended, they again attempted to leave. Stalin said, "Now my favorite, the jazz movie *Volga, Volga*." As these movies were shown, everyone's eyes followed Stalin to see when to laugh or clap. It was after six in the morning when the delegation finally left the Kremlin.

On the morning of October 10, Katerina, with tears of joy, welcomed Antanas home, discussed his historic trip, and read the newspaper headline: Vilnius to revert to Lithuania. The article stated the USSR ceded this city to Lithuania by special decree, giving the ancient capital back to its rightful owners.

Two weeks later, the Lithuanian army gloriously entered the streets of Vilnius, marching past the cathedral and up Pilsudski Street. Jubilant throngs of Lithuanians, some in their native costumes, waving the tricolor Lithuanian flags of yellow, green, and red, met the soldiers with flowers and Lithuanian songs. A frenzy of happiness infected the Lithuanian onlookers; however, other natives of Vilnius interpreted the event with hostility and suspicion.

Antanas, in his uniform, returned home from observing the Lithuanian parade and meeting with colleagues in city hall. "Mother, by chance, I got a tremendous political appointment. The Russians appointed General Kuzas to be the acting mayor of Vilnius, and since his assistant does not speak Russian, he asked me to be his assistant."

Katerina hugged him as Vytas shook his son's hand and poured all of them a toast. Katerina wondered if the cloak of good luck was to envelop Antanas throughout his life. "Wonderful news! But you must be careful to distinguish what is best for Lithuania. The Russians chose General Kuzas to be a puppet for USSR interests."

"The general already did what is best for Lithuania. He released me from the Polish army and gave me a Lithuanian colonel's rank," Antanas added, laughing.

"My son, I'm bursting with happiness. I can't wait to see you in the Lithuanian uniform," Katerina exclaimed with joy. Her eyes shining, a beautiful peach glow of excitement coloring her face, she twirled like a young girl and shouted, "To Vilnius!" Observing her with a smile, Antanas confirmed his father's opinion of Katerina's attractiveness.

Antanas, in the midst of this excitement, suddenly realized, "This city must be returned to its Lithuanian roots! Our work is enormous. All documents must be changed from Polish to Lithuanian. The currency must change from the zloty to the litas. Lithuanians must be hired to fill all important city posts. My god! We must change the names of all the streets and parks and redraw all the maps!"

"Darling, take a breath!" said Katerina, laughing. "There will be enough time. You know the saying 'Rome was not built in a day.'"

The Eimontas family enjoyed the festive supper Paulina prepared. The discussion centered on Katerina's plans for a party marking this historic occasion. She planned to invite her friends from Kaunas to attend and debated the decorations, the program, the menu, and a new dress. "Of course, Antanas is to come in his new Lithuanian uniform," she added with a proud smile.

Antanas, working at his desk in the mayor's office, received a cable from Moscow: Germany and the USSR had partitioned Poland, officially setting their borders. He rushed the cable into the mayor's smoke-filled office. The general, in full Polish uniform, still uncomfortable in his new position as mayor of the city, observed Antanas in his new Lithuanian uniform. He saw the incongruity of their appearance and said, "As of tomorrow, only civilian dress in this office."

General Kuzas, a chain smoker (although his snow-white mustache denied his habit), pointed out a chair to Antanas with a wave of his hand. Antanas gave him the telegram and sat down. Kuzas squinted to read the cable, smiled, and said, "Good news. Perhaps all will be stable now. In case of further encroachment by either, of course, Lithuania would be in play. We must defend ourselves."

Antanas, taken aback by his naïveté, stated with a smirk, "Defense would be a disaster." He stood up and lit a cigarette. "As a reserve officer, I know how weak the Lithuanian armed forces are. They have inadequate arms, few uniforms. Their air force consists of six airplanes, and the soldiers are poorly trained. My god, we are still dependent on cavalry and outmoded artillery."

Kuzas threw down the telegram. "When freedom from Russia came in 1918, the money and all efforts went to education and infrastructure, raising the hopes and opportunities of a whole generation. The spare money spent on the military was useless since it did not prepare us to fight and left us vulnerable to attack."

Antanas, aware of the implications, said, "Even if we were armed, what could a small country of three million inhabitants do? It's hopeless." He picked up the small Lithuanian flag on the general's desk and inspected it. His eyes fell on a small bottle of peroxide half-hidden by the flag. Antanas surmised the bleach was used to maintain the pure white of the mustache.

The general, lighting another cigarette, said, narrowing his eyes to slits, "True, we must hope for the best and not antagonize the Soviets. Our main concern is to return this town to its Lithuanian roots. That is our assignment and our priority."

In the evening, Antanas found his father in the library, smoking his pipe and reading. Greeting Antanas, Vytas got up from the leather chair, placed his copy of Homer's *Odyssey* in Greek on the side table, and poured glasses of cognac for them. "What's new in the mayor's office?" he said as he returned to his favorite chair and filled his pipe with fresh tobacco.

Antanas downed the cognac and observed the painting of Vytautas the Great, a ruler who was supreme when Lithuania was in its glory, the biggest country in Europe. The precarious position of his country was uppermost in his mind as he gave a detailed report of the contents of the cable. He concluded, "The idea of Lithuania being eaten by these two giants is horrific."

At first, Baron Eimontas was silent. Then he stood and replied in a voice full of pity, "Son, it's always been so. The partition of Poland is probably just the beginning of what will happen to this part of the world. There's a good chance that Lithuania will be under Russian rule."

"Father, what can be done?" Antanas walked over to his father and put his hand on his shoulder as if to join forces against this unimaginable tragedy. Baron Eimontas shook his head.

Katerina, standing by the door with Astrid to call her family to dinner, overheard them. "No! There's no way the Soviets would occupy the whole country. The world could not let that happen! Being under Russian occupation would be a crime! That can't happen again!" She embraced her daughter as if to protect her.

Astrid grew up hearing stories of life under the Russian occupation, the horrors of subjugation, the persecution of the Catholic Church, the effort to extinguish the Lithuanian language. Children were taught to fear the Russian bear as the specter of evil. Astrid echoed her mother, "No, Daddy, it cannot happen again."

"We must be realistic. It is happening," said Vytas as he put down his pipe.

Katerina, with misting eyes, said, "Enough, dinner is ready."

Antanas and Vytas followed the women into the dining room. Astrid walked crying toward the dining table to their dinner of roast duck. "I was starting to live life as a Lithuanian," she said between sobs. "I don't want to become a Russian peasant."

Katerina said, "Astrid, don't worry, we will never be Russian, peasant, or aristocrat. However, the Soviets eliminated the aristocracy, so you would do better becoming a peasant." Katerina took her shawl and draped it over her head in likeness to the Russian babushka. "This will be the new fashion," she said, making Astrid laugh through her tears.

Suddenly Dalia, Vytas's sister, who had a separate apartment in the mansion, appeared in the dining room and, even after a plea from Katerina, did not join them. She only said, "Days of tragedy are beginning." The laughter was silenced as Dalia fled upstairs. Katerina found Dalia mysterious, having heard hints of a tragic love affair that led her to be eccentric and renounce the world. At their first meeting, Dalia peered deep into Katerina's eyes and made a whispered prediction, "You will be the mistress here, but your heart will always be elsewhere."

When Katerina questioned Vytas about Dalia's psychic powers, Vytas answered, "Extreme sensitivity, tragic circumstances, and mental frailty do not make a resilient human being." After learning of Dalia's weakness, Katerina treated her with care.

After the awkward dinner, Vytas and Katerina undressed in their bedroom and slipped into the down quilt bed. Looking at the huge cross above the bed, a family heirloom from the fourteenth century, Katerina said a silent prayer. The bedroom had heavy, dark, carved furniture from the previous century. Katerina longed to redecorate it in a modern style, but Vytas's mother, Baroness Maria, remained the real mistress of the house. Mostly silent, Maria could indicate her wishes with a nod. Everyone knew she ruled. Vytas's parents had a separate apartment in the mansion, and Baroness Maria refused to socialize with their guests, saying, "We are too old to mingle with young people. Let us alone with our memories."

Vytas took Katerina in his arms and found she was trembling. "Don't worry, my love, my position and yours will survive politics. Physicians will be needed no matter who runs the country. My only fear is for Antanas because of his army commission and political connections. If the wind blows the wrong way, he will be caught in the crosshairs. Astrid is too young to be in any danger, my parents are too old, and Dalia is hardly there. We will survive, my love, I can assure you."

"You can't guarantee our safety." Pointing to the cross above their bed, Katerina said, "Our only guarantee for safety is there."

"We can only hope the Russians keep their promise," Vytas said.

"Mother Maria invited me to tea today and said there was an aura of doom over this household. I think it's the pessimism of the aged."

"Or the forecast of experience."

Antanas, garbed in his best civilian clothes, appeared at the mayor's office the next day and initiated a frenzy of activity. Ruta, his secretary, a whippet lean blonde from Kaunas, already seduced and bedded by Antanas, slavishly followed his instructions. "Schedule a meeting on the renaming of all the streets of the city. Make sure the Office of the Budget declares the Lithuanian litas as our only official currency. Call a meeting of the top economists, merchants, and bank owners to establish a new financial policy." Ruta wrote rapidly and rushed to fulfill her assignments.

In the town hall, newly decorated with the seal of the grand duchy of Lithuania and Lithuanian flags, the financial elite of Vilnius met. The twenty men, Polish and Jewish, bankers and shopkeepers, listened as Antanas explained the change in currency from the Polish zloty to the Lithuanian litas.

Mr. Rothstein, a tall man with bright red hair and beard, stated, "I know I speak for all of us when I say we welcome the Lithuanian litas. It is a stronger currency than the Russian ruble or the Polish zloty. The litas is backed by gold and cannot be printed at will. With Vilnius under Lithuanian control, the economy will prosper." All present nodded in agreement.

Antanas dictated a report, proud of his first independent success. To celebrate, he went to Bernstein's to order his fur hat.

"Where is Madam Bernstein?" he inquired after entering the store.

"She's left for the day. Perhaps I can help you? I'm Daniel Bernstein, the owner's son, and this is Rachel, my sister." The young man was plagued by a facial deformity, but the girl was a beauty with dark curls, flashing black eyes, and a buxom figure. However, she was not more than fifteen and Sarah's daughter.

"May I help you?" Rachel insinuated herself in close proximity. Antanas was the most attractive man she had ever seen. "I would be glad to help you with anything," she whispered.

Antanas answered curtly, "I will only deal with Madame Bernstein." He turned and went out into the street, amused that his Sarah had grown children. The disappointment of not seeing Sarah was quickly gone in the company of officers who all found girls to be with that night.

Abraham Bernstein met some elders from his synagogue. "I think this geographical shifting of Vilnius is a joke," commented Samuel Stein. "How can they expect to change the character of a city? Are they going to drive people out? Are they going to import some Lithuanian pig farmers to run it?" He laughed as he slapped his thigh.

"It's not so hard to clear a city. Klaipeda is an example," Abraham said as he chewed on his lower lip.

"But those people left mostly of their own accord. There is no reason for us to pick up our skirts and run," Stein provoked hilarity in hiking his coattails and mimicking a run.

"The Lithuanians are renaming the streets and arguing violently. Everyone wants their own opinion to prevail. The Lithuanians are inexperienced in governing," Rabbi Gold concluded. "And without us, there would be no commerce since they feel it is beneath their dignity to be merchants."

Shlomo Weiss, the richest businessman, agreed. "Certainly, the Lithuanians will leave business to us and not soil their hands with commerce. Let's hope they are in power and not the Soviets, who are nationalizing the economy of Russia."

"One thing for sure," interjected Abraham, "they will not let us have any say in the running of the city. The idea of a Jew in government is foreign to the Lithuanians."

In Klaipeda, Stefan had been passing for a German by perfecting his German accent and inventing a fictitious family background in Prussia. Now completely comfortable with his new identity as Katas, he followed the news closely, concerned about his family. The German papers barely alluded to the transfer of Vilnius to Lithuania. However, rampant gossip spread that the Russians wanted army bases in the country as a bulwark against Germany. *They are afraid of Germany*, Stefan thought. The flotilla of mighty armaments flowing on the Baltic Sea gave evidence to Stefan of the power of Germany, an industrial giant.

His recent promotion as supervisor of the loading docks for armaments led to his acquaintance with a friendly, fat German officer, Hans Schmidt.

"The German factories must be working day and night to produce this quantity of arms," Stefan commented after sharing a few beers.

"We are an industrious people," Schmidt responded, standing, almost stretching to full imperial height. "German might will transform the world."

"You are already prospering and expanding. What other transformation is needed?" Stefan asked as he marveled at Hans eating two huge sausage sandwiches while drinking his fifth beer.

"We Germans believe the high culture of our Aryan race is meant to rule the world. We have given the world Beethoven and Wagner, Schopenhauer and Nietzsche."

"But the idea of a superior race?" Stefan asked, taking another beer.

"We did not originate the idea, only the Aryan signature. The English believed in their superiority over the heathens of their colonies in India and Africa. America believed in the superiority of the white race over the black, and I think it still does," he concluded with a wink while taking another beer.

After a brief silence, he continued, "So why would our thoughts be so different? We believe certain people are inferior: the Jews, the gypsies, the mentally disabled, the Slavs." He took a cigarette and pointed out a blonde girl approaching another table. "Now, there is an Aryan beauty. Why should she be contaminated by scum?"

Stefan, seeing Schmidt speaking too freely after too much beer, tried to steer the conversation away from racial superiority, "So where are you going on your next leave?"

Hans, slurring his words, looked at Stefan and whispered, "You don't fool me. You're not German. You're a Pole, a Slav. I can tell by the way you pronounce certain German words. But it's OK. I told everyone you're a Lithuanian. You won't have any trouble." Then Hans passed out.

Stefan, frightened, helped Schmidt home through the dark streets. If Schmidt suspected Stefan was Polish, other people might think so also.

Stefan heard how Germans referred to Poles and how they treated them. He must watch his accent and keep his job. He must do everything to appear more German or at least Lithuanian. Lithuanians were considered Aryan enough to be Germanized, and now his last name was the Lithuanian Katas.

Entering the apartment complex where Hans Schmidt lived, he rang the bell, being unable to find keys in Schmidt's coat pockets. After a few minutes, an extremely tall girl in a yellow bathrobe came to the door and faced Stefan. Confronted by such a large woman rendered Stefan speechless. "I see you're bringing Hans home from a celebration," she said in an incongruously small voice. "This often happens."

Her soft voice made him ignore her height and plain face. "Sorry to wake you, but I couldn't find his keys. I'm Stefan Katas. We work together."

"I'm Monica Faust, and our family lives in the next apartment." She looked at him in the eyes with admiration since few men met her height. His good looks compelled her to say, "We keep an extra key to his apartment. Let me help you get him to bed. He has the weight of an elephant."

She waddled away and returned from her apartment, smiling and holding up a key. Entering the spotless apartment, they removed Schmidt's shoes and jacket, laid him on his bed, and covered him with a blanket. They laughed at their mutual chore to the music of Hans's loud snoring. Monica made tea, and an easy camaraderie developed between them. As he was putting on his coat, Monica turned to Stefan and said, "Since you are alone here in Memel, why don't you come join our family for dinner on Sunday?"

Stefan, tongue-tied as ever, was silent, and this pressed Monica into further pleading, thinking he was shy. "You must come. I would really like to have you meet my parents." Stefan could not explain that he avoided all social occasions that might expose his background.

"Please, you must come, I insist. Why would you refuse?"

Stefan, caught, could not devise an excuse and nodded yes.

The following Sunday, the Faust family welcomed him, knowing their daughter, their only child, did not have much of a social life. The dinner of headcheese, pork roast with potatoes and apple strudel was a welcome change from the sardines and sausage that Stefan prepared for himself. Stefan hardly said two words, but Monica explained it away as his shyness. She left Stefan alone on the curved sofa in the ornate sitting room. The dinner and Monica's adoring looks evoked a feeling of affection in Stefan. He squeezed her hand as he thanked her and said goodnight. Monica, excited and happy, took his gesture as a sign of affection and started to weave dreams of romance.

Sunday family dinners became a welcome habit for Stefan. In compensation for her size and lack of looks, Monica had developed a compliant and quiet personality desperate to please. But these motherly qualities attracted Stefan, who longed for comfort and safety far from home.

One Sunday after dinner, as Stefan was getting up from the sofa, Monica bent over and touched him on the cheek. Stefan was so moved that, as he stood, he quickly brushed Monica's cheek with a kiss. This fulfillment of Monica's imaginative longings exploded into a rush of emotions. "Mother, he loves me!" she joyfully sang out later that evening.

Mr. Faust inquired about Stefan at work. His background was hazy, and he was not a Nazi. This limited his future prospects, but he appeared of good character and a hard worker. In discussing the matter with his wife, they both agreed that, considering Monica's shortcomings, Stefan would be welcome into the family. In short order, he was considered her fiancé.

CHAPTER 6
DECEMBER 1939

Glistening in the cold morning sun, the forty-seven snow-coated churches of the city appeared as a sugar confection. New street signs changed Pilsudski Street into Gediminas Street. Anxious to change the face of this city, the new government replaced Polish with Lithuanian signs, ignoring the confusion that it may cause for most residents. Business thrived with the change in the currency to the litas. Lithuanian officials assured merchants that they would not interfere in their business practices.

Antanas, deluged with projects, met with the different factions of the city. He assured Polish employees they could keep their jobs if they learned Lithuanian, but there was opposition to this policy. Nationalistic Lithuanians objected: "Lithuania for the Lithuanians." They wanted to discharge all Poles. Polish residents bemoaned the vast numbers of people who might lose their jobs. Finally, twelve thousand Poles were granted Lithuanian citizenship, but one hundred and fifty thousand Poles were considered aliens. Antanas established an office to evaluate qualified Lithuanian candidates for available positions.

Government information was published only in Lithuanian, and the Lithuanian flag of yellow, green, and red appeared everywhere. Lithuanian peasants came from the countryside and, feeling entitled, started to demand jobs and mistreat the local inhabitants. Resentments increased, and fights broke out constantly.

Vytas, appointed director of health services for Lithuania, frequently traveled to Kaunas to integrate medical services between the new and the old capitals. He started programs to coordinate student projects, lectures, and facilities under the umbrella of Lithuanian Medical Services. He retained some prominent Polish professors by certifying they spoke adequate Lithuanian.

One of the most outstanding Jewish professors was Dr. Rubenstein, an ophthalmologist, who restored the sight of Polish President Pilsudski and Vytas assured him of no change in his position under Lithuanian rule.

Katerina assumed her new duties as director of the Lithuanian Red Cross. One morning in the clinic, a Russian colonel approached her. The colonel in the tan garb of the Red Army, blessed with the authority of the prominent red star, said, "Dr. Eimontas, here is a list of USSR army bases in Lithuania requiring auxiliary medical services. Please provide the personnel, equipment, and medication to adequately care for them."

Katerina, writing rapidly in her notebook, replied, "I'll write a protocol for various conditions and indicate which could be taken care of locally and which would require transfer to Kaunas or Vilnius." The colonel thanked her and left. Most of the young Russian soldiers were healthy farm boys, so providing medical services was not a problem. In listing the various disease classifications, she saw "war wounds" but decided to skip that area of concern.

Most Lithuanians had been kept out of Vilnius since 1922, and now with the transfer of the capital to Vilnius, many Lithuanians in government had been arriving from Kaunas. Vilnius Cathedral, located on a plaza adjacent to an ancient tower, embodied the heart of the city and was the center of all events. On Christmas Day, Bishop Venclovas would celebrate the official Mass of Thanksgiving for the return of Vilnius.

Katerina and General Kuzas's wife, Nina, planned an official New Year's Eve party to be held in the official state residence, Napoleon's headquarters, during the war of 1812. After a thorough purging of all Polish symbols, it was now designated for the Parliament and the President of Lithuania. The guests at the dinner followed by a ball would include all of Lithuania's most important people, plus foreign diplomats.

Katerina in a sable coat and Nina Kuzas in a black Persian lamb coat met to discuss the menu and decorations at the state residence. The construction noise of the neglected building made conversation impossible, so they adjourned to a nearby café. After ordering a light lunch and finalizing plans for the party, the subject turned to politics. "Katerina, there are rumors my husband is to be dismissed as mayor because he is Polish and they want a Lithuanian," said Nina Kuzas with a wrinkling of her translucent skin and trembling of her double chin.

Katerina, surprised at the statement, answered, "The Russians were wise to appoint him to calm the Polish population and don't fear for his position. The Russians surrounded him with Lithuanians. So everyone is pleased." Katerina found herself to be at the center of influence and adopted a condescending attitude toward the Poles. Nina smiled in gratitude.

Astrid, with her head held high, sauntered on the newly named Gediminas Street, passing many newly arrived Lithuanian students who sang and laughed, infusing a festive atmosphere. At last, Astrid did not feel inferior to her Polish friends; her birthright to this city practically made her royalty. She spoke only Lithuanian now and laughed at her friends when they tried to speak Lithuanian, and she corrected their pronunciation. Many of the Polish students were expelled and relegated to Warsaw or Cracow by the new Lithuanian regime. She skipped with joy at the admiring glances she received on her new gray fox coat, a recent birthday present. Her blonde curls bounced as she scrunched the snow in her new leather boots from Paris. Her entourage followed as she smiled with happiness. Across the street, she received an admiring intense look from Pranas, who saw her beaming smile that seemed directed at him, surprisingly free of the now common Polish prejudice. He crossed the street and said, "Astrid, hello."

She turned and hissed, "How dare you address me, you one-eared Polish peasant." Nearby students laughed at him. Astrid saw his face burn.

Rector Dielka was appointed Minister of Foreign Affairs, and Katerina invited Elena to lunch to discuss their move to Vilnius. Elena entered the Astoria Hotel dining room in a cloud of Chanel No. 5, wearing an impeccable gray winter suit decorated with Persian lamb. Her chestnut hair cut perfectly in a sleek, shiny bob glistened as she occupied the sunlit window seat. Katerina admired the creativeness of this woman in becoming one of the most attractive women in the city and a powerful social figure. She was compared to the duchess of Windsor.

After they ordered chicken Kiev and reviewed the decorating plans for Dielka's Vilnius apartment, the talk turned to a serious nature. Elena said, "Zygmond is troubled by the events between Germany and Russia. He believes a complete takeover of Lithuania by the USSR is imminent."

Katerina glanced around the high ceilinged room and replied, "Elena, you worry too much. Antanas said a top Russian official from Moscow praised the progress our new Lithuanian government is making."

"You must understand what is at stake." Elena continued, "A communist takeover would take our wealth and transform our way of life. It would mean exile, even death. Wake up from your dreams, Katerina." She rose from her chair with the dignity of a queen and the grace of a ballerina and turned to leave but hesitated. "You are so happy with the return of Vilnius, you are blind to reality," Elena said in her modulated voice as they parted.

Paulina, on her knees, scrubbed the Eimontas mansion kitchen floor when the parlormaid, Nina, almost stepped on her swollen red hand. "Watch where you're going!" shouted Paulina looking up at her. She noticed the girl's eyes filled with tears. "What happened?" Paulina asked as she raised her body into an upright position by holding on to the kitchen table.

"I've been let go," the girl blurted, wiping her nose on her sleeve, "and I have a child to support since my husband died. I hear there are no jobs for Polish workers."

"Why? You've always been an excellent maid, and you've been here as long as I have. I'm Polish too and have not been told anything."

"Baroness Maria was told to employ Lithuanians for her household, and they let me go. A new girl from Kaunas is to take my place, and I'm to train her. How can I do this when she speaks Lithuanian and I speak Polish? Sima has also been let go. Watch out, Paulina. You may be next."

Paulina got back on her knees and finished scrubbing the floor. She felt tightness in her chest and a cold, clammy feeling on her skin. Casimir already lost his job at the railroad to a Lithuanian. Now what she earned was barely enough to feed them.

On her way home, she again fell on the snow-covered cobblestones before the Virgin of Vilnius. "Dear Mother of God, I plead for your help.

Save us from disaster. We are hard-working people and do not expect too much, but please, give us our daily bread." Paulina spent a long time on her knees, combining prayer and tears in equal measure.

When Paulina returned home to make their meager supper, Pranas winced at the sorrow written on his mother's face. "Don't worry," he said. "I found Father a job after he was fired by the fascist Lithuanians. They needed a night security guard for communist party headquarters, and I recommended Father. He had to sign a standard loyalty oath to the party."

Feeling faint, Paulina stumbled to a kitchen chair and sat down. "Holy Mother of God! Tell me this isn't true! The communists are destroying the churches in Russia and putting priests into prison."

"Mother, we have no time for superstitions. We are promoting justice for all people of the world. Why should most people have nothing and a few people live like kings off of their labor? I know Jan is studying for the seminary, and you are good Catholics. But where is it getting you? The Church takes your prayers, your son, your donations, your faithfulness unto death—and what does it give back? Some nonsense story of a heaven no one has seen. The Church takes advantage of your ignorance." Pranas took a piece of black bread, slathered it with cold bacon drippings, and liberally applied salt. "Communism is my religion because I'll receive the fruits of my beliefs in this world."

Valeria, her cheeks red from the cold, stood by the door, holding a bag of potatoes retrieved from the cellar. Her blue freezing hands barely held on to the heavy bag. "Pranas, stop. You're upsetting Mother," she pleaded.

Valeria set down the potatoes and started to peel them. "There are many changes. With the Lithuanians in charge, there are no jobs for the Polish. I don't want to go to the countryside to mow hay and feed pigs. I'm seventeen. My parents shouldn't have to support me. I wrote to Stefan. He has a friend who could give me the required racial papers if I change my name to Katas. I could live with Stefan and get a job near the docks."

Paulina, with a red blotchy face, sighed and asked, "What kind of job?"

"Stefan said there was a bar by the wharf looking for a waitress, and there are good tips to be had. I would send money home," Valeria said with a toss of her hair. She opened the door for little Anna home from school.

"Dear Mother of God! My oldest daughter a prostitute!" Paulina wailed as she hugged frightened little Anna to her copious bosom.

Pranas took the news in stride. "It's better than farm work, and she'd be with Stefan. They could live together, and she could take care of him. He'd protect his sister from any bad influence."

Paulina, thinking about the benefit to her beloved Stefan, composed herself and finally acquiesced. "I know your German is pretty good, your best subject in school. With your light hair and blue eyes, you could pass for German. My Stefan would be joined by family and not be alone."

As the family discussed this possibility, Casimir came home from work in his new uniform. "I look and feel like a general in this uniform."

Paulina just sneered, "Communist flunky at most, but at least it's work. Since the Poles are to be replaced by Lithuanians, even my job with the baron is not safe. Valeria wants to get a job in Klaipeda and live with Stefan."

Taking off his uniform jacket, Casimir said, "If the baron lets you go, you will find other work. Those damned aristocrats, no loyalty! The communists will help us now. May the baron and his ilk go to hell! My salary as a guard is not much, but with Valeria gone, there will be one less mouth to feed."

After a sleepless night, Paulina approached the baron as she served him breakfast. "Please, sir, I understand all Polish employees are being replaced. My husband has already been fired from the railroad, and we have children to feed. I beg you, sir, not to let me go."

Vytas, taken aback by this plea, tried to explain the situation to anxiously hovering Paulina. "This law was meant to fill the higher positions of government with Lithuanians in order to change the culture and language of the city. If a current Polish employee learns Lithuanian, they could keep their job. The law does not apply to domestic workers."

"But, Baron, they are being let go by Baroness Maria," Paulina insisted.

"No, Paulina, your job here is safe. I assure you of this since both the baroness and I are pleased with your work. I will speak with my mother, the Baroness Maria. She did not understand the new law."

Coming home, Paulina shared the good news of her safe job with Casimir, Jan, and little Anna. When the whole family sat down to a dinner of potato pancakes, Paulina prayed, "Thank you, Virgin of Vilnius, for your miracle today." Casimir and Pranas smirked at each other.

Abraham did the accounts late into the night. Numbers started to blur in his head, but they gave evidence of an excellent sales season. The Polish zloty, a floating currency, was losing value, being printed day and night by a government in crisis. People who had savings were trying to spend their zlotys on items that would keep their value, and fur was a perfect commodity, expensive and useful.

A light in the storage room outlined Daniel hunched over rare tiger pelts. "Enough, son, let us go home." Abraham closed the ledgers and locked the store, and they stepped out into the street. Walking in the eerie quiet of Gediminas Street, he noticed the profusion of Lithuanian flags. "No more Polish flags."

Daniel nodded in agreement. "Things will change."

Abraham turned to his son and said, "People and ideas change, money is printed, land is occupied, and armies march. Most items of value are variable according to politics and fashion. Remember, the only permanent things are furs, jewels, and gold. Valuables are the essence of life, able to buy power and safety, and in hard times, they buy you shelter and food. When all else fails, they could buy your life. I will always treasure my wealth, my lifeblood."

"Father, I think you're wrong. Money cannot buy acceptance for the Jewish people. Why these ancient hatreds? We have been discriminated against for two thousand years. The Germans hate the Jews on racial grounds, but the Russians also hate us. We are blamed for the death of Christ and our refusal to integrate into society."

They walked through the street in silence, and finally, Abraham spoke, "The Germans, fed by Nietzsche's philosophy, believe in the superman of the Aryan race. But why is the Aryan race superior?" Abraham chewed on his lower lip, thinking so deeply he almost collided with an oncoming Russian officer. He apologized.

Daniel wanted to impress his father. "I recently read an interesting book, Darwin's *The Descent of Man*."

Abraham interjected, "Aha! The same author who wrote *On the Origin of Species*."

"Yes, in evolution, certain species are stronger and deserve to survive. Translating this theory to humans, the Germans believe they are superior and want to hasten their rise to dominance by removing the weak and inferior. Does this have anything to do with wealth? Of course, they hate out of envy the rich Jews, but they also hate the poor ones."

Abraham shook his head as he reached home. "No, the Germans are jealous of our brains and our proclivity for profit. After all, we own over eighty percent of all businesses here in Lithuania. It was the same in Germany. It is we who are superior. There is always safety in our wealth."

Sarah met them at the door in a dark-blue velvet dress. She put her arms around Abraham and gave him a passionate kiss. Surprised, Abraham took off his coat. "You look lovely. What was the wonderful kiss for?"

"A Lithuanian officer brought in a whole squadron of army officers as customers," Sarah explained, and they ordered nine fur hats.

"Business success is good for my marriage!" Abraham beamed. "Also, my beautiful wife is good for business."

Sarah blushed at the memory of Antanas trying on his hat. He was so tall she had to stand on tip-toe close to him to position the brim, and as she did so, her body came in contact with his. For a fraction of a second, this union of their bodies evaporated all layers between them. She then turned and introduced Antanas to Rachel. Antanas looked at Rachel and said, "Yes, your daughter, she is a beautiful copy, but nothing can compare to you, the original work of art." He kissed Sarah's hand, and she melted and beamed at his compliment.

Jacob was in his usual place on the sofa, reading the paper but stood up when his father entered. "A partition of Poland!" he exclaimed. "I had wanted all of Poland to be under communist rule to participate in the greatest human experiment of all ages, to celebrate the equality of man!"

Daniel looked up from a map of Siberia. "Jacob, you're dreaming. The Russian pogroms, the riots against the Jews, forcing them to live in confined regulated areas! I am apprehensive about going there next week on my buying trip. But we are low on fur, so I must go."

Abraham appeared puzzled, "Our inventory seems adequate. Why make this trip?"

"No one goes this time of the year, so there are tremendous bargains," Daniel argued. He was unsure whether to tell his family of his entanglement with a Russian girl, his first love, for she was not Jewish. Since he had met her, she had never left his thoughts, and memories of their time together left him with paroxysms of acute longing. He kept silent, remembering his encounter.

Two months ago, a snowstorm had been raging when Daniel arrived in Moscow. The clerk at the travel bureau, a small girl with short dark hair, affronted by the ungainly, snow-covered young man, suppressed her disgust when she noticed his face with the disfigured lips. Daniel shyly asked, "Could you please tell me the price for a ticket to Irkutsk?"

"Why are you going there? Isn't it cold enough for you in Moscow?" she teased and, ignoring him, returned to her paperwork.

Daniel laughed, "Yes, it'll be colder there, but my business is fur."

The minute she knew his business, all disgust vanished. The yarmulke identified him as a Jew, and she knew all Jews in the fur trade were rich. With his ugliness, he should be an easy mark. "There's a train in two days, and in the meantime, you could stay in warm Moscow." Svetlana flashed a smile. "You could let me show you Moscow." Daniel was thunderstruck. Knowledge of his disfigurement and embarrassment at his awkwardness made him painfully shy. The Jewish girls he knew were chaperoned on excursions. Never in his twenty years had a girl flirted with him. Romance existed only in dreams and thoughts, not in life.

The day in Moscow was magic. They toured the Kremlin grounds, went into the GUM department store, and had hot tea at a warm, dimly lit restaurant. Svetlana never seemed to be aware of his face. The time with her fulfilled his wildest dreams. Her eyes and lips were perfect, as were her small and soft hands. Her figure, with its high bosom and slender waist, was alluring when she removed her thick wool coat in the café. She spoke to him in a soft, seductive tone mesmerizing him. The fog of attraction hid the facts of the girl. She had a narrow sly face with small brown eyes roofed by overplucked black eyebrows. Her long nose shifted to the side, and her hair was thin and dirty. She spoke with an uneducated accent and walked with a limp. Sexual availability had turned her into a raving beauty.

As darkness approached, she said, "Come spend the night in my room. Hotel rooms are hard to come by and expensive. Don't worry, I live alone."

They entered an area of ruins and garbage until Daniel said, "No! Is this where you live?"

"I've been on my own for a long time. My parents were killed in Kazakhstan," she said sadly.

Daniel felt a great protectiveness toward her. She was like a helpless kitten, and he sympathized with the abandoned and the injured. The cold, dank room became a heaven for Daniel, who felt her soft lips for his first kiss, a miracle he never expected. His heart pounded. She pulled him to her on the filthy mattress and took him to paradise. A pretty girl loved him! He promised her a better life in Vilnius, and she felt she had caught a prize—a rich Jewish fur merchant. Svetlana's prejudice against poverty far exceeded her prejudice against Jews and deformities.

The problem of integrating her into his family consumed him. "Father, I must go. It is my business decision." Daniel's thoughts were only of returning to Svetlana.

Sitting down to dinner after his prayers, Abraham turned to the news of the day. "If Lithuania becomes occupied, we must leave. Neither of the powers will respect our rights. We must prepare to leave for Palestine. I am already taking appropriate steps." The family's stunned looks indicated their inability to respond. They finished their meal in silence.

Christmas, primarily a joy for children, in the Kataski household was a quiet affair with a traditional Christmas Eve feast. Anna no longer believed in Santa Claus but carried the excitement because she expected a present. Stefan and Valeria sent their greetings and money, but it did not assuage Paulina's sorrow at not having her whole family under her wings.

Casimir, Pranas, Jan, and Anna sat at the Christmas Eve table, prepared by the exhausted Paulina, who had, for the last two days, cooked nonstop for the baron. Their meal began with a prayer asking for God's blessing. The ancient custom of breaking and ingesting bread wafers as if it were Holy Communion followed. The Feast of the Twelve Fishes, one for each of the twelve apostles, began. There were sardines, sprats, herring in wine sauce, herring in tomato sauce, smoked trout, gefilte fish, smoked eel, whitefish in aspic, and fried smelt—all accompanied by rough black bread, cucumbers in sour cream, pickled cabbage, pickled beets, and a potato salad with red beets. The meal ended with a clear cranberry pudding and small pieces of dough with poppy seeds covered with cream.

A small fir tree with homemade straw ornaments stood in the corner of their living room. After the feast, Jan helped put away the food as Anna helped Paulina with the dishes. They planned to attend Midnight Mass. Anna opened her package under the tree and exclaimed with delight at the fluffy blue sweater Paulina had knit for her. Anna did not know the beautiful wool was unraveled from a sweater Astrid Eimontas had thrown away because someone remarked the color was not flattering. Pranas had seen the unraveling of Astrid's sweater. "The Eimontas garbage becomes the Kataski treasure," he cursed under his breath. "No, I'm not going to church," Pranas stated.

"Pranas, you can't mean you're not going. It's one of the holiest days of the year. Your brother is almost a priest, and I pray every day. You have nothing if you lose your eternal soul," Paulina said in a trembling voice.

"What has your religion given you? Mother, you slave away scrubbing pots and pans and floor on your knees. Are they better than you—the baron and his wife and children?"

"My dear son, Christ teaches that blessed are the poor, for theirs is the kingdom of heaven." Paulina said with tears in her eyes. Resigned to Pranas's decision, she led a browbeaten Casimir, a happy Anna wearing her new blue sweater, and a meditating Jan to church. "Dear God, where have I failed you? What more can I do? My apologies for my failings since I should have tried harder to make my child, Pranas, love you, Lord."

The Eimontas household, sparkling with silver and candles, flowing with champagne, also had a traditional twelve-seafood dinner, but it included caviar, shrimp, and lobster. Vytas in his smoking jacket appreciated Katerina in her long dark-blue velvet dress and said, "Remember this Christmas well, my love, because I don't believe we will see the likes of it again for a long time. The world is on a collision course, and I'm afraid our lives will change forever."

The table had been set for eighteen guests, including the bishop, Rector Dielka and his wife, Elena, Dr. Beata Rosenfelt and her husband, various ambassadors, Professor Rubenstein and his Polish wife. Old Baron Algirdas and the Baroness Maria made a rare appearance. Even Dalia condescended to partake of the meal.

After the bishop's prayer, Baron Algirdas spoke, "The news is tragic. The Great War is to continue. The intermission was only twenty-one years, long enough for a new generation of young men to be raised by their mothers to fight and to die. I remember 1914 and the unease with the Kaiser's Germany and the Tsar's Russia. It was to be the war to end all wars, but humanity needs the periodic cleansing of a bloodbath."

"Algirdas, please," pleaded the Baroness Maria, "it's Christmas Eve."

Dalia softly whispered, "The noise of war will forever ruin the silence of our peaceful house. The blood of this war may wash away the guilt from my hands."

Noticing the confused looks of the company, Antanas interjected, "Aunt Dalia, you are tired. Let me help you to your rooms."

To brush off the gloomy pronouncements, Vytas made a champagne toast of thanks for the return of Vilnius. A contingent of Antanas's fellow officers arrived in high spirits and delighted Astrid all evening. The company, fueled by champagne, trooped out into the snow for church. The two Jewish couples went home, and the old baron and baroness retired to their apartment since a Mass had been said for them in the mansion's chapel.

Returning from Midnight Mass at the Cathedral, a man in the shadows smoked under a streetlight. Astrid recognized him as the boy from the university who worked in the library. Pranas waved to her, and she walked by him. Astrid pointedly turned her face away from him and shouted to her companions, "There is a pig who doesn't know his place. He acts as if he knows me. I spit on his arrogance." Antanas and all the officers laughed.

Pranas was mortified and angered yet again. The hiss of humiliation fired his mind, never to be extinguished. He vowed to get power through the communist party so he could extract his revenge.

A severe ice storm raged on Christmas Eve in Memel as Valeria welcomed Stefan and Monica. Removing their wet coats, Valeria looked in disbelief at the plain giant girl chosen by her handsome brother. Valeria had prepared a simple version of the Christmas Eve meal for Stefan and Monica. She had decorated a small tree and arranged fir boughs in the dining area.

After their traditional meal, Valeria gave her brother a hand-knitted cap in return for a silver brooch. Valeria gave Monica a fashion magazine, which she had already perused. Monica looked at the magazine as if the gift were an insult, the pictures meant to mock her. Stefan and Monica gave Valeria a box of chocolates, but Valeria gave the box of chocolates back to Monica, saying, "I really don't eat sweets anymore." Monica, uninterested in the magazine, happily consumed the whole box.

Monica felt Valeria's disapproval at her weight and lack of elegance but tried to ingratiate herself. She helped in the kitchen, washed the dishes, and complimented Valeria on her meal.

Valeria sang a few Christmas carols from their childhood and told some funny stories about Pranas and Jan. "Remember how their gifts got mixed up, and Pranas got a rosary and Jan got a book on hunting?"

"Remember how excited Anna was when we gave her a small rabbit?" chimed in Stefan. Instead of brightening up their small holiday, the memories of family Christmas in Vilnius made Stefan and Valeria homesick.

As the evening ended, Monica said, "Stefan, we must say goodnight to your sister. We are expected to spend Christmas day with my parents."

Stefan looked over at Valeria and realized that she would be alone on Christmas Day. "Monica, perhaps Valeria can come also."

Valeria answered, "No, it is fine. I want to be alone, and you already have your plans."

Valeria decided to celebrate Christmas Day by exercising, not eating and sewing a new blouse. She wanted achievement and success in the new world of Memel. The symbols around her proved the superiority of the German way. She would copy the order and cleanliness of her new station in life, leaving behind her ignorance and poverty.

Her gift to herself would be bleaching her hair blonde to achieve the ideal of Aryan beauty. She would be slender and her posture perfect. There was no one to help her, so self-sufficiency and self-reliance were her only keys to happiness.

Chapter 7
January 1940

Pervasive winter ice and snow did not quell the surging joy, bolstered by bottles of champagne, at the return of Vilnius to Lithuania. The euphoria escalated with the holiday season of Christmas, and palpable desperation existed to celebrate New Year's Eve in an apex of bliss. But the celebration only shrouded the beating heart of incipient tragedy.

Katerina Eimontas and Nina Kuzas organized the event of the season, a New Year's Eve party. Two hundred people in formal wear—the men in white tie and tails and the ladies in long gowns sparkling with jewels—attended the grand dinner in the Presidential Palace. Government officials entered to the rousing sounds of a military band as soldiers carried in regimental flags. The guests with tear-stained faces, overcome with emotion, sang the Lithuanian national anthem, their heritage resurrected in this ancient city. The bishop started with a prayer for continued blessings.

General Bulgarin, representing the Russian troops in Lithuania, attended with his adjutant and two other officers. Katerina seated them with some important dignitaries and, as an honor, also put her own Astrid at the table. Adjutant Norgolov, a young man from Stalingrad, approached Astrid with a rakish grin. Astrid, in her new green velvet gown complementing her golden hair and green eyes, sat down after the bishop's prayer. She observed the tall, brown-eyed man looking at her with familiarity. "I would like to introduce myself. I am Georgi Norgolov on the staff of General Bulgarin." He kissed her hand as they sat down to dinner.

Blushing deeply, she answered, "I am Astrid Eimontas, daughter of the baron."

"Titles are foreign to our government, but you deserve one, not for your birthright but for your beauty," Georgi said, smiling.

"Only my papa is an aristocrat. My mama is from a poor family in Kaunas," explained Astrid to ingratiate herself to the presumed proletariat.

"My beginnings are humble. My father was born in Georgia, in Gori, also Stalin's birthplace. My father met Stalin in prison when they were both fighting the tsar as Bolsheviks. My father is now on Stalin's staff in Moscow, so I suppose I have a mark of favor as good as any aristocratic title," Georgi proudly conveyed.

"Have you met Stalin?" asked Astrid, impressed, as she took a bite of smoked salmon with a topping of caviar.

"Many times. He held me on his knee when I was a child and later told me never to let my heart rule my brain. He said the only thing in life worth pursuing is power," Georgi said, admiring Astrid's exquisite table manners, an aristocratic trait.

"I heard he has very strange customs—never sleeping in the same bed twice in a row, sleeping during the day, and being up all night. I also heard he could be brutal." As the other Russians at the table gave her startled frowns, Astrid started to wonder if she was insulting the Soviet leader. She took a sip of wine.

Georgi, to cover her faux pas, took Astrid's hand and said, "May I have this dance?" and led her away. He whispered as they were dancing, "You should never even think what you just said aloud. By thinking this about Stalin, you are apt to say it as you did now, and it is dangerous. You can never tell who will report you."

Astrid did not understand his comment. "Am I to hide my thoughts?" She was in his strong arms being twirled about.

"Don't talk of things that do not concern you but can harm you," Georgi cautioned as he led her back to the table to continue their dinner.

As the bells of the cathedral robustly rang out at midnight, everyone stood up and sang the Lithuanian anthem, followed by a champagne toast, and started greeting friends with the New Year. Astrid, unused to the effects of champagne, did not resist when Georgi kissed her. She closed her eyes, responded, and let out a deep sigh. She left childhood behind and came alive as a woman.

"Is this the first time a man kissed you?" asked Georgi, surprised, with a grin.

"No, it's not the first time, but it's the first time I kissed with desire." Astrid basked in the joy of attraction and danced the rest of the evening in a private cloud. Hours of drinking, eating, and dancing followed with the music becoming louder as the happy crowd lost more inhibitions. The ball reached its apex in a lively Mazurka before coming to a close. As people were leaving, Katerina came to their table and said, "Please, everyone, come to our house for breakfast."

At the Eimontas mansion, Paulina and Nina were waiting at a table with steaming tea, coffee, and omelets filled with jams. Paulina noticed the way Astrid hovered by a young Russian officer and thought that Astrid should wake to the reality of the Soviet: a godless communist, an occupier of their country, a friend of the evil Stalin.

At daybreak, putting on his coat, Georgi asked Astrid, "Would you have time to show me the place where thirty thousand French soldiers are rumored to have been buried after the war of 1812?"

As Georgi was saying farewell at the door, the cold winter sun illuminated him. The bitter morning wind tried to wake Astrid to the reality of Georgi, but the dance and the kiss blurred perception. "I will have to ask Papa," Astrid answered as the baron approached. "Please, Papa, may I show Colonel Norgolov some Napoleonic historic sites in Vilnius?"

"Yes, show the adjutant the presumed burial grounds. It's a good lesson for anyone trying to invade Russia."

Before bed, Katerina warned Astrid, "Norgolov is older than you and a communist. Be polite, but don't meet with him privately after this one time."

Several days later, Georgi arrived in a large black car. Astrid met him in the doorway in her gray fox coat and hat with her new boots. "You look like a Siberian rabbit, good enough to eat," Georgi said with a grin.

"You are a Siberian wolf!" Astrid answered with laughter.

In the car, Astrid sat close to him and smelled his cologne and tobacco, perceiving the presence of a real man. "Here is the map of the site, and I could read to you the archeological report." She babbled the numbers, dates, and metric measurements, not noticing that Georgi's mind was elsewhere. Arriving at the site, they walked, and Astrid pointed out the various features. She lectured, "The cold winter took its toll because of the inadequate clothing and food these men had received during the campaign. A quick summer victory became a prolonged winter disaster."

Georgi explained the military history and, after a short silence, turned to Astrid and asked, "Is it true the Lithuanians felt the French occupation was a relief from Russian occupation?"

"Of course, the Russians are not as cultured and are brutal people," Astrid said, remembering all the stories of the Russian occupation.

"Do you think I am brutal?" Georgi asked with a smirk.

"Of course not. You're an educated officer. I'm talking about the general population, which differs from the higher classes in any country. The Lithuanian, Polish, German, Russian, and French upper classes have more in common with one another than with the masses of its people."

"So, you don't believe in equality?" Georgi asked, brushing snow from her hair.

"People can never be equal. Some are better than others," Astrid quickly replied, getting back in the car.

"You believe in the racial superiority idea of Hitler?" Georgi asked in surprise as he started the car.

"No! Not racial superiority but cultural sensitivity, knowing great ideas, operas, fine clothes and food," Astrid answered from the heart.

"That's not the superiority of anything, except money. The rich can afford higher education and items of luxury, and the poor cannot." They drove in silence as this thought was evaluated from each of their perspectives.

Arriving at the Eimontas mansion, Astrid, flushed with cold, invited Georgi in for a hot drink. Paulina prepared the refreshments and excused herself to do the marketing. With her parents and brother at work, the house was deserted. Astrid and Georgi removed their coats and boots and went by the fire to the small table set with hot chocolate, a bowl of whipped cream, and a plate of cookies. They sat down on the blue sofa, drank the sweet liquid, and fell silent as Georgi ate three cookies. Astrid peered at Georgi in his uniform. She sat close to the fire in her black velvet fitted dress with a white lace collar, admiring their reflection in the wall mirror. Georgi got up and inspected the portrait of Baroness Eimontas placed above the fireplace. "Who is this beautiful woman? It's not your mother."

"It's my father's first wife and my brother Antanas's mother," Astrid answered coldly since she had asked her father many times to remove this prominent insult to her mother.

Sitting down next to Astrid, Georgi took her cup and set it down on the small table beside the sofa. She turned to face him, thinking he would take her in his arms and kiss her, a repeat of midnight on New Year's Eve. Her heart was racing so loudly she hoped he would not hear it. Her half-closed eyes and wet lips would make him realize she was welcoming his advances. The next step should be a passionate embrace. She waited and waited, but nothing happened. The silence was deafening, and as she fully opened her eyes, she saw him focused on the snow outside the window. The surprise of his indifference chilled her body. She turned from him with tears in her eyes. "It's better if you go now."

Georgi stood, kissed her hand, and left. Inadequacy and rejection overcame her, and she became obsessed with what did not happen.

In Memel, work at the waterfront café pained virtuous Valeria. She felt degraded with sailors on leave harassing her, pinching her buttocks, and asking her to sleep with them. She could not affront them since her tips depended on her demeanor. Soon she learned how to flatter them and then slip out of any entanglements. With time, the men understood her ruse and became more insistent.

Stefan, however, easily integrated into life in Memel, and Monica, a compliant, needy person with many problems, considered Stefan her savior. Kindhearted Stefan, glad to play the hero, after numerous Faust dinners, felt obliged to propose to Monica.

"Yes, darling, yes!" she eagerly accepted. "But you must also join the Nazi Party. It's the best way to get promoted, Stefan," pleaded Monica.

Monica's parents, overjoyed, congratulated him. Monica's father said, "Now you're only a manual laborer on the docks, but you are an excellent worker. If you joined the national socialists, I could make you a director at the seaport and increase your pay substantially."

The marriage presented a problem since Monica was Lutheran and Stefan would only marry in the Catholic Church. Discussions and arguments resulted in a compromise, a small civil ceremony attended only by Monica's parents and Valeria. Monica wore a light-blue suit with a matching hat. Valeria, in her best gray dress, said, "Monica, your hat makes you taller than Stefan." Monica removed it.

The reception held at the Faust residence included Faust relatives and friends. Subdued music played during a dinner of Wienerschnitzel with potato dumplings and escalated joyfully when the black forest wedding cake appeared. The young couple left for their small apartment, where Stefan, exhausted by the proceedings, promptly fell asleep.

Stefan accepted his home in Memel, but Valeria, since becoming blonde, received even more unwanted attention and suffered humiliation and fear daily. If it were not for the drunk sailors, she liked living here among the Germans, who were clean, orderly, and efficient, so different from the Poles with their open emotions and their vodka. The Germans thought of themselves as superior, and Valeria saw no reason to disagree. There were stories of the Nazi mistreatment of the Jews, but she rationalized that the Germans had their reasons.

A week after the wedding, Valeria said, "Stefan, you must find me another job. I can't stand what I'm doing now." A drunk had waited for her outside the tavern and had followed her after work. Only her screams stopped him from entering her apartment.

"Valeria, the pay is good, and you never mentioned any serious incidents before." Stefan did not welcome trouble or change.

"Don't you understand it's only a matter of time before someone attacks me? You are so busy with Monica you're not even aware of what's happening to me. You're involved with work and the Nazi Party. I don't fit into any of your future plans. No matter how I try, I can't find other work here. Perhaps I should leave."

"There is definitely no work for you back home, but there must be other alternatives. I'll talk to Monica's father."

After a few weeks, with no progress about another job, Valeria wrote of her unhappiness to her mother, who panicked. "My sweet daughter is in trouble!" After a night on her knees by her bed in prayer, Paulina hesitantly appealed to Katerina Eimontas for help finding work for Valeria.

"Why, Paulina, I understand your concern. Our good friend Count Doban lives in Memel, and I will contact him," Katerina said, wanting to help.

Paulina wrote the good news to Valeria and told her to approach Count Doban.

Count Doban, pleased at his ability to grant favors, invited Valeria to his office for an interview. Valeria, now a light blonde, in her best gray dress, spoke German as a native and answered his questions intelligently. "Count, I am a hard worker, and I will do whatever is necessary to be good at my position here."

"I could find you a position here in my office at the Nazi headquarters, but you would have to cut off all contact with your Polish family and pass for a German. You do believe in our cause?" Count Doban stood up and looked down at Valeria with a commanding air.

"I understand your cause. Germans deserve to rule others because they are superior in cleanliness, orderliness, and intelligence," stated Valeria.

"You will do, you will do fine." Count Doban smiled with satisfaction. He thought, even this uneducated Polish girl understands why we should rule. "You will start on Monday. Come here to the national socialist headquarters, give them my name, and fill out the forms on the fifth floor."

Her path was clear. She couldn't go home where there was no work. She couldn't continue being pinched and propositioned at the café, in danger of being raped. So, she would work at the Nazi headquarters. She was sure they would treat her well. Stefan thought the Nazis were going to expand and occupy all of Lithuania, so they could go home in triumph. Relieved at having reached a decision, a letter to Mama was still a difficult task:

Dear Mama,
Stefan and I are both healthy and doing fine financially, but since
we are passing as Germans, it is difficult for us to write to you.
Stefan married Monica Foust, a German girl, a week ago in a small
civil ceremony, and I attended the wedding. He was promoted to
be a director at the wharf, and I got a secretarial job in the office of
Count Doban. Please know you are in our hearts and prayers, and
we wait for the day when Germany will rule Lithuania. We will
return and show you a much better life. All our love to you, and
Daddy, Jan, Pranas, and Anna. How we miss you! Heil Hitler!

Valeria

Paulina's life was over—to lose contact with her children. But if it would help them to have a better life, she was ready for this sacrifice. Her oldest son, Stefan, guilty of not having his marriage blessed by the Church, was living in sin. She had lost Pranas to the communists and now Stefan and Valeria to the Nazis. Casimir, in his pride of being a guard, did not care. Why was God punishing her? These godless evils were tearing apart her family.

Count Doban, celebrating his successful career and their wedding anniversary, planned a lavish party at the end of January. Sitting in his paneled study, he smoked a cigar and sipped cognac as he mentally reviewed his guests and added names in Berlin. Even if none of the Nazi hierarchy could attend, he was sure to gain favor by his friendly gesture. "Gretchen, are the invitations sent?" Gretchen, her green satin robe caressing her body, walked by him as if she did not hear.

"Gretchen, tell me how the plans for our party are going. Did you write to the guests on the list I gave you? I gave you some very distinguished names in Berlin." Doban grabbed her arm but only held green satin as she looked down with disgust at his baldhead and obese body.

She freed herself from her husband and said, "Stop hounding me with requests." She had seen his secretary and continued, "Order your secretary—you know the skinny bleached blonde—to address them."

Doban replied with a sly smile, "Valeria is intelligent and the brightest secretary I ever had, and I am sure she would write proper invitations."

Gretchen felt a passing envy since composing letters was difficult for her. "Then have her find the correct terms of address of all these important dignitaries. I have appointments to keep."

The count knew better than to pursue his argument if he was to bed her later. Gretchen was unfaithful, but as long as she was discreet, he would not lose face or make it an issue. The reward was his own pleasure.

Valeria Katas was an excellent employee—taking on her tasks with furious determination, not at all deterred by Nazi ideology. Comparing his opulent wife with this slender, hardworking girl, the count felt sorry for Valeria and decided to invite her to the party. He approached her as she busily wrote his invitations in elegant penmanship.

"I would like you to attend this party also," he said, munching on a chocolate bar.

"Count, it would be my pleasure to accept, but my brother Stefan, recently married, has already invited me for that evening."

"Well, bring him and his new wife along. Didn't you say he married Monica Faust? I've already invited her father and his wife. He is a high-ranking party member."

"Then we would be delighted to attend." Valeria smiled at this unexpected honor.

The cold, brisk wind from the Baltic blew Stefan, Monica, and Valeria into the brightly lit, warm Memel mansion for the anniversary celebration. The Countess Doban, attired in a tight satin flame-colored gown, greeted them at the door with a sniff at the plain black gowns worn by Valeria and Monica. Monica, noticing her parents in an adjacent room, took Valeria's hand and went to greet them, leaving Stefan with the countess.

Her eyes took on a lascivious look when she was introduced to Stefan. Here she saw a real man—tall, muscular, blond, and blue-eyed. She licked her lips and gave him her gloved hand to kiss. "Stefan Katas, you are Lithuanian? From Prussia with German blood?" asked Gretchen as a maid took his coat.

Stefan, with his limited background, had never been exposed to a woman like Gretchen. He could not summon his tongue to do his bidding as his eyes were glued to her figure.

"Oh, so you are the strong and silent type. I appreciate silence. A man who talks too much is too feminine for me. Let me show you around," Gretchen said as she took his arm and pressed herself to him. The maid, coat in hand, rolled her eyes.

She went up the stairs to the second floor, pointing out paintings and antique furniture as they passed through several rooms. At the end of the corridor, they went up the back steps to the third floor, seemingly deserted.

"This is a beautiful house," Stefan said, his mouth growing dry. They entered a bedroom, small, apparently used by the staff. After the countess shut the door, she reached down and put her hand on Steve's crotch. She got her desired result.

He panicked in his confusion. Everyone was downstairs, including Monica and her parents and the count! She fumbled with his pants as she slid down the top of her gown. She pressed his head to her breasts. "Now," she said. A man used to following orders fulfilled this direct order.

Straightening out her dress, she leered at Stefan. "You suit me grandly, and I will tell my husband to help your career. I would like to repeat our friendship." They went downstairs as if nothing had happened, rejoining the company.

Stefan spent the next few days unable to sleep, feeling the slow drip of acid conscience on his brain. Did it really happen? Do women act this way? His wife of a few weeks, should he confess? Does the countess expect him to return? If the count finds out, will he kill him? Sometimes he could not sleep due to the lust aroused in him as he played over and over details of her body and her actions. The golden-red hair with the heavy perfume, the softness of her skin, the lushness of her breasts, the wet suction of her sex—he must have more.

At breakfast, Monica, plump and pale in her old bathrobe, handed him a bowl of farina with milk. Her eyes were moist with the tears of rejection from the night before when she tried to kiss her husband and he abruptly turned away. Stefan saw Monica in the bland, tasteless mush. As she stroked his forehead, he shuddered at her touch, seeing her plump white forearms jiggle. Now the bowl of red apples on the table—round, juicy, tempting, asking to be bitten, was like Gretchen.

"Why aren't you eating? Why are you staring at the apples? Have you not slept at all?" Monica's sharp voice stabbing at his mind woke him to reality and the danger of his thoughts.

In Vilnius, Pranas was on his way to work at the communist party headquarters, an imposing cement building in the city center. Since the agreement between Lithuania and the USSR, the communist party was officially accepted. As he approached the large gray building, he saw his father standing proudly in the freezing weather. "Father, are you still on duty?"

"Simon is sick, so I'm working his shift also. It's OK. I can already hear the jingles of extra litas in my pockets. My replacement is coming, so wait and join me for some coffee. It's been a long, cold night standing here."

When relief arrived, they went around the corner to a small café. "Mother is so upset about Stefan and Valeria in Klaipeda. She's not much happier about us and the communists," mulled Pranas.

"I took the communist oath to get the job. I don't believe in anything political. I don't even understand what the fuss is about. People like me suffer under any system. Believe me, the Soviet generals and the Nazi generals live well, and Hitler and Stalin live like emperors, even though they are no longer called tsars and kaisers. And we live like we always lived, by the sweat of our brow." Casimir picked up his coffee cup with shaking hands. His icy mustache started to defrost and drip water onto the table.

"No, Papa, the communists will make a much better society. You'll see. The wealth of the country will be equally distributed to all of us." He placed his hand over his father's cold hand as if to offer truth and assurance.

"Pranas, you keep dreaming," Casimir replied, his voice sad.

"There'll be a communist takeover in the near future, and if that happens, I'll be in a position to advance, to help them nationalize the wealth of this country, and distribute it to all." Pranas stood and helped his father to his feet.

"Well, make sure to distribute some of it to me," said Casimir, rising slowly, leaving to go home.

In a dacha on the outskirts of Moscow, Stalin rose from sleeping at two in the afternoon and called for Karolina. The lumbering gray-haired woman laid a big mug of black coffee and eggs scrambled with mushrooms, a side dish of herring, onions, salami, and a basket of black bread on the small table. Stalin ate, sitting on the sofa. He then rose, went to the adjacent washroom, threw some water on his face, examined his pockmarked skin in the small mirror, blotted it with a towel, and sat down. Karolina returned and removed the dishes, put out fresh clothing, and left the room thinking, *Poor man, everyone is out to kill him. So many guards are stationed, not even an ant could get in here. He must be afraid to die, to face judgment. Perhaps he fears the devil.*

Stalin's first law was kill or be killed. His force of will and command could dispense with any enemy, but still, his most faithful friend since his revolutionary days in Georgia was his gun. Nothing is as precious or needs as much protection as power. Only the powerful instinctively know the vulnerability of power, desired by all. He had only one faith to live by, and that was to promote world revolution. His only god was communism.

Stalin went to the desk in his study and started to read the voluminous papers always arriving. His efficiency and grasp of facts was legendary. He carefully read and made notations on all of them. Secretary Bulganin approached, holding yet another sheaf of papers. "This is the situation in Lithuania. Those people seem to be under the impression that they are independent now and accept Vilnius city as a gift. Most believe our troops are stationed there as a defense against Germany. Only a minority of dissidents are suspicious of our intentions."

Stalin, walking to the wall-sized map, used a pointer. "We are only doing our historical duty to end the control of the bourgeoisie in the Baltics. These are our army bases in Lithuania with 20,000 Soviet soldiers stationed there. Our present border is not defensible. It must be on the Baltic seacoast. This is self-evident," he stated as he raised the pointer to the sky. "The Lithuanian army is a joke, still using cannon and horses, and it will be an easy victory, but we need the right opportunity to convert the country. We must make our takeover acceptable and need a reason for the official occupation of the country," Stalin said in a soft, gentle voice at odds with his savage personality.

Stalin ran his hand over his thick black hair, squinted, went to the window, and said, "Defense! Lithuanian nationalists will attack our Soviet garrison. With so many bases in Lithuania, it will be easy to stage an incident, and then we must defend ourselves. Defense is always justified under international law."

"Yes, a plan of genius," said Bulganin since there was ultimate safety in agreement. The plan to incorporate the Baltics was a cornerstone in the spread of communism, and Stalin was fulfilling the plan.

"Take some vodka and herring," ordered Stalin, and Bulganin ate the food and drank the vodka since he knew of one refusal that led to the firing squad.

"We need to supplant their current administration with our people. Of course, promote some of theirs since we do have a party down there." He winked at Bulganin. "Karolina, bring me some beet juice." Karolina came rushing in with the dark-red liquid, confused at the inedible request.

Stalin stuck his right hand into the bowl, went to the map with the USSR already in red, and spread the red liquid over Finland, Estonia, Latvia, and Lithuania. "Looks better, no?" Stalin smiled.

Bulganin clapped his hands and exclaimed with glee, "Excellent future! Congratulations." The map looked like it had been smeared with blood.

CHAPTER 8
MAY 1940

In Vilnius, melting snow and longer days offered no relief from the crackling tension in the air. A few apologetic flowers fearfully forced their way out of the earth. The news of a lightning-rapid German conquest of Paris buzzed as people tried to predict the future of the great standoff between Germany and the Allied powers. After his breakfast of ham and eggs, Vytas, reading a thick pile of newspapers, commented, "The Russian and German papers write as if their relationship were a romance, but this is propaganda. The British are hysterical over the advance of Germany."

Katerina had coffee, farmer's cheese with preserves, and black bread. She picked up the Lithuanian paper. "Chamberlain seems to believe Hitler is satisfied and will go no further," she said.

"The French think Russia is the only savior from German expansion," Vytas said, putting down LeFigaro. "How stupid these politicians are. Don't they realize Stalin's ambitions? Stalin or Hitler—that is our choice?"

That morning, Antanas, impeccably dressed, stood at attention as the mayor of the city, General Kuzas, welcomed the prime minister. The gilt-edged table in the mayor's office hosted official discussions about the Russian garrisons. Antanas wrote down every word of these historic meetings. "The Soviets are not here to change our way of life," the prime minister insisted. "They are just here to form a bulwark against any fascist aggression."

General Kuzas, rotund and red-faced, contradicted him, "The government is blind to the slow erosion of principles and acceptance of communism. The Jewish population is welcoming the Soviets."

The prime minister was taken aback by this criticism, "This is a free country, and some people's thoughts on economic preferences are not our concern. And of course, the Jewish population in Vilnius prefers the

Russians to the Germans!" By the middle of May, Red Army trucks circled the streets of Vilnius as supposed protection against Nazi invasion.

A visiting Russian professor, Victor Kuznetsov, approached Zygmond Dielka for discussions about Lithuanian economic policy. The rector, a professor of economics, welcomed the exchange and invited him to dinner at his home with his wife, Elena. Dielka participated in many official discussions because he spoke Russian and few Russian officials spoke Lithuanian.

The dinner on May 22 was focused on Kuznetsov, the guest of honor—a short bald man characterized by quick movements. Intelligent small brown eyes struggled to peer out from under bushy black eyebrows. Both Dielka and Elena, his wife, were tall, and therefore, the rector immediately sat down because of the discomfort of talking down to Professor Kuznetsov, whose head barely reached his shoulder. Kuznetsov, dressed in a brown suit and a red tie, boasted, "This tie was given to me by Stalin himself."

Roast goose and plentiful vodka and champagne graced the table. Dielka noticed that Kuznetsov drank multiple vodka toasts to the bottom as he tapped the floor with his right foot. The more he drank, the more openly he leered at Elena in her flowing light-blue chiffon gown. At one point, he attempted to put his hand on her knee. Elena, a lovely, cold, unapproachable goddess, compared favorably to his fat, loud, old Russian wife and annoying, ignorant young mistress. After three hours of discomfort at the blatant lusting of this short man, Elena excused herself and left. Kuznetsov asked if he might have a serious talk with Dielka, and they went to the library, where Kuznetsov paced the Persian rug.

Kuznetsov slid into his main theme: "There is a request for the University of Vilnius to give a series of lectures on Marxism and Leninism. These lectures are to demonstrate that Marxism is superior to all other economic theories. The request comes from Moscow, Stalin himself."

Dielka retorted angrily, "To ignore teaching Adam Smith and Keynes seems to be an imposition on the freedom of speech in Lithuania. Education requires the teaching of all economic theories."

"Stalin questioned me closely about Lithuania and was concerned about the disposition of Lithuanian intellectuals and of university professors. He would very much want them to learn true Marxist theory,"

Kuznetsov said and quietly added, "I could send you to Moscow for courses because of your stature and fluent Russian, and when you return, you could give instruction." He had more vodka. "Your president may not last long in his position. This would put you in the forefront of the leaders of this nation." Kuznetsov finally sat down and drummed the nearby table with his fingers.

Dielka replied, "I don't know if Moscow would be a possibility since my wife, Elena, would have to come with me." Seeing Kuznetsov's surprised expression, he realized this was not a discussion but an order. "I spent much time traveling through Western Europe and have seen a variety of economic systems. I am not familiar with living under communism, so it would be hard for me to proclaim its superiority."

Kuznetsov shifted in his chair and stood up. "There are some shortcomings and various imperfections in our system, but these deficiencies will be quickly overcome and prosperity will flourish. There is a great future in store for communist ideology. The fateful hour has come when communism will bury capitalism. The war between Germany, France, and England is the last gasp of capitalist nations. Fighting among themselves, they will prepare the ground for their own graves, and from here, socialism will blossom and flourish as it spreads through the world."

Dielka, alarmed, said, "A complete communist takeover!"

Kuznetsov sat down again, smiled, and said, "Your wife is an attractive woman. I could see why you would want her by your side, but I think it would be better for her to stay in Vilnius, where I could make sure she is safe," Kuznetsov said as a concerned uncle.

Terror struck into Dielka's heart. "Are you preparing for an occupation of this country?" Dielka asked, choking with emotion.

"Of course not." Kuznetsov stood and patted Dielka on the back in a comforting gesture. "We are not changing your way of life and have no desire to bring down the state. We respect Lithuanian sovereignty. We only want to have leaders in this country who understand our ideology. Your new prime minister, as well as some of his colleagues, certainly understand and are friendly to our views."

"You think communism will flourish in Europe, but what of the United States?" Dielka asked, pouring some cognac in both their glasses.

Kuznetsov sat down again, relaxed at last, and with a smile said, "An interesting question, and I will give you an answer. The United States, because of capitalism, has a great profit motive and will want to expand their industries for the manufacture of war materiel. When the war ends, they will have to close their factories, resulting in millions of unemployed people. There is nothing better than a hungry population to affect a socialist revolution. In one day, America can be transformed."

Kuznetsov took another glass of cognac and, not seeing Dielka's discomfort, continued, "In the government takeover, immediately, by decree, all the money in financial institutions will be confiscated. This will break the back of the American governing class. It is on the basis of the dollar the capitalists exploit and govern millions of workers. The rapidity of the change will be a firestorm!" Kuznetsov clapped as if watching the change before his shining eyes. "All loans and indebtedness will be abolished, and a standard amount of money will be issued to all the people. Entire industries, businesses, and services will revert to the people."

Standing, he looked down on Dielka and proudly concluded, "All prisoners in jails will be released, and being grateful to the government for their freedom, they will be our most reliable enforcers. Soldiers are taught to obey, so the army would also enforce orders from the government. All taxation will be abolished since it punishes the poor and exempts the rich. America will have free medical care, inexpensive food, housing, and four-week vacations. This will be a paradise for Americans!" The excitement of the plan made Kuznetsov sway. "I seem to be unsteady—the cognac. I think it is time for me to leave." Dielka stood up from the sofa and held Kuznetsov's arm to steady him as he breathed a sigh of relief.

"Let me know when you are going to Moscow. Please extend my thanks and farewell to your wife. You are a lucky man to have her," Kuznetsov said as a servant helped him put on his coat. He then entered the cool May night and was met by his chauffeur.

"Elena!" shouted Dielka entering the bedroom where Elena was reading on the chaise lounge. He repeated the conversation with increasing alarm. "Kuznetsov wants me to be a student of communism in Moscow and then propagate these theories in Lithuania. He also has his eyes on you. We are in mortal danger."

Elena put down her book and said, "Calm down, darling. We'll figure something out. Remember the financial crash of 1929 when all our money was invested in bank stocks. The crisis wiped us out. You tossed and turned through a hundred sleepless nights. I told you everyone was suffering equally. We'll survive this also." Elena tugged at the belt of her pale beige satin robe and removed it, revealing a matching negligee. Dielka always appreciated her mysterious and elegant sexiness. He reached over and held her hand.

She smiled and continued, "If we are invaded, we'll all be invaded, and you will still be the rector of the university only under a different regime." She kissed her husband. "Remember the proverb that it is better to have a bad year than a bad husband because a bad husband makes you alone suffer, whereas during a bad year everyone suffers."

Dielka smiled at the thought of comparing a Russian invasion with a bad year, but he tried to put it into perspective. "This will not be only a bad year, Elena. There will be a fundamental change when this country is again under Russian rule. Maybe they won't change education, but there will be a reign of terror for the population to force a collectivist regime upon us." At these words, he felt her trembling and embraced her.

They made love but with a hint of desperation, fearing the future might not be as safe and familiar. As Elena fell asleep, Dielka's fears exploded. He feared for the country but mostly for Elena since Kuznetsov was definitely interested in her.

One morning at work, Katerina, surrounded by a contingent of interns, examined a Russian soldier with burnt corneas. Joseph Rudis, her admirer, slid into a space nearest to her. Katerina asked, "Dr. Rudis, what is the treatment for this condition?"

Joseph blushed but managed to come up with "Sulfa ointment."

"What about steroids? Did you forget?" Katerina said in a harsh voice as she moved on to the next patient, disappointed at his incomplete answer.

The next day, Joseph approached her in the cafeteria and asked if she could meet him after work at the Luna Café. "It is vital I speak with you about a grave matter."

Katerina, seeing his tear-filled eyes, agreed to meet him, speculating that either he wanted to apologize for his failure to answer her question during rounds or his infatuation could be serious. She walked to the Luna Café and found Joseph sitting at an outdoor corner table with a crocus and hyacinth bouquet at her place. Katerina wondered how she could reprimand him for his mistake or divert his affection. This handsome boy, so young and sensitive, had sparkling blue eyes—just like Jonas's eyes. She greeted him with coolness, and they ordered coffee and cognac.

"Doctor, thank you for coming. I'm breaking a vow of secrecy and endangering my family to give you a warning. I'm doing this because of my deep respect for you," Joseph stated in a quiet tone.

"Warning?" Katerina's mind raced as to what type of warning this could be. Katerina thought she was hearing the ravings of a madman and rose to leave to avoid any further interaction.

Joseph caught her arm and, in a low voice, said, "My uncle is an official with the NKVD, the Soviet Secret Police. I found out about some of their plans."

"What has this to do with me?" Katerina shook off his arm.

"Uncle Vlad, whom my father had not seen in twenty years, came to visit from Moscow. They talked in Russian while drinking one glass of vodka after another. I finally left because I don't understand Russian. Late at night, my father woke me. He needed help to get uncle into bed."

"Your family history of drunkenness is of no concern to me," Katerina scoffed.

"Katerina! As I half carried him to his bed, he said to me, 'Well, all the pigs on this list are to have a very cold time of it.' I was curious and removed the list from my uncle's sleeping hand and read it in Russian. I know only enough of the Cyrillic alphabet to make out words. The heading was Siberia, and the only name I recognized was Eimontas, Vytas."

"Are you insane? You're losing touch with reality. It was a mistake for me to meet you. Goodbye." Katerina stood up and left, leaving the flowers.

Returning home, she took a long bath and tried to relax and forget this incident. As she was getting into bed, she told Vytas of her strange encounter. "I met a young intern for coffee this afternoon. He told me a crazy story of getting a list of people destined for Siberia from a drunken uncle who is an NKVD agent. He said you were on that list." She told the story in a joking manner, hoping to elicit a laugh.

Instead of laughter, Vytas jumped out of bed. "My god, we are lost. My darling, promise me to go with the children to the country tomorrow. This is no joke, and the young man probably saved your life!"

Katerina sat up in bed, stunned at his reaction. "What would the Russian NKVD want us for? We are not political nor criminals."

Vytas went to the fireplace and lit a fire. "It's a warm night. What are you doing?" asked Katerina, her mind racing with possibilities of danger.

Without answering her, Vytas went to his desk and grabbed a pile of papers and started to burn them. The flames illuminated his deeply etched, haunted face. "Katerina, could you please meet this young man again and ask if he could provide us with a copy of the entire list?" He threw more papers into the fire. "Start packing. You must stay with your Aunt Teresa."

"Why go to my aunt and not the Eimontas estate? It's spring. We always vacation at Erelis."

"The NKVD knows about the estate. Very few people know about your aunt."

"Vytas, please, you're upset at what could be nothing, a fairy-tale made up by a boy trying to get my attention." Seeing the sorrow in Vytas's eyes, she took his warning seriously. They spent a sleepless night as Vytas, in telephone conversations with his friends in government, became more and more agitated. Katerina became aware of the reality of danger.

The next day at work, she looked for Joseph to get more information, but he was nowhere to be found and was told he had left the clinics.

In the evening, Katerina telephoned Antanas to come home as soon as possible. "There are serious political developments regarding your father, and I want the whole family at dinner."

The desperation in his mother's voice compelled him to obey in spite of his plans to go to Bernstein's after work to see Sarah.

Astrid, stretched out on the blue velvet sofa with a compress over her forehead, daydreamed of Georgi. Since her rejection by Georgi, contemplation of her perceived inadequacies resulted in headaches. Life was so boring. Nothing ever happened, only eating and sleeping and going to school. Each minute had the weight of hours. She wished for something exciting to occur, and now her mother's urgent voice could be the answer to her ennui.

Astrid sat up at attention as Antanas entered, sat down, and lit a cigarette. Katerina, entering distraught, announced, "Children, your father will be here soon for a serious discussion about how to keep our family safe."

Vytas, entering the grand salon, removed his jacket. His family looked at him with anticipation. The portrait of his first wife seemed to gaze down upon the scene. The aroma of Paulina's dinner and bouquets of spring flowers made the coming discussion surreal, an intrusion of an obscene foreign matter into the loving, familiar household.

Vytas cleared his throat and asked Katerina to recount her afternoon meeting with Joseph. Vytas then said in a hoarse voice, "This is rather credible information that we are in danger because of my actions. To take precautions, it is best for all of you to leave the city. The safest place is with Aunt Teresa in Prienai. If this news is untrue, you could return after a few weeks, but right now, there is no reason to take a chance."

Antanas jumped up from his chair. "Where did you hear such nonsense? I am the assistant to the mayor, and there have been no discussions of any arrests."

"Of course, the mayor has little to do with the politics at the highest levels of government. It is the ambassadors and ministers and the president who might know. And sometimes even they are not informed. There is no reason for the NKVD to have discussions with the mayor of Vilnius. It concerns warrants for arrest. The NKVD is in charge of the matter."

"Father, these are rumors. I will not leave. I'm not a child. I'm the mayor's right hand as well as an officer in the Lithuanian army. You cannot expect me to leave my post on the basis of what some crazy intern said."

Astrid, red in the face, rose from the sofa and said, "I can't leave my life here for Prienai. Aunt Teresa lives a primitive life on a farm. When I was little, I liked playing with the animals and helping with farm work, but now I'm in society. It's outrageous. I would be in exile! I'd rather die!"

Vytas, wiping his brow, said, "Antanas, I can't make you leave. You must decide, but upon my life, I tell you, if I am on a list of the NKVD, your lives will also be affected. Astrid, you're leaving with your mother tomorrow morning for Prienai." Dinner that evening was a quiet affair with each Eimontas family member lost in their own thoughts of the future.

Paulina, arriving to serve breakfast the next morning, encountered the tear-stained faces of Katerina and Astrid. "I hope you enjoy a hearty breakfast since last night's dinner was barely touched," she said.

Antanas, with dark circles under his eyes, drank some coffee, rose, and left for work. Paulina, hovering by the phone, heard Katerina asking for sick leave from the Red Cross and Astrid being excused from school due to illness.

"Are you going somewhere, madam?" Paulina inquired, seeing several large packed suitcases and hoping to receive an explanation.

"Astrid and I are going to the country for a few weeks. Take good care of our gentlemen while we are gone," Katerina said in a low voice. Paulina started scrubbing the kitchen floors. What could have happened? Such a strange and sudden trip. They were no more ill than she was. Vytas, working on some papers, told Paulina he would be driving them to the country but would be home for dinner.

As the car was being packed, Paulina put in some of her specialties for Aunt Teresa. Vytas picked up the basket filled with cheeses, sausages, and baked goods and warned Paulina, "You are to keep this information secret. No one must know where they went."

That evening at the Kataski dinner, as they finished their potato pancakes, Paulina described the unusual events at the baron's home. Listening intently, Pranas made a jump in logic, "Astrid must be pregnant, and they had to get her out of the city."

Casimir, smearing sour cream on the crisp pancakes, thoughtfully said, "No, that's not the reason. If it were, they would just send the pregnant girl away. But now the mother, who holds an important post, is also gone. They must be running away from something."

Paulina looked at Casimir and said, "You don't know anything."

Casimir answered, "I don't read, but as a guard at headquarters, I can sense things from the comings and goings. Something is afoot—how smug the Russkis are, as if they found their place in the sun. I can smell danger."

Paulina did not take any of Casimir's pronouncements seriously. *What danger?* she thought. Steve and Valeria were safe with the Germans in Memel, Jan was safe at home, and little Anna was . . . well . . . little. Could Pranas be in danger? He was working with the communists, so how could they be a threat to him? *Nonsense,* Paulina realized as she helped herself to more pancakes.

Pranas mulled over his father's explanation and realized there could be something to it. So Astrid would be out on a farm and away from all her fancy friends. He took out a map finding the village of Prienai.

The next day, Pranas attended a general meeting in the main hall of the communist headquarters in Vilnius. The full auditorium had people standing along the walls. He considered this new ideology his road to status and power. Rachel, on fire with the idea of equality, also attended. She saw Pranas. "Hello, I thought you would be here."

"Rachel, good to see you. You look pretty in your blue dress."

Rachel, pleased at the compliment, smiled at Pranas. The missing left ear he tried to hide by a long lock of hair marred his average looks, but he had helped her with her bicycle and introduced her to Marx. They found seats among the crowd where Rachel saw many of her friends from the Jewish quarter. The guest lecturer on the evening of May 29 was Professor Kuznetsov. Although not physically imposing, his booming, authoritative voice mesmerized the audience.

"Lithuanians must know there is no greater calamity than the evil of fascist thought. They seek the opposite of equality and fairness. The Germans are stealing land in the name of reunification of the German-speaking peoples. The British and French are cowards ready to be eaten alive by Hitler's forces. The capitalists of the Western world only want to provide arms to shed blood in the conflict. The USSR is the beacon of fairness, and the love for its citizens is paramount. Stalin will protect us from the savage Huns."

The mood in the room was enthusiastic as all stood to applaud. His speech was finished in half an hour, so there was no boredom—only inspiration.

Rachel ran home to invite her parents to attend the next lecture. "Father, I learned the most exciting new way of looking at the world at the communist lecture," she said breathlessly, as she found her parents reading. "We should live our lives in this just, new way."

Abraham stood up and slapped her. "You're never to go there again or to believe communism is the answer," he said. "You're an ignorant girl. You don't know about communism and real life and what the Soviets are doing to their people. There's massive starvation in Ukraine and Russia. There are killings all across the USSR and a population living in fear of the NKVD. I raised you to be a religious girl. Communism is godless. Under communism, you could end your life in Siberia."

Sarah was uneasy observing this scene. She left politics to Abraham since the head of the family should decide political orientation. Her concern was for both Jacob and Rachel, who seemed to be brainwashed by communism. Thank God, Daniel was still faithful to his family and religion.

Jacob embraced the crying Rachel and said, "Father, punishing Rachel does not change the fact of a dawning of a new world order. You are the ignorant one."

"Jacob, how could you be a communist? What does your yeshiva teacher say about this?" an astounded Sarah asked.

"Mother, I've changed my mind about being a rabbi, and I left school. I think bringing communism to enslaved people is a more worthy calling."

Stunned, Abraham turned and looked at his son. "You're insane! If only you had studied the history of our people better, you would not be making these crazy statements. We must never follow any other beliefs except those of our fathers in the Torah. If you accept communism and have the gall to draw your innocent, ignorant sister in this, you are rejecting everything we believe in. If you do not reject these ideas, you are no longer my son!" With tears in his eyes, Abraham bit his lower lip so hard a trickle of blood started running down his chin.

Jacob was taken aback by his father's vehemence. "Father, I'm a student of the Torah, and there is nothing in my studies to condemn communism. You're the one who is ignorant with your mind being only on furs and business!"

"My furs and business are what has given you a roof over your head and food in your mouth. We will see what your communism will give you!" Abraham yelled as he opened the front door. "Now, get out of my sight!" Abraham opened the door, pushed Jacob out, and slammed the door so hard it vibrated.

As Jacob left the house, Sarah, sobbing, got her shawl, opened the door, and ran after him into the cool spring evening. She ran as far as the park by the Niemen River but could not find Jacob anywhere. She sat on a bench in the small park and wept at the prospect of her fractured family.

Antanas had gone outside for fresh air, debating his father's warning to escape to the country. Walking down a path by the river, he saw a small dark-haired woman in a black dress and a violet shawl. Sarah, sitting alone, looked up at the tall stranger. "Mr. Eimontas!" She quickly wrapped the shawl around herself and wiped her wet cheeks.

"Madame Bernstein?" Antanas observed her efforts at decorum as the aroma of eucalyptus escaped the folds of her shawl. He bent down, reached for her hands, and with great concern, said, "Please tell me what happened. How can I help?" He sat down on the bench beside her.

Sarah poured out her story, telling Antanas she needed help to extricate her son from the communist movement. He focused on her eyes, her lips, and her face as if every word emanating from her was a priceless jewel. He profited handsomely from this technique of passionate, intense listening to women in his art of seduction.

"Madame, as the assistant to the mayor, I assure you, your son Jacob will be fine. The balance of power will be on the side of the USSR, so being a communist would provide him safety." Antanas was still holding her hand and felt the slight return of pressure as a sign of encouragement.

His soothing low voice calmed Sarah; she did not object when he put his arm around her. Her eyes shone with gratitude at his protective demeanor. "Thank you," she said. "Would you help me find Jacob?"

They walked up and down the streets, looking into bars and cafés, reaching the communist headquarters, where Casimir stood guarding the door. The building, an enormous block of gray concrete, contained offices and a basement prison. Casimir, shocked to see the baron's son, ran up to him. "Sir, you can't enter! I'm Casimir, your maid Paulina's husband."

"I'm looking for Jacob Bernstein. Can you help me?" Antanas appealed.

"One moment." Casimir disappeared inside for a few minutes and came back with Jacob, surprised to confront his mother.

"Jacob, Father threw you out, but I must know where you are," Sarah said as she embraced him. "Please come home. All will be forgiven."

"Mother, I intend to stay here. I intend to make this my life's work. I've never believed in anything as strongly as I do in this idea of equality, and I intend to live with my comrades," Jacob walked back into the headquarters.

Sarah started crying and shaking. Antanas held her and led her to a nearby café, where he bought her a cognac. She drank the unfamiliar drink and took some deep breaths to calm herself. She also felt rushing dizziness and rested her head on Antanas's shoulder. Inhaling the fragrance of eucalyptus, Antanas reached down and kissed her forehead. Startled, she got up and fell against him once more, disengaging her long hair from her scarf. Antanas could not resist touching the black glistening waterfall escape confinement. Sarah jumped back at his caress.

"Sorry, I don't know what came over me. I will take you home," Antanas said as they walked to the entrance of the Jewish quarter.

Sarah entered the apartment to face a furious Abraham. "Where were you? Is that alcohol I smell? Have you no shame? Today I saw my son renounce his faith and family, and now I see my wife, who was above reproach, coming home disheveled and drunk!" Abraham sat down, holding his head in his hands. "I feel like Job." Sarah's happy family life was hurled toward destruction.

Vytas, Katerina, and Astrid arrived in Prienai, a tiny village where Aunt Teresa had raised Katerina. This small, round-faced, wrinkled, white-haired woman, a cousin of Katerina's mother, expressed joy at seeing the Eimontas family. She wondered what prompted this unexpected visit and noted how worried Vytas had been as he brought in their suitcases. He apologized for the intrusion and soon left.

Aunt Teresa apologized for the premises since Katerina and Astrid would have to share one bed in the small room upstairs. Katerina had fond memories of that room with apple blossoms visible through the window where she had dreamed dreams of her future.

After unpacking, they went to the warm kitchen, where a rough-hewn table was set with homemade sausage, potatoes, and sauerkraut. The city guests did not have much of an appetite, but with prolonged urging from Aunt Teresa, they ate.

A fat gray cat sleeping by the oven was the only thing that brought a smile to Astrid's face. "Lulu used to be an outside cat and a great mouser, but now she is retired, as I am, so we spend most of our time in the kitchen," Teresa explained to Astrid.

The next morning, Astrid refused her mother's invitation to go for a long walk to the nearby forest, so Katerina went alone. Forests of pine and birch covered most of the flat Lithuanian countryside and were a joy to walk in because of the lack of undergrowth. Following a path on a lush carpet of pine needles, she looked up at the shimmering sunlight filtering through the green birch leaves and breathed the fresh country air and aroma of pine.

Katerina, lost in memories of her youth being raised by Aunt Teresa after the death of her parents, heard the snapping of a branch. Startled, she looked up, and it was only a deer. A little further, she saw a rabbit warren and stopped to observe it. All the rabbits ran away, but one tiny rabbit, so frightened, froze in place. Seeing it tremble, she avoided going near it, and it hopped away. Spring rains had produced a variety of mushrooms, and she vowed to return with Aunt Teresa, a mushroom expert. She found it hard to imagine that in this beautiful world, there could be any danger.

Returning for lunch, she found herself alone with Aunt Teresa. Astrid had gone to a neighboring farm to visit childhood friends. Eating a fresh omelet with mushrooms, Aunt Teresa told her the gossip of the village. Katerina paid scant attention as she did not know the local people. Aunt was a talker who spared no detail. "And so her nephew, Jonas, has now moved in with her. Could you imagine a grown man moving into the Saulis household and not doing any farm work?"

At this, Katerina was startled. This must be Jonas, her true love. "Have you seen this Jonas Saulis? How old is he? Is he an attorney?"

"He comes to church on Sunday. I could introduce you," Aunt Teresa said in a hesitant and puzzled voice. Perhaps her instincts were right, and Vytas and Katerina might separate since Katerina showed such interest in another man. "I believe he is an attorney."

"We need no introduction. I knew him in my younger days," Katerina said.

That Sunday, Mass in the small stone village church was as Katerina always remembered it—the choir singing the ancient hymns in Latin, the priest in his vestments, the incense and the sermon extolling the afterlife.

Exiting the church with Aunt Teresa and Astrid, she felt a touch on her shoulder. It was Jonas. He greeted all three women and evinced surprise at learning Astrid was Katerina's daughter. Aunt Teresa saw the tension between them and, to give them privacy, took Astrid aside to show her the pastor's beehives in the back of the church.

"Katerina, how beautiful you look!" Jonas said, and as they shook hands, his eyes traveled over her face. "I hear you are a baroness now."

Even though she was expecting to see him (the reason for her best violet spring dress), the encounter still took her by surprise. "Jonas, what are you doing here? The last I heard, you were in France on some legal project," Katerina said, trying to remove some of the excitement from her voice. She saw he had lost weight and had some silver hairs among the blond. "You didn't join the army. What are you doing here on your uncle's farm?" Katerina asked.

They walked side by side from the church, down a forest path. "I came back when I heard rumors of war. The Russian occupation is imminent.

You know I would defend Lithuania to my last breath. I'm organizing a guerrilla army. My recruiting is in the farmlands, and I'm trying to obtain weapons for the coming conflict. The forests of Lithuania will serve as our battlefields, so at present, I'm working on strategic maps for our troops."

"You? Impossible! Are you telling me you think you can organize an armed resistance to the Russians?"

"No! Not an armed force. I'm too realistic to think that. But diversionary guerrilla tactics until we could get help from friendly democracies like the United States. We must show the world our intent to remain free so they would come to our aid."

"Jonas, I think you are dreaming," Katerina said as she touched his shoulder. "But you're always so compelling, just, and idealistic. I'll always share your dream."

Jonas devoured her with his eyes full of pain at their unfulfilled future. "My dear, what are you doing here? How can the country do without your medical knowledge and administrative expertise?" They stopped and sat down on a tree stump. Spring in Lithuania was God's masterpiece, with the blue cloudless sky, the fresh green leaves of the birch trees, multitudes of wildflowers, and music from the bubbling stream.

In a low voice, she said, "My husband believes our lives are in danger and wanted me out of the city." Her body shivered with unwanted thoughts of a dark future in store.

"There may be no safe place in the near future, but I will always be here to protect you," Jonas said as he took her hand, and the touch inflamed all her feelings for him. Katerina's heart leaped upon hearing these words since it was an indication he still cared for her. Surely he still loved her.

They returned to the church where Aunt Teresa and Astrid were waiting and took their horse cart back to the farm. "Who was that man?" asked Astrid, confused by her mother's bright-red cheeks.

"An old friend I had not seen in twenty years," answered Katerina with her heart pounding at the unbidden attraction, which she had thought was long buried.

CHAPTER 9
JUNE 1940

The rumbling of Soviet tanks entering Vilnius drowned out the sounds of thunder at the start of this cool and rainy June. The phalanx of Soviet soldiers pounding their boots into the city's streets sounded out regime change and occupation. People, shocked and terrified, remembered the brutal Russian occupation before the Great War. The fever pitch of speculation about a predicted takeover ended with doomsday finality. The Red Army crushed the city as a sledgehammer.

Interruption in all services led to massive layoffs and unemployment. Gold, art, and museum treasures were stolen; equipment and machinery were removed as factories were nationalized. Supplies from hospitals, vehicles, and trains were requisitioned. Women were raped, and prominent citizens were arrested. An ignorant, ill-disciplined, brute force plundered the helpless city. The citizens of Vilnius faced the terrible consequences of loss, hunger, displacement, and fear of the unknown.

In the mayor's office, Antanas blanched when a cadre of Soviet officers entered. He greeted his visitors in Russian and went into the mayor's private office to inform him of their presence.

"What's the meaning of this?" Antanas asked the mayor.

Mayor Kuzas stood up red-faced, trembling with rage. "The politicians settled matters and have given up the country without a shot being fired. The communists have all their pieces in place, and now it is up to us to follow their rules."

Antanas led the delegation into the mayor's private office and sat down, stunned. It was a fait accompli. The USSR had occupied Lithuania. His future, after all his career successes, now was shrouded in uncertainty.

Returning to Antanas with sheets of paper, Mayor Kuzas, his voice quavering with emotion, blurted out, "Our first assignment—to remove the litas to be replaced by the ruble. The exchange rate stinks of extortion. The bastards are going to destroy our currency! The Soviets said it would be justice for the rich to find their hoarded money, their litas, now worthless. Type up the orders and send it to all newspapers and banks in the city."

After a non-stop day of intense work, Antanas left the office to return home in darkness. He sensed the change in the streets, full of Soviet soldiers and tanks, with no inhabitants in sight. Only a sudden breeze in the swaying trees expressed the city's trembling fear. In the dark house with no servants or prepared meal, Antanas ate a piece of black bread and sausage in silence, comforted that his mother and Astrid were safe in the country. He briefly visited his grandparents and found them braced against the future, stoically living through yet another regime change. His Aunt Dalia did not even seem to be aware of what had happened.

His father returned late, and Antanas told him about the changes already put into effect by the new regime. "Mayor Kuzas is still in charge, so I think my work will remain the same but with different goals."

Vytas sat down and said with a sigh, "When I first became aware of a possible Russian takeover, I had spent an evening with my friends discussing what we could do to defend our country. The use of force is a joke, considering we don't have a functioning army. So we all signed a letter of protest to be delivered secretly to England, France, and America to help us since the invasion of a sovereign nation is an international crime! Because of my involvement with this document, I became alarmed by your mother's friend who claimed that my name was on a list. There could be some truth to it, and therefore, I wanted our family out of Vilnius."

Antanas observed his father's haggard face harboring dark circles under his eyes. His father's signature on a letter seeking help against the USSR alarmed him. "I know you're a patriot," said Antanas, taking a glass of vodka and pouring one for his father, "but it's dangerous to pick a fight with an overwhelming force. You're already on a list of enemies of the people since Soviet tactics include removing the intelligentsia, the leaders of the country. If anyone finds this document with your signature, not even God can help you. Warn all your co-signers they are guilty of treason."

"Did you expect me to do nothing?" Vytas stood and raised his hands in the air in a gesture of surrender. "They are all my closest friends and would die before betraying me."

"I expect you to tell these friends to destroy any evidence. Keep away from them and any activity that might be interpreted as subversive," Antanas warned. "Our whole family could be in danger."

"You're right. I put this family in danger, and I could be arrested. If that ever happens, you should have the means for escape. I will show you where our family valuables are." Vytas asked Antanas for help in taking down the portrait of Jadvyga. Both struggled with the weight of the portrait in its heavy wooden frame. Antanas suspected a safe in the back of the portrait, but there was only a reinforced wall. Putting the portrait face-down, Vytas carefully removed the side and bottom slats of the intricate woodwork. There, wrapped in gauze, were hundreds of gold coins as well as a king's ransom in diamonds. They carefully replaced the slats and the portrait. "I had this frame specifically made after your mother died."

"Where are the servants?" Antanas asked as both returned to the library. Antanas was pleased to discover so much unknown family wealth in such an unusual place.

"Casimir came and told Paulina to go home since masters and servants do not exist under communism. Paulina cried as Casimir pulled her away. As he left, he whispered to me, 'Wherever your wife and daughter are, they should not come back to Vilnius.'"

"Casimir knows some things since he works at NKVD headquarters, but I would not take him seriously. Will you be leaving for the country also? It would be safer for you to be out of the city," Antanas said with a heavy heart.

"I can't leave my position at the university. I'm staying for the faculty and students. A change of regime does not change the need for education and health care. I am also helping your mother's temporary replacement."

By "mother," Vytas was referring to Katerina, but she was not Antanas's mother. His mother was Jadvyga, the woman in the portrait, the beautiful lady he saw dying. As a young boy, he saw this beloved, dark-eyed, dark-haired woman shrinking before his very eyes. His grief at losing her would never leave him. He tried to find her in every woman he met.

Katerina was a good, kind person, but he didn't feel the same intense love. The portrait struck a familiar chord. There was a resemblance to Sarah Bernstein—the same classic dark features crowned by shiny coal-black hair. He felt a pang of longing to see Sarah.

Vytas followed his son's eyes to the same portrait. Jadvyga was a tempestuous artist who had captured his body and soul. He sat down in contemplation.

Vytas and Jadvyga had lived in neighboring estates, but because of the Lithuanian-Polish conflict, their parents discouraged their childhood play. Years later, he arrived for advanced studies in Paris, already a practicing physician. Fate and mutual friends threw them together at a formal dinner party where he was struck by Jadvyga's uninhibited laughter and overt sexuality. Her dark, flashing eyes mesmerized him, as did her supple body with its seductive scent of gardenias. "Let's get out of here. It's so stuffy," she said to him as he followed her, hypnotized. They went to an artist's garret where a wild party was in full swing. Jadvyga made him the center of attention, and he had the most interesting, carefree evening of his life. He felt joy; he felt alive.

After that night, he was addicted to her. He fought with his parents for two years for permission to marry her. The birth of Antanas occurred too soon after their wedding, according to gossip. Her hedonistic, free lifestyle excluded more children since the birth of their son, the heir, established her rank and ensured her position. No need for more encumbrances.

Jadvyga never changed her ways of being charitable to men with her body, to Vytas's deep pain. But even the agony of her faithlessness did not make her less attractive to him. The cancer diagnosis crushed Vytas. Jadvyga had been the center of his life, and the enigma of her seductiveness lived on. Vytas turned out the lights and went to bed, chastising himself for his lustful memories and forcefully thought of Katerina.

Antanas left early for the mayor's office. When he arrived, Ruta informed him that Mayor Kuzas had been replaced. Antanas knocked on the mayor's door and entered. A young man wearing a wrinkled, somewhat soiled tan uniform emblazoned with the red star of the USSR sat at the mayor's highly polished desk. A red flag with the hammer and sickle was now prominently placed on his desk, as well as a nameplate: Commissar Yuri Sabanov.

"So you have experience in turning Vilnius from Polish to Lithuanian?" he asked Antanas as he stood to full height, revealing a muscular, fit body.

"Yes, in a period of six months, we effected an almost complete change," Antanas answered in Russian, evoking a smile from Yuri, who lit a cigarette.

The commissar had dark hair, his brown eyes were bloodshot, and he badly needed a shave. "So much to do, I have not slept in days," he said. "You will work with me to convert this city under the auspices of the USSR. Your Russian is excellent, and my Lithuanian is weak, so we will make good partners in this assignment from Stalin. I will continue your appointment as assistant mayor of Vilnius. Let's drink to Stalin!" They both toasted their new arrangement.

To maintain the same position was a godsend and a miracle. The knowledge of Russian saved him. He vowed to increase his study of German and French since communication was a key to being indispensable. Antanas marveled at his good luck. He could seduce all women, including the goddess of good fortune. "Thank you, comrade."

Pranas ran up to Casimir stationed at his post at headquarters. "Father, I got you promoted to city inspector for internal security. You'll get a new uniform, and your pay will double!"

"What is this work? What do I do?" asked a puzzled Casimir.

"You will go around the city asking questions and recording the answers."

"How can I do this? You know I can't read or write and speak only Polish."

"Easy, memorize these questions I will tell you, get the answers, and have a soldier I assign to you write them down. Vilnius residents know Polish."

Casimir put on his uniform, proud of the red star. But leaving for the first address, he hesitated until his assigned Polish-speaking Soviet soldier arrived. Becoming a boss conferred importance and confidence. He strode out into the beautiful June day, passing by a park full of green leaves and lively flowers where a sparrow chirped to its mate in the silent absence of any people in the streets.

He approached the first house on Lombard Street and rang the bell. "Is this the residence of the Meska family? You are Jonas Meska?" he asked of the short, overweight man who opened the door. He looked inside. The room was covered in Oriental rugs with gleaming silver on the table. The filthy rich were to be exposed.

"Yes, I am Jonas Meska. I am the proprietor of the Vilnius Porcelain Factory," the hesitant voice answered.

"How many of you live here? How many square meters do you have?" Casimir asked as his aide stood by him with paper and pencil.

"My wife and I and her elderly mother. About 1,600 square meters." answered the perspiring Meska.

The aide scribbled this information. Casimir smiled at how easy this was.

"An unjust occupation of the people's housing. Be prepared to share this apartment with the USSR Army," Casimir declared the memorized script.

Casimir and his helper went around the city to determine who had "bourgeoisie housing." In the evening, he met with friends, also in his unit, who had visited factories and tabulated the numbers of employees of every enterprise. All the inspectors had some beer to celebrate their newfound power, and Casimir could not wait to go home to impress Paulina.

"Paulina! Congratulate me!" shouted Casimir entering the kitchen. "I'm an inspector for internal security at twice my pay! This was my first day, and they commended me for visiting the most households and exposing the theft of space by the rich cockroaches. I'm a success!"

"You stupid man! How could you be proud of being a spy, of turning in innocent people to the communists? They'll be deprived of what was theirs and forced to share with the beasts from the north. I couldn't enter church today for my daily Mass because they closed all the churches."

"Paulina, you are the stupid one. Working for the rich has clouded your mind. Of course, they're going to take away from the rich, but it's to give it to us—the workers—who have toiled for so long and suffered so much!" Casimir looked in the pot on the stove to examine this evening's dinner and said with pride, "Our lives will be much, much better."

"How can our lives be better when churches are closed and all the goods in the stores disappear? I had a difficult time today buying enough for supper." Paulina stirred the thin beet soup with a few potatoes in her pot. "The grocer told me all his supplies were confiscated by the Red Army. What little he had was at an exorbitant price. Exchanging the litas for the ruble, it took a week's worth of our currency to get enough rubles for tonight's soup and bread."

Paulina shook her head in disgust. "I can understand why you, an illiterate, may think things are improving. But my brilliant son, Pranas, who reads so much, why couldn't he understand the consequences? He's late, probably doing more of the work of the devil."

Jan Kataski was sitting in the corner, reading the New Testament while following the conversation between his parents. Putting his book down, he said, "It really is the work of the devil. The seminary closed permanently today because of the edict against all religious institutions. The director told us school records were destroyed to protect us from interrogation."

Paulina's eyes misted. "Be careful, my son. May God protect you."

Jan said, "I will carry the cross of Christ and walk in his footsteps. How could anyone live without the love of God? Only God's love can absorb the cruelty of life. If happiness comes as a raindrop, sorrow comes as a deluge."

Although Casimir expected a celebration for his promotion, the meager dinner proved to be a quiet affair. The blessing given by Jan and ignored by Casimir led to harsh words from Paulina. They ate in silence, only interrupted by little Anna's complaint that they could no longer say their prayers in school and were supposed to learn Russian.

As they were finishing, Pranas came in with a face flushed with triumph. "I'm now the assistant to the head of the communist party of Vilnius. The party will have all the power, reporting straight to Moscow. I know the politicians think Mayor Sabanov is important, but the party will control what goes on. They had a talk with me and were impressed by my knowledge of Marxism and my commitment to its ideals. I already applied for better living quarters for us."

He noticed his downcast brother. "Jan, don't be sad. Didn't Christ tell his followers, 'Blessed are the poor' and 'Give away what you have and come and follow me'? Marx outlines a far more Christ-like attitude in giving to the poor than the rich Catholic priests with all their property and churches decorated in gold by the sweat of the poor." Pranas, proud of his brilliant explanation, made communism more Christian than the church. This logic was completely lost on Jan.

Abraham opened his store, noting that in the past few days, there had been no customers. People, paralyzed by uncertainty, could not decide on the best and safest use of their money. Anticipating the currency conversion, always prepared to store his wealth in a transportable form, Abraham had hidden his bags of gold coin rubles. The Soviets, with the aid of Lithuanian communists, inspected Bernstein's living quarters and concluded the Jews did not possess excess living space.

Bernstein's Furs had appeared on the list of businesses to be confiscated, but Antanas convinced Yuri Sabanov to exempt the furrier who could provide furs for their wives. Abraham rejoiced that his business escaped closure, not aware Antanas had acted out of concern for Sarah.

Daniel walked into Bernstein's, stooping as always as if the weight of the world rested on his thin frame. Daniel hesitantly spoke with his face turned away from his father, "We have been saved from losing our business and should feel safer now with the USSR to protect us against the fascists, but the end is not certain. The Soviets are in a desperate fight with Finland, such a small nation, and they are losing! Even worse, Hitler has conquered Norway and France."

Abraham looked up from his accounts and said, "I despise communism. It's bad for business, but for now, it seems we have survived. Our business, our home, our family are intact, except for Jacob, who is too fond of our enemy. But he's my son—he will come to his senses."

Even with Jacob's betrayal of his family and religion, he was still the beloved son to be forgiven and loved. Daniel's chest ached with grief at this lifelong injustice. He wanted to be worthy, to impress his father with his political acumen, to warn his family.

Daniel continued, "This is a death struggle between two great powers and two ideologies that cannot compromise. There is a belief these two cats will share the mouse and go away. But this will not happen. They are both equally hungry—one will win."

Abraham laughed at Daniel's description of world events and said, "Jacob's standing with the new regime will offer some protection, no matter how distasteful. But the only real protection for us is our wealth and the possibility of a homeland."

"But what about the Nazis? Hitler is moving east and is getting ready to attack Russia," Daniel countered.

"A customer told me Stalin heard this and answered that it is a damned rumor to break his alliance with Germany," said Abraham with a dismissive wave of his hand.

"What if the Germans attack and win, Father? Then what?"

"My plans are laid for an escape to Palestine. With my plan, we will survive. Daniel, the only thing of value is our wealth. I will show you where I hid it. I wanted to show Jacob, but his crazy Marxist ideas could make him betray us. For now, we are safe, but if anything happens to me, I want you to know where to find our wealth. Come with me."

They walked to the ghetto and to the adjacent small cemetery. The gardener's shed had a trapdoor, and descending a ladder, they found a labyrinth of dark passageways under the entire ghetto built centuries ago. As they approached with their flashlights at a second right turn, Abraham stopped and counted twenty bricks from the bottom. He took out a penknife and scratched out the caulk. He eased out the brick and removed a long leather bag. Opening the bag, the sparkle of hundreds of gold rubles and napoleons shone under his flashlight. A smaller bag was full of loose diamonds. "These underground areas have served as a safe bank for the residents since ancient times."

Daniel looked around and said, "This is a terrible place. In case of a crisis, everyone will run here to claim their gold. You must find another place."

Abraham took the heavy bag, for once impressed with the foresight of his son, and said, "What do you suggest?"

"A place where you can grab the gold while escaping and not be caught in an underground crowd. A place far from the ghetto," Daniel said, thinking.

They went home, found a metal box to hold the leather bags, and took a small shovel. They walked to a wooded area by the Neiman River. "See the column of the Zoo Bridge?" They approached the supporting post closest to the ghetto. He paced twenty steps into the woods. The wet ground splashed around their shoes, and rain from the trees dripped on them. Abraham stopped by a massive rock at the side of a large oak tree. Daniel and his father pushed the rock aside and brushed away a thick covering of leaves. They dug a hole in the soft, wet ground big enough for the metal box. They covered the box with earth and pushed the rock into place.

"Daniel, this is for our trip to Palestine. Now only you and I know where to find our gold and diamonds, my profits of a lifetime. If I'm not here, take care of your mother and sister. I know you'll also take care of your brother."

Daniel inwardly shouted with joy at this first instance where he took precedence over his brother Jacob in his father's eyes.

A sham election to install a new government, boycotted by most inhabitants of Vilnius, had been held. The results, Vytas noted, had the communists win by 113 percent of the vote. Moscow installed a Lithuanian puppet government, and Mayor Sabanov organized a celebration to welcome the new communist prime minister of Lithuania.

Antanas in a tuxedo attended alone, a handsome addition appreciated by the diplomats' wives. The tub of caviar donated by Mayor Sabanov enhanced the champagne and vodka reception in the Astoria hotel. After a few drinks, Mayor Sabanov took Antanas aside. "Your house is one of the biggest, but it'll escape registration because I'll make it one of my official residences for visiting dignitaries. This will be a reward for your service." Then Sabanov frowned. "There's a problem, though, with your father since he signed a secret letter sent to the Western Powers, asking for armed help to overthrow our regime. You know this is an act of treason. I want you to be prepared for the consequences."

Terror struck Antanas. He could not imagine who would have betrayed his father. "Where did you get this letter?"

"The NKVD who alerted us had intelligence from our spies in England. There were eight names that signed it," Yuri Sabanov said.

"I don't believe this," Antanas scoffed as he lit a cigarette.

Sabanov reinforced the truth, "We had a report of this letter arriving in England, seeking help against the USSR, but we needed proof. It seems there had been an incident between Professor Kuznetsov and Elena Dielka, and in order to keep it quiet, Dielka gave us the original copy of the letter. There is no question of the names on the list."

Antanas's mind raced. His father's best friend? Sabanov said an incident between Kuznetsov and Elena. There was nothing Dielka treasured more than Elena. Was she unfaithful? What happened to make Dielka betray his father? Antanas sat down at the lavish table with little appetite. He tasted a few mouthfuls of zakuski, Russian appetizers of smoked fish, eggs, ham, and herring. He consumed the bouillon with piroshki, but he only moved around the portion of roast suckling pig with potatoes on his plate. "Consequences" meant prison and death with this regime.

Coming home to the empty, dark house, he felt like a stranger. He walked up the steps to his father's bedroom, opened the door, and saw he was asleep. He turned on the lights. "What's the matter?" Vytas sat up, rubbing his eyes as he reached for a bathrobe.

"I was at a state dinner with Mayor Sabanov, who told me you are guilty of treason. The NKVD has a copy of the document you signed and sent abroad!" Antanas shouted this accusation in hopes of a rebuttal from his father.

Vytas got out of bed, went to the bathroom, and splashed cold water on his face. "Dear God! How could this be?" asked Vytas, now fully awake. "We're all friends and swore our secrecy upon our sacred honor. There may have been rumors, but there couldn't be any proof! Who gave them the copy?" he asked, returning while wiping his face.

"Zygmond Dielka," Antanas spit out the name.

"Impossible. I don't believe it!" Vytas, his face white, went up to Antanas and shook him by the shoulders as if to shake out the lie.

Antanas took Vytas's hands from his shoulders and said, "I know this is a shock. Dielka is a patriot of the highest order. Mayor Sabanov told me they blackmailed him with an incident between his wife and Professor Kuznetsov, and the price was a copy of the document."

Vytas said with a shaky voice, "Dielka is only vulnerable where it concerns Elena. They have no children, and she is the world to him." The baron dressed, throwing his shirt on so rapidly it ripped at the shoulder. He told Antanas they were going to Dielka's house immediately.

Antanas, wanting to delay the tragedy, said, "Father, it's two in the morning. This isn't the time. Let's wait until daybreak." The danger to his father made him shiver.

"There is no time. By daybreak, I may be arrested for treason. I want to find out why my best friend betrayed me." Vytas rushed out and got into the car, a ten-year-old American Ford, as Antanas sprinted after him.

Vytas drove their car through the mist-shrouded, deserted streets of Vilnius glazed by a fine rain. Antanas, calm and sober, tried to analyze the situation. "Arrested for treason! You hold an important position here in the city. It would be an outrage."

"You have no idea of what people brainwashed by ideology and ambition are capable of. My life is dust." They screeched around a sudden turn.

The Dielka apartment was in the old town behind the ancient city walls. They rang the bell a few times before they were let in and climbed the stairs to the second-floor apartment. Dielka, in pajamas under a hastily-thrown-on robe, came to the door, visibly shaking. "Thank God, I thought you were the NKVD to take me away. You see, I cannot leave Elena. She is under sedation."

"Zygmond, we have been friends since youth. What in God's name have you done? I never took you for a traitor," the baron shouted in the entryway.

"Vytas, calm down. It's done. Come in." Dielka closed the door and turned on the lights in the elegant, sparsely decorated sitting room. He proceeded to pour some vodka, striving for a reasonable discussion.

"You understand not only you but my father and all your colleagues are also accused of treason," Antanas spat out as he accepted a glass of vodka.

"I can explain." Dielka turned to Antanas with his arms out in supplication and then offered a glass of vodka to Vytas.

Vytas refused the proffered vodka with a cut of his hand as if it were poison. "The penalty for treason is harsh, and my hands are tied because of the evidence you provided. What made you do such a hellish thing? Betraying your colleagues and your country! You are not worthy to be called shit!" Vytas shouted.

Antanas, hearing his father, felt sorry for the pale cornered Dielka. Silence fell on the trio since the oppressive realization did not leave room for words.

"I understand it concerns your wife," Vytas broke the silence with tears in his eyes, remembering this room in happier times. "What could you possibly have to say for yourself? You could implicate yourself for your goddamn reason, but why involve me and the rest?"

"Vytas, no apology can take away the loathing I have for what I've done. I was a man drowning, and I would have drowned myself, but it was for Elena. I would die a thousand deaths for her," Dielka said, taking a gulp of vodka before finally sitting down.

"What happened?" Antanas asked.

Dielka took a deep breath, "We had dinner on May 22. I introduced Kuznetsov to Elena, and the small toad was practically licking his lips. He became obsessed with her and tried to contact her numerous times with no success. The more she refused, the more his desires were inflamed. Elena was repelled by him. He even stopped her in the street once and made lewd suggestions to her. Since then, she never went out alone."

Dielka poured another glass of vodka for Antanas and himself. He gestured to Vytas, who waved away the offer with disgust. Dielka, hesitant and ashamed to continue, took another drink of vodka. "Last Monday, when I was at the office, she was home alone in the morning having breakfast in her negligee." She interpreted a loud knock at the door to be an expected delivery of food. As she opened the door, Kuznetsov burst in and said, "I see you are ready for me," grabbed her, and ripped off her negligee.

Dielka lit a cigarette with shaking hands and continued, "He forced himself on her! Raping her right there on the dining room table! When she started to cry, he said, 'So you did not like it this way, so let us try something else,' and sodomized her. When she was bent over, she reached for her breakfast knife, quickly turned over, and stabbed him. He shrieked and collapsed. In spite of the blood and shock, Elena called the police to report the attack."

Dielka let out a long sigh, covered his face with his hands, and started to sob. "Soon after, two men from the NKVD came, called an ambulance for Kuznetsov, found out his identity, arrested Elena, and took her away. I got a call at the university to come to police headquarters. My wife had been arrested for an attack on a Russian official!"

Dielka's voice croaked, "You could imagine how I felt. I saw my Elena behind bars naked and covered in blood and bruises. The NKVD interviewed me and informed me Elena would be executed or sent to Siberia. There was only one way I could prevent this. They said USSR intelligence intercepted a document I signed asking the Western Powers for help. What they needed was proof of the co-conspirators. I wanted to kill myself. What choice did I have? You all can still escape. Elena was helpless. I was able to bring her home," Dielka pleaded, lowering his head in supplication.

"You have condemned all eight of us in order to save your wife!" Vytas hit the table with his fist as he stood up.

Antanas saw his father's face blanch as he grabbed the table on the verge of collapse. He rushed to help him and pleaded, "Come, Father, there is no further discussion. We know our answer." They stood up and left without saying goodbye, slamming the door behind them.

As they were driving home, Antanas said, "What a fool. It was probably an orchestrated NKVD ploy to compromise the weakest member."

After Vytas and Antanas left, Dielka closed the door, went to their bedroom, and fell in bed beside Elena. He tried to close his eyes, but the pounding in his head and the taste of vomit in his mouth made sleep impossible. Death would be a welcome end to the pain. The relief of an eternal void was impossible now since, first, he must help Elena. Dawn started to break when a loud knock on the door made him jump up. Elena, sedated, was asleep, and he covered her with a quilt before he opened the door. Two NKVD men ordered him to come with them; he was under arrest for treason. The NKVD handcuffed Dielka and dragged him to Red Army Headquarters.

"Remove all your clothes!" a voice blared as he entered a gray room filled with members of the secret police and a Red Army officer. Dielka tried to summon some dignity in his naked state, "I deserve a trial."

The Red Army officer held up a piece of paper on his desk, smirked, and said, "A trial? Why? It's clear. The evidence is here. Do you think you are innocent?" He turned to the other officers, and they all burst out laughing.

Dielka realized he had already been condemned. "Please, do what you will but spare my wife. She's innocent and was not aware of anything."

The guard pushed him out of the interrogation room into a dingy corridor and down the steps into the cellar. He was last in a line of naked men. The first person in line was shoved through a door. Dielka heard a shot. A minute later, the next in line was forced through the door. Finally, it was his turn. The door opened, and he stood in front of a wall covered with blood and bits of tissue. His feet splashed in liquid, and he looked down at a pool of blood. On the wall to his right was a large poster of a blood-splattered Stalin with a kindly grin. He felt the cold gun barrel at the back of his head. As Dielka's body was thrown on a cart, an official took his papers and stamped "traitor."

Antanas sat at his desk, waiting for the mayor, who was still out after the previous day's festivities. He read the announcement that Lithuania would now be called LSSR—the Lithuanian Soviet Socialist Republic and to expect one hundred thousand more Soviet troops into the city.

He had also brought a large wooden box closed with a lock and wrote a note:

Comrade Sabanov,
My father is an academic, not a politician. Zygmond Dielka
ensnared him into treason. I know the NKVD answer is execution,
but with your influence, he could be imprisoned instead. His life
is in your hands, and my indebtedness to you personally would be
limitless for the rest of my life. Your wish would be my command.
Antanas Eimontas

He put the note and the key on top of the box and placed them on the mayor's desk.

Sabanov read the letter and opened the package containing the Eimontas family jewels and gold. They managed to hide these well, thought Sabanov. There must be at least a million here. Antanas would be indebted to him over and above party loyalty. He could be of use as a personal guard. He picked up the telephone. "Comrade Zuikinov, regarding the Eimontas case, there are some facts . . ."

Elena woke in an empty apartment from her sedative-induced sleep and cried out for her husband. Staggering out to the drawing room, she saw the door ajar. She knocked on a neighbor's door and was informed of the arrival of the NKVD in the predawn hours and her husband's arrest. She dressed quickly, without her usual care, and took a taxi to NKVD headquarters.

A uniformed officer took her to a room where she saw many people anxiously waiting. She was given a number, 52. After five hours of terror eating away at her heart, a buxom Russian woman called out her number. Entering a booth, a small gray-haired man searched through some folders. "Zygmond Dielka. Yes, he was here," oozed the man. "But he is here no longer."

Elena shrieked as she fainted. A Russian woman officer came into the room, shook her, and splashed her with a glass of water. Pulling herself together, Elena asked, "Where could I look for him, in prison, in Siberia?"

The Russian woman looked at the pained eyes of Elena and had pity. She helped her outside and said in a whisper, "My dear, do not waste your time on looking for ghosts." Elena understood Zygmond was dead.

Returning home, Elena collapsed into a stupor. Her intense pain seared her mind, and the throbbing insanity of the events proved to be completely incomprehensible. She needed some explanation, some comfort. Knowing Katerina was away, she reached Vytas on the telephone.

Her voice was so weak at first Vytas did not recognize it.

"Vytas, this is Elena. Zygmond is dead." She wanted an explanation, gentle human contact and understanding.

However, she was met with a frosty response from Vytas, "He condemned eight of his friends to save you. He deserved death."

Elena put down the phone and looked at her surroundings still beautifully intact. The clock continued to tick, although she was frozen in time. She shivered in the now profound realization that her whole life was gone. The ultimate sacrifice of her husband due to his love for her made her guilty.

She filled her bathtub with warm water, took a straight-edge razor, and placed it on the tub ledge. Holding the razor, she remembered giving it to Zygmond one Christmas and saying it was so expensive it should be sharp for one hundred years. Memories of their years together played like a movie in her mind, and removing her husband from the scene extinguished all desire to continue. There were no doubts about her action; there were no alternatives.

Elena combed her hair and put on her makeup. She had been a homely child, pale and skinny, inheriting no natural beauty. Her will, intelligence, constant striving, and vigilance produced her pleasing looks. She was one of the rare women who improved with age, each year yet another hard-fought victory toward beauty. Creams, makeup, diets, exercises, and slavish adherence to style were her guidelines for the physical illusion. But also her reading, study of psychology, and intelligence combined to give her charm, a quality which masked any remaining imperfections.

The routine of grooming, honed by years of practice, had given her so much pleasure. Now it was bittersweet since death, no matter how elegant in preparation, manifested ugliness in its result.

Putting on her favorite perfume, she stood naked in front of a mirror and bid herself adieu. She then entered the warm water and opened her veins.

Chapter 10
September 1940

How many nothing days need to be strung together to make a nothing life? Jan Kataski asked, after hours of prayer, kneeling by his bed, facing an icon of the Vilnius Virgin. Since the party ordered the seminary closed, Jan had not found an alternate outlet for his life. "Please, all-powerful God, forgive my sinful family. Father and Pranas are doing the work of the devil." He rose slowly, his knees aching, went to the kitchen, sat on a chair, and focused on the family crucifix. Cold and darkness descended with the setting sun, but instead of lighting a fire, he wrapped himself in his heavy black sweater.

Pranas returned from work, found his brother sitting in the dark kitchen, and turned on the light. He shook Jan by the shoulders. "What the hell are you doing, Jan? You could at least start supper or a fire. Mother must be working late. Do something practical, for God's sake! You're a sad excuse for a man, as sensitive as a girl, always on your knees, as if that could change anything."

Jan glanced at the robust, flushed face of his brother, startled to confront this complete stranger. Pranas, in his Soviet uniform, physically embodied a rational form that excluded a spiritual life. Jan smiled at his brother, lit a fire, and started to peel potatoes.

"Find another field of study and forget the priesthood," Pranas said, cutting a chunk of sausage. "The churches will never reopen, and I don't want my brother wed to a ridiculous idea that'll only bring grief."

Jan's whole being lashed out, "No, I'm going to be a priest! God has shown me the way. What has being a communist done for your soul?"

"Look at this!" Pranas shoved out his arm, and Jan saw a big gold watch on his wrist. "My reward for catching a bourgeois factory owner trying to hide some of his machinery," Pranas mumbled, chewing the salami.

"That watch is yours only by theft," Jan whispered.

"Action is the only way to survive, by taking what you want and getting as much as you can out of this life. There should be more to life than just suffering. Communism gives our family an opportunity to advance ourselves and not to be stuck in poverty all our lives."

"Communism condemns riches. It is greed and not your philosophy of equality that made you steal the watch," said Jan, peeling the potatoes.

"Don't be naïve, Jan. Of course, equality is promised, but there will always be people with more power. Power without a gold crown and servants, but with power, you get the best of what's available, the best apartment, the best food, the best goods."

"I'm not looking for power. I only want to follow the example of Christ and help the poor and the suffering. Following Christ is my happiness." Jan's knife slipped, and the cut finger started to turn the potatoes pink. He rinsed his hand and pressed down on his wound with a cloth.

Pranas noticed the cut. "You will bleed far more for your stubborn denial of the facts of life. Your fantasy of a reward in heaven does not exist by any measure of reality." Pranas grabbed the potatoes from him, finished peeling them, and started to grate them at high speed.

As Jan was sitting on the sofa, holding his cut finger, he heard a racket on the stairs. He rushed to the door and swung it open, and two strangers staggered in, supporting between them an unconscious Paulina.

"Mother!" both sons shouted as they joined the awkward procession, moving Paulina to the sofa. "What happened?" Her hair matted with blood; her face cut, bruised, and swollen; and her clothing torn and muddied rendered her almost unrecognizable. Pranas got a pillow, and Jan got a blanket.

One stranger, a tall bearded man, said, "We found her like this in front of the Gates of Dawn. I recognized her as Casimir's wife, so we brought her here." As Jan washed her wounds, Pranas ran to the doctor next door for help. Paulina started to regain consciousness, moaning with pain.

Pranas returned in minutes with Dr. Zubrickas, who took a syringe from his black satchel, gave her an injection for pain, and examined her wounds. Removing her blouse, he said, "She has broken ribs. She was kicked so hard they left the imprint of their soles on her chest." Jan had never seen his mother's naked chest and turned away, but not before seeing the huge black bruises. "She also has head injuries." He wiped away the blood from her face and said, "I will suture the cuts to stop the bleeding."

The other stranger, so light-skinned and blond he appeared to be an albino, sighed in relief and said, "Thank God she's alive. At least I didn't waste my time carrying a corpse." Pranas took this as an insult and grabbed the man by his lapels. "This is my mother. Tell me what happened! Who attacked her?"

"We were walking to work and saw an old lady kneeling in the middle of the street at the Gates of Dawn. Who is to say if that's against the law? So we decided not to report her. Two NKVD agents approached her and asked her to move on. She refused and started to fight them off when they took their clubs and started to beat her and kick her repeatedly. I think they left her for dead."

Casimir entered, expecting a warm supper, only to find a room full of strangers and commotion. "What the hell is this?" he shouted.

Jan pointed to Paulina on the couch and explained, "Mother was praying at the Gates of Dawn, and two NKVD agents beat her. These two men brought her home."

Casimir thanked the strangers and the doctor, and they left after the doctor gave Casimir instructions. "She is to rest."

"We have no recourse against the brutality of the NKVD," said Casimir, looking at Paulina. "She's been told not to pray publicly, but the stupid woman will not leave her superstitions. This will be reported to the authorities, and a black mark will go against our names, Pranas. We may even lose our positions."

His father's cold and selfish remarks shocked Jan. His mother had worked, cooked, cleaned, read and wrote, and borne five children for this man. "Father, why are you so cruel to your wife? You show no sympathy or concern for her pain. You only focus on the chances for your own advancement in the party. How can you live with yourself?" Jan asked.

"I've lived a stupid life listening to your mother whose instructions were only to pray and obey." Casimir looked at the prone body of Paulina with a mixture of sorrow and disgust. He sat down, lit a cigarette, and continued, "Pranas showed me I don't need to be a slave. On the railroad, I fixed machinery and cleaned wagons. Now I go to the biggest, richest houses in Vilnius and eject the owners who tremble when they see me at the door. As a party member, I have power. I don't want to lose what I gained."

Pranas was torn between his father, proud of achieving success in his work for the party, and his mother's broken body on the sofa. "I love Mother and see her need for religion. But she blows it out of proportion, praying loudly, always stopping and kneeling in front of the Gates of Dawn. Why can't she pray silently in her room?" Pranas asked.

"She's too old to change, but she'd better not destroy the good changes in my life," Casimir replied with a scowl. He went to the stove, put some lard in a pan, and started the potato pancakes.

Little Anna, back from school, frightened at the commotion and her mother's condition, crawled to her mother's side, crying. Jan placed a cool compress on Paulina's head and tried to give her a sip of water. Paulina, finally reviving, tried to sit up slowly and whispered hoarsely, "Thank God for my family."

Casimir lowered his head and turned away as he put his dinner on the table. Jan broke the silence. "Pranas, what are you going to do about this assault on Mother? It's clear to me Father will do nothing. He blames her for what happened. You should find out who did this and bring them to justice."

"You're a fool! Mother will recover. Her wounds aren't fatal, and maybe you've both learned a lesson. No more religion! It leads people like sheep to think only of the next life, while in this life, the Church and the capitalists rob them blind."

"The only robbery I'm aware of is the robbery perpetrated by Father and you as you steal the property of people," Jan countered.

This comment enraged Pranas, who raised his fist to hit Jan but instead went to the crucifix on the kitchen wall, tore it down, and threw it to the floor. "This is what I think of your 'goodness.' There is far more good in the equal distribution of property." This action of defiling a cross brought a moan from Paulina, a scream from little Anna, and even a look of disbelief from Casimir.

During the entire night, Jan sat at his mother's side, praying and grasping the broken crucifix so desecrated by his brother. "Mother, you suffered for Christ. You'll be a saint. These trials are a test of our faith. We have a chance to be martyrs for Christ," he gently whispered in her ear.

In the next few weeks, an angry Casimir continued to ignore Paulina, scowling as he passed the sofa. How could he condemn a system that provided him with his first glimpse of good fortune? But he felt guilty for not defending Paulina and rationalized that she would heal and forget. Finally, to apologize, one evening, he returned with a small statue of a rabbit he found in a vacated apartment. Paulina, touched by his gift, forgave his coldness.

Jan's world completely collapsed. His thoughts ran in torrents. He must avenge his mother's attackers. Christ said to turn the other cheek, but he also preached justice. He must at least confront the devils. Jan's whole being throbbed with the desire to express his faith publicly. He thought, *This life exists only as a trial from God to prove we are worthy of eternal life. How can Father and Frank value some uniform and rubles above paradise?* Christ wanted him to spread the message of his love and salvation and denounce this godless communism.

For spiritual help, Jan made an appointment with the bishop and hurried along the dark streets to an address at a rundown apartment building. Bishop Venclovas now wore civilian clothing and was confined to a small room with two other priests. Three mattresses on the floor and a stool in the corner constituted their quarters, almost a prison. Jan kissed his ring and said, "Your Excellency, thank you for seeing me. You told me to come late at night so I wouldn't be observed. I need your guidance."

"Jan, you came in time. My arrest and deportation to Siberia is imminent because I gave a sermon in which I asked Germany to be our liberator. I understand my punishment, but many of my colleagues, innocent of any subversive activity, have also been arrested."

Jan told him his family's story. "I need to avenge my mother's attack. How can I see injustice and not do anything? Is there no righteous anger?"

"My son, no. Anger and revenge are not in God's plan. We are in the grip of a terrible evil starting its course of destruction. They stripped our churches of art, precious metal, chalices, crucifixes, and statues. Our beloved St. Casimir's church is now the Museum of Atheism. But you have the right to protect your life and not anger the authorities by public displays of faith. God also loves those who pray in silence."

Hearing a loud knock on the door, a young man said, "They are here for you." Three soldiers in tan uniforms with red stars entered the room. "Bishop Venclovas?" one of them asked. The bishop stood. The soldiers pushed him to the ground and tied his hands behind his back. One soldier with a large, freshly stitched cut on his cheek spat on the bishop as another rolled him over and kicked him.

Filled with rage, Jan went after the soldier with the sutured cheek, punching him in the face. He only managed to open the scab and start it bleeding. The soldier brushed him away, but after touching his face, he saw blood on his hand and laughed. "You mosquito," he said, "how dare you attack me." They handcuffed Jan and led him away.

Arriving at the prison in the center of town, Jan was photographed, documents were filled out, and his identity papers were stamped with the word "criminal." Pushed down a long, dank corridor to a cell so crowded only standing was possible, one of his cellmates said, "Don't worry, there will be more room when the next group leaves for Siberia."

After three days with no food or water and only one overflowing bucket in the corner serving as a latrine, the steel gates opened. Names were called out, and most of the prisoners were led off to trains heading east. Not hearing his name, Jan continued his imprisonment.

Paulina slowly recovered and asked Pranas more and more questions about Jan's disappearance but found Pranas's answers unconvincing. Finally, to appease Paulina, Pranas went to the prison, appeared by the steel bars, and cursed at Jan. "So, you have finally gotten us in trouble. I don't see a promotion in my future with a brother labeled 'criminal.' Come, I got you out by saying you were mentally incompetent."

"What happened to the bishop?" Jan asked as tears rolled down his cheeks.

"He's on his way to Siberia. He'll be taken to a forced labor camp if he is lucky. If unlucky, the train will stop, and he'll be told to get out."

"But they don't have supplies or food or warm clothing. Temperatures at this time of the year are below freezing." Jan looked at Pranas in horror. "But that's murder."

"If you don't understand reality, that's your fate also. Stop your fantastic delusions. I won't be able to help you again," said Pranas, spitting on the ground.

"Brother, you are the devil's enforcer. I don't want your help. I want to help you. Are you too blind to see what they did to Mother and now the bishop? How can you side with them? And for what? You are losing your eternal soul for a few crumbs of earthly rewards. Please listen to me as one who loves you, who is your blood," pleaded Jan.

Pranas slapped Jan's face so hard it knocked him back. "You're not my brother. Only a mental incompetent."

Jan, weakened by the prison ordeal, almost crawled home, appearing so ragged and dirty it brought tears to Paulina's eyes. She saw the huge red mark emblazoned on her son's face. "So the monsters in prison hit you in the face!"

"No, it was my brother," said Jan, hanging his head down in shame.

Jacob Bernstein, a party member in good standing, clever with words, wrote some pamphlets for the communist press. Initially enlisted to write anti-religious propaganda articles, he became influential in the atheist movement, giving lectures and even attending some meetings in Moscow. He rose quickly through the ranks and earned the title director of the Division of Atheism for the Lithuanian Communist Party.

Commissar Ivan Ivanov, a tall, middle-aged man with thick black hair streaked with gray, arrived from Moscow to be the chief of the Lithuanian Communist Party. Rumor had it he was the best drinker in all of Russia. His eyes were always bloodshot, but his habit never seemed to impair his ability to function at work or—as gossip had it—with women. His relentless pursuit of pleasure did not disguise the facts of his ruthless nature.

Ivanov requested to meet all the directors and started with Jacob, an important functionary in the conversion of a religious country to communism. Sitting down in Ivanov's office, Jacob found himself in what appeared to be a chapel to communism. The walls were plastered with pictures of Karl Marx and Lenin and large propaganda posters. Numerous large red flags with the hammer and sickle were on every wall. A large bronze hammer and sickle under a portrait of Stalin seemed to be at the center of worship. *One god replaced by another, one religion replaced by another*, thought Jacob. The urge to worship was universal.

Ivanov started the meeting. "Jacob, you wrote an excellent article on the closing of the cathedral. No one needs a place with gold and statues. Now we have a museum of art that can be appreciated by everyone for free." Jacob took this praise with pride. Ivanov paced the room while talking. "In Vilnius, the urban population understands our orders. However, some resistance groups continue to fight us. Priests are holding secret services, trying to keep the population under subjugation. My directive is to end these practices. If you find dissent, you are to eradicate it under pain of death. I mean to be thorough."

"Comrade Ivanov, I am a writer, not an enforcer," Jacob stammered, horrified at the thought of physical violence.

"Jacob, this is an order. Obeying is the first principle of an effective organization. You know Stalin appreciates effective organization."

Jacob, in view of this assignment, visited the recently closed churches, mostly empty. The Church of St. Peter and Paul inspired awe in him by its rococo splendor. The beauty of the architecture, the high gothic arches pointing to the sky, the sun streaming through amazingly intricate stained-glass windows took his breath away. In this place, in this silence, he could imagine Rachel playing her violin. He could see why churches mesmerize poor people confronted by the ugliness of their daily lives. The few old babushkas he found he chased away. He should probably arrest them, but what's the use? Their ancient bodies and sclerotic religious thoughts were not worth the effort.

Commissar Ivanov returned one afternoon in a vile mood with angry red eyes and breath smelling of alcohol. "Jacob, I assume you're on top of this plot to subvert our work."

"I have no information on a plot." Jacob, pale and breathing rapidly, did not know what he was talking about. "Commissar, I'm sorry, but how could I kill some old lady on her knees?"

"You must be an incompetent idiot. Didn't I put you in charge of eliminating religious displays in this city? Are you ignorant of an uprising being planned at the Gates of Dawn? We must remove the opiate of the people for the glorious revolution. Don't you want to exterminate this vile superstition? Your ignorance and stupidity are incomprehensible. Stop this demonstration, or I will have your head!" He pounded on his desk. "Siberia will be too good for you!"

"I know nothing about an uprising," admitted Jacob with the acrid stench of failure clinging to his body. "Commissar, there's a rumor of a protest, but still no evidence." Jacob, his head throbbing, answered to this pounding pressure of the daily request for results. In terror, Jacob scurried away, and from bits and pieces of gossip, he gleaned some priests were planning a protest against the closing of the cathedral and the arrest of the bishop.

The next morning, the commissar strode in and shouted, "You'd better come up with something, and soon. These are orders from Moscow! If you do not succeed in uncovering this subversion, you become a co-conspirator, and there will be grave consequences."

Jacob's life depended upon exposing this plot and arresting the religious fanatics trying to outwit the regime. He could not sleep thinking of ways to achieve his goal; his life depended on exterminating them. He sank in a whirlpool of paranoia. He was nervous and jumpy, and his eyes darted about as he sought to pick up evidence of secret plans.

Jacob, in desperation, fantasized a plan to secretly start a demonstration himself. He would hire a few hooligans to bring a mob to the Gates of Dawn, and then he would arrest everyone and shoot the ringleaders. By successfully accomplishing his mission, he would be done with this torture. He woke from this nightmare in a shroud of sweat.

The person organizing this religious event loomed to gigantic proportions in his mind as "the enemy" out to destroy him. He stood at the Gates of Dawn for hours in the cold, approaching people walking down the street and questioning them. He was possessed.

Jan, always introverted, became even more so. He lost weight fasting and said the prayers of the Benedictine Order every three hours. He almost never slept or ate. He was aware of the way the world worked and hated it. The only way out is to be a martyr for Christ so that he could escape to sweet heaven and union with the Lord. The Gates of Dawn was the answer. It was the heart of faith in Vilnius, where his mother was almost martyred. It was where he must make his stand for his faith.

Physically never the same after her attack, Paulina worried about Jan in his downward spiral. She turned to her only salvation and fell on her knees in prayer by the kitchen table. Jan walked in and found his mother on her knees in front of the stove where soup was boiling. Embarrassed, Paulina slowly rose and said, "This is such a poor place to pray. How I miss my Gates of Dawn and my beautiful Madonna." She broke out into heartfelt sobs accumulated within her since her attack. The prohibition of religion, her husband's cruelty, the loss of Stefan and Valeria, the arrest of Jan, and the fanatic communism of Pranas was beyond her control. She was heaving with sorrow.

Seeing his mother's agony, Jan went to his bedroom and, after heartfelt prayer, changed into his seminarian's vestments. Looking at the broken crucifix, he loudly stated, "Thy will be done," and walked toward the front door.

"Where are you going dressed like that? It's forbidden," Paulina said.

"I'm going to the Gates of Dawn, where I will make a public profession of faith. Don't try to stop me, Mother."

"My child, my beloved Jan, don't do this. They will do worse to you than they did to me. Stay by my side. I need you. Casimir and Pranas are draining my soul. You are all I have left. Little Anna is so sad at all these things." Paulina grabbed his arms, clawing at him desperately to stay.

He gently pushed her away as he said, "This has been my destiny since birth, my sacred duty." Praying the rosary out loud, "Hail Mary, full of grace . . ." he walked slowly to the Gates of Dawn, oblivious of the people staring at his vestments. "God, give me the strength to endure what is to be. Christ, I will be with you in paradise."

Jacob was at his desk when a furious Commissar Ivanov strode into his office, brandishing his pistol. "Why are you sitting here on your ass when there is a demonstration starting?" he screamed. "You are in charge of stopping it. I should shoot you right now!" He fired a shot into the ceiling. "You idiot! I received a report of a priest wearing vestments at the Gate of Dawn. The demonstration is about to start. Stop it!"

Jacob took two soldiers in a police car and sped to the Gates of Dawn. He saw one young man in priestly garb on his knees with hands outstretched on the cobblestone street. Jacob's eyes bulged out. "That's him, the leader of the demonstration! That's the enemy destroying my life. The snake. I will destroy him!" He ran up to him, brutally grabbed him, motioning for the soldiers to take him.

Jan, expecting this, did not resist. Arriving at the prison, Jan, stripped of all of his clothes, was pushed into a cold room stinking of blood, urine, and excrement. The soldier's questions did not make any sense to him since he knew of no "other criminals wanting to destroy the state."

Jacob decided he would get to the bottom of this demonstration. "Chain him, and I will start my interrogation." With adrenaline coursing through his blood, he felt the high of achievement. Finally, he caught the bastard who was responsible.

"Who are your co-conspirators?" asked Jacob brandishing a cudgel.

"I don't know what you're talking about. There is no conspiracy. I am only a servant of the Mother of God," Jan answered in acute embarrassment at his nakedness.

"Don't play with me. I know you're the ringleader of a rebellion against our rule. Who are your followers? What are the details of your planned demonstration? Confess, or you will suffer greater pain than you can imagine."

"I have no followers. Only God has followers as his servants on earth. Our only demonstration is to do his holy will," Jan said with resignation. He always knew it would be like this. He was ready to die for his faith. He felt calm and peace.

Jan endured the day: starting with blows to his face, stomach, and back with a wood cudgel and electric shocks to his genitals. With no confession forthcoming, this was followed by the extraction of his nails one by one with rusty pliers, submersion under water until he had to be revived from drowning, breaking the bones of his fingers and his feet with a hammer.

By the second day, suffering horrible pain and heavy blood loss, he became lightheaded. In his delirium, he saw visions of the Virgin of the Gates of Dawn. "Mother of God, take me in your arms and free me from this suffering."

Commissar Ivanov came in and patted Jacob on the back. "Success! You got the ringleader. You cut off the head of the snake, and there is no demonstration." This commendation made Jacob more determined to extract the truth from this piece of shit. The more silent Jan was, the more furious Jacob became to know the co-conspirators. "This is a tough one. He will not give up his friends." Jacob smirked, showing off before the guards. He took an awl. "See this! If you do not confess, you will never see again!" Jacob plunged the awl into one eye and then the other. Blood gushed onto his face, splattering Jacob.

Jan whispered, "I do not need eyes to follow the journey of my soul to God," and collapsed into a heap.

Duty done, Jacob was revolted by the bloody mutilated remains. He took out his revolver and shot Jan in the head. "Take him away!"

Jan's tortured body mingled with the other victims of communism in a common grave.

Jacob, still furious he did not get more information, decided to publicize Jan's death as a warning to others and published an article: enemy of communism gets just end. The article was widely hailed and reprinted. It was to be a chapter in a new book to be published in Moscow. Jacob got a promotion and felt justified. His only regret was that he could not unsee what he had seen in the last moments of Jan's eyes. Guilt infected his conscience, and this indelible stain would never leave him.

When Pranas received a report of his brother's murder, he felt sorrow, but he blamed Jan's fanatic religious beliefs rather than the communists. As details of the torture leaked out, however, he started to question communist tactics. "It's sadists like Jacob Bernstein who are turning this economic struggle into slaughter," he told Casimir, who was angry but quiet, in the vise of an overwhelming dilemma between family and fortune.

When Jan did not return, Paulina suspected the worst, but Pranas spared her the horrid details of the torture. He told her only that Jan had died. Paulina knew her Jan had died for his faith. She placed his picture on her bedroom dresser and always put a few flowers in a small vase beside it. In this homemade chapel, Jan was her saint, and she prayed to him.

CHAPTER 11
JANUARY 1941

Like the freezing winds from the Baltic Sea, the German occupation blew away the past history of Klaipeda, the area amputated from Lithuania. The city, now called Memel, became more industrious and German by the day. Every building carried a swastika, and people greeted one another with "Heil Hitler." Triumph saturated the air.

The harsh breeze also dissipated Valeria's memories of life in Vilnius. She missed her parents and Anna, Jan, and Pranas but had no regrets about leaving the Polish hovel in Vilnius. She stopped going to church and considered her mother's fanatic religiosity shameful in this new, enlightened atmosphere. The mistreatment of the Jews bothered her, and she thought she could hear her mother saying, "We are all God's children," and Jan telling her, "Christ was a practicing Orthodox Jew all his life." Her old and new values were at odds since the Catholic dogma of love of neighbor branded her.

She had come to love the German way of life—the precision, cleanliness, and efficiency. Order and dedication to the Reich became the chief virtues to cultivate. Her ambition was to bring this superior, advanced system of life back to Vilnius when the Reich finally ruled all. She lost weight and continued bleaching her hair to a platinum blond, inspired by posters of "Aryan beauty." She obtained a small apartment and enough money for a fashionable wardrobe. Newspapers, radio, and books filled her hours, transforming her into an informed and interesting conversationalist at social gatherings. Young German officers found her attractive and asked her out for dinner and dancing. She basked in happiness because a bright new future beckoned her.

Her assistive work for Count Doban at Nazi headquarters included typing, answering the phone, keeping his schedule, and running errands but producing a daily précis of news gleaned from the world's press became her favorite task. She knew Russian, Polish, and German; with the help of a dictionary, she also could read the headlines in English and

French. Count Doban preferred a verbal litany of local, national, and international news while he drank a cup of coffee from his Rosenthal china. The count, hungry for an audience, then gave his own opinions to his secretary.

One evening, after work, Valeria was struggling into her boots and coat when Count Doban approached, "Valeria, I was able to secretly obtain a preview copy of Soviet propaganda. Please read this book and report in the morning." He threw a brown paper-wrapped book on her desk: *Religious Activity in the Lithuanian Soviet Socialist Republic.* Valeria sighed since she had plans with her friends that evening but now had to cancel them to read this thick, uninteresting book.

After a simple supper of cold roast pork and tomatoes, she curled up on her small sofa, turned on a bright light, put on her reading glasses, and opened the heavy book. After reviewing a list of Lithuanian church closings and religious prohibitions and needing to finish this book and prepare a short report in the morning, she skimmed the rest of the pages. A chapter included a newspaper reprint by Jacob Bernstein, entitled "Enemy of Communism Gets Just End." This got her attention since Bernstein had a reputation as a brilliant writer of propaganda. The Germans valued propaganda and considered Goebbels a genius in the field. A comparative evaluation of Bernstein's talents in promoting communism was called for, so she perused the article. Reading the name Jan Kataski dilated her eyes; this was her brother. Jan had been accused of trying to overthrow the communist regime by instigating religious riots.

In turning to the next page, a slip of paper fell out of the preview copy, and it was the editor's note:

> *Delete all information of torture as the USSR does not condone this, and it will not appear in the final version. The official version should include the information that this Kataski was a leading terrorist in support of fascism. Please rewrite the text to include these changes before publication.*

She intently, slowly read every word before the full impact of her brother's torture and death sank in. My god, beaten, tortured, blinded! She screamed at the images in her head, those sweet hazel eyes sightless oozing with blood. Jan was the most gentle and loving of all of God's people. Her chest felt crushed, and she could hardly breathe. She sank to the floor in a torrent of tears from the sorrow impaling her heart.

After an hour, exhaustion wrung out the last of her tears and left her in a dry desert of despair. She read the pages to be deleted again. This torture was at the hands of Jacob Bernstein—a Jew! A vortex of hatred she had never felt in her life rose from her bowels to her heart, to her brain. Despair turned to determination. She must tell Stefan of this outrage and demand justice. In her fury, only vengeance would cool her blood.

Valeria put on her coat and boots and walked through the snow and strong wind for the two miles to her brother's house. In the bitter cold, her hatred for Jacob Bernstein and the whole Jewish race boiled, and her milk of human kindness froze. Revenge throbbed through her veins.

Stefan opened the door in his robe, with Monica towering behind him. "What's the matter? Are you sick? You look terrible. Did you lose your job?" they asked in unison.

She shoved the book with the note wet with snow and frost at Stefan, "They murdered Jan! Read!" Her frozen fingers marked the page where the article appeared. Valeria, filled with venom, did not even take off her coat as Stefan read the article and note out loud to Monica, who, plump in a pink robe, was confused by this unexpected horror. When he finally read the by-line, Jacob Bernstein, he let out an inhuman cry. "And I had some sympathy for these Jewish communists and their suffering. What an idiot I am! They tortured and killed my brother, the most harmless person on earth who wanted nothing but prayer and silence! Those bastards!"

Monica, although she had never met the saintly young man, also fell into the hurricane of hatred. All three of them spent the whole night spewing their outrage at not only the crime but the hypocrisy of the denial.

The next day, Valeria, a sleepless night etched on her face, gave her report to Count Doban. "This book describes the Soviet occupation and how complicit the Jews are in the extermination of Christianity. Lithuanians are intimidated and prevented from the simplest gestures of their faith. This article has deep relevance to me because it describes the torture and murder of my brother, Jan, by Jacob Bernstein, a Jewish communist, and their official lies to suppress the evidence," Valeria concluded.

The violent hatred in her voice took Count Doban aback. "Valeria, my deepest sympathy. Now you understand our stance on the enemy. The Jews are out to kill Christianity. They take control of all the media to propagate their immorality. They constituted the majority of criminal activity in our Fatherland. They take charge of all financial areas to be powerful. They are the parasites of the world and should be eliminated from the family of man."

"Count, I always favored Nazi ideology but not one hundred percent because I could not justify its racial condemnation of Jews. After reading this book and knowing the fate of my brother, I am more than happy to work for the party and exterminate this vermin from the face of the earth."

Count Doban, looking at the haunted face of Valeria, conceived an idea, "My dear, your words are so heartfelt. I would like to send you to Berlin to attend a youth conference on the Jewish question. I believe your personal insight would be a commendable addition to instructing our people on the evils of this race."

"I don't think I could speak at a conference. I don't possess the education or stature to adequately speak for the correctness of Nazi philosophy," Valeria demurred.

"Your passion will trump all your perceived shortcomings," said Count Doban. "The National Socialist Party does not promote religion, but the extermination of religion is not one of our goals. We only wish to show the superiority of our Aryan race and have it dominate the world. If any religion is in agreement with our goals, we leave it alone. We target only certain clerics that oppose our rule. I must tell you, our Führer Hitler still pays tithes of ten percent to the Catholic Church."

In three days, Valeria was on a train to Berlin. Entering Germany, the rich farmlands, large cities, and smoke-spewing factories impressed her. In Berlin, magnificent buildings and the wide beautiful boulevards awed her, especially one named Under den Linden. Order and cleanliness predominated in the giant city. Store windows were stocked with goods, and well-dressed people went about their lives with vigor and determination. From her hotel window, she saw a plethora of flags with the Nazi symbol waving in the wind, symbolizing the face of victory.

On the way to the conference, she saw Jews walking in the streets with yellow stars emblazoned upon their sleeves. Recently, she would have felt compassion for their plight, but now, since her conversion, she was glad not to share her sidewalk with them. Swastikas and a banner "Welcome Hitler Youth" proclaimed the conference hotel. Her lecture, "Jewish Communists Rule Lithuania," scheduled on the last day of the conference, detailed the horrors of communist tactics.

"My fellow members of the National Socialist Party, I come from Memel, already under the genius rule of our Führer. However, the USSR rule in Lithuania is gruesome. There, in Vilnius, my brother, a meek and holy young man with no political motivation, chose to pray in public. He was arrested and tortured in a most horrific manner, including gouging out his eyes. The official version not only denied the torture but falsely accused him of being a fascist terrorist. The perpetrator was a Jewish communist, the vermin who occupied Lithuania and now maim and kill your Aryan brothers. I call upon our supreme leader, the Führer, Adolph Hitler, to free the Lithuanian people from the Jewish communist scourge. Heil Hitler!" She received a standing ovation.

She called Count Doban to report on events and proudly told of the Nazi trophy she had won for an outstanding presentation. He was pleased with her success. "You have a bright future with us."

The day after her triumph, she was invited with a select group of Hitler Youth participants to meet with Josef Goebbels, Reich minister of propaganda. She dressed in her best navy-blue suit, expecting this occasion to be the highlight of her life. In the Berlin Nazi Headquarters, their group was invited into a large room filled with many delegations. They were provided with refreshments and told to wait since Goebbels had been delayed in a meeting with the Führer.

While waiting, a Lithuanian priest approached Valeria and congratulated her on her speech. To her surprise, she also saw a large delegation of Lithuanians who told her they had come to ask Germany to expel the Soviets from Lithuania. Speaking with them, she understood that if only the Nazis would expel the Red Army, Lithuania could be independent.

After several hours, an impressive, highly polished, perfectly regimented group of Nazi officers arrived. In their midst was a very short, extremely emaciated man whose head was too large for his body. In addition, a noticeable limp, the result of a clubfoot, rendered him almost comic. A murmur went through the crowd, "Goebbels."

Goebbels spoke to the select Hitler Youth group about the invincibility of the German Reich and the inevitable force of history. ". . . but a war between the Judaic and Germanic races; that is the essence of this gigantic struggle." Valeria, seduced by his voice, mesmerized by his message, by the end of his speech, thought him an attractive man. She stood in line to shake his hand, noticing he barely came up to her shoulder. The touch of his hand was electric as she looked into his eyes. "Miss Katas, you are the one who won the trophy. You are from Memel. I count on you to propagate the truth." The personal persuasion was effective.

As she stood with Goebbels, a huge contingent walked by. "Look! Look! There is Hitler!" The crowd of happy Germans screaming for their savior went into a frenzy of excitement. As he passed closely, Valeria saw a man of medium height with a small mustache who wore an immaculate gray uniform and a hat with the silver eagle. His shoes had a mirror-like polish. Followed by a German shepherd, he smiled, turned, and patted the dog. Hitler glanced at her with steely-blue eyes. An aura of power and invincibility emanated from him. Hitler stopped by Valeria and said to Goebbels, "So this is the trophy winner. Fraulein, you are the pride of the Aryan race." He shook her hand and continued with his entourage.

"My god, how impressive! To have seen him so close in person! I can't believe it! And he spoke to me!" Valeria gushed to the young man beside her. "His superman qualities are obvious to anyone who sees him. Now that I have seen him, my greatest wish now is to serve him all my days."

Another young man said, "He is truly the good father of our country. He has no children since he says he is married to Germany. What dedication! So gentle with the dog, Blondie, and you know he is a vegetarian." The huge throng surrounding them, ecstatic, with tears of joy in their eyes, shouted after him with all their might, "Heil Hitler!"

Valeria returned to Memel, seduced by Nazi thinking. Faithful attendance at all Nazi meetings attracted the attention of Colonel Helmut Obermeyer. His inquiries led to Count Doban, who gave a glowing recommendation of Valeria and attested to her Prussian background. The colonel, a careful man, observed her at a distance for a few weeks before he invited her for a private discussion of an important project.

The colonel was a striking, tall, blond man with a distinguished profile and aristocratic bearing. The gray uniform with the eagle and the swastika endorsed his authority. Valeria looked into his green eyes, and her goal was to impress him with her work. They started to meet every week, and she became more familiar with *Mein Kampf.* His project was propaganda on the Eastern Front, reporting directly to Goebbels. Valeria immersed herself in the project, and when the colonel asked her to dinner, she was pleased by the prospect of familiarity beyond work. A surge of passion overcame her: she was possessed by the anticipation of love.

Vytas alone survived and languished in prison for six months since all the co-conspirators had been shot. Antanas, on his first visit to the prison, had told his father, "Mayor Sabanov took my bribe, and in return, instead of execution, you'll stay imprisoned. Just survive, and I'll do everything possible to release you." Since June, Antanas visited his father, bringing him news and food and tried to convince everyone of his innocence.

Vytas said, "Thank God, Katerina and Astrid are in the country and did not see my arrest or know of the life sentence."

"I'll keep them and my grandparents and Dalia safe," promised Antanas.

"Antanas, I saw Bishop Venclovas imprisoned here, and he said he was on his way to Siberia. Is there anything you could do to help him?"

"It's out of my hands," Antanas said as a prison guard signaled the end of their visit.

In Prienai, Katerina prepared a breakfast of eggs and farmer's cheese. As she took the freshly baked bread from the oven, she said to Aunt Teresa, "Since Vytas's arrest, I've written numerous letters to Antanas, but Jonas destroyed them. He told me Astrid and I would be arrested if the NKVD knew where we were. The most difficult thing is not knowing. Is he sick? Is he suffering?"

Aunt Teresa took Katerina in her arms and wiped her tears. "I know you love your husband. All we can do is pray." They sat down to breakfast.

Astrid came down wearing three sweaters. "We are in a frozen hell."

"Sweetheart, sit by the fire and eat," Katerina indicated, plumping a pillow.

"Will life ever return to normal? I am so bored." Astrid fumed, not noticing her mother's tear-stained face. After breakfast, they sat to read novels by the fire as Aunt Teresa went upstairs to rest. After a while, Katerina started cooking lunch.

At noon, Aunt Teresa walked down the steps slowly on her painful arthritic knees and said, "I was looking at the snowfall from my bedroom window, and I saw a man approaching our house."

As they all peered through the frost-covered window, to their horror, they saw a man in a Soviet uniform. "Both of you, hide in the cellar," said Aunt Teresa lifting the rug in the kitchen to reveal a trapdoor. As Katerina and Astrid climbed down a primitive ladder, they found themselves in a large earthen hole used to store potatoes and winter vegetables. Aunt Teresa closed the trapdoor and replaced the rug. She quickly hid the plates and cups set out for lunch and turned off the stove where Katerina's pork stew simmered.

Suddenly there was a loud knock on the door. "I'm here to inspect the premises," Pranas Kataski said as he entered the cozy farmhouse. Pranas had known of Astrid's presence in Prienai from his mother, but not until he had obtained a record of Vytas's arrest did he have the official excuse to make this trip. He spent days studying possible Eimontas connections in Prienai since he had the authority as NKVD to question and arrest any relatives of subversives. He arrived on the morning Vilnius train to Prienai.

Smells of lunch whet his appetite, but food was inconsequential with the enticing possibility of finding Astrid Eimontas. She was an unobtainable princess, but some acknowledgment, a smile, a nod would have satisfied his fantasies. But ignoring him, insulting him, and rejecting him turned his fascination into vengeful hatred. Did she not consider him human? She humiliated him in front of his friends. She personified all the pain he felt for his mother having to scrub the Eimontases' dirt on her knees. What gave Astrid the right to be rich, to be superior, and to receive everything without even asking? She challenged his manhood, his pride, his essence.

"Where are your guests?" asked the soldier, taking off his coat and stomping the snow from his heavy boots. He imagined Astrid's look of surprise upon seeing him in power. Aunt Teresa turned white at the question. Lulu, the black-and-white cat, played the role of the traitor by meowing loudly and scratching near the corner of the rug.

"I know guests are here," he said. "Look at all this food." Pranas poured himself coffee and, removing the pot from the stove, piled a mound of pork stew on a plate. He cut a chunk of bread and sat down to eat as an honored guest. "Your guests are lucky to have this delicious feast."

"Please, there are no guests," Aunt Teresa said as she pushed Lulu to a less conspicuous place, but Lulu immediately ran back to the corner of the rug and continued pawing, looking up at Teresa with a loud *meow*.

"Let's see what this cat is so anxious about," said Pranas as he finished eating. "Perhaps there is a rat under the rug." He raised the rug and discovered the trapdoor. He opened it. At last, revealed in the dark was his prey—two frightened women. At his command, Katerina and Astrid emerged from the cellar and stood trembling in front of Pranas, who, full of authority, pronounced, "Katerina and Astrid Eimontas, I arrest you under the charge of enemies of the state."

Astrid further inflamed him when she instinctively and scornfully said, "I know you, the boy with no ear who slinks around the university." At this ultimate insult, to show his power, he put his right hand on his gun holster and his left hand on his crotch as his face flushed in anger.

Seeing his actions, Katerina understood his intentions and quickly thought, *He is alone, there are three of us, and we can overcome him.* She reached over and grabbed the pot still full of pork stew and threw it at Pranas. Pranas ducked, avoiding the hot pot but was splattered by the food.

Pranas drew his revolver and fired, hitting Katerina, who fell in a heap. Terrified, Teresa bent over Katerina, grabbed a kitchen towel, and pressed it to Katerina's bleeding shoulder. Despite her shock, Astrid saw her mother move and realized her mother was alive.

Pranas shoved Astrid aside and yelled, "You two get in the cellar!" As Teresa helped Katerina down the steps, Pranas commanded Astrid, "Get me a hammer and nails." He nailed the trapdoor shut, ignoring the screams of the women, and pushed the heavy wooden kitchen table on top.

"The rats are captured, cat. I should thank you." He picked up Lulu and petted the cat as he gently placed it on the sofa near the jumble of abandoned books. Inspecting Astrid, downcast and sobbing, he remembered all the hours of thinking about her golden hair, green eyes, and slender waist, but her bitter insults provided more vivid memories.

Pranas then grabbed Astrid, dragged her upstairs to the bedroom, and threw her on the bed. "What are you planning to do to me, swine?" she yelled with a look of disgust. She tried to spit, but her mouth was too dry.

Pranas straddled her and smiled. He pulled off her sweaters and started to fondle her breasts. A look of horror came on her face. "No!" she screamed. She scratched his face. "You cannot touch me, you dirty peasant. Go find your own kind for sex. Did your last victim bite your ear off? I will bite off your other ear."

Pranas slapped her hard across her face. "That is the last insult from your mouth. Now I am your master. Astrid, obey me and don't say another word. If you try to fight, I will kill your mother. Do you understand?"

The reality of the situation finally dawned on her. Her nod of assent represented both fear and terror. Ripping her clothes off, he started biting her breasts, and when he plunged his fingers into her vagina, she screamed, and a stream of blood stained the sheet. "So you waited for me, a virgin."

Astrid curled herself into a ball and closed her eyes as he unzipped his trousers. She screamed, "Help!" He drove his engorged penis into her vagina as the pain made her scream louder. Katerina heard the screams and begged him to rape and kill her instead but to please spare her child. Pranas only heard muffled noises as blood rage pounded in his ears.

After a bout with anal intercourse so traumatic the sheet was wet with blood, he stood over her. "So you thought you were better than me? See what I think of you." He turned her face up, stood above her, spat, and sent a stream of piss on her face. He then punched her until she was senseless. "Now I am in charge."

Astrid regained consciousness, freezing and in throbbing pain. Fumbling for her clothing, she slowly dressed to see what happened downstairs, but she found the door locked. So she curled up on the floor, whimpering, avoiding the bed that exemplified the last circle of hell to her.

In the morning, the door opened, and Pranas walked in after having made himself a hearty breakfast. Full of energy, he forced himself upon her for a repeat of yesterday's pleasures with the added torture of a broom handle. By noon, she was so incoherent, stained, and bloody that he lost his appetite for her. "You are an ugly, smelly, used-up bitch. No one will want you now. Do you understand?" He then knocked her unconscious.

He washed, dressed, and ate the bread and sausage that was on the counter. He gave milk to Lulu, petted her, and whistling, left the cottage.

Astrid awoke in the dark and realized she was alone and the door was open. Dragging herself to the kitchen, she moved the kitchen table with great difficulty. It took her hours to pry out the nail heads of the trapdoor with a knife. Once she got the head of the nail exposed, she used a fork to grab it, rotate it, and pull it out. There were six nails, and after pulling out three, she sat down and cried in hopelessness. Only her mother's moans made her resume her task. Finally, she opened the trapdoor with Teresa pushing up from below. Teresa emerged but said Katerina had lost so much blood she was unconscious.

Teresa put on her coat and boots and staggered to the Saulis farm to get help. Jonas, astounded to see Teresa struggling through the snow, heard the horrific story and ran to get a doctor. All three returned to Teresa's farm in a horse and buggy.

Jonas and the doctor were able to lift Katerina from the cellar. The doctor cleaned and sutured the wound. "You were lucky it went right through and missed the brachial artery." He gave her codeine and sulfa and made a sling. He examined Astrid and gave her an injection while shaking his head. "In all my years of practice, I have never seen such a brutal assault. This man wanted to kill her."

Antanas noted in a routine incident report filed by the NKVD that family members of an arrested traitor in Prienai had assaulted an NKVD officer.

Antanas saw "Prienai" and realized this must refer to Katerina and Astrid. He could imagine their terror and needed information. Showing the report to Mayor Sabanov, he asked, "Why were these people who assaulted an NKVD officer in Prienai not arrested and brought to prison?"

Sabanov smiled. "The arresting officer probably did something to them he did not want entered in an official report or have them examined. It's understood the culprits were punished. From your concern, I gather this was your family?"

"Yes, my mother and sister. Could you not ask this officer what he did to my family? Could not the officer be punished for his actions?" Antanas had visions of Katerina and Astrid being tortured.

Mayor Sabanov smiled at Antanas's naïveté. "This was done by an NKVD officer who remains anonymous. The city government concedes to the communist party, and the NKVD has the final authority. Calling for an investigation will put pressure on your father and even you. Keep away from them and let the incident pass."

Katerina, hysterical over the raping and beating of Astrid, blamed herself for letting that animal capture her daughter. Since their location was no longer a secret, she asked Jonas to call Antanas from the village where there was a public telephone.

"Antanas? Why not your husband?" asked Jonas.

Katerina finally told Jonas of Vytas's arrest for trying to get help from the Western Powers and Dielka's betrayal. She had been sworn to secrecy about the matter, but her need for understanding trumped her promise.

Jonas said, "Since your husband is in prison, I will move into Teresa's farm and protect you from a return of the NKVD." He put his arms around her, careful of the wounded shoulder. "At last, will you let me love you and take care of you?"

Astrid did not get up from her bed and spent days staring at the ceiling or whimpering. Teresa fed the animals, cooked, and cleaned. Katerina cried and was comforted by Jonas. She said, "You're the only one who is helping us. Of course, Vytas is in prison, but I don't understand Antanas. Why is he not here?"

A week later, the late January weather brought sheets of freezing rain blowing sideways. Jonas Saulis's cousin came with a message received in the village post office. Katerina recognized the handwriting on the wet, frozen note:

Mother, please do not do anything. I cannot come to help since the NKVD would accuse me of helping subversives. I finally obtained the arrest report accusing you of assault on an NKVD officer who shot you in self-defense. You are all enemies of the state, and he is in charge. As a family member, if I visit, I will be seen as being complicit in the family's traitorous activities mirroring the main criminal, Father. I am only doing this because Father's life is on the line and any further aggravation of the authorities is sure to condemn him.

Katerina wanted to escape. She trembled at every noise, at every sudden movement. The beast was going to come back to arrest them. She knew it. The depth of his hatred for them was not extinguished. But what were her options? She had none, only to pray.

Astrid changed from a privileged young woman into a crushed, depressed victim of life. All the joy and anticipation of living left her as the cruel realities of life became evident all too clearly. Having lost the protection of her powerful father and being denied help by her influential brother made her realize her vulnerability. Memories of happy days in Vilnius seemed as distant as a mirage. She longed for her days of boredom.

Chapter 12
February 1941

The red-brick Vilnius train station, surrounded by long lines of wagons emblazoned with the hammer and sickle, served as the center of deportation for thousands of people accused of anti-Soviet activity. Multiple trucks transported the arrested people, packed together one on top of another, and deposited them at the station. The emerging prisoners shivered in the gusting snowfall and huddled with their meager belongings. Russian soldiers formed a barrier separating the inner group of prisoners from the pleading, crying relatives and friends outside the circle of doom.

"Kneel!" shouted the short Asiatic soldier to all prisoners in a heavily accented Russian. He held a rifle and observed his charges with eyes half-closed against the swirling snow. Mongolian soldiers from Russia near the Chinese border were considered savage and feared by the population.

Bishop Venclovas, tall and gaunt with deep-set black eyes, did not understand the order and asked the prisoner next to him, "Why? To pray?"

Smirking, the fellow prisoner answered, "Your cassock identifies you as an innocent. I've been arrested before. No, fool, not to pray. Sudden movements to escape are more difficult from a kneeling position."

A Soviet officer shouted, "Silence!" He raised his rifle and swiped the bishop across his back. "Names!" he shouted as Venclovas knelt.

"Bishop Venclovas. I'm innocent. I answer only to God and the Church."

"We have no bishops. We will call you Bandit because you're guilty of filling your pockets with gold in the name of God, but there is no God."

"There is no God only in your soul," whispered the bishop with downcast eyes.

The soldier kicked him as he hissed, "Silence or I'll shoot you."

Forced into cattle cars, the victims cried out, "Where are you taking us?" and "Please, I did nothing wrong," as soldiers padlocked the doors. Many shivered since they had been arrested without warm clothing. The prisoners remained standing with no water, food, or sanitation. Their crime consisted not of what they did but of who they were.

The snow ceased, and the afternoon sun illuminated an old man in a park across from the train station sitting on a bench feeding bread to the birds. As he passed a train at the station, he heard cries for water and bread. He crept up to the end cattle car and pulled out slices of bread from his pockets. He slid the bread through the splintered wood slats. He bent down, cupping snow with his hands, and pushed it repeatedly between the boards of the train. Murmurs of thanks from the people inside silenced as crunching boots of an oncoming soldier approached. A gunshot rang out, and the Good Samaritan collapsed in a montage of blood on the snow.

Silence reigned on the first day of travel, broken only by some sobs and children crying, but by the second day, the sounds of hell erupted in screams and moans. Crowding prevented room to stretch out, making sleep impossible. A hole cut out in the bottom of the car served as the sanitary facility, and when need overcame shame, a line formed for its use. The freezing train made its way north through a wasteland of snow.

After five days, the train stopped. The bishop peered through the wooden slats of the wagon. Blinding sunlight, sparkling on the fresh snow, glistened as a field of diamonds. Attention shifted from moaning to silent terror. A soldier, emerging from the first-class compartment, unlocked the doors and called out names. Twenty people, lightly dressed, with no food or provisions, were herded out onto the snow and lined up.

One pale young woman in a sable coat holding an infant fell down, fainting in the snow. No one moved to help her until Venclovas jumped off the train and picked up the crying infant. A soldier raised his gun and shot the bishop in the arm, causing him to drop the baby. Another soldier came up to the crying baby and smashed the infant's head with the butt of his rifle. A fellow passenger dragged the bishop back on the train and tied a rag around his arm to stop the bleeding. The desolate lines of people left behind in the frozen wasteland faded into the horizon as the journey continued northeast.

Venclovas prided himself on his vast reading to understand human nature but never envisioned such barbarity. Can these soldiers simply be following orders? Or is this the eternal evil forever simmering under cover of civilization boiling over at the slightest excuse? Here was proof of original sin, the existence of the devil, the inherently evil nature of man.

At numerous stops, people were discarded, but hundreds of prisoners still remained. Was death preferable inside or outside the train? A young woman died giving birth, and the soldiers threw her body and the newborn infant from the train. A Lithuanian man, Donatas, who had been comforting the heavily pregnant young woman throughout their journey, sobbed.

"What was her crime?" Venclovas asked Donatas.

"She was raped by a Soviet official, but when she complained, she was arrested. Punishment is the outcome of trying to get justice."

An endless panorama of snow and ice stretched out for miles. At the next stop, eight adults and two children were evicted. The prisoners cried and screamed as the train moved on as if the tortures of the train were preferable to the unknown frozen desolate landscape. "What's to become of them?" the bishop asked Donatas.

"If they know how to survive, they will build a hole in the ground, cut down trees and use logs to make a roof. If they are lucky, they will find some berries, mushrooms, and wild creatures to eat. But since they have no tools, it's most likely that if they don't freeze to death, they'll starve to death."

After a silence, Donatas asked the bishop, "What was your crime?"

"I'm a Catholic priest."

"A hardened criminal for sure," snickered Donatas. "I was a stationmaster in Vilnius and was caught reading some telegrams. They decided I was a spy, so here I am. I know where our train is going. We are headed for Vladivostok."

"Is there a prison there?"

"Prison? You would be lucky to get into one. No. We are headed for a gulag. Vladivostok is only a way station."

"A gulag is a work camp, a concentration camp."

"I would call it a death camp, but yes, we will work there."

The train ride with long stops continued for a seeming eternity. On occasion, they were fed salted herring, but burning thirst ensued from a lack of water. Any container brought from home became an envied treasure. The owner could sip the precious fluid throughout the day while the rest had to be satisfied with the single gulp at the distribution of a water bucket. In desperation, people licked the dirty condensation icicles off the roof and sides of the wagons.

In Vladivostok, after not having eaten anything in days, the prisoners were given bread and water and walked to waiting boats with English names *London* and *Voyager* painted on their sides. Yuri explained the Russians had bought the vessels from their allies. "A sea voyage, a cruise!" Donatas shouted as they were forced below deck to even more cramped conditions as other survivors of train wagons joined them.

The rough winter seas caused seasickness and vomiting. Lack of sanitary facilities led to an unbearable stench. "Can't we open the hatch and get some fresh air?" the bishop asked Donatas.

"We are sailing north near the coast of Japan, and our masters do not want the world to know their cargo." A bucket from the deck lowered down water and some bread. Occasionally, a screaming woman was gang-raped by the crew. If she did not survive the assaults, her body would be thrown overboard.

The torment stopped with arrival at the Port of Magadan, where the sick, hungry, and freezing prisoners, now referred to as zeks or weeds, were let out of the stinking hold. The bishop took a long breath of the stinging cold fresh air and saw in the distance an endless vista of nothingness. Once the prisoners were herded back into trains, the journey continued. Three more weeks of torment ensued.

The trains reached their final destination—Kolyma, the northernmost gulag. A land of uranium and gold mines dug beneath the tundra. In the long winters above the Arctic Circle, temperatures fell to minus sixty degrees centigrade at night. Stalin's plan to use natural resources in exchange for Western armaments only succeeded with the utilization of slave labor, a program named "re-education through work."

With the exception of two corpses, everyone left the train for roll call. The women, bedraggled and worn, were herded in one direction with the sick and infirm. Children, clinging to their mothers' legs, screamed and cried as they were separated. Able men constituted the prime fodder for the machine of slave labor.

A rectangle of primitive wood buildings with an open plaza in the center constituted the camp or zona, the perimeter enclosed by thick barbed wire. Armed soldiers with guard dogs patrolled the area dominated by a large watchtower.

Herded to a large rough wooden hut, the men were told to strip "so we could sterilize your clothes." The prisoners filed into another room and stood under ice-cold showers, washed with a sliver of black soap, and were shaved to remove lice. Clothes were provided: long underwear, black tunic, quilted pants and jacket, felt hat with earflaps, boots, and mittens. Since the distribution did not take sizes into account, everyone scurried to exchange their garments for better fitting clothes. The bishop belonged to a class of prisoners that did not deserve these "presents from Stalin" and put on the mutilated cassock in which he had been arrested. A guard threw Venclovas a rough leftover felt coat and a pair of thin mittens.

"I have no shoes," said Donatas, who had been shortchanged.

A seasoned prisoner, Filipp, a German, pointed to his feet. "This is what you do. There are old rubber tires here. Cut them to fit your feet. Cover them with birch bark and tie them to your feet with rope—better than naked feet on the ice."

A meal of hot cabbage soup and bread preceded an order to sleep well before work tomorrow. "Why food and rest?" asked the bishop, pale and emaciated.

"They want you to be able to work," answered Filipp. I have been here a long time and know the system.

"What was the reason for your arrest?" asked the bishop.

"I am a German who chose the wrong time to go see my girl who lives in Poland. A neighbor accused me of espionage, and so here I am."

Space and privacy were at a premium. The barracks had slats along the walls piled three high. The narrow slats could not accommodate an entire back, so the turning from side to side made a creaking symphony all night. The criminals took the areas on top with the warmest air. Intellectuals and political prisoners were on the lower rungs, and priests had the ice-cold floor. On the first night, the bishop discovered that lice not only pervaded in his clothes but swarmed on the walls of their barrack.

The latrine consisted of a bucket in the corner. The bishop stood and looked at the empty bucket. "Where is the stench coming from?"

Filipp smiled and answered, "Diarrhea from the food. They can't void outside since the shit freezes and rubs their asses raw, so they shit in their pants. In the barracks, it thaws and leads to the perfume of Kolyma."

In the morning, in minus-fifty-degree weather, the roll call took one hour. Assigned to a brigade of six men and led by three guards with dogs, Venclovas walked an hour to the uranium mines. Everyone hurried to keep moving to avoid frostbite. Their goal was for each prisoner to sift through 150 huge wheelbarrows of sand a day to extract the uranium. Work only stopped when everyone met their quota, so one person could cause overtime for the whole brigade. Although fear of repercussions enhanced their speed, they were only finished, exhausted, after midnight.

The next morning, a winter storm attacked the area with white fog and a blizzard of ice and snow. Prisoners stayed in the barracks. "We are lucky," said Filipp. "If we had been outside when this started, some of us would not be found until the spring thaw."

"Summer must be a blessing, an escape from this hell of cold," the bishop speculated.

"You'll be wishing for the cold when you see our summer. The tundra turns into a massive swamp, breeding millions of huge black mosquitoes that eat you alive," Filipp laughed, his jagged smile exposing a few black, broken teeth.

After several weeks, the bishop could no longer work due to the frostbite of his fingers. Medical treatment in a barrack dubbed the infirmary included wrapping his black fingers with dirty rags and being given a slug of vodka for pain.

Attending roll call, a new officer approached Venclovas. "Why are you wearing that dress? Why not pants if you are a man?"

"I am a bishop from Vilnius, and this is my cassock."

"I'm Colonel Shakulov of the NKVD. I know your city. I'm familiar with the Baltic provinces. While you can't work, you won't get any food. You could be fed if you work. Your specialty is religion, so you could give some lectures to your comrades on the non-existence of God." The colonel laughed at his bitter request.

For seven days, the bishop had no food and survived by melting snow and some small pieces of bread brought by Donatas. He made pellets from the bread and soaked them in the water to make them last all day. By the eighth day, he could think of nothing but food. The longing for any scrap of food possessed him. He even chewed on a piece of bark. He learned the tyranny of the flesh and its dominance over the spirit. The gnawing in his stomach won out. He consented to lecture.

The pangs of conscience also ate away at his insides. Why had God created an existence where there is so much suffering and agony and any human escape into oblivion, whether through women or drink or sin, is prevented by the promise of even more suffering in hell? Is this truly the guideline of a religion to which he devoted his life? He came to the seminary from an intellectual family honored to have a priest in their fold. He graduated with honors and spoke five languages. He wrote the most profound sermons in Vilnius. He administered the Church with distinction. So why, God, are you punishing me now?

He prepared his lecture, and in the hall, after dinner, to the tired, dazed, starving prisoners, he delivered his message.

"'God is dead,' says Nietzsche. The God of our fathers has deserted us, and our leader Stalin is able to provide for us a paradise here on earth. Why wait for a non-existent heaven? The religious books speak of God loving everyone. Do you feel loved? Is everyone equal? Did not the Old Testament books say that Jews are God's chosen people? If this God does not love everyone equally and raises some above others, is this not evil? If God created and loved all mankind, why did he choose only some to be his people? How can he be a good and just God for everyone? Now Stalin loves all people equally."

The bishop considered this babble ridiculous and not worth intelligent attention. Calling Stalin's present life a "paradise"?

Lev, a small man with a high forehead and ears that jutted out from his head, approached him. "Did you really mean all that you said? I heard you were a bishop."

"I was a bishop in Lithuania, but here I am Bandit."

"I was a thief in Vilnius, part of a robbery ring, and this is my third time in prison. I went to the city prisons twice, which are much easier to take. Here I won't survive, but lately, I've thought about what it'll be like after my body disintegrates here. I started to think of God and heaven, and here you are, an authority, and you tell me it's all nonsense. Belief in God was my only reason to continue."

Venclovas did not answer him but went back to his barracks, tortured by his guilt and betrayal of all his beliefs.

In the morning, Lev was missing. Escape meant certain death since there was nowhere to go and no one to help. Starvation and freezing were means of suicide in Kolyma.

Lecturing to the prisoners fed the bishop and kept his healing hands exempt from crushing labor. Tortures of the body dimmed, but his mind took the punishment. Guilt racked him. Lev died because of his words. He had never before consciously harmed a living thing. He tried to silence his mind by thinking of all the poems he knew and reviewing the lyrics of operas he remembered.

Friendships developed, especially with the arrival later in the month of a group of Lithuanians from the coal mines and the logging camps. Andrius, a tall blond farm boy, told of felling trees and sawing logs with no equipment: "We had to improvise saws by cutting jagged edges into plates of steel, but we had quotas to meet for food rations. The speed to finish our assignments cut many fingers and hands, and felled trees killed many comrades." Andrius paused with a downed head.

"Russia gets one-half of its gold, uranium, and timber from our labor. These camps, started by the tsars, extend from the Siberian forests to the Kazakh deserts," chimed in Zuvili, a Tatar and an engineer.

"At least it was possible to do your assignment," interjected Liudas, a clown with a bushy black beard. "I was part of a brigade sent out with equipment to build a bridge. There must have been a hundred of us. It was only when we got there in the blowing blizzard after a trip of four weeks that we discovered that, of all of us, not one of us had any idea how to go about building a bridge. Not one architect or engineer in the whole group." The recital of another catastrophic insanity led to hilarious laughter.

The bishop laughed but came to the realization that German torture was through order, whereas Soviet torture was through chaos.

Survival became the singular goal for the bishop, and he became convinced that good habits reinforced character. He noticed prisoners who did not care how they looked disintegrated faster, so Venclovas reinforced his hygiene. He washed with his ice-cold cup of water daily and shaved with a thin steel strip honed on a stone. He rubbed clean his torn cassock in the snow. For a few pieces of bread, a woman repaired some of the holes in his clothes by using fish bones made into needles and thread from unraveling other fabric. This sense of control replaced prayer as his life force.

His hands healed, and his nails reappeared. He was put to work again in the uranium mines. This time, he acquired thick felt mittens and had advice from experienced comrades.

The air was so cold that swishing his hand through it made a sound as if cutting through paper. Walking, he tried to remember the prayers of the Mass. No words came to mind. He panicked. "Our Father . . ." What was the rest? He focused on the poems of Mickevicius, the lyrics of *Tristan and Isolde*, *La Traviata*, *Aida*—they all came back clearly, but prayer escaped him.

In the bitter-cold Siberian winter, exposed to man's inhumanity, his frozen soul no longer contained the love of God. He had lost his faith.

Chapter 13
March 1941

In Prienai, the melting snow exposed a bleak country landscape of brown earth and leafless trees. No young shoots or buds dared poke through the still-frozen crusted earth. The weather-beaten farmhouse, marked by the ravages of a savage winter, enclosed inhabitants crushed and transformed by the brutal events. The hope of better days diminished, and the past seemed a distant memory.

Astrid's effervescent personality transformed into a fragile shell of silence. Her eyes, in turn, communicated the pain of intense suffering or the vacant stare of annihilation. Katerina's sorrow over her daughter's condition evolved into a growing concern over Astrid's missed menstrual periods. Katerina tried to think of reasons; it could be depression and severe stress.

The closeness of living with Jonas these past few months made Katerina aware of her intense physical attraction to him. The domesticity of the small cottage fed their intimacy. His aquamarine eyes and his response to her every need led to sleepless nights filled with longing, a thirst for love. The force of her desires surprised her. She dreamed of waking him on the parlor sofa and leading him into her bed. Only Lulu, the cat, jumping up, purring, and licking her face extinguished her dream.

Katerina opened her eyes to the wan sun and the desolate landscape through the farmhouse window. Astrid, next to her in bed, turned over to avoid the light. Katerina picked up Lulu, the black-and-white cat with green eyes sleeping at the foot of the bed, and stroked her silky fur. Katerina rose from her bed and carried Lulu downstairs to prevent her from waking Astrid. She concluded animals bring so much satisfaction, perhaps because they lack the complications of humans. Aunt Teresa was making breakfast as Jonas indulged in apple pancakes. "Good morning," Katerina said as she sat down at the table, longing to kiss him.

The dangers of the brutal occupation sharpened the feelings between Katerina and Jonas. The religious virgin of twenty years ago, denying herself the physical pleasures of love, had matured into a woman. She smiled at Jonas as if in apology for her past avoidance of their attraction. Jonas, aware of the change in Katerina, looked at her across the table and knew the love he wanted from her twenty years ago was now his. Teresa, offering more pancakes, broke their connection.

Most nights, Jonas returned only at daybreak, dirty and exhausted. His weary aquamarine eyes reflected suffering and hopelessness. Katerina confronted him one morning as he entered the kitchen. She prepared tea for him at the kitchen table, still scarred with memories of the attack. "Jonas, please tell me where you go at night."

He looked up at her, smiled, and said, "I told you I would defend my country unconditionally. Now I've put my ideals into action."

"What are you doing? Why is it so secret?" Katerina said, trying to keep her voice low as Aunt Teresa prepared breakfast. When Aunt Teresa went upstairs with a tray for Astrid, they were alone.

"The political situation is dangerous. A few prominent Lithuanians fled to Germany and formed the Lithuanian Activist Front to convince Germany tó liberate Lithuania from the Soviets. Katerina, whatever happens in my life, there is only you and Lithuania. I've joined the Lithuanian Activist Front. My duty is to report to the Germans the number of Lithuanian partisan fighters recruited to help them in case of an invasion."

"This is suicidal! The Soviets will kill you," Katerina hissed, white-faced.

Jonas stood up and embraced her. Their bodies entwined. She felt his desire, and her whole body demanded union, but she heard Aunt Teresa's steps and pushed Jonas away. He sat down, shaking his head.

Katerina's voice trembled as she sat down again. "How do you make your reports?"

"We meet in the cellar of a local farmhouse and get a tally of partisans. We published *A Proposal for Lithuanian Liberation,* a manifesto outlining how to expel the Soviets by fighting for Germany."

"What assurances exist that a German occupation would be better than a Russian one?" Katerina asked, giving Jonas another pancake from the stack in the middle of the table.

"One of our members is a priest who said Mass last night and prayed for Germany. He said he counts on Hitler to save Catholicism from communism."

Katerina, understanding the danger, placed her hand on Jonas's arm. "How will we ever survive?"

"Katerina, I'm not naïve. Hitler is a megalomaniac out to conquer the world, but there's no question that Hitler is a better protector of the Catholic Church. Hitler sends ten percent of all Catholic Germans' income to the Pope."

"Really?" Katerina said with surprise. "I thought the Nazis were against religion."

"Nazis are not against religion, only the Jews and anyone against their regime. The Nazis don't care about the religious beliefs of their occupied subjects. They don't want to make everyone a Nazi. They only want obedience and order. It's the communists who aim to make everyone a communist."

"Then Lithuania would be much better off with Hitler than with Stalin," concluded Katerina. "If we help him, he would free us of this bloody red plague." Katerina realized she was still clutching Jonas's arm.

Katerina removed her hand reluctantly from his arm, feeling as if she were cutting a surge of electricity, a force of understanding deeper than love, between them.

One night, Katerina, awake with anxiety, went down to the kitchen for a drink of water when she heard the door open. She saw Jonas at the door clutching his arm, which was bleeding profusely. She quickly cut open the bloodstained shirt and cleaned the wound. As she applied pressure with a bandage, she asked, "What happened?" in frustration and anger at his disregard for safety.

Jonas explained, "I've formed my own band of partisans living in the forest. We plan and execute raids on the Soviet troops. We sabotage their tanks, steal their weapons. Not very effective, I'm afraid, but at least we're doing something against the occupation."

"Thank God the bullet went straight through the muscle. If the bullet had struck a few millimeters to the right, it would have shattered your arm."

"A measure to the left, and it could have been my heart." Jonas joked.

"Where did this happen?" She touched the bandage, now soaked through with blood, and said, "This will need stitches." She got her medical kit, sutured the wound, and applied a thicker bandage.

Jonas looked at her with admiration. "I'm not an accountant. I couldn't just write down names and tally numbers. I had to do something."

"So you decided to take an enormous risk! We are in enough danger just living here. We can't attract more attention to our situation. What made you endanger all our lives?"

"The Soviets caught three of my men, killed them, and threw their bodies in the village square. When their relatives came, the Soviets refused to let them move the bodies, saying, 'You must leave them to rot in public so the whole village would know who the traitors are.' I tried to pull my dead friend Klimas out, and they shot at me. A bullet grazed my arm as I escaped."

Katerina, tears clouding her eyes, emboldened with admiration and desire, took his face in both her hands and kissed him. "My darling, I'm so sorry I wasn't brave enough years ago to risk it all and love you. Now, when I see your bravery, I'm so ashamed. Why was my passion so anemic then and so robust now? I'd do anything to turn back the hands of time."

Seeing the love of his life so vulnerable, so passionate, made him desire her as never before. This was the moment to enjoy Katerina fully—physically, mentally, and emotionally. He wanted to truly live with no regrets. They deserved this moment of fulfillment.

He started to undress Katerina, removing her lilac silk robe slowly with one hand. As the robe fell to the floor, with no hesitation, as if it were destiny, she rapidly removed her nightgown. His need for her was so intense he could hardly breathe. Katerina, in her nakedness, with glistening skin and shiny hair falling over her shoulders, drove him to a fevered response.

But in a split second, a thought entered his head like a forceful bitter wind, and he pushed her away, saying, "No! Think of your husband."

The unexpected physical rebuff and his words stunned her. She tried to make sense of his action but only felt the presence of her husband between them. Damn his thoughts! Why did he consider her husband?

Jonas saw pain and confusion on Katerina's face. But Vytas was a patriot, in prison for signing a letter requesting help from the Western Powers. How could he betray a hero by sleeping with his wife? How could he betray the sacred principles by which he led his life?

Katerina, conscious of her actions and deeply wounded by his rejection, silently gathered her nightclothes, dressed, and went back to her room. That sleepless night, tears of shame flooded her eyes. For a week, she could not meet his direct gaze. She thought it foolish to think that love could be free and without consequence.

Katerina's sadness since that fateful night when he turned her away tore at Jonas's spirit. If he had consummated his love for Katerina, he would have had physical peace and psychological happiness, but it would have been accompanied by a spiteful conscience churning out acid thoughts of failing his ideals.

After a few weeks of avoidance, Jonas had come back early and found her on the sofa reading a book, *Magic Mountain* by Thomas Mann. Smiling, he said, "Katerina, I have good news. German troops are spreading throughout Europe in Belgium and France, now even in Denmark and the Netherlands. The German army is building up on our southern borders. If they invade, there is hope of a free Lithuania again!"

Katerina looked away from him and remained silent. She could not correlate the freedom of her country with the freedom she wanted, a release of her helpless longing for this man. She continued to read.

Getting no response, Jonas went out to walk in the foggy afternoon and to think. Every person has a set of principles, an internal core. If he compromised his principles, who was he? He loved Katerina because he saw the same strength in her. The torture of her daughter clouded her mind, but when she recovered, she would realize he was not rejecting her but preventing a permanent wound to her essence. The agony of adulterous guilt would poison their relationship. She must understand this.

Katerina put her book down and started shredding cabbage on the ancient wood table for their soup as Teresa hobbled into the kitchen. "Child, we must talk," Teresa said as she sat by the window in the harsh sunlight. Katerina noted her deterioration. Teresa had been an old but jolly, plump, white-haired woman with boundless energy. Now she had shrunk, her face withered, wrinkled, weathered by their brutal winter.

"There is no doubt in my mind. Astrid is pregnant. She has healed from her injuries, but now her whole future is at stake," Teresa said.

Katerina's worst nightmares of irreparable harm to her child had come true. "Perhaps we could get her an abortion? It would be the only solution."

"Abortion? In this Catholic country? Who would perform it in this village?" Teresa asked, blessing herself against this evil.

"I must get Astrid back to Vilnius. There are more possibilities there." Her mind swirled with the complications of obtaining an abortion in secret.

After their meal of cabbage soup, Katerina's conversation with Astrid was one-sided. Katerina outlined some options, all with negative consequences, and Astrid, with shame burning her cheeks, sat as if in a trance. When Katerina said that abortion was really the only solution, after an ocean of silence, Astrid nodded as she petted Lulu.

A week later, Jonas, returning from his patrols, saw Katerina with two suitcases. "Where are you going? To the Riviera?" he asked with a laugh.

"We must return to Vilnius. The NKVD knows about us, so what difference does it make where we live?" Katerina's voice had an edge. "I must do something to help Astrid. She's so unhappy here with the horrible memories. We must return home."

"You have no home. It's occupied by the Soviets," Jonas countered.

"Antanas lives there. He still has an important position in the city."

"You're inviting tragedy. Have all my arguments fallen on deaf ears? Here at least I can protect you."

"No one can protect us," Katerina said, still in a fury from Jonas's rejection.

"When are you leaving?" Jonas said, picking up the open train schedule on the kitchen table.

"Early tomorrow. Please keep an eye on Aunt Teresa," she said coldly, as if speaking to a stranger.

After packing and tearful farewells to Aunt Teresa and Lulu, Jonas took them to the train station with his horse and buggy. They rode in frigid silence and then boarded the train.

Jonas sighed in relief. At least he would not be tortured by Katerina's presence and how his work, if discovered, could condemn them.

As the train entered Vilnius, the city—empty stores, dirty streets, and teeming with hundreds of Red Army soldiers—seemed foreign. The devastation brought bitter tears to Katerina. They made their way to the Zoo district in a dilapidated taxi. Approaching the Eimontas mansion, they were crestfallen at the outward damage and decay to their home and garden. Their house, unloved and abused, cried out to them; inanimate beloved possessions acquired life.

They rang the front doorbell, and a fat woman with a rose-printed kerchief opened the door. When they asked for the Eimontas family, she said in Russian, "Go away." Katerina and Astrid indicated they did not speak Russian; the woman went in to call someone. They were able to peek through the half-open door to the wasteland inside—all furniture, carpets, and paintings gone, the parquet floors scratched and dirty.

Katerina sighed and remembered her first visit to the Eimontas manor and the beauty of the rooms, the richness of the silver and the Persian rugs, the breathtaking art, the aroma of polish and flowers. Beauty exists in the care and love lavished on inanimate objects and on living beings.

A young woman came to the door and told them in Polish, "The Eimontas family lives in the basement in the back." They went around the back, saddened by the cut-down stumps of the orchard. There would be no apple and cherry blossoms in the spring. The logs were piled up as firewood.

In response to Katerina's knocking on the basement door, two eyes appeared through the crack. It was Baroness Maria. "Katerina! I thought I would never see you again." Katerina started to cry seeing this aged noblewoman in rags. She let them into a small windowless area with a table, a shabby sofa, a stove, and a sink. The stench of sorrow had sucked out the light, leaving only darkness.

Behind a curtain, she saw the outlines of three crowded beds. "The baron is very sick and confined to bed. Dalia does what she can, but she is not a strong woman. We would both be dead, but Antanas, who has his own apartment now, comes by regularly with food and supplies."

Dalia, in the strange garb of a gypsy, came out from behind the curtain, acknowledged the visitors with a nod, and silently put on some water for tea. A loud hacking cough came from the bedroom. After serving them tea, Dalia left to get medicine for the old baron. Responding to the baroness's questioning eyes, Astrid poured her soul out to the baroness describing the attack in Prienai.

"The worst thing, Grandmother Maria, I was raped by a Soviet animal, and now I am pregnant," Astrid said with a trembling voice.

"My god! The end of your future," the baroness said with a stifled sob.

Katerina and Astrid made a makeshift bed of blankets that night on the kitchen floor, but sleep was interrupted by the baron's continuous cough.

Katerina's thoughts stung her like glass shards through the night. She would find a gynecologist to perform the abortion. Abortion was murder in the eyes of the Catholic Church, and she considered herself a good Catholic, but love for her child made her forget her religion. Did necessity void principles? Was that why adultery was easier to accept now, as she thought of Jonas? Twenty years ago, the thought of sex with a divorced man was anathema, and here she was, a married woman, eager to consummate her physical desire. Acceptance of adultery, abortion! Her life of black and white had melded into gray.

The next morning, at breakfast, Astrid silently sat down by the small kitchen table. Her physical changes were obvious. She had lost weight and looked older with dark circles under her eyes. Mirrors had always proclaimed her reflected beauty, but after her rape, she perceived only ugliness. The psychological changes were even greater. The shame of her helplessness during the rape eliminated the beauty of happiness.

But the days of silent suffering in the country strengthened her character and resolve. She began to accept reality. Astrid approached her mother. "I know you're trying to help, but it's no use. I must try to help myself since I'm a whore with a bastard child. How can I overcome this and survive?"

"Darling, have faith and belief in God. We will dig out of this somehow."

As they finished breakfast, they had a joyful reunion with Antanas, who brought cheese and bagels. Seeing the sad changes in the faces of Katerina and Astrid, he wanted to lighten their suffering and said, "There's good news. Father is surviving in prison. At least he's not tortured. I visit every week and make sure to bribe the guards."

"What news of the criminal NKVD officer? Is he still after us? Astrid asked with the hateful face of the rapist imprinted on her mind."

"I don't know, but I could try to find out. It would be useless information since they wouldn't punish him," Antanas answered, knowing the whole incident would be best forgotten.

Antanas took Katerina and Astrid to see his small but adequate apartment in government housing. The two-room apartment consisted of a bedroom and a sitting area, which included a never-used kitchenette. A bookstand cordoned off a small study area. Not luxurious, but it retained a few artifacts of his former life—furniture, rugs, and household items. Much to her chagrin, Katerina once more faced the portrait of Antanas's mother, Jadvyga, hanging prominently on the wall. Antanas winced at Katerina's reaction since she would always consider Jadvyga her rival.

Studying the premises and worried about Astrid's mental state, Katerina said, "Antanas, take in Astrid to live with you. You have a small study area, and if you move the small gray sofa here, it would suit Astrid. She needs younger company, and living with your parents and depressed sister in the dark isn't helping."

Antanas surmised the two women had been subjected to horrors, but the only physical manifestation was his mother's scarred shoulder. Astrid had not yet started to show her pregnancy, so he was confused that his previously happy, carefree sister had turned into a haunted, quiet woman. "Share my apartment, impossible! Mother, I can't. This isn't a suitable place for a young girl." His lifestyle would have to change.

Katerina insisted, "Antanas, you must help Astrid. Your sister was raped and is now pregnant with that monster's child. You must help us!" Antanas blanched at the thought of Astrid's rape. But what could he do? The idea of revenge against an NKVD officer was ludicrous.

Astrid, running her fingers over the plush sofa, smiled, "This would be a wonderful place for me." Antanas, in the face of the two pleading women, consented with a sigh.

Astrid welcomed the distraction of moving out of the dark, dank hole and into the new apartment of her brother. Antanas, as a member of the Soviet regime, had many privileges, and one of the greatest was access to the store for USSR personnel. He took Astrid shopping for some fabric and cosmetics, items impossible to buy in the empty markets of Vilnius. The Red Army had emptied all the local stores like a plague of locusts. In the special store, hefty Russian women grabbed the most outrageous gaudy print fabric and red and platinum-blond hair dyes. Astrid did everything she could to differentiate herself from these crass women. Astrid found a dark-blue fabric and, with the help of a neighbor seamstress, turned it into an elegant loose-fitting dress.

After a week, her mother's plan of abortion had not materialized. Abortion, legal under USSR laws, needed registration, and above all, Katerina wanted a secret abortion. Astrid imagined the slight growth of parasitic life within her. She tried hot baths, herbs, and jumping from a wall, but nothing dislodged her shame. She decided she must get someone to marry her and give his name to this unwanted baby.

One day, leaving Antanas's apartment for a walk, a familiar face appeared. "Adjutant Norgolov!" Astrid's heart leaped at the thought of a desirable, possible savior. He was more handsome than her memory of him.

"Astrid, she of noble beauty!" teased Georgi. "What are you doing here? I thought you would have escaped to Paris." She had the same smile and honey hair, but the lost weight made her features more chiseled and beautiful. She had acquired an air of mystery.

Tears rolled down her cheeks, and she said, "No, we are still here."

Immediately, Georgi realized her precarious position. "Come to the Moon Café with me." They ordered lunch. He noted how this aristocrat's eyes devoured the food, although her pride dictated minuscule portions. He understood the Eimontas family was in the vise of difficult times.

A physical relationship with Astrid was impossible when they last met. He remembered her closed eyes and pliant body ready to yield to him after their Napoleonic history outing. Then she was a daughter of an important leader of the country, a condemned aristocrat, and Georgi was, first and foremost, a communist. There was no possibility of liaison, no matter how inflamed his desires were. Besides, he was married. Natasha, his wife, lived in Leningrad and had no desire to follow him on his tours of duty.

But now, Astrid, reduced in status to just another beautiful girl in Vilnius, could certainly be his mistress while he was stationed here. If Natasha did not serve his needs, he certainly was entitled to another woman. He smiled, realizing the benefits of a changing situation.

"Where are you living?" Georgi asked with a plan in mind, a plan that did not include the information that he was married.

"My brother Antanas has an apartment in this building, and I'm staying with him. My mother is helping care for my grandparents in our old house. As you probably know, my father is in prison."

She studied him, returning his smile. Georgi was an eligible male and, considering her previous attraction to him, a likely candidate to rescue her.

They met a few times for dinner and drinks, and he even took her to see a film with Greta Garbo. When he asked her to come to his apartment, she consented, much to his surprise. She made sure he had a few large glassfuls of vodka, and she had a few drinks also. The drunken sex was step one in what Astrid believed was a solution. A Russian took advantage of her, and she would take advantage of a Russian.

The next morning, seeing sunlight streaming on Georgi sleeping innocently made Astrid reevaluate her plan of ice-cold revenge. She remembered their happy times in Vilnius and the kiss that never took place. A spark of affection began to worm its way into her forgotten dreams and abused heart.

"Come back to me tonight," pleaded Georgi, wildly pleased with his conquest.

"I will," she answered and plotted how she could leave Antanas at night to pursue her affair. It was less difficult than she thought. She made an excuse of being with friends in the evenings, and Antanas was only too happy to have the place to himself. They established a policy of silent consent.

Katerina beseeched all her medical friends for someone to perform a secret abortion but was unsuccessful. None of them wanted to take a risk. She was struck how her closest friends, in times of fear, built a carapace of protection meant for them alone. Astrid seemed less depressed in her living arrangement with Antanas. Katerina suspected a lover, perhaps someone to take responsibility for Astrid's child.

Katerina tried to get Dalia's help with the elderly couple, but Dalia was lost in a fantasy world, out of touch with reality, forever repeating stories of a grand youth. Katerina became the primary caretaker of the elderly couple and diagnosed the baron's hacking cough as lung cancer. "We must get him to a hospital," Katerina said with concern.

Baroness Maria, shedding silent tears, said, "We tried, but the Russians generally refuse any treatment for people over sixty. His designation as an enemy of the people would put him in such a long line he would die before he would get any treatment." Katerina, never before comfortable with the imperious Baroness Maria, instinctively took the downcast woman in her arms. "These are hellish times, and it is probably better to wish for a rapid death than slow torture under this regime."

This simple, warm gesture released a torrent of intimate memories from the old baroness: "I never imagined my life to end so bitterly. When I was a young girl, my parents took me to all the capitals of Europe. It was the belle époque, and the world glittered. At twenty, I was the darling of so many handsome young European aristocrats, and my only thoughts were dresses and parties."

Baroness Maria went to a drawer and took out some yellowing and broken photographs. They showed a beauty with a wasp waist, lovely bosom, and a dress of voluminous satin. She had a headdress of feather plumes. The multiple strings of huge pearls fell to her knees. Other photographs in fashions of later eras showed her with Kaiser Wilhelm, one with the king of Romania, and another with President Pilsudski.

She sighed as she said, "How miserable I was when my parents told me I was to marry Baron Eimontas and live in Vilnius, a backwater hole compared to London, Paris, and Rome. In those days, there was no such thing as a choice in marriage for a girl of my social standing. A young Polish prince had caught my eye, but my father refused to let my ancient Lithuanian blood be bastardized by Polish blood. How I cried." Baroness Maria's head sagged as if she still felt the weight of the decision.

"So I married Baron Algirdas and played the role of wife and hostess and mistress of his estate. I grew into the role and became what I had played at. After a year, my pregnancy filled me with joy, but the delivery was so brutal I was told I could have no more children. I treasured our life since Vytas was a good child, and I could see day by day he mirrored the goodness in my husband." The baroness smiled at this reminiscence before she continued. "But predictions are sometimes wrong, and a year later, a miracle, Dalia, was born. No one had seen a more beautiful child."

"The Lithuanian aristocracy held a low position in the tsar's court but still enjoyed considerable privileges. Our estate was minuscule compared to the grand Russian estates, but thank God, we were not prominent enough, so the murderers in the Great War and Red revolution overlooked us."

The old baroness took a sip of tea and continued, "Vytas had originally fallen in love with a Lithuanian farm girl we considered unsuitable. Our Polish neighbor's daughter, Jadvyga, met him in Paris, and since she had noble blood, we consented. That we preferred Vytas to marry a noble Polish girl was ironic in view of my past history. When Jadvyga died, I thought he would never venture into romance again. His life was his country and work, so when he told us about you, we knew we would accept you with open arms."

Katerina hugged the baroness and said, "I will always be grateful for the unexpected, warm welcome you gave me." She offered a piece of buttered bread with jam to the baroness.

The baroness continued, "When Lithuania was declared free in 1918, we continued our lives quietly. Of course, there had been Dalia's unfortunate romance. It changed her forever."

Katerina had always wondered about Dalia, "What happened?"

"Dalia, a miracle child, was overprotected by us and turned into a high-strung, sensitive creature. We made a brilliant match for her—a young, handsome prince who seemed to truly love her. As an extremely shy girl, she was completely seduced. I think she was not stable, to begin with, but she witnessed his betrayal and suffered a mental breakdown. She has not been normal ever since."

They embraced, Katerina overcome by this outpouring of intimate details. Katerina repeated in detail the story of their time in Prienai. She confessed to being unsuccessful in finding a doctor to do the abortion, and time was running out. There was a new man in Astrid's life, but it was unknown if it would lead to her salvation. "Mother Maria, what can I do?"

"You must do the abortion. You will be able to do what countrywomen have done in this country since ancient times," the old baroness said sternly, with thoughts of a bastard child to sully the family name foremost in her mind.

The next time Astrid came to visit, Katerina said, "Astrid, I could get some anesthetic and instruments from my friends, and I myself will do the abortion."

Astrid, shocked, replied, "Mother, no. I know your morals and your faith. There is no way you could live with yourself if you do this. I'll take care of it my own way." She smiled at the thought of Georgi.

One drizzly, misty morning, Astrid was standing in a food line when she saw the next person in line was Paulina, and seeing her faithful servant from her past life, Astrid burst into tears. They walked down Lenin Street, formerly Gediminas Street, to a cafe. At a table, Paulina stroked Astrid's hand.

"How are you, Paulina? It cannot be easy for you these days." Astrid, in her troubles, was for the first time aware of the sufferings of others.

As Paulina enumerated her problems, she asked, "How can I help you?" This gesture of kindness released Astrid to unburden herself, "Paulina, I was brutally raped in Prienai by an NKVD officer. He also tortured me."

Paulina blessed herself. "I will pray for you every day," Paulina promised, horrified at the news that the victim was her employer's sacred daughter.

"Prayers will not help. The monster should be shot. I know for a fact that there were other victims. He even had his left ear bitten off by one of them. I wish it had been me who took off his other ear."

Paulina gasped at this description. "Miss Astrid, I must go home now. I'm not feeling well." Paulina knew the rapist was her son Pranas.

CHAPTER 14
JUNE 1941

June's warm breezes and spring flowers marked not only the transition of seasons but also the transition of regimes. At the start of the month, German victories and Soviet unease portended changes, but Vilnius, the capital of the LSSR, the Lithuanian Soviet Socialist Republic, remained subjugated. Russian prevailed as the official language, and the ruble served as its currency. Exploited and humiliated, the citizens of Vilnius trudged on with their dreary lives in contrast to the hope and joy of spring.

Antanas, secure in his position with the Soviets, remained in the pleasant cocoon of his daily life, not disturbed by Astrid, now visibly pregnant. The dangerous subterfuge of carrying Georgi's child was a high-stakes gamble she intended to win. Months ago, Georgi took the pregnancy in stride with only a slight comment on accidents in contraception. They discussed abortion, but Astrid insisted on maintaining her religious beliefs.

Returning late one evening, Antanas, encountering a morose Astrid, asked, "What happened? I hope you didn't have a fight with your lover."

"Georgi says he'll be leaving for Leningrad soon, but he won't be taking me," Astrid answered in a shaky voice before breaking into tears.

"There must be troop movements. A possible Russian need for reinforcements in Finland," Antanas speculated. "Well, as an army officer, of course, Norgolov must follow orders. But what will happen to you? You must get married before he leaves. I don't know why you haven't yet. I thought that was the plan for your pregnancy."

Astrid, ashamed to tell her brother the truth, recalled her last conversation with Georgi. He surprised her earlier by coming to her apartment with a bouquet of blood-red roses. Smiling, she put the roses into a crystal vase, thinking he might be ready to propose marriage.

Georgi, eyes cast downward, stammered out, "I'm leaving Vilnius. My duty is to go to Leningrad with my company." He took off his army jacket and avoided Astrid by pouring a drink of vodka from a bottle on the bureau and lighting a cigarette. He drank the vodka in one gulp as he faced her.

Astrid, with the blood draining out of her face, screamed, "You can't leave. I love you. You know I'm carrying your child. We must get married!" Astrid panicked as she put her hands on his shoulders and looked into his eyes. She reached up to kiss him, but he pushed her away.

"Our arrangement was never permanent. I was here on assignment. Marriage was never a possibility." Georgi cracked his knuckles as he turned away and looked out the window. His words cut her breath.

"I always thought we would marry," Astrid blurted out in the dead silence of rejection. She sat down on the gray sofa, lacking the strength to stand.

"Marry! Are you insane? My life is my army career. There was never any hint of marriage as a possibility." Georgi paced the room like a cornered wild animal.

"Your career! What about my life? What about our child?" whimpered Astrid, clutching her unwanted distended stomach.

"The last thing I need is a child. I told you before, get an abortion—they are free." He stopped and looked down at her crying on the sofa. "Besides, I am married and already have a child."

"Married! Why did you not tell me?" Astrid screamed in shock. "What did you take me for?" Astrid's house of cards collapsed. She took the vase with roses and smashed it to the floor.

Georgi shook his head, turned, and left, closing the door behind him. She had been a pleasant diversion on this assignment, and he did enjoy her, but for her to expect marriage? Never. There was the question of the child, but Astrid was clever: she would find a way and survive.

The next day, Antanas walked home in sunlight after a long workday, preoccupied with the story Astrid had told him. His sister's sad plight seemed at odds with the multitudes of peonies and hyacinths lining the park exuding an aroma of spring and love. Why was Astrid so unlucky in love? He wanted to help her, but his rage at Norgolov was impotent in view of his Red Army deployment to Leningrad.

Passing the main train station of Vilnius, he saw a huge mob of people frantically motioning and yelling to people in trains. He approached the crowd and asked a nearby man in a dark suit, "What's going on?"

"The communists have started a panicked wave of mass arrests and deportations to Siberia. Didn't you know last night thousands of people were arrested? They identified forty thousand who they think may help the Germans. With the approaching German front, they can't leave 'anti-Soviet terrorists' in German hands."

"I live in government housing, and I wasn't aware," Antanas answered, puzzled. He knew the communists were always arresting the "enemies of the state." The NKVD did not inform the city government of its actions.

"If you live in Soviet housing, you are one of them." The man walked away.

The people in the train cars were pleading and holding out their hands. As Antanas approached, one woman screamed, "Please, milk for my infant who has had nothing all day. Please, sir, here is my wedding ring, gold."

Antanas bought a bottle of milk at a nearby grocery store and ran back to the train. He tried to hand the bottle to the woman through the slats. An Asiatic Soviet soldier approached and said, "Nyet!" as he pointed a gun. Antanas explained in Russian that he only wanted to give milk to the baby. The soldier, not understanding Russian, raised his gun. Antanas turned and, in anger, smashed the milk bottle to the ground, shouting, "Your occupation is criminal! The civilized Germans are coming to throw you bastards out." The soldier, seeing him yelling, fired a shot in the air, and Antanas fled.

Anna Kataski, her little braids tied with pink ribbons, skipped to the Klimas apartment on the next block to play with her best friend, Elona. As the two girls were playing with their dolls, a thunderous knocking caused the girls to jump up. Soviet soldiers barged into the Klimas apartment, and an officer shouted, "You're all under arrest. You have five minutes to get dressed and leave."

Mr. Klimas, a slight, pale man, stood up from reading on the sofa and removed his glasses. "What's the charge?" he asked. "I've done nothing wrong."

"Your neighbor said you listen to foreign broadcasts on a short-wave radio," accused a Soviet soldier, scratching his mustache.

"My neighbor, Pauksta, asked for my radio on which, I swear, I only listen to music. I refused to give it to him since he has never returned anything he ever borrowed. So this is his revenge for not getting my radio. Arrest me, but leave my family." Klimas answered, starting to tremble.

As a very young soldier grabbed the two little girls, Anna screamed, "I'm not a Klimas. I'm a Kataski. I'm only visiting." Her blue eyes dilated with fear.

The two soldiers pulled out their guns and said, "Only five minutes, or we start shooting."

The family put on all the clothing they could, especially winter coats since they knew Siberia to be the destination. Anna did not have any extra clothing, so Mr. Klimas wrapped his heaviest sweater around her. Maria Klimas took a pillowcase and stuffed what food she had with some family pictures and prayer books. Mr. Klimas tried to explain that Anna was a neighbor's daughter, but there was no response from the arresting machine.

A truck with its engine running in front of the house swallowed the entire family, including Anna, who continued to scream, "I'm Kataski. I want my mama."

When Anna did not return for supper, Paulina went looking for her at the Klimases' apartment. She saw the broken door and the empty rooms. "Where is my Anna?" Paulina, ashen, screamed in the empty corridor.

"The NKVD arrested the whole family," a next-door neighbor said, peering out her door. "They took all of them away in a truck about two hours ago."

"But my Anna was here playing with Elona!" stammered Paulina, in shock, hurriedly looking in all the rooms of the small empty apartment, praying that Anna was left behind, hiding. Prayers mingled with curses as she opened doors and even drawers. She saw Anna's favorite doll on the floor.

Running into the street, she saw another truck rounding up frightened people. "Where are you going?"

"Orders. Traitors are to be rounded up and put on trains to Siberia," answered the truck driver with a spray of foul breath.

When the truth exposed the horror, Paulina, crying and huffing, ran to the train station. In the dense crowds with everyone focused on their own fright, she could find no one to ask about Anna. She flailed about like a fish out of water. Soviet soldiers completely surrounded the train. The sounds of crying and moaning in the wagons came from hell.

"Anna, Anna, Anna!" she screamed. "My daughter!" she appealed to people too terrified themselves to care. "My Anna has been taken by accident with another family," she explained to the soldiers who looked at her with complete incomprehension.

Paulina ran down the tracks, grabbing any little girl until she saw it was not her Anna. She screamed, "Anna! Anna!" as hundreds of people were herded into the enclosed wagons. Crying, out of breath, she ran up and down the tracks without seeing her daughter until late at night when the wagons were locked, the engine started, and the train left. Paulina ran along the tracks after the train until it disappeared into the horizon, and she collapsed on the ground as if her heart had been cut out.

Jacob Bernstein received recognition and another red star for being an effective organizer in stopping subversive activity. Since a German attack was rumored, he was assigned to supervise the deportation of seven hundred thousand Lithuanians accused of anti-communist activity in a speedy manner. Jacob had to oversee that the maximum number of victims who screamed with terror and anguish were forced into the cattle cars.

With this promotion, his future success was guaranteed. But the worm of conscience wheedled itself into his head. The agony of the current victims touched Jacob's conscience as they reminded him of his torture of the seminarian. Unbidden memories of what he had done to the seminarian haunted him, and many nights, he woke to the gruesome sight of blood gushing out of the sightless eyes.

Jacob had difficulty communicating with his soldiers from Uzbekistan and Kazakhstan since they knew little Russian, so his entreaties for less crunching of bones and spilling of blood fell on deaf ears.

Among the last truckload of deportees, a familiar face arrived, his father's friend, Shlomo Goldstein. "What are you here for?" Jacob asked.

"I got arrested this morning because I'm a business owner, as were many of your father's friends. Not all of us are believers in communism as you are. I curse you for your actions against your own people."

"Mr. Goldstein, I am not an evil man. I am just promoting the benefits of communism," Jacob answered in a hollow tone, remembering the bloody eyes.

"Jacob, may the curse of your father and the whole Jewish race be upon you forever. Your ignorance of your evil is the greatest evil of all."

Jacob was struck with the lightning realization of truth. All that he had been taught by his parents and religion, all he previously believed in, he had desecrated. The communist cause forced him to take actions against his conscience and humanity. He must escape and seek salvation.

On June 21, Germany launched Operation Barbarossa with three million German troops. Stalin, dumbfounded after his complete trust in Hitler, was unprepared to counterattack his former ally. His past purges of senior USSR military personnel had weakened his military capabilities. In the first few days, the Nazis destroyed hundreds of Soviet aircraft and most of their tanks and decimated the poorly commanded Red Army. The victorious German army raced north and east as the Soviets fled. The Lithuanians close to the border welcomed the German liberators and rejoiced.

Aunt Teresa, in her small cottage, caught in the crossfire, saw Soviet snipers at her kitchen window and the Nazis from her bedroom window. Bullets broke one of her windows. Lulu, the cat, never left her hiding place under the bed. One German soldier dipped into Teresa's well for water, received a bullet, and fell with blood spurting from his neck.

After three days, all was quiet, and Teresa left her cottage. Inspecting the dead German soldier, she cried, thinking of the pain to be felt by his mother. She decided to go to the village to get help to bury the soldier.

The village center buzzed with discussion. "The Germans differ from the Russian troops," concluded her neighbor Rita. "They are orderly. They set up a tent in Prienai and politely asked if they could fill their basins with water so they could wash and shave."

Adolfas, the grocer, agreed, "This is a civilized army, not like the Russian animals."

The official news of impending German liberation reached Vilnius on June 23, and Lithuanians in the streets staged an uprising against the Soviet authorities. They fought the communist invaders in a murderous frenzy.

The mayor's office, a shambles from the rapid evacuation of all Soviet personnel, was empty but for Mayor Sabanov, packing his belongings and burning documents in a tin wastebasket. "Are we in official retreat?" asked Antanas, opening the door to his office.

"My car is waiting. Come with me, and we'll avoid any military action in the city. There'll be fighting in the streets in a few hours. The Nazis are at the outskirts of the city."

Antanas hesitated. "I can't leave my elderly parents and my sister. Also, where would I go, and what would I do?"

"You're clever, and you speak Russian as well as a native. There'll always be a place for you in our system. You can't stay. The Nazis will kill you."

Air raid sirens blasted, and bombs exploded. The walls of the city administration shook. Antanas crawled under his heavy desk. A bomb hit the roof, and a wall collapsed in a mass of falling plaster and wood shards. After five minutes of terror at the creaking of the unstable structure, the bombing stopped. As the dust settled, Antanas realized he was alive. Next to him was Mayor Sabanov's body covered by debris. Pushing aside the rubble, he saw Sabanov's crushed head and realized he was dead.

Soviet soldiers rushed to the scene. Antanas instructed them, "Remove the commissar's body and bury him."

"Hurry, we must make a rapid retreat!" they shouted, carrying Sabanov's body through the rubble.

"I'm staying," Antanas answered. He built a fire in a metal wastebasket and finished burning the papers marked "confidential." After a few more hours of sporadic street fighting, Antanas heard people cheering, went to the broken window, and saw a swarm of Germans arriving. He stood in the middle of the office and evaluated the damage. It could still be functional with removal of the debris, a new wall and window. He brushed the plaster dust off of his jacket and tore down the picture of Stalin.

The Lithuanian Activist Front, bent on revenge, helped the Nazis and killed as many Soviets in retreat as they could. Citizens with cudgels and knives attacked anyone with the Soviet uniform as the sickle and hammer flags burned.

During the evacuation of NKVD Headquarters in Vilnius, Casimir Kataski retrieved a gun, a new coat, and a full wallet left behind in the rush. As he left, a Soviet officer stopped him and ordered, "Stay and guard the remaining property. We'll return soon. After we beat those bastards, you'll be compensated."

Casimir, compliant, followed his instructions and observed the German Army enter the city—first the motorcycles, then the cars, then the trucks, and then the heavy artillery. This army consisted of young men marching with precision as Swastika flags waved in the breeze. He realized the Soviets would not return, so he left with the gun, the new coat, and the wallet.

Casimir saw thousands of people in the street with flowers waving Lithuanian flags welcoming the liberators. Throngs of people yelled, "Heil Hitler!" and sang the Lithuanian national anthem. Freedom at last!

When the Germans arrived, they officially turned the country over to the Lithuanian Activist Front. However, on the same day, Lithuania formed a provisional government that declared its independence and released all political prisoners, among them Baron Vytautas Eimontas.

Antanas, with a crowd of supporters, met Vytas released from prison. Katerina, in the forefront, kissed him. Astounded by how thin and ill he looked, she said, "We will return you to health. You are now a member of the new provisional government. How I prayed for this day!" She avoided his eyes for fear he could see her betrayal with Jonas. "Now we have a future," she said.

Leaving the crowd, Vytas turned to Katerina and whispered, "Don't be too confident of our future. This is war, and we're in the midst of it. The Germans will do what they need to do, not for the good of Lithuania but for Germany." He looked around and said, "Where is Astrid?"

"I will tell you later," said Katerina, dreading the horrendous truth.

Antanas, being the only lucky survivor, placed himself in charge of the mayor's office. He took the responsibility of getting a construction crew to rehabilitate the damages and had Ruta supervise the cleaning of the premises. A week later, he was pleased as he examined the results as he sat by his highly polished new desk covered with German newspapers in the mayor's office. A knock on the door announced Gebietskommissar Hans Heinz, who introduced himself. "I am to be in charge of Vilnius."

Antanas immediately stood up and gave him the Nazi salute. "Heil Hitler. Welcome, Gebietskommissar Heinz. We Lithuanians have waited for this day of deliverance," said Antanas in faultless German.

Heinz smiled. "All government positions held prior to June 15, 1940, when the Soviet occupation began, are to be reinstated and their functions resumed. I know you were in this office prior to the communist takeover, so you will remain." Heinz, a tall, thin stooped man with round glasses, seemed colorless and phlegmatic. He saw the small Lithuanian desk flag and smiled.

Antanas, as assistant mayor, assumed he was to be kept in the same position due to the German edict to reverse all the USSR orders. "Thank you, Gebietskommissar Heinz. I will do my utmost to help you for the glory of the Reich. Heil Hitler."

Heinz, with a wry smile, realized Antanas had kept his position with the Soviets. "Yes, you are an excellent deputy, and I understand you must have been under tremendous strain to keep your position under the Russians. But you are the son of Vytautas Eimontas, a supporter of the LAF, and therefore, I know your true feelings are with Germany. We are aware of his prison sentence for anti-Soviet activities."

Antanas answered, "Yes, we eagerly waited for your arrival every day. Because of my knowledge of city affairs, I was forced to serve the occupying regime. The communist rule was one of chaos, and I look forward to helping you in any way I can."

Heinz strutted around the office and lit a cigarette. "The Lithuanian Activist Front is in good standing with the Fatherland. It is a Lithuanian self-defense battalion of only fifteen thousand soldiers, but we have plans for them to help us clean this country of your criminal Jewish-communist element."

He placed a flag with a swastika on the desk and said, "All prior laws are to be obeyed with a restoration of private property." He looked at the freshly painted walls. "I will request a large color portrait of Hitler for this wall." Visions of this same office under Polish, Lithuanian, Russian, and now German authority appeared to Antanas as he thought; this was so much like the change of scenery in a series of tragic plays. As the leading actor in all the various productions, his character could be called Lucky.

Under the new decree, the Eimontas family ascended from their cellar and reunited in their abused mansion, harboring scars of the rapid evacuation of the Soviets. "Look"—Katerina pointed—"there are burn marks as if they cooked on the parquet floor. What uncultured, primitive animals!" She looked around with tears in her eyes and said, "All the furniture and curtains are gone. My god, there seem to be human feces!"

As they surveyed the mansion, Vytas calmed his distressed wife, "We're all alive, and what's more important, the devils were beaten."

Antanas told of his meeting with Heinz, "Death warrants are issued against all the communists who helped the Red Army. Also, there's an order to pay all partisans who fought the Russians." Katerina took a deep breath. If only she could tell Jonas this good news that all his partisan brothers are to be compensated. But now, with her family at home, her romantic reunion with Jonas faded into the background.

As Astrid removed her coat, her father registered surprise and asked, "Did you get married while I was in prison?"

"No, Daddy, I am neither married nor even in love, but I am with child. A communist animal raped me." She told in detail what happened in Prienai.

For Vytas, the mental image of his only daughter desecrated by the enemy tore at his emotions and brought out a fury of revenge. "I will help the Germans exterminate every last one of those communist vermin."

Astrid continued, "I thought another Russian, a gentleman officer, would marry me, but the Soviets are all pigs. He deserted me."

Katerina comforted her daughter, "We'll find a way. The criminals are gone." Antanas, aware of Astrid's tragedy, had made it a point to ask his new boss Heinz to make sure that no German soldiers fraternize with the local females. The discipline of the German army came to the forefront in an edict obeyed throughout the occupied country. Rapes by German soldiers were extremely rare events punishable by death.

A hesitant knock on the door by Paulina was followed with joyful greetings. She said, "I heard you had returned," and soon broke down in anguished tears. "My little Anna was arrested by accident with a neighboring family on the way to Siberia. Baron, could you please help me? Or you, Mr. Antanas? You both have so much power. Please help me."

Both Vytas and Katerina tried to comfort her but explained the reality, "The Soviets have retreated. There's no one to appeal to. Pray that Anna will survive and the Germans win the war."

Antanas, the bearer of good news, said, "Paulina, your family can return to your apartment. The Germans have annulled all Soviet laws and returned private property."

In a flurry of thankfulness, Paulina returned to her most basic instinct. She looked around the mansion, went to the cellar, got a bucket and some rags, and started washing and waxing the premises, murmuring, "Pigs!" She did not leave them for the next few days, putting in a semblance of order until she decided the home was habitable enough for "her" family. Although exhausted, she managed to peel, grate, and fry her potato pancakes for a celebratory dinner.

Leaving the Eimontas mansion, Paulina met Casimir and told him of the repatriation of property. Holding on to one another, staggering under the burden of grief at Anna's fate, they returned to their old apartment in the Polish section. A Russian woman, left behind in the retreat, met them at the door. Her large face, half-hidden under a large peony printed babushka, confronted them.

"You must leave. We are the rightful owners of these premises," commanded Casimir as she stood her ground. She started to argue in Russian, but intimidated by Casimir's raised big stick, she hurriedly put her few belongings into paper bags and left the apartment.

Now there were only the two of them in the premises left a pigsty by the hurriedly retreating Soviets. Paulina grabbed a broom, soap, and rags and spent the day scrubbing and crying, but the activity assuaged some of her grief. The lovely surprise came when Casimir, understanding her weariness, brought home bread and some bacon for dinner.

"Casimir, you are not to return to headquarters. The Nazis are hunting communists," Paulina stated, having overheard conversations at the baron's home. She took his hand and placed it on her cheek in a loving gesture. The recognition that he was hers and the bond of many years together filled her chest with love.

"I'm not a communist. I'm a Polish worker trying to earn my bread." Casimir's guilt at the items stolen from communist headquarters bothered him.

Before sunrise, there was a knock on the door. Casimir, in his underwear, opened the door, expecting the evicted old Russian woman begging for shelter, but instead, there were two German soldiers. "Are you Casimir Kataski?" They produced a document stating Casimir was a member of the communist party. "You are arrested in the name of the Reich for your communist activities."

Paulina tried to stop the soldiers from taking Casimir away. "Leave him alone! He's harmless. He can't read or write. He's not your enemy!"

"I put an X there so I could get work to feed my family," Casimir explained. The two soldiers shoved him out the door, leaving Paulina struggling for breath.

Casimir was driven to an outdoor barbed-wire enclosure with a few hundred people. He thought he was arrested for his theft from headquarters. "Are we going to Siberia?" he asked a prisoner next to him.

"Are you stupid? These are Nazis!" shouted a voice in reply.

Casimir saw a young woman at his side. "Why are you here? What did you do?"

"I worked for a Jewish pawnbroker who joined the communist party. I'm a Catholic and needed work, so I cleaned his shop. They arrested both of us, and even though I was not Jewish or communist, they called me his whore and arrested me. My baby is at home alone!" She started to cry.

The soldiers paced around them, avoiding eye contact. Casimir looked up at a tree and saw the young green leaves and two birds flitting about in the sunshine. These terrorized people in this enclosure juxtaposed with the free birds made Casimir think that Paulina was right—communism was not the answer, but neither were the Nazis.

Casimir saw a priest on his knees praying, and Casimir joined him. In a few hours, they were asked to line up in rows. Ten soldiers approached with rifles, and the prisoners were systematically shot dead. Soldiers from the Lithuanian Activist Front dug graves, and the bodies were pushed in and covered.

When Casimir did not return, Paulina feared the worst and ran to the Eimontas mansion. "Casimir was taken away!" Antanas, afraid to tell her the truth of the death sentence for all communists, said, "It'll be OK, Paulina. Perhaps he escaped and went looking for Anna."

Paulina saw through Antanas's dissimulation and went home. She was now utterly alone, and her thoughts pounded in her head in tune with her footsteps on the cobblestones.

Jan, her favorite, was a martyr, killed by the Soviet beasts. At least he was now a saint. Casimir, her husband, was missing, arrested by the Nazis. She knew he would not return. Casimir was never her ideal, but he was hers, a part of her life that now was a void. And the most painful loss was her youngest, Anna—her sweet, innocent baby. Was she alive? Was she hungry? Was she hurt? Was she freezing? How can a mother's heart overcome such sorrow? And Pranas? She was sorry he started this family on the path to communism. He must be with the retreating Soviets. Valeria and Stefan, do they know they are working for another devil? Do they realize their high and mighty perfect Germans arrested their father?

Paulina suffered in the depth of depression. She went to the Gates of Dawn, got on her knees in the shadow of a doorway, took out a rosary, and spent the night praying. "Mother of God, I have lost all hope. Please take my life, for my pain is too great to survive. Let me know what to do."

Returning in the empty streets at dawn, she sat at her kitchen table, the heart of her family meals. She drank some tea, ate a piece of bread, and sat down to write a letter:

Dear Stefan,

There is so much tragedy here even after the murder of your brother Jan. The Russians have left, and the Germans have arrived. I have returned to work for the baron. Your father was arrested as a communist by the Nazis and has not returned. Anna was taken by accident with a family to Siberia. No word from Pranas, who probably left with the Red Army. Honor the memory of a mother who loves you. Please come home. You and Valeria are all I have left in this world, and without you, I will die.

Love,
Mother

After posing the letter, she returned and scoured the floors as if to remove all traces of the sorrows in her heart.

CHAPTER 15
JULY 1941

Freedom for Vilnius! With the dreaded Red Army vanquished, hope loomed for renewed independence. Long hidden Lithuanian tri-colored flags of yellow, green, and red emerged. Streets filled with people walking with heads held high. Sounds of children playing and people singing filled the air. Animated discussions of the future, with plans for a new government, restoration of the economy, and rebuilding of destroyed landmarks resounded in the cafes.

For Vytas, long warm nights of summer at home replaced months of confinement in a dark, dank prison cell. The provisional government choosing him as one of their leaders instilled a sharp desire to do all for his country. He studied government documents to craft a contract with Germany for a free Lithuania.

"Vytas, stop working on those papers and come eat. Antanas procured bacon and eggs for you," Katerina said, almost skipping into his study, holding a coffee pot. "I even got some coffee."

Vytas smiled, giving an exaggerated sniff. "How did you manage that? The German allotment requires a king's ransom in ration cards for coffee."

"Those damned ration cards were printed within days of the German arrival. The German sense of order is fanatical," Katerina said, shaking her head.

"Food, in general, is scarce. I officially objected to their distribution of available food—thirty percent for Lithuania and seventy percent for Germany," Vytas said. "Germany thinks of their war needs first."

"Dear, I'm familiar with all the strict constraints. Shopping is a nightmare. They allot so many points for milk, for bread, for sugar, meat, salt."

"We've already exceeded our family's quota. So, how did you manage the coffee?" Vytas asked, raising his eyebrows as Katerina poured him a cup.

"The exception to the rules is a special store, MAGAZIN, with better card quotas for German officials. Antanas qualified for food there," Katerina explained, observing Vytas savoring his coffee.

Vytas chuckled. "Our son is a chameleon. I know he's talented and charming but to survive under three different regimes requires more than a facility with languages. He possesses that most elusive of all God's gifts—luck." Vytas took more coffee and continued thoughtfully, "And besides the gift of luck, he also does so well because he possesses no core of strong beliefs. He can serve any master." Vytas added with a wink, "Also, he can love any woman."

Leaving the dining table, Vytas embraced Katerina and said, "Perhaps that is best, survive and have pleasure. My only son is unscathed by tragedy. My daughter received all the misfortune. What can we do?"

Katerina sighed, thinking about her daughter, and confided in Vytas, "I already concocted a solution. By wearing loose clothes and claiming morning sickness, I will be the pregnant one."

"You! Impossible. How could you perform this feat?" Vytas laughed.

"I confessed to Beata, a gossip, about my symptoms and that I don't want anyone to know my condition since the child could not be yours."

"So, I'm going to be seen as a cuckold! Have you thought about that?"

"Do you have a better idea to save your daughter's reputation?"

"Do you really think it could work? You would be considered a faithless wife. Think not only of my reputation but also of yours," Vytas said, frowning.

"Of course I would mind, but I know I am innocent before God, and you can be confident you have not been deceived. We must not think of ourselves. We must think of Astrid and her future."

"Of course, our daughter is worth any sacrifice, but tell me how we could pull this off."

Katerina explained, "I have thought this through. In a few months, I'll take Astrid to the Eimontas estate, where she will give birth. I'll return to Vilnius, claiming the baby as my own. You will forgive me for the indiscretion brought on by my grief at the thought of losing you."

"Are you sure there is no other way?" Vytas, now serious, pushed away his plate and his pride.

"An abortion wasn't possible in the midst of war, and now it's too late. Astrid will give birth, and I will claim the child as mine. This is the only way to help Astrid and save the child from the stigma of illegitimacy."

Vytas nodded grimly. "I guess you are right."

Vytas attended meetings of the provisional government. One morning, he approached his thin, pale, wispy-haired secretary, Mr. Simkus, who seemed to fly about rather than perambulate around the office. "Simkus, we sent our declaration of freedom to Berlin with all our aims. Any reply?"

Shimkus, shuffling papers, answered, "Berlin said their aims must supersede any of ours in wartime. The fifteen thousand Lithuanian activist defense soldiers are to help them eliminate the communist Jews."

Vytas, taken aback, said, "The Lithuanians who joined these battalions did not do so for the sake of German aims but only to fight for freedom for their own country. They'll never agree to fight for Germany."

Germany, in charge, meant to use all the resources of Lithuania to help win the war with the USSR. Private property was nationalized for German purposes. Lithuanians, initially grateful for the German liberation, witnessed one occupation replace another.

Katerina received a notice for all physicians to present themselves at the Red Cross Hospital, where she was reappointed director, her previous position. Commander Beck, a handsome blond officer, clicked his heels upon meeting her. "Doctor Eimontas, the Vilnius University Medical School will be closed as of next week."

Katerina, stunned, said, "Why? Our physicians are trained to the highest standards with German equipment and books."

"The Reich needs soldiers. The students must all join the German army."

Katerina panicked at the thought of the end of Lithuania's medical education and, thinking quickly, said, "Commander, this would not be the best course of action for Germany. Your army is at war and will need our

Lithuanian physicians to help your wounded. By conscripting students, interns, and residents, you would be putting your wounded soldiers at risk."

Commander Beck reviewed his notes, studied Katerina, and after a long silence, said, "I agree. Our wounded heroes deserve the best of care. The army can recruit others of less value. Physicians are valued by the Reich and will not suffer any consequences if they stay out of politics." Beck concluded with another click of the heels and kissed her hand. The medical students and personnel were left alone.

Katerina, at dinner with Vytas, recounted her meeting with Beck and said, "Today, I saved Lithuanian medical education."

Vytas kissed her. "You are an amazing woman, and not only I but the whole country should be proud of you. My only concern is still the challenge to your reputation with your scheme to save Astrid. You of all people to be gossiped about as a common adulteress is deeply painful for me."

With challenges at work, constant worry about Astrid, and her husband's psychological trauma at the publicly presumed infidelity of his wife, no thoughts of Jonas existed.

Antanas received new orders from Heinz. "You are now part of the Reich war effort. As of today, please inform all banks the ruble is no longer a valid currency, and the reichsmark is the only means of exchange at a rate of ten rubles to one reichsmark."

With this third conversion of the currency, the paper with different imprints was blurring. Antanas mused, *What's money anyway? It's what you are told it is. There's no intrinsic value in the paper or even in gold and diamonds. You can't eat it or wear it or sleep in it. It only represents what you believe it to be, and yet people live and die for it. Belief is everything.* "Ruta," he instructed his secretary, "send the same memorandum we used for the ruble to all the banks. Change the wording from 'ruble' to 'reichsmark.'"

Going home, Ruta, thin and birdlike, was exhausted from fulfilling the rush of orders issued by Antanas, but she smiled, remembering the last time they made love. She knew he had other women, but she could forgive him since his love of women came from a generous impulse. He wanted to make them happy by sharing himself with them. How could she condemn his altruism?

Entering her small apartment on Gediminas Street, Ruta saw her brother, Mindaugas, packing a small suitcase. "Hi! What are you doing?"

"I'm leaving on the next train to Frankfurt. About five thousand of us are being sent to Germany for the war effort. The Germans requested scientists, engineers, electricians, carpenters, and technicians—anyone in a skilled trade."

"How did they know you're an engineer?" Ruta asked suspiciously.

"The German war machine requires workers. Everyone over fifteen received a work card and registered their occupation."

Ruta remembered filling a work card out herself, but she thought it was only to get ration cards. Apparently, they had no use for secretaries. She bristled at her brother being conscripted, "No! They have no right to take you. I'll talk with my boss, Antanas, who can talk to his father, Vytas Eimontas."

"Ruta, don't be dumb. Lithuanians have no say. We are under German occupation. Be happy I'll be a worker in Germany and not a soldier on the front in Russia."

When Ruta at work complained to Antanas about her brother, Antanas answered, "They're stripping the country of all goods—machines, oil, and gas. Even tobacco, furs, fabric, glass, and furniture are sent to Germany. The biggest theft is our educated, needed workers such as your brother."

After a late night, Antanas woke and drank coffee while sitting on the sofa. He looked across the room at the portrait of his mother, Jadvyga, comparing her to Sarah with an ache of realization that Sarah was a Jew. Knowing Hitler's persecution of Jews, he approached Gebietskommissar Heinz and asked, "What is the Lithuanian policy toward Jews?"

Heinz lit a cigarette and told Antanas to sit down. "There are a few facts you should understand. The German Reich is here to Germanize Lithuanians and to colonize the East with German natives. Hitler got the idea from America. The first English settlers realized America was an open land with just inferior natives as inhabitants. They cleared the land and occupied the territory. The natives were killed or put on reservations. Hitler plans to do the same with all the territories to the East. The first people to be eliminated are those found to be scientifically inferior, and our first aim will be to identify them. I want you to issue the same edicts that are in place in Germany." He took a sheet of paper and read the following:

1. *All Jews are to wear a yellow Star of David on their outerwear.*

2. *No Jews on sidewalks, benches, public places, or public transportation.*

3. *Jews cannot own radios, printing presses, cars, pianos, or cameras.*

4. *No Jews can be employed as a lawyer, banker, agent, or realtor.*

5. *Jews are prohibited from commerce.*

6. *All Jewish property is to be seized.*

7. *All Jews are to be confined to two self-governed ghettos.*

Antanas didn't realize the extent of the prohibitions in everyday life. Heinz gave a copy of the edicts to Antanas, then went to a map of Vilnius, outlined two areas, and drew Stars of David over them. "You are aware of how the Lithuanians attacked Jews during the Soviet retreat. We must put the Jews into these ghettos for their own protection."

"Whose law prevails in any dispute?"

"Lithuanian civil law and self-rule prevails for all citizens. Only German military and police courts will supersede Lithuanian courts in cases involving the Germans and the Jews."

"When we were occupied by the Soviets, their laws were the only authority. They eliminated all Lithuanian laws."

"You cannot compare the Reich to the outlaw, primitive Soviets."

"Gebietskommissar Heinz, how do you define a Jew?" Antanas asked while taking notes on his orders. "Who is confined to the ghetto?"

"A male Jew has three Jewish grandparents. A female Jew has one or two Jewish grandparents. If anyone marries a Jew, they must also live in the ghetto."

Katerina walked to the Red Cross hospital and saw people in the middle of the street with the yellow Star of David on armbands. She felt no compassion remembering the rape of her daughter. Her Catholic faith shuddered at the thought of revenge since Christ instructed one to turn the other cheek. She headed for the cafeteria in search of strong tea. Standing in line before her was Father Vilas, a physician who was also the hospital priest, a fact not known to the communists. "Good morning, Father. Would you join me for breakfast?"

"Doctor Eimontas, with pleasure."

"My conscience bothers me, Father. The Communist Jews are ostracized because they are our enemy, but now on the street, I saw all Jews, including children, being blamed for our year of sorrows."

"The Germans have their racial policy, and it's certainly not in conformity to Christianity, but it only targets the Jews. The Soviet policy targeted all of Christianity and was, therefore, the greater evil to our country."

"You don't think that the Germans will turn on the Lithuanians?"

"Lithuanians, according to their racial policy, are Aryan enough to be incorporated into the Reich. Nazi policy is not interested in making every citizen a Nazi, whereas the Soviet policy was to make every citizen a communist. If Hitler wins, he will free Lithuania as an independent protectorate. Our bishops fear the destruction of the church by a communist victory. At least under the Reich, the Church will be free," Father Vilas concluded as Katerina finished her breakfast.

Mr. Simkus ran into Vytas's office, waving a piece of paper. "About three thousand members of the fifteen thousand strong Lithuanian Activist Army have rebelled. They would only fight for Lithuanian aims and refused to fight for Germany."

"What happened? Did they just resign?" Vytas said, surprised.

"About twenty-five hundred soldiers ran away to hide in the countryside or in the forests to avoid fighting for Germany," Simkus said with a frown. "About five hundred were shot as deserters for disobeying orders."

"What about the rest? What about the twelve thousand others?" asked Vytas.

"Hard to say. There are those who are eager to help the Germans destroy their common enemy, the Soviets, the Bolshevik Jews, so they will fight for the German cause."

"So the Baltics want revenge," Vytas said, shaking his head. "The reputation of Lithuania will suffer if our people engage in the blood lust. I can understand segregation if Hitler wants a pure race, but this policy of destruction is not a part of the conditions of war but pure extermination. How can we avoid participating when to disobey means a death sentence? The only way is to avoid all service to the Reich that deals with the extermination of the Jews."

The Bernsteins remained in their ghetto apartment, although six more persons were ordered to move in. The newcomers were like frightened rabbits, and the two women, sisters, cried all day, tending to their four children. Their husbands, scientists, had been deported to Germany.

In the overcrowded ghetto, Sarah assumed Jacob, missing since the German takeover, had joined the Russian retreat. They had not heard from him for weeks. Daniel's absences were sporadic and without explanation, and the aroma of cheap perfume led her to believe a woman was involved. Abraham chewed his lower lip bloody, contemplating all the events. Only Rachel brought relief to their despair by playing her violin.

Sarah, as required, walked in the middle of the street to visit Rachel's music professor to negotiate a lower fee for her lessons. Money was tight since the confiscation of Bernstein's Furs. Also, walking in the proscribed middle of the street, a ragged, hunchbacked woman with a scarf covering her face approached Sarah. She tugged at Sarah's armband with the yellow Star of David. Sarah pushed her back and came to the realization it was a man who whispered, "Mother, it's me."

Sarah, stunned, saw it was Jacob in disguise. "My god, I didn't recognize you. Bend over and pull your scarf lower so your face is not seen, and follow me." At the barbed-wire fence of the ghetto, they passed the guard who did not pay attention to two incoming women.

They walked down the narrow paved lanes bordered by houses with people bursting out of the windows, trying to avoid the heat. Filth from overcrowding was everywhere. Sounds of children crying, people screaming and arguing filled the air with a cacophony of noise.

Reaching the Bernstein house, Jacob said, "My disguise worked. I stole this outfit from a dead gypsy and tied a pillow on my back. I have been hiding in the forests, and I am starving. Please give me some food."

Sarah's reply was a look of disgust, but she gave him cheese and bread. "You should have stayed with the communists. The Nazis will kill you for being a communist and a Jew." Seeing the desperate look on his face, she added, "Come to the basement with me." Opening a small door, they entered the damp ill-smelling place Jacob remembered from his childhood.

"Help me," Sarah said as she knelt down in the dark cubicle and pried open a trap door. Jacob followed his mother down the dark secret steps into a maze of passageways ending in an alcove. "Stay here. I will bring you food and water. It's dark, and if you hear anything cover yourself with this." She picked up a large torn blanket and handed it to him.

Sarah was too frightened to reveal Jacob's whereabouts to anyone, even Abraham. She brought him food, but increasing traffic in these tunnels made it only a matter of time before someone, trying to save their own skin from the Nazis, would turn Jacob in. She had to save Jacob, her son, at all costs.

One morning, Sarah combed her hair and applied some color to her face. She put on a red dress, her best high-heeled shoes, and perfume. Studying herself in the mirror, she broke into tears. The yellow Star of David on her dress ruined all of her efforts. Taking courage, she stationed herself in the street near the mayor's office where Antanas would have to pass on the way to work.

"Good morning, Mr. Eimontas. What a pleasant surprise," Sarah forced a smile as she approached the sidewalk.

"Good morning, Madame Bernstein." Antanas's heart raced as he saw the panic in her beautiful, bottomless brown eyes. He had learned her fate.

"I implore your help. I'm desperate," she said between deep breaths.

"What could I do for you?" asked Antanas in a flirtatious manner.

"Save my son," Sarah said as she started to sob. Antanas took her elbow and walked to a nearby park. He found a secluded bench and put his arm around her to hide the Star of David.

Sarah spewed out her tale, "My son, Jacob, was an NKVD officer originally in charge of suppressing religion. In June, he was promoted to supervise the transport of all prisoners to exile. While he was putting people in railroad cars, he received orders to deploy with them to Siberia. He found the torture of the prisoners hard to bear, hard to believe since I never considered him a sensitive soul. In a split second, he made the decision to defect and has been hiding in the forests ever since. If the Nazis find him, they will kill him."

"Where is he now?" Antanas asked with his mind racing at the danger.

"Our ghetto has ancient tunnels deep underground reached only by secret doorways. I've taken him there and occasionally bring him food, but he can't stay there any longer. Please, please help me." She grabbed his arm with such force she was not aware of Antanas wincing.

"Do you realize what you're asking of me? Probably a death sentence." Antanas furrowed his brow and closed his eyes, thinking, why the hell should he help? His life was good, and here she was confronting him with a potential disaster. Why should he get involved? He didn't give a damn about her son. "Sorry, Sarah, it's too dangerous."

Sarah dug her nails into his arm and said, "Wouldn't your mother try to save you? Don't do this for me, but for the memory of your mother." She thrust a photo of Jacob into his hand.

Antanas removed her arm and, as if stung by poison at the mention of his mother, who seemed embodied in Sarah, hoarsely said, "I'll see what I can do."

After a few inquiries, Antanas found an active trade in false documents and discovered a passport of a dead priest, Viktoras Vebra, killed by the communists. The blurred picture of a dark-haired, bearded man with a flat nose was the best he could do when he compared it to Sarah's photo of Jacob. He paid dearly for the passport.

Sarah walked by the mayor's office every day with no sign of recognition from Antanas. After nine days, he motioned to her, and they again met in the park. Seeing no one was around, he gave her the passport. "Make him look exactly like this and know about the Catholic priesthood. When he is prepared, have him visit me at the mayor's office. If he can pass my identity test, I'll find him a place to stay. However, if he is found out, he will be killed. Do you understand?" Sarah nodded yes.

In the black market, Sarah bought a priest's long black robe and hat, a rosary and a Catholic prayer book. She visited a nearby church and sat in the back, observing the actions of the priests, how they prayed and how they blessed people. She bought him a Latin dictionary.

"Jacob, you must grow a beard and read these books." She gave Jacob the clothes and religious articles. According to the passport photograph, she cut his hair and dyed his eyebrows black, but his very prominent nose was all wrong. There was no way he could be Father Vebra.

Sarah, after much pleading, brought her friend Dr. Blumenthal, a white-haired surgeon sworn to secrecy, down into the tunnel. With Sarah holding a flashlight, he gave a few jabs of local anesthetic and made a small incision. With a sharp chisel, he pounded and removed a large piece of bone. After a few sutures, he left some medication and departed. Jacob moaned and swallowed the sulfa and codeine pills. Sarah said, "Better to lose your nose than your life."

Two weeks later, Jacob's nose was still swollen and black and blue. He had to leave the ghetto because the elders had heard rumors of people living in the subterranean passageway. If the fugitives were found, there would be no hiding place for their gold and money, so they evicted all stowaways in the tunnels. Jacob found a safe hiding place under a bridge.

After a month, Sarah brought Jacob home in full disguise—a huge beard, glasses, and the disfigured nose. "Who the hell is this?" shouted Abraham through blurred eyes. She had hidden Abraham's glasses that morning. Sarah smiled at the deception but put her finger to her mouth to indicate Jacob should not speak since his voice would be recognizable. She told Jacob to sit at the table and said, "Eat this chicken and kugel." The sounds of his munching made his silence natural.

"Abraham, this is a Catholic priest who wants to convert Jews so we could avoid persecution by the Nazis," Sarah explained.

"Get the hell out of my home!" shouted Abraham as he stormed out. "I was born a Jew, and I will die a Jew."

Sarah gave Jacob all the money she had and said, "Go, go, to Antanas Eimontas at the mayor's office. He will help you from here." Sarah kissed Jacob and bid farewell.

Rachel was in the next room, and after the priest left, she whispered to her mother, "The priest was Jacob. I could tell by his eyes."

In the assistant mayor's office, Ruta jumped back, startled when the man entered. His large hat and enormous beard could not hide the black eyes and disfigured red nose. She thought he was a drunk who had been in a fight, but she could not reconcile this image with his priestly garments. He spoke in a garbled way, "I am here to see Mr. Eimontas. Please tell him Father Vebra is here." He sat down and started to mumble the beads of his large rosary. The aromas of the unwashed made Ruta think he was some sort of holy hermit.

Ruta went into Antanas's office. "There is a very curious priest to see you, a saint probably. He must have been tortured for his faith. He is still disfigured from his wounds."

Antanas colored and said, "Send him in." Amazed at Jacob's bizarre appearance, Antanas boomed, "Father Vebra, good to see you again. What brings you here?"

"The Lord Jesus Christ places his blessings on you." Jacob made a large sign of the cross. Ruta knelt at the blessing, and Antanas, satisfied with the disguise, sent her out, saying, "I want to go to confession."

After the door closed, he whispered, "You are Sarah's son?"

"Yes. Thank you for my new identity. Even my father did not recognize me."

"The wounded nose is a great disguise. You are not recognizable at all, and the passport will work. In Vilnius, you would be exposed because of the registry of passports. You must leave the city. In the near future, my family will be going to the country with a servant, Paulina. You can go with them, live simply, and survive. What you do is up to you. I've fulfilled your mother's request."

"What will you tell your family?" asked Jacob, worried about intimate contact with the Eimontas family.

"I'll tell them you're a priest hunted by the Nazis because you objected to their treatment of the Jews," Antanas said with ironic laughter.

"Where should I go now?" Jacob asked with a sigh of relief.

"Go to the kitchen door of the Eimontas mansion. I'll call my mother and tell her to let you stay in the basement. You had better memorize all your prayers since my mother is very religious and the maid Paulina is even more so. In the country, pray, read religious books, and keep out of their way. Perhaps you will survive."

CHAPTER 16
AUGUST 1941

The August sun scorched Vilnius as its citizens lived the nightmare of occupying German soldiers and the suffering of the abused Jews. Paulina kept returning to the Eimontas mansion like a faithful dog. The house, now thoroughly cleaned by Paulina and somewhat refurbished, still appeared a shabby cousin of its former self with no remains of the merriment, laughter, and sparkling luxury of prior years. Nursing the old baron and baroness became Paulina's primary purpose, but her thoughts never strayed far from Astrid hiding in her room, heavy with child.

Paulina observed Astrid's depression and felt pangs of guilt for the crime committed by her son, Pranas, during the year of Soviet terror. Paulina recalled the conversations about the brutality of Astrid's rape. How could that devil, Pranas, be her child? He had been a good son before political power became his only aim in life. Could God forgive her for raising a monster? And yet a new life was beginning. Would this innocent baby be forgiven or cursed with life so evil in its conception? These thoughts swirled in her mind as she cooked and cleaned, interspersed with prayers to heaven, heartfelt and constant.

Vytas worked day and night, constrained by his role of following German orders, signifying a more strict and onerous occupation by the month. Katerina wore loose dresses with a small pillow inserted into her girdle while working long hours in the hospital full of wounded German soldiers. Dalia had not changed, floating through the house in her negligee, sometimes muttering nonsense.

When the Germans needed more room in the government apartments for Nazi officers, Antanas moved back home. His work and pursuit of women ensured his absence at the mansion. Astrid never left her room and spent her days reading and writing sad poetry.

The old baron's white, shriveled body was shrinking daily in the big, dark bed. He had stopped coughing, but his breath had turned raspy.

Paulina put cool compresses on his head, and Katerina gave him shots of morphine. One day, Paulina called Katerina to come home at lunchtime because of the baron's labored breathing. Katerina rushed home from the hospital, took his pulse, wet his lips, and pronounced, "The end is near."

Baroness Maria, shrouded in black, prayed at his bedside, "Please, God, take us together. We have not been apart in sixty-five years. I don't want to spend a minute of my life without him." She held and kissed his cold, wrinkled, brown-speckled hand and felt a return of pressure. Antanas and Vytas entered the room, followed by a crying Astrid.

The old baron whispered, "Do everything you can to avoid the return of the Soviet hordes. They are always our enemies. Be careful with the Germans. They have their own agenda. Someday all this will end. Remember, you are Lithuanians." There was one last exhalation before Katerina closed Baron Algirdas's eyes. Antanas took his grandmother in his arms as she collapsed. Vytas cried, holding his father, a rare show of emotion.

Ceremony and tradition marked the old baron's funeral. The German military made an honor guard bringing the coffin, draped in Nazi and Lithuanian flags, into the cathedral. The Catholic Mass, accompanied by a choir, resounded against the sacred walls. Throngs of people attended the ceremonies and extended their sympathy to Baron Eimontas and Doctor Katerina, as well as the frail old baroness. Heavy black veils shielded the desolate faces of the women. Many notables delivered eulogies praising Baron Algirdas's life and mourning the passing of an era. A mountain of flowers marked the gravesite.

After the ceremony, refreshments were offered to the mourners at the Eimontas mansion. People mingled, talked, and laughed. Katerina overheard gossip of her pregnancy but found innuendoes going no further because of the loving attitude of Vytas. When asked about the absence of Astrid, Katerina told everyone Astrid was studying medicine in Berlin.

As guests were leaving, Katerina excused herself and ran up the back stairs to the maid's room where Astrid was hiding. Katerina brought food and told her daughter about the funeral. Astrid, hearing the ongoing roar of guests, started crying since she had never experienced death before. "Mama, it sounds as if they are celebrating."

"Darling, life goes on, no matter what," Katerina said. "It's just an ancient custom. When people traveled long distances to funerals by horse and carriage, the hosts had to feed them before their return."

Soon Vytas also came to Astrid's room, exhausted from the emotions of the funeral and the heat. "The last guest has left, but now we must discuss our future." Vytas removed his coat, looked at his very pregnant daughter, and mopped his brow before he continued, "The best solution is for my mother, Dalia, Astrid, and you, Katerina, to go to the country."

"To Aunt Teresa's?" asked Katerina, shaking her head, thinking of Jonas Saulis.

"I'd rather go to hell than to return to that place of horror," Astrid hissed.

Vytas, confronted with the rejection of Aunt Teresa's home, said, "The only other available place is our estate, Erelis, although I don't know what condition it's in now after the war. With your medical help, Astrid can give birth there in a few weeks. After the birth, Katerina, you would return with the child to Vilnius. Astrid would stay at Erelis until the association of Astrid with the child blurs in people's minds. Paulina can go with you to help. I would also like my mother and Dalia to accompany you. It is safer there."

Antanas, standing at the door, said to his father, "I would also like to send along a priest who is escaping the Nazis for protecting Jews. He could provide some protection and would be no trouble since he could do farm work and live in the barn. His name is Father Vebra."

"Yes," Katerina said, "I think we must save the priest who is now hiding in our basement."

The trip to the estate, 200 kilometers away, required strategic planning. Antanas would drive Astrid and Father Vebra to Erelis secretly at night. The rest of the family would follow by train with much fanfare as Vytas publicized the great favor the Germans did in returning the estate to them. He had some trepidation about its condition but was sure the thick stone walls had withstood the occupation. The estate was named Erelis, or eagle, in honor of the numerous ancient Lithuanian victories in the region.

During their night drive, Astrid recalled her enchanted summers at the estate, the enormous stone manor with a large wood-carved eagle above the massive entry door. There were acres of fruit trees and flowers, and the surrounding forests of fir and birch were full of mushrooms, deer, and rabbits. She looked forward to Erelis as in her happy, hopeful days.

Father Vebra, scrunched in the corner of the car as if to disappear, did not speak a word and was mumbling the rosary all the way there. Astrid observed the strange priest: he looked Russian, but that was impossible. And his nose! He must have been injured or beaten by the Nazis.

The nighttime arrival shrouded reality, and Astrid did not notice too much devastation in the moonless night. Inside, however, lighted candles revealed the destruction and desolation. Partisans, Soviets, and Nazis had occupied the house as they fought their way through the countryside. Not only was the house stripped of all furniture, rugs, and curtains, but filth and garbage were evident everywhere. As Astrid stumbled along in the dark, clinging to the walls trying to avoid shards of broken furniture, she screamed as a rat ran by, "Holy Mother of God, how can we stay here?"

Antanas took Astrid's hand, trying to calm her, but she was overwrought, gasping for air through her tears. She suddenly bent over and yelled out in pain. "The baby, I think it is coming." A viscous fluid started to run down her legs and made a puddle on the floor.

Father Vebra told her to lie down, but there was nothing except the wood floor, so he said, "I'll get some straw from the barn. And, Antanas, we brought some blankets and sheets—you can put some bedding down."

With Astrid whimpering in pain, Antanas and Father Vebra made a makeshift bed from straw and the linens they brought. The nightmare of giving birth began with both men at a complete loss. "It wasn't supposed to happen so soon," said Antanas, pacing and smoking one cigarette after another, trying to ignore the sounds of Astrid screaming at intervals.

"We'll need clean cloths and hot water," Father Vebra said as he tore up a large sheet, shaking his head at the bottle of vodka proffered by Antanas.

"Whatever for?" asked Antanas, completely helpless at this event not expected for at least a few weeks. He took a slug of vodka for himself.

"I saw childbirth in the movies," Vebra offered. "There's some wood logs here, so I'll light a fire in the stove and get things ready." He found a pot and filled it with water from the well, found by luck in the dark, and set it on the stove. "We also need a knife sterilized by being passed through a flame to cut the cord."

After hours of suffering on the straw bed, Astrid jumped up, squatted, let out one horrendous scream, and an infant—red, wrinkled, covered in blood—emerged. Father Vebra ran into the room and took the baby and, as he had seen in the movies, took his knife and cut the cord. He took the baby by the legs and gave him a slap on the buttocks. Both men noticed the child was male. Antanas wrapped the screaming child in a towel.

Astrid was bleeding heavily between her legs, and Father Vebra pushed another towel there. Not knowing what to do with the baby, Antanas handed him to Astrid, who looked at the child with disgust. "Take it away," Astrid said as she closed her eyes. Antanas held the baby as a foreign intruder wrapped in a towel and mused on how life begins.

Daylight soon approached when the child, still held by Antanas, began to scream again. "I think he's hungry," observed Father Vebra.

Antanas woke Astrid and said, "You must feed your child." Astrid took the bloody bundle with a look of disgust and placed it on her breast, where blindly, it started to suckle.

Antanas and Father Vebra were smoking cigarettes getting ready to make breakfast with provisions brought from Vilnius. "I'll cut some more wood for the stove so we can make tea," Father Vebra said as he went out. Collecting branches and twigs, he heard a rustling in the woods and panicked. The Soviets would kill him as a deserter and a priest, and the Nazis would kill him as a Jew. He panicked, but after ascertaining it was only a dog, he exhaled and went back inside. After some tea and bread spread with jam, a sense of relief came over all three. They had faced a major crisis, but Astrid and the baby were alive.

At noon, an old local farmer, Leonas, met the Eimontas family at the train station with his horse and wagon and helped load the suitcases and provisions. As the rest of the family approached Erelis, Leonas mumbled, "Forget this place from before. There's been so much destruction. No crops were planted, and all the animals have been killed. It's a miracle the place is still standing." At the entrance to Erelis, Katerina got out of the wagon and looked around at her beloved estate in ruins.

Through her tears, she saw Antanas opening the door and running to her, shouting, "Mother, the baby is here. He was born last night!"

Katerina ran into the house to see her daughter lying on straw with a bloody bundle in her arms. Katerina, taking her medical kit, immediately removed the placenta, cleaned up mother and child, and gave Astrid some medicine. "My darling, I'm so sorry I wasn't here." She looked at the infant and saw he was perfect.

Paulina was a hurricane of activity trying to make the place habitable. The old baroness, forgotten in all the excitement, looked at the infant and said, "This child, conceived in terror, born in squalor, what can possibly become of him?"

"Mother Eimontas, the child will be mine, and his future will be bright. We are all born in pain, so he will just be part of the human race," Katerina said, holding the infant.

Paulina enlisted Leonas and his three sons to put some order into the house and surroundings. She commandeered Father Vebra, whom she considered a lazy man always off by himself mumbling prayers, to do physical work. "Father, you can work as well as pray. The Eimontases feed you and give you a roof over your head. You certainly should help them on the farm."

Jacob, in his Father Vebra disguise, plotted to get out of this circumstance. His only hope remained a rapid Soviet victory and reinstatement into the ranks of the NKVD. Perhaps he could construct some story about being a prisoner of the Nazis. In the meantime, he had to act this role of a religious. What irony! He had been in charge of ridding the country of superstition, and now he was saving his life under the guise of a believer.

In cleaning the trashed library, he ran into some interesting books, novels, history, philosophy, but the hawk eye of Paulina and her look of disgust made him read only religious books. Soon he had worked his way through Aquinas and the Confessions of Saint Augustine. He started to read the New Testament with new appreciation. He had been a good student in the yeshiva, and now he immersed himself in Christianity.

Paulina held the infant, her grandchild, with mixed emotions. But mingled in her joy and affection, she also saw the result of her son Pranas's crime. She longed to confess and throw herself on the baron's mercy, admitting the criminal was her son, but how could she condemn her own child? This new life had come into the world under a burden of forced terror.

Astrid refused to feed the child, so Paulina found a lactating woman in the village and enlisted her help. Father Vebra, after reading a prayer book about the sacraments, spilled some water on the child's head, made a sign of the cross, and named him Adam. Antanas observed this baptism with barely suppressed laughter.

To Astrid, the house, now clean and habitable, remained a prison with expectations for her future collapsed. Listless and unhappy, she harbored depressing thoughts. She had become a worn-out shell, a shamed exile.

Two weeks later, with baby Adam bundled, Katerina and Antanas left for Vilnius with a long list of requisitions to send to the estate. Vytas met her at the station with a bouquet of flowers. A nursery and a wet nurse waited at home, and in a week, Katerina was back at her post at the Red Cross. Few people questioned her directly, considering the embarrassing circumstances, and to good friends, she whispered, "Yes, a baby boy, and his name is Adam." Vytas, to good friends, explained that at one time, Katerina believed he was executed, and in seeking comfort, she succumbed. The man was a soldier who was killed, and Vytas said he decided to forgive and forget. His friends nodded at this being one more tragedy of war, and soon, all gossip ceased.

Vilnius was in the midst of a heatwave with many citizens retreating to Palanga, a haven of endless birch forests and magnificent mountains of sand dunes on the shores of the Baltic Sea. Antanas, drowning in work, remained working in Vilnius, striving to be an exemplary assistant mayor. Home was boring, with life totally revolving around the new infant. Antanas longed to be in Palanga, swimming in the Baltic Sea and meeting lovely girls in their summer frocks on the boardwalk.

One morning on the way to work, he spotted Sarah. Since she was not allowed to use the sidewalk, she passed him on the street and dropped a note in his direction. He lit a cigarette and threw a match in the direction of the note and went to pick up the scrap of paper.

Dear Mr. Eimontas,
Give me a signal if my Jacob is alive. When I pass you tomorrow,
if you wave with your left hand, I will know he is OK. I will be
forever grateful to you for taking this risk.

Sarah

The next morning, Antanas, walking with Ruta, gave a wave, as if brushing away a fly, with his left hand. Sarah beamed with joy but did not tell the rest of her family about Jacob. Abraham had not forgiven Jacob for joining the communists, Rachel assumed he had left with the Soviet retreat, and Daniel was too immersed in his romance to care.

At Erelis, the old baroness spent her days in bed, in sorrow and remembrance of her life in former years at the estate. The fields had been rich with crops, and the fruit trees had hung heavy with apples, cherries, and pears. Bushes of berries abounded, to be eaten with cream at teatime in the fragrant afternoons, sitting in the shade of magnificent birch trees. She closed her eyes and saw herself laughing with her husband as young Vytas chased little Dalia around the table. Where had those days gone?

She went to the window and saw Dalia ambling, almost sleepwalking in the garden. So many years ago, Dalia walked with a young German prince in this garden. The old baroness shivered at the memory. During the Great War, Germany occupied Lithuania and the kaiser appointed a German as king of Lithuania. Baroness Maria wanted Dalia to marry into the aristocracy. The newly appointed Lithuanian king had a son, Prince Franz, the goal of all matchmakers. The baroness connived to have Franz meet Dalia, an innocent child, at Erelis. Dalia developed an all-encompassing love for Franz, and her love seemed to be returned. Baroness Maria, pleased, started negotiations with Franz's parents.

One night, Dalia, descending the staircase, heard moans and sounds completely unfamiliar and saw two naked people enmeshed. Shocked, she raced upstairs screaming. She could not process what she had seen and could not even speak of it to her mother. She did not have the words. After the incident, she avoided Franz. Baroness Maria suspected Franz of an indiscretion. Perhaps he had tried to force himself on Dalia, or Dalia had seen Franz with a servant. Baroness Maria blamed herself for being overprotective.

A few months later, the kaiser deposed the king of Lithuania, and Prince Franz went back to Germany. Illness prevented Dalia from attending the farewell dinner, but she never fully recovered. Her mother did not pursue any reconciliation with the young man since, without the prestige of the Lithuanian title, he was just another young German. She planned another match, but Dalia was broken. As she blamed herself for the unfortunate events, the memories brought tears to Baroness Maria.

In the morning, Paulina made a bowl of farina for Baroness Maria. Entering the bedroom, she saw her open staring eyes and almost dropped the tray. She touched her cold cheek and closed the baroness's eyes before calling for Astrid and Father Vebra. Astrid ran in and saw the pale, lifeless body. Father Vebra followed. "Father, give the last rites," Paulina said to Vebra.

Never having seen the "last rites," Vebra had no idea what to do. In his confusion, he started to mumble the rosary and said, "Paulina, it's too late. The baroness is dead," he said.

"You must give the last rites," demanded Paulina as Astrid cried by the bedside.

"Dominus Vobiscum, in aeterna," he said, making the sign of the cross, his fallback gesture. He looked up for approval.

"The oils and all the prayers!" Paulina could not believe a priest would not know this sacrament. "Do you want to bless some of my cooking oil?"

"I'm sorry, I can't continue. I'm overcome with grief," Vebra said as he left the room.

"Some priest!" harrumphed Paulina. "They must have thrown him out of the seminary." She thereafter became very suspicious of him.

Father Vebra sighed with relief when Vytas, Katerina, and Antanas arrived from Vilnius with a priest for the funeral Mass. Vebra avoided everyone, claiming illness. The humble funeral for the widow at a nearby village church with burial at the estate contrasted with her husband's ceremony.

Her mother's funeral devastated Dalia, now an orphan. She sought escape from sorrow and found relief in solitude. She left the funeral lunch and walked along a forest path immersed in memories of her childhood at Erelis. She cried, remembering how the happy early years had morphed into intolerable pain. As she was faced with the mortality of her parents and her own mortality, her thoughts swirled around the turning point in her life, her deep love and engagement at sixteen to her dream prince and the moment of confronting two naked bodies—Franz and her sister-in-law Jadvyga. Shame loomed large, shame for herself as the witness, shame for Franz at his faithlessness, shame for Jadvyga for her sinfulness, but most of all, shame for her beloved brother Vytas in having a faithless wife. To confide in anyone would open her brother to ridicule, and this ensured her eternal silence. The unexpressed rage played havoc with her mind.

Passing the edge of the forest, in a clearing by the river, Dalia encountered the strange priest sitting bent over on a tree stump, and when he lifted his face, she observed tears rolling down his cheeks.

"Father Vebra, what's wrong? Are you still ill?" Dalia asked in sympathy.

Startled by Dalia's presence, he answered, "I committed terrible deeds in my life, the torture of a seminarian. I realize I can't be forgiven by God."

Dalia sat down on the log beside him, unable to believe his comment. "As a priest, what you say is heresy. Christ came to this earth to take away our sins. You must find another priest and confess."

The sensible comment startled Vebra. Father Vebra looked up into her eyes, comforted by her concern since they shared the bond of being outcasts. "I think my sins are too horrendous for forgiveness."

Dalia had found a kindred soul, someone who shared her experience. "Father, I've never confessed my own terrible sin to a priest because I didn't think it could be forgiven. But since you, as a priest, understand sins too grievous to be forgiven, you are the only one who could give me absolution. Father Vebra, I confess to the sin of murder," Dalia whispered.

Vebra looked at this slight, sensitive, middle-aged woman and could not reconcile her image with murder. Dalia, not fully mentally functional—how could she have killed anyone? "How did this happen, my child?"

Dalia hesitated, looked at the sunset over the river, and said, "To my horror, I saw a young man I was very much in love with committing adultery with my brother's wife, who personified evil," Dalia sighed.

"You're not guilty of the sin of your sister-in-law. The only murder you have committed is hatred in your heart for this woman," Vebra said as Dalia started to cry, shaking with heaving sobs.

"No, Father, let me finish. Years later, Jadvyga had cancer and was dying. My brother, blind to all because he loved her, did everything he could to save her. What a fool!" Dalia spewed out.

"Did you think your hatred of her caused the cancer?" Vebra tried to reconcile the presumed action of murder with the guilt of hatred.

"Father, you don't understand what I am confessing. My sin was not of thoughts but one of action. One day, I came into her room as she lay near death, still beautiful. I told her, 'Vytas is in pain over your condition. I fear for his health.' Jadvyga answered me with a smirk, hissing, 'Tell him all his hand wringing is not helping. A good fuck, like I had with your Franz once, would do more for me than all of Vytas's whimpering and praying.'"

Dalia started to cry hysterically, and it was some time before she continued, "I had a rush of pounding blood to my head that blurred my eyes, and I grabbed the pillow from under her head."

"What happened?" Vebra asked.

Dalia blurted out, "I pushed the pillow against her face with all my strength to stop the evil. I held it down as she struggled against me, but she was weak. After what seemed like a long time, she stopped struggling and lay still. I replaced the pillow and smoothed out the bedclothes and sat by her side for hours."

"So you did kill her," Vebra said.

"When the maid came in, she was already cool to the touch. I said I had fallen asleep. No one suspected anything. How could God forgive me?"

Vebra made a sign of the cross. "You are forgiven in the name of the Father, and the Son, and the Holy Spirit."

Chapter 17
December 1941

The prospect of a cold, bleak winter crushed the citizens of Vilnius with minimal food and clothing allocations imposed by extreme rationing. The media flooded the city's inhabitants with reports of the furious, rapid advance of the German army across western Russia. German officers strutted with pride for their invincible war machine and their infallible leader, Hitler. The spectrum of the people's suffering ranged from the dismissive attitude the Nazi officials directed at the population in favor of the regime to the life-threatening changes for its most vulnerable citizens, the Jews.

Injuries from the front increased at an alarming pace and filled hospital beds. Katerina constantly juggled assignments in the operating theater. Young German boys returned wounded and frostbitten, their summer uniforms offering little protection against the savage Russian winter. She suffered a sense of hopeless resignation as her staff performed a crushing number of amputations. After completing yet another futile surgery on a young man whose blue eyes would never see again, Katerina stopped for a late lunch of cabbage soup and potatoes in the small hospital cafeteria.

As she sat down, Beata Rosenfelt, a friend, a whirlwind of a large woman in a nurse's uniform, greeted her, "Congratulations on your son! We had not even realized you were expecting." Beata had no discretion or subterfuge; her words were as transparent as her thoughts. Katerina, always protecting herself by secrets and nuances, found Beata's open personality refreshing and delightful.

Over the years, since the first day of medical school, Katerina and Beata shared a multitude of joys and sorrows. As students, they discussed the advantages of the various specialties as Katerina chose ophthalmology and Beata chose psychiatry. Beata, a big-breasted, broad-hipped, blonde woman, bleached her hair in an effort to look less Jewish. Her beaming smile radiated comfort, good humor, and warmth. "Beata, come sit with me and tell me how you are doing." Katerina patted the seat beside her. "To be demoted from chief psychiatrist to surgical nurse must be devastating. Surgery is so different from psychiatry."

Beata sat down beside Katerina with her tray of potatoes with yogurt. "I went into psychiatry because I couldn't stand the sight of blood. But the new regime does not believe in the Jewish science of psychiatry, so here I am assigned to assist the surgeons day and night. I get so nauseous and know that it's not my pregnancy because I am too late in my term for that."

"You're lucky that you hardly show even at this late date."

"That's because I am so large that a tiny fetus is not too evident," laughed Beata. "How did you, so petite, hide your pregnancy so well?"

"I wore the tightest girdles and fullest clothing to conceal the fact. I didn't want anyone to know my condition and lose any professional respect. Our colleagues consider pregnancy a shameful condition since it makes us appear less intelligent and capable."

"You're right," Beata agreed. "Although there are many women physicians since the schools are tuition-free, the top positions remain held by men. It's not discrimination in medicine but in leadership. It's difficult enough being accepted as a female, and a pregnant female in authority is even harder to accept. You, as director, did well to hide your condition."

"I'm happy to have my position but even happier with my son. The child is a healthy blue-eyed boy. We named him Adam, and the baby brought back youth to our lives," said Katerina.

Beata whispered, "How's your husband taking it? I know he was in prison for over a year, so the child couldn't be his."

Katerina, taken aback by the crudeness of her statement, nevertheless answered, "Vytas, being the kind, generous man he is, decided to forgive my indiscretion, the result of stress and depression, and consider the child his. At first, I never even suspected pregnancy. I thought it was menopause. And now I'm a mother again!"

"What about the real father?" asked Beata, finding illicit passion a hard trait to reconcile with prim, religious Katerina.

This direct question took Katerina off guard. "He was a partisan from the countryside who was later killed. A true hero of Lithuania."

Beata nodded, understanding that this would have been the only irresistible temptation for her patriotic, idealistic friend.

Harsh winds blowing across the desolate landscape of the Erelis estate painted a bleak setting for Antanas's visit from Vilnius. Asked by Katerina to provide Christmas cheer to Astrid and Dalia, he came with greetings and presents. He found Astrid haunted and in despair with no reaction to the Vilnius gossip that Antanas provided. She looked at him incomprehensively as if he were a stranger. But Aunt Dalia, with combed hair and a decent dress, seemed much better with even a whiff of happiness. Antanas decided to surprise them with a Christmas tree. He ventured into the woods with Father Vebra to cut down a fir tree. During their excursion, Vebra, asked, "Any news of my parents?"

"Bernstein's has closed, and I hear the Nazis, with help from the Lithuanian Activist Front, are arresting known communists. Your family is confined to the ghetto. Of course, living conditions there are horrendous with little food to sustain survival."

"Do they know I'm alive?" Vebra asked as they cut down the fir tree. The vigorous ax cuts caused the snow-laden branches to disperse flurries of snow. Vebra thought of this snow as tears of the dying tree.

Antanas, wielding an ax, looked over at Vebra standing still in contemplation, "I gave a signal to your mother that I helped you escape. I don't know how much she told the rest of your family." Antanas found the story that Jacob had told him of being a murderous communist hard to reconcile with this gentleman in front of him.

"You saved my life," said Vebra as the tree fell, and they roped the branches together. "I just don't know if it was worth saving."

"You should be grateful to my family for taking you in. It's dangerous for them to harbor deserters. Winter will curtail much of your farm work. In a few months, the women will be returning to Vilnius. You must stay here alone to avoid detection," Antanas informed him as they trudged back.

"Perhaps the war will end, and I'll be able to escape," Vebra said as they stopped so Antanas could smoke a cigarette.

Antanas, striking a match, asked, "Why did you desert your comrades?"

"I loaded the train wagons with their human cargo and was to get in the last car with the Soviet officers. My assignment was supervising these prisoners in Siberia, and I dreaded torturing people in that frozen hell. I said I had to get cigarettes and left the station. I bought a civilian outfit and threw away my uniform. In the confusion of the Nazi advance, I escaped."

"Is anyone here suspicious of you?" Antanas asked.

"Only Paulina since she's very familiar with Catholic practices. Otherwise, my disguise is almost too good. I officiated at a baptism, a death, and a confession."

Antanas couldn't stop laughing. "You? Impossible! From a Jew to a Catholic priest! What a transformation!"

They dragged the fir tree to the drawing room of the estate. Astrid, Dalia, and Paulina had made rudimentary ornaments from straw and found a few candles. They decorated the tree, exclaiming its beauty and aroma.

The traditional Christmas Eve supper consisted only of herring, sardines, and bread. Antanas could hardly contain himself listening to Vebra perform lengthy prayers in Latin. Aunt Dalia appeared transfixed by holy fervor listening to Vebra. She had begun to undertake some chores around the house and appeared to be returning to some semblance of normalcy.

The next day, for Christmas Mass, they traveled by sleigh the few miles to a small chapel. The sun sparkled, and the frozen landscape gleamed. The sleigh crunched through the snow, and the horses' breath created fogs of vapor in the chill, crisp air. The white purity of the fresh snow created a mantle of forgiveness. In church, Vebra prayed with sublime sincerity, and Antanas concluded Vebra was the best actor he had ever encountered.

Antanas had brought a canned ham for the holiday, a great luxury. Presents for the women consisted of toiletries and warm clothing. Astrid managed a wan smile when she received Katerina's old fur coat, and Dalia cheerfully accepted some new clothing. Paulina's inventive cooking transformed their meager provisions into a feast. She managed to combine a little flour, a few eggs, and some sugar to bake a cake.

As Antanas was leaving for Vilnius, Astrid asked, "What of the child?" The question showed no more emotion than asking, "Will it rain tomorrow?"

Surprised, Antanas answered, "Our little brother, Adam, is doing well. Mother is very happy, and Father loves the boy. All is well." Antanas found his sister's attitude understandable since the child was a symbol of her tragedy.

The Bernsteins lived in constant fear, forbidden to leave the ghetto without documents, as the confined enclave grew more crowded. The two sisters and their four children who had moved into their apartment disappeared one night. The Bernstein family now shared two small rooms with newcomers, the Eisensteins from Germany. Abraham never referred to his son Jacob, only introducing "my son Daniel and my daughter Rachel."

Abraham rued Jacob's disappearance from their lives. Even though he disowned and evicted Jacob, he remained his favorite child. He had accepted the rumor that Jacob was to supervise the deportation of subversives to Siberia and was with the Soviet Army.

Sarah, aware of Jacob's fate, did not share this information with her family, hesitating to reveal her active role with Antanas and the final degradation of Jacob acting as a priest.

During dinner, Benjamin Eisenstein, taking a piece of challah bread, said, "In Germany, we were treated worse than animals, confined to the streets with our armbands. Many of our neighbors were shipped to work camps where they endured twelve-hour shifts under brutal conditions. We fled to Vilnius to escape those horrors, but it is the same. There is no safe haven."

Abraham started his litany of "The only safe haven is Palestine," and Sarah left the same endless discussion to clean up after supper. Rachel left the table to open the door and greet Daniel, who had been absent at supper.

Following Daniel to his room, Rachel teased, "Daniel, where do you go? Our parents ask, and you refuse to tell them. I'll keep your secret."

After a long silence, he relented, wanting at last to share his newfound joy. "Rachel, I'm in love for the first time in my life. Whatever you do, don't tell our parents. I met Svetlana in Moscow. She's not Jewish, but I'd rather die than give her up. She is perfect, the most beautiful creature on earth. She lives close by, and I visit her whenever I can."

"Are you sure she loves you? You're no Prince Charming. Be careful with this foreigner. How did she get here if you met her in Moscow?"

Avoiding her eyes, Daniel answered, "Svetlana came to Vilnius to visit her friend Vera, and her husband, a Red Army officer from Moscow. I was so happy to see her." Daniel's face turned red as he remembered Svetlana's arrival, their passionate reunion. Her lithe body contorted into paroxysms of ecstasy. "Rachel, I had never been loved before!"

Rachel understood his feelings of inferiority and his desire for acceptance but had many questions. "Where do you visit her? Will she move here?"

He sighed and continued, "The German invasion forced her Russian friends to leave Vilnius and Svetlana threatened to return with them. I'd rather die than lose her." Rachel saw tears rolling down Daniel's cheeks as he said, "I found her a place nearby."

How could he tell Rachel he was supporting Svetlana in a small room even before the German occupation? He had taken a cache of furs from Bernstein's and sold some of them on the black market. When Abraham asked about the furs, he lied and said Soviet officers requisitioned them.

"How is she living? Where is she working?" Rachel wanted to know. "You can't keep it a secret forever. If she is beautiful, maybe Father would understand," Rachel speculated.

"No! Father would disown me. You saw how he threw out Jacob, the perfect son."

"Perhaps then you should consider giving up this Svetlana for the sake of your parents," Rachel said, knowing a breach in her family already deprived her of Jacob.

Daniel took this remark as an insult and a painful attack on his love by his sister. He would never confide in Rachel again. "I would rather be thrown out and never see any of you again."

There were practical matters, as well. With all the money held in common for the family, Daniel had no money of his own. What if he could not get his share? Money matters had been discussed at length with Svetlana, who was extremely curious about the Bernstein finances. He had shown her the now empty store, but she saw it was large and located on the main business street. Confident that there was money to be had, she insisted on more and more luxury items. To please her, Daniel took more furs he had hidden to sell on the black market and changed the inventory records.

The infant Adam embodied Christmas happiness for Katerina. The little one was a miracle. The wet nurse, Maria, remained as a loving nanny and simple toys for Adam brought forth the holiday spirit in everyone. The traditional Christmas Eve repast, meager compared to previous years, had a way of confining tragedy and inspiring hope. Midnight Mass at the cathedral attended by Vytas and Katerina provided a welcome respite to the ubiquitous presence of swastikas in the snowy landscape. Fervent prayers for Lithuanian freedom were silently said.

Outside of severe financial restrictions for the good of the Reich, if one did not actively oppose the Nazis, life was tolerable. "The Germans have had tremendous victories. They've almost taken Moscow," Vytas commented on Christmas Day, having finished their luxurious dinner of rare chicken and potato pancakes.

"If the Germans win the war, we'll be living under the Nazis for the foreseeable future. What would German hegemony be like?" Katerina asked, holding Adam in her arms and smiling at the baby's giggles.

"After the war, Lithuania would be Germanized. We would have to speak German and adhere to all their racial policies. All Jews, gypsies, Slavs, the infirm and insane would be deported to somewhere like Madagascar."

"But that would not affect us," Katerina concluded but stopped short, remembering Dalia's mental difficulties. "Their goal is to establish a new, better race of people, is it not?" She poured tea for them both, and they enjoyed silence while considering the hypothetical future.

Vytas, finishing his tea, rose from the Christmas dinner and said, "I believe their plan is to take over the world and establish a thousand-year Reich. Their expected result could be an ideal world of supermen enjoying the best living conditions and highest cultural standards."

"It is not in keeping with Christian principles, but it sounds like progress according to the latest science. Could that be so bad?" asked Katerina.

"If you are not one of the ones to be deported," concluded Vytas.

Returning to the hospital the day after Christmas, a nurse approached Katerina. "Your friend Dr. Rosenfelt delivered a baby last night."

Katerina took a spray of decorated fir branches and went to the maternity ward at lunchtime. A beaming Beata held a tiny baby. Next to Beata sat her husband, Moses, an engineer Katerina remembered as a fat, tall, jovial man. Now, his lost weight and shrunken stature made him appear as if he suffered from a wasting disease. He slouched as he stood to greet Katerina. "Congratulations, Moses, you have a son," Katerina said as she placed the fir spray on the bedside table.

"Such happiness at having a son, but we wanted to bring him home to our nursery. However, the Nazis confiscated our home and forced us into the ghetto. Somehow, we managed to make a small space for the child."

"The living conditions in the ghetto are brutal," Katerina said, looking around to make sure no one heard her. "Are you working?" she asked Moses.

"Because of my profession, I've been given a work order to reinforce the security fence around the ghetto, a terrible job. Every day more of our people disappear, never to return. But work in the ghetto is better than to be sent away to death in a concentration camp," Moses mumbled.

"You in a concentration camp! You're not a communist," Katerina reacted in disbelief.

"How can you be so unaware of what is happening under your nose?" asked Moses as he stalked out of the room.

With tears in her eyes, Beata interceded, "Forgive him. He believes our son, his first child, deserves a better future. I'm worried his temper and emotional outbursts will get us into trouble."

That evening, Katerina approached Vytas in the library, reading, and told him about Beata and Moses. "Is it true there are concentration camps?"

"Of course, my dear, war always leads to prisoners and enemies. The Soviets had concentration camps for Lithuanians, and the Germans have concentration camps for communists. After the attack on Pearl Harbor this week, there are calls for Japanese concentration camps in America."

"What justification can there be for people who had lived together in peace for years to suddenly start torturing and killing one another?" Katerina asked.

Vytas put aside his newspaper and said, "Although propaganda conveys self-defense, wars always start with someone's idea of superiority and desire for control and follow with attack and retaliation. Revenge follows, and so it goes an ever-increasing spiral of hate."

"What happened to Christ's instruction to turn the other cheek?"

"Darling, that's not one of the rules of war," Vytas said, returning to his newspaper.

A knock on the door of the Eimontas residence after midnight forced an irritated maid to rise from sleep. She opened the door and saw a large woman in a snow-covered fur coat holding a bundled infant. "Please tell Dr. Eimontas that Beata Rosenfelt needs to see her." The maid let her in and closed the door against the stinging wind. The maid ran to the second floor to wake Katerina, who threw on a robe and hurried downstairs.

"Beata, what brings you here in the middle of the night?" Looking closer, she saw the bundle wrapped in a blanket. "I see you brought your son."

"Katerina, you must help me. You must take David. You must save his life."

"What happened?" Katerina asked, shocked by the request as she took the infant in her arms. Beata passed her coat to the maid while Katerina removed the wet blanket from the baby and wrapped him in a soft throw from the sofa. "Maria, bring some warm milk for the baby," she told the maid as she led Beata to the drawing room.

After settling on the sofa, Katerina handed the baby back to Beata, who gave the baby a bottle brought by Maria. "Now," Katerina said to her friend, "tell me what happened."

"It's my husband," Beata began. He accused a ghetto guard of being a criminal for keeping innocent people, including his child, inside the ghetto. He said, "If the problem is communism, why punish a newborn with no political thoughts or affiliations?"

"All Jews are communists," the guard had answered as he spat.

"That's not true, and it shows the ignorance of this occupation!" Moses screamed at the guard.

"The guard went away furious and later came to our apartment with the commandant. He accused Moses of being a communist. The more Moses argued, the worse it got. They arrested him and took him away." Beata tried to keep from sobbing as she continued. "I ran after the commandant, begging him to reconsider since my son had just been born. The commandant said the poison of Jewish communism was in our blood, and my son was as guilty as Moses," Beata concluded in a whimper.

"This infant, guilty?" asked Katerina, her voice filled with disbelief.

"You must help me. They took Moses, and I'm sure they will take David to a certain death. You can keep him with you, and he would be protected." Her eyes pleaded as she took Katerina's hand.

"Compose yourself, Beata. I'll have some tea brought while I wake Vytas."

After listening to Beata's desperate story, Vytas shook his head. "Sorry, we can't take your son. We have one infant registered with the authorities. Because of our positions, we are under constant surveillance and could never keep another infant a secret. If we try to hide your baby, the Nazis could take Adam and subject him to the same fate as David to punish us. We can't do that. He is our son."

"Katerina, please!" Beata begged as she fell to her knees. "You must help me. I love this child more than life itself. Could you not hide him?"

"Beata, Hide him? Where? In a closet? This is an infant requiring constant care. We could not leave him by himself and drop in some food at times, as some people have hidden adults," said Katerina, shaking her head. "We have servants and visitors who would report us."

"If the danger is specific to your boy, could not someone else in the ghetto take him in? You could say he was a cousin from the countryside. After all, he would fit in better with your people," advised Vytas.

"Fit in better with my people!" Beata hissed. "So you believe in racial purity also, just like the Nazis! I should have known." Beata got to her feet and studied the two people whom she considered her last resort. She put on her coat, took her sleeping infant David, and opened the door. With tears in her eyes, she turned to Katerina and said, "We promised to be friends forever, but that wasn't true, was it?"

"Beata, he would be safer with you than he would be with us! We simply cannot take the risk. If we did, we are likely not only to lose David and Adam but our lives as well."

Beata looked at Katerina with a crestfallen face and tortured eyes and ran back to the ghetto.

Antanas, having returned from the Christmas holidays at Erelis, entered the mayor's office with the latest economic numbers as Heinz perused a report. They started to discuss the latest Marlene Dietrich film when Ruta interrupted, announcing visitors for Gebietskommissar Heinz in the boardroom. Alone, Antanas, out of curiosity, glanced at the open file marked confidential Heinz left on his desk. The report stated the Nazis, with the help of the Lithuanian Activist Front, had shot tens of thousands of people in the Panarys forest in July. Most were Jews. Antanas quickly put the report back. He was aware of deportations of Jews from the ghetto, but he assumed them to be in prison camps outside the city. The report provided proof of the systematic extermination of a civilian population.

At dinner, Katerina recounted to Antanas her story of Beata and her heartbreak at not being able to give shelter to her friend's child.

"Mother, you did the right thing. Taking Beata's child would have meant not only death for Adam but perhaps for all of us. I found out today about the mass shootings of Jews from Vilnius. Jews are not taken to prison camps but to nearby forests to be shot in groups of twenty and thrown into pits. It's a killing machine and not directed just at communists but all Jews."

Katerina began to cry as he spoke. "If all Jews are slated for death, they may destroy the entire Rosenfelt family."

"Be realistic. There's nothing we can do. The punishment for harboring Jews is death," said Antanas.

"Couldn't we even make an attempt?" Katerina asked.

"To whom do you owe the greater obligations? Your neighbor or yourself?" asked Vytas. "Christ said, 'Love your neighbor as yourself,' implying you must love yourself first. You would be committing suicide to oblige Beata."

"Did not Christ die for us?" Katerina said, blessing herself.

"Avoid the arrogance of comparing yourself to God," Vytas said. "That was his anointed mission. Even if you were to sacrifice Adam and our whole family, you cannot save humanity, not even the Rosenfelts."

Katerina shuddered at her helplessness in the face of great evil.

Chapter 18
April 1942

The few daffodils raising their cheery heads seemed displaced this gray, dreary April as Vilnius became a venue of sorrow for its seventy thousand Jews under Nazi attack. Vilnius citizens harbored a spectrum of reactions to the brutal treatment of Jews under the new occupation, ranging from collaboration to acquiescence to condemnation. The Lithuanians' desire to avoid confrontation, punishment, arrest, and even death overcame any impulse for attempting heroics, which proved to be useless in most cases.

Sarah, ashamed of her "Juden" patch and proscribed path in the street, spent her days inside her room sketching and reading. The Eisensteins had been arrested one night, so the Bernstein home, now empty of enforced company, contained an oppressive and tomblike aura. *Our turn will come,* thought Sarah as Abraham walked in from one of his numerous meetings. "I miss Jacob," said Sarah after greeting Abraham.

"We lost Jacob long ago," said Abraham, stroking his beard and frowning. "Even Daniel is lost to us. Where is he? I hardly ever see him."

"A woman is the reason," said Sarah with a sigh, putting down her sketch pad. "Rachel told me in secret. He's keeping a Russian whore."

"How can he be so stupid? A woman! With Daniel! Impossible! He's never had a woman in his life. And a Russian! Our lives are at stake!" Abraham shook his head as if unable to reconcile the image of Daniel with any woman alive. "What woman could possibly be interested in him?"

"Furs and the smell of wealth could be an inducement for a woman," Sarah said. "Passion and lust often win out over reason, especially for a vulnerable, inexperienced man. I think he supports her and gives her gifts."

Abraham collapsed on the tattered blue velvet sofa and held his head in his hands. "That could be an explanation for all the missing furs. Daniel always claimed they were requisitioned. Now I think he stole them to support his whore." He took a deep breath and, with a heavy sigh, said, "We must leave on Hitler's birthday, April 20th. The guards will be celebrating and might not be as vigilant. First, we need to take our gold and diamonds from hiding. Only Daniel knows where we buried our wealth, and now I regret that my stupid son, the liar, has the information."

Sarah stroked Abraham's shoulder. "This woman could have seduced our naïve son. Ask Daniel if he discussed our family's money with her. She could have already extracted information about our wealth."

"My son, betraying his family? I could understand stealing some fur coats for his insanity, but our entire family fortune? Never! He's my blood," said Abraham, trembling at the thought.

Sarah rose to start supper as Abraham continued to describe his plan. "I bribed a tavern owner to take us, Rachel, and Daniel to the countryside in his wagon. Then we must trek for a long time through rough terrain before we reach the port on the Baltic Sea. I paid Ezak Frankel an exorbitant amount for passage to Sweden. From there, we can reach Palestine."

Sarah shuddered, imagining the dangers of this plan. If caught, they would be arrested, and she did not know of anyone who returned after being arrested. There were rumors of starvation and brutal treatment in the work camps. "Are you sure this would work? Who else would come with us?"

"The Stein family and Rabbi Horowitz, eight people total. The Stein boy is eighteen, so there would be no small children to worry about."

Rachel was in the adjacent room, playing the violin. Music, the only beauty remaining, soothed her anxiety and lifted her out of a morass of problems. Her parents' business confiscated, the puzzle about Jacob's fate, the acrimony with Daniel, and her parents' constant anxiety made home an anguished prison. As she finished the Mozart concerto in D major, she clearly heard her parents' whispered conversation. "Father," she said, emerging from her room, "you can't mean Aaron Stein!"

"You've been listening to us!" said a frightened Sarah. "You must swear never to reveal what you overheard."

"Escape, it's all anyone talks about these days. I know Aaron, but he said his parents are safe because his father is valuable to the Nazis. He's a scientist who specializes in chemicals for warfare. If his father were to be sent anywhere, it would be to Germany to design chemical weapons."

"Stein told me he wants to escape with us because these chemicals would be used to exterminate unwanted populations," Abraham stated.

"God! Unwanted populations, they must mean to poison us," Sarah whispered in shock as she sank into a kitchen chair. Bracing herself against the kitchen table, her hand overturned a cup of tea.

Rachel looked at her careworn mother with wrinkles and gray hair wearing a baggy brown dress and sighed. This last year had turned her beautiful mother into an old woman. "Mother, don't be so dramatic," Rachel said as she wiped up the spilled tea with a towel. "The unwanted populations are the enemy Soviets, not us. The Nazis hate the Jews, and there are rumors of death camps, but still, their main enemy is the Red Army."

Svetlana was wiry and slender with bowlegs and a caved-in chest. A long, slightly off-center nose divided her narrow face. Her eyebrows, plucked into a pencil line, formed thin half-moons over her small eyes. She never smiled since her few remaining teeth had deep black cavities. She noticed even Daniel wince, encountering her breath. The hair, thin and dyed a lusterless black color, was cropped short. The slightest admiring glance eluded her, and this outward lack of favor instilled a burning ambition to better her position in life by any means available. Without formal education, she was cunning and had the survival instincts of a viper.

In exchange for crumbs of affection, Daniel had brought Svetlana expensive presents, but since the closing of the Bernstein shop, Daniel had less access to furs, and his offerings diminished. He tried to take some goods from home, and Svetlana deduced some gift clothing items with the lingering scent of eucalyptus were those of Sarah, his mother.

Boredom invaded Svetlana, and the predicted prospect of beautiful gifts from her Jewish boyfriend dimmed, as did marriage since she did not want to share the future of Jews under the Nazi regime. In this stalemate with Daniel, she missed excitement and the rich future she deserved.

Daniel took some smoked fish and bread from home and went to see Svetlana, who grabbed the food and started to eat. When she finished, he approached for an expected kiss, but she shoved him away and stated her crafted ultimatum, "I'm thinking of going away. A few people still manage, by money or sex, to get through the German lines." She smirked.

"There's a war! You'll never make it alone!" Daniel had a vision of Svetlana bartering sex with a German in order to escape. Removing a pile of old papers, food wrappings, and dirty clothes, he sat on her unmade bed smelling of decaying food remnants and unwashed sheets, never daring to criticize her hygiene or her housekeeping. "You must not leave me!"

Svetlana also sat down on the bed and, taking Daniel's hand, murmured, "Not that I really want to leave you." She glanced at him for his reaction. "I want to go to the West. Daniel, let's get out of this hellhole. But if you can't figure out a way for us to get to Europe, I'm leaving alone. There are ships on the Baltic sailing to Sweden. Once I get there, I can go anywhere and have what I want—a good life," Svetlana said with a smile. She put her arms around Daniel and gave him a passionate kiss.

"You can't be thinking of leaving me. I love you. You're everything to me. I can't live without you," Daniel pleaded. "What can I do? I would do anything to be with you. You are my life." Daniel put his head down and heaved with sobs of anguish, not seeing Svetlana smirk with satisfaction.

Svetlana decided on one more turn of the screw, "Don't you want me? What's the matter with you? Go to your father and demand your share of the family money. It's ridiculous for them to have all the wealth. They just sat in the store and talked to customers. It was your labor, working hard, haggling in the wilds of Siberia that made the money. How could you be so stupid! Be a man if you want me. Take what is yours!"

Desperate to keep from losing Svetlana, Daniel's fevered brain started to focus on the family treasure. "Svetlana, our family has a store of gold and jewels, and some is my share that I earned. I would take just my share, much less than what I deserve from the profits of Bernstein's Furs. But it would be enough for us to leave here and go to Sweden, maybe eventually to Britain or America, and start a life there." Seeing Svetlana's happy face, Daniel continued, "I've decided that since Jacob abandoned the family, he does not deserve his share, so I will take one-fourth of the gold and take you across the Baltic. I'll leave the rest of the gold and all the diamonds for my parents and Rachel."

Svetlana, brimming with happiness, rewarded his decision by an invitation to sex. "Darling, you are my prince, and I will always love you."

Daniel, exhausted by emotion, arrived home late at night, and Abraham, waiting for him, said, "God forgive me, I think you are guilty of lies and theft of furs from our family business, but we have no more time. We must escape to Palestine. I spoke to the Steins and Rabbi Horowitz and hired a boat on the Baltic. There is room for only the four of us Bernsteins on this ship, no one else. Ezak Frankel left for the coast some days ago and is now arranging passage for us."

Daniel, taken aback, realized the implications of "room for only the four of us Bernsteins." Father must have been told, probably by Rachel, about Svetlana, and then Abraham must have connected his love to the theft of the missing furs. Damn his sister! Now he was specifically excluded from bringing Svetlana to escape. Daniel panicked. Without the gold, there would be no future with Svetlana.

"When do you plan to leave?" he asked, thinking how to get his share.

"On April 20. The guards will be occupied celebrating Hitler's birthday," Abraham said with a smile at his cleverness. "We must be prepared."

Racing to Svetlana's small room, he found her celebrating, smoking and drinking vodka. His only desire was to please her. "Svetlana, escape plans are for the day of Hitler's birthday when the celebration will distract the guards. I'll get the gold and take our share. We'll escape to the coast where my father's friend, Ezak Frankel, will provide passage. We will be free." Svetlana's eyes sparkled with excitement, and she submitted with a grimace to his deformed lips for an unpleasant wet kiss. *Our gold*, she thought.

On April 20, Sarah and Rachel packed their most valuable items in small bags to avoid alerting the guards. They found the bags too heavy to be carried long distances, so beloved things were left behind—Jacob's Torah, photographs, and a silver menorah. Sarah felt a pain in her heart at leaving all she had known in life. With a worried expression at Daniel's absence, Abraham repeated his plan. "Our group must be very careful. We will stagger, leaving one by one showing our identity cards: first Daniel, then me, then Sarah and Rachel to dispel suspicion. The Steins and the rabbi will leave by another entrance before us. We'll meet by the river on the other side of town where Liudas's wagon will pick us up. From there, we'll journey to the countryside and the long trail."

Daniel returned home to the disgusted faces of Sarah and Abraham at his unexplained absence and saw the preparations for leaving. Sarah said, "Well, I hope you went to bid farewell to your whore. Pack your most precious things—whatever you can carry a long distance. Son, your most important people are your family."

As Daniel put together his parcel, Abraham said, "It's getting dark. Now is the time to get the gold. Daniel, we will now go to dig out the buried box."

Daniel hurriedly found a small shovel and added it to his bag in desperation to uncover the treasure alone and take his share before his father arrived at the treasure. "Father, it is raining. I will go first to do most of the digging," Daniel said as he bounded out the door and raced off.

"Daniel, wait!" shouted Abraham, but his son was already out of sight, and he sat down at the kitchen table.

"Abraham, don't wait. Follow Daniel. He needs the information where Liudas's wagon will be waiting at midnight." As Abraham stood and hurried out the door to stop Daniel, Sarah warned him, "Be careful. If his Russian whore shows up, get rid of her."

Abraham took off toward the river after Daniel. He would get rid of that woman! The thought of her seducing his son and maybe even boldly wanting passage to Sweden infuriated him. Anger pounded in all his steps.

Instead of going to the river, Daniel first ran to Svetlana's place. Waving his small shovel, Daniel said, "We're going to dig up the gold, and I'll give you my share. Bring it back here to your room. I'll take the rest of the gold to my family. They won't even know any is missing. I'll make some excuse to join them later. I'll return here, and we can leave for the coast. To avoid my parents, we'll go to a different port to cross the Baltic. Gold will buy us passage. Then we can go to Sweden and get married!" Svetlana jumped up and down and kissed him with passion for fulfilling her desires.

Rain fell as the lovers rushed off to the bridge in the dark, holding hands, hearts pounding with excitement. Their feet splashed the rain-soaked earth. Reaching the area, Daniel paced off the steps to the tree and recognized the large stone. With some effort, they pushed the rock aside, and taking out his shovel, Daniel began digging as Svetlana held a flashlight. He removed the covering of dead leaves and excavated the soft earth. Soon a metallic sound indicated he'd reached the metal box. "Oh, let me see! Let me see!" whispered Svetlana. Daniel knelt down and started to remove the dirt with his hands to free the box.

Abraham, with his arthritic knees, moved in the dark at a snail's pace on the moonless foggy night. Not seeing Daniel, he nevertheless knew the direction of the assigned place. He crept carefully to avoid falling in the dark shadows. He saw a faint light, so he continued in the direction of what he assumed was Daniel's flashlight. Through the wet foliage, he made out the figure of his son on his knees, bent over, digging. The rock had been moved to the side, and Abraham thought, *Thank God our treasure is safe.*

In the next second, in spite of poor visibility, he also saw the outline of a woman by the tree at Daniel's side. *There's the witch who poisoned my son*, thought Abraham as his head started to pound. I will make sure she doesn't come with us. He clenched his fists and stealthily moved toward his son, ready to explode with anger at the woman.

Svetlana saw the shadow of a tall man walk toward Daniel, who was bent over, lifting the box. She stepped behind the tree and pulled out her knife. As the stranger put an arm on Daniel's shoulder, she stepped out from behind the tree and plunged the knife deep into the man's neck. Abraham screamed in pain as Daniel, holding the metal box, looked up in horror at the familiar face contorted in agony.

"What have you done?" Daniel shouted in terror, throwing down the box. "This is my father." Blood spurted from Abraham's carotid artery as he collapsed.

"I thought it was a thief! I never met your father. I didn't know!" Svetlana screamed, holding the bloody knife.

"Get some help! The police! Hide the box! Leave! I'll say we were attacked by thieves," Daniel sputtered in horror.

"I'll take the box," hissed Svetlana as she picked it up.

Daniel knelt by his father and pressed down on his spurting wound as blood bubbled through his fingers. He grabbed a shirt from his knapsack and tried to apply pressure to the wound. "Father, forgive me, don't die," Daniel said, covered with blood, as he held his father in his arms.

Observing the bloody scene, Svetlana opened the metal box and beheld the sparkle of gold and diamonds. She quickly sized up the situation: Daniel would never leave his dying father. If help came, she would be charged with murder. A lightning calculation gave her only one solution, and she took off with the box.

Daniel, paralyzed by shock, sobbing, held his father until his heart ceased beating. Then hard reality came upon him. His father was dead, his lover a murderer. To report the incident to the authorities became impossible. He could not bring his father back to life. He knew Svetlana had taken all the gold to safety and was waiting for him. But what to do with the body?

Daniel knew Jews had been rounded up and killed in a forest outside the city. He would hide the body there. It would be considered one more atrocity committed by the Nazis. He searched through nearby gardens until he found an old, rusted wheelbarrow. Straining, he folded his father's body into the wheelbarrow and covered it with branches torn from nearby bushes. He ran with all his might for hours, drenched in congealing blood and sweat, rolling the wheelbarrow along the dark, deserted paths to the place where the SS killed Jews.

In the forest out of town, Daniel approached a clearing with many trenches. He saw a large rectangular area of a multitude of corpses. He stared at the dead men, women, and children. He wanted to turn around and bring his father home, but a movement in the forest of a man with a flashlight made him overturn the wheelbarrow and slide his father in with the rest. "God forgive me, but what could I do? I've been cursed since birth."

He ran through the empty streets to Svetlana's place, perspiring, covered in blood, not believing his actions until he realized his hands were still clutching the empty, bloody wheelbarrow. He threw it down. Svetlana would be grateful for the rest of her life for saving her from a charge of murder. Had he sacrificed his father for Svetlana? Love was worth it.

He raced up the stairs to her room. Empty! "Svetlana!" he shouted. Svetlana was gone. Only the fetid odor of her presence remained.

Sarah panicked when neither Daniel nor Abraham returned. The rabbi and the Steins waited outside the gates, but when the Bernsteins failed to appear, they went back and, finding Sarah, said, "We will try another time." When they left, Sarah felt confused and desolate. She found Rachel sleeping curled up with her violin and covered her with a blanket. Anxiety dispelled sleep, and Sarah made some tea. She paced the kitchen floor, distraught, until a disheveled and blood-soaked Daniel pushed in the door. "Mother!" he cried, sinking to his knees. "Father has been killed!"

"Murderous Nazis!" she cried, deep sobs excoriating her soul. She felt pain stabbing her heart. She closed her eyes in disbelief at the collapse of her life, her universe, thinking, how could the other half of her be gone? "Daniel, you must take me to him."

Daniel washed off the blood and changed his shirt. His thoughts jabbed as needles painfully into his head. He must wake up from this nightmare. "Mother, you can't go near there. The soldiers will be digging and covering the bodies by now. You would be killed also!"

"I must go to him, see him, my love, my Abraham, one last time." Sarah ran outside in her tears, and Daniel was forced into following her. "Where is he?" She looked around as if she were a rabbit surrounded by wolves.

"I will show you the area where they kill the Jews," Daniel said as he took her arm and led her, stumbling, the few miles to the killing area. The weight of the tragedy flooded her chest. Her breaths were airless, shallow, small inhalations. She was drowning in a vortex of sorrow and collapsed a few times along the interminable way.

After miles of pain, they arrived at a forest where large trenches dug into the ground abounded with corpses of men, women, and children. The horrific scene was scorched forever into her soul, changing her perception of humanity. Sarah's eyes searched the scattered bodies but could not identify Abraham. The rising sun marked the approach of soldiers with guns. Sarah, oblivious to the sounds of soldiers' threats and barking dogs, wandered the edges of hell trying to locate her Abraham.

"Let's get out of here, Mother—it's dangerous. They'll kill us also," said Daniel as he dragged his mother away.

Resisting his pressure, Sarah asked, "Did the Nazis catch you digging the gold? Did they shoot him at the riverbank and transport him so far away? Did you follow the Nazis and your father's body? Is that what happened? How did you escape?" Her questions were met with silence.

Sarah, eyes widened in surprise at Daniel's silence, asked, "Did the Nazis kill Father? If Abraham was shot by the Nazis, why were you spared? Was he arrested? He was going after you when I last saw him. Why were you covered in blood if the Nazis shot him? You have no wounds. Tell me what happened."

The depth of deception overpowered Daniel, who was physically and emotionally spent. He took her aside and whispered, "Mother, there was an accident."

The admission confused Sarah, "What kind of an accident?"

"I mistook him for a thief trying to steal our gold and stabbed him accidentally when he crept up on me as I was on my knees digging. I had to bury him immediately so I would not be charged with murder."

He was not about to implicate his true love in this tragedy. His mother, in time, would forgive him, and Svetlana was just trying to protect him from a thief. How could Svetlana know it was his father? She was innocent.

Sarah, stunned, speechless, tried to comprehend this unspeakable horror. Daniel did not recognize his father! Her son, a murderer! The motive must have been that whore, the she-devil. She fainted as Daniel wept.

Daniel picked up Sarah's limp body and carried her home. He put her down on the sofa and covered her with a blanket. Rachel trembled at the sight of the drawn, pale face of her mother. "Where's Father? What happened to Mother?"

Daniel could not answer. The weight of guilt split his head into two. His muscles were twitching in agony, and he could not breathe. His thoughts were in hell. No, hell would be too good of a place for him. He wanted oblivion. He wanted to cease to exist. He could not grasp a sliver of hope. He was cursed. A cursed, misshapen failure deluded by thoughts a woman could love him and he had a future. He was a doomed cosmic joke. It would have been better if he had never been born. A patricide—he killed his father in his greed to make a life for himself as if he deserved one. He could not exist. He must kill himself. That way, the pain would stop.

Daniel grabbed a straight razor from his father's bed stand and ran out of the house. In the middle of the street with his yellow star, he passed children playing, dogs barking, and people laughing. He breathed in hope: perhaps Svetlana had returned and was waiting for him.

Daniel walked again to Svetlana's room and found the room empty. As he sat there dazed, the landlady with mops and rags arrived to clean for the next tenant. She recognized him as the one who paid the rent. "Get out of here," she said. "You no longer have any right to be here. There is so much cleaning to do after that pig lived here. She was a filthy, lazy tenant who had all sorts of strange men here. Good riddance!"

Clarity came to Daniel as a strike of lightning—Svetlana was only after one thing, the family's wealth. The thief. He should have known that he could not inspire love. What had he been good for, bartering fur pelts in Siberia? His parents were always ashamed of him. He brought only tragedy and death to their lives, and now he was a patricide! Death was too good for him, but life was impossible. The searing pain demanded an end.

Walking in an incoherent fog of despair, he arrived at the SS killing fields to beg for his father's forgiveness. He searched for Abraham's body in the trenches and found him where he had left him. He sank to his knees by the edge of the trench and, looking down at the corpse, said, "Father, forgive me. I will join you." Daniel, faint, lay down, angling the razor blade to his throbbing neck artery but heard the voices of approaching Nazi soldiers and became still.

"We must guard the bodies until morning when the SS will come to extract their gold teeth and remove their clothes," said one gruff voice.

"Let's look through their pockets for money," said another soldier. "It's a bonus for being with these stinking corpses."

"There may be some reichsmarks in this pocket. They'll never know it's missing," a soldier laughed, approaching Daniel, and reached for his pocket.

Daniel moved. "Look, here is one who is not dead yet!" shouted the gruff voice. The soldier withdrew his pistol and fired two shots into Daniel's head and kicked Daniel into the trench on top of his father. "Success, another dead cockroach."

Svetlana paid a gold coin for a buggy ride to the seashore. After several inquiries, she was directed to Ezak Frankel. "You were going to help the Bernsteins escape?" she asked a fat bearded man who nodded in response.

"I'm Daniel Bernstein's wife. His family left earlier and got an alternate ship. They told me to come later with you. I'm late because I had to pick up the Bernstein belongings. I'm to meet them at the Swedish wharf."

Frankel did not believe her story. "I'm not convinced you should take their place. I'll wait for Abraham and Sarah."

Svetlana went behind the departure shed and came back smiling. "Here is the passage for all the Bernsteins," she said, handing him four gold coins.

Frankel looked at the sparkling coins and said, "OK, get on board." After disembarking in Sweden, Svetlana disappeared along with the Bernsteins' fortune.

CHAPTER 19
JULY 1942

The fragrant, brilliant red roses in the parks of Vilnius appeared victoriously vibrant, as if fertilized by the bloodshed of war. Catastrophic changes did not mar the continuity of comfort provided by the blue sky and warm breezes of a sunlit summer. Children played tag while mothers hung laundry out to dry. People shopped in the almost vacant stores, the empty shelves testifying to hardship and want. Bizarre accusations led to arrests and the disappearance of citizens resulting in a pervasive fog of fear. While the savage battles raging in Russia dominated most conversations, in Vilnius, the front existed only in the myriad of wounded soldiers in streets on crutches or in bandages on their way back to Germany.

Pranas Kataski, NKVD member, in a burst of patriotism, enlisted in the army. He blended in with the massive chaotic retreat of the Red Army heading east into the interior of Russia. Paulina received his note about deployment and prayed for his safety, although her greatest desire was for God's forgiveness for his criminal behavior toward Astrid.

During one bitter battle with the Germans, he inadvertently became a medical orderly in a baptism by fire. An exploding bomb lighting the night sky had burst, sending limbs flying everywhere. The horrific screams of the wounded permeated the aroma of gunpowder and blood. Algis, his newfound friend, lost his left leg to shrapnel and looked at Pranas with pleading eyes filled with terror. Pranas tied off his gushing stump with his belt and constructed a makeshift gurney from two tree limbs and rope. With the help of another soldier, they carried Algis into the nearest medical staging area. "Help bring in the rest!" barked the doctor in charge. Pranas retrieved many wounded soldiers and became adept at triage. He made himself so useful the doctor attached a Red Cross badge to his Soviet uniform and enlisted him in the medical corps.

The number of casualties increased each day, and Dr. Virshup, a mustachioed, wrinkled man in a dirty bloodstained smock, shook his head at every new arrival. "It would be better to shoot the seriously wounded. There's no way we can help them. We have nothing left for pain." Virshup and Pranas smoked cigarettes to the background screams and moans of the dying soldiers.

"There's only one hope," said Pranas. "A day ago, we passed a German medical station containing only corpses from the bombing. Since the Germans continue their advance east and deserted the medical station, we could go back and retrieve any medicine remaining."

Dr. Virshup stamped out his cigarette. "Kataski, go back and search the area. We need medicine, especially morphine."

"That's still German territory. If anyone sees me, I'll be killed on the spot."

"There's a farmhouse about a mile back. I searched the place, and the farmer is alive. Demand a change of clothing and the cow and walk back to the medical station. If anyone approaches, say you're a farmer taking your cow back home. The cow will be your excuse for movement. Do not speak Russian and answer only in Polish."

Pranas followed orders, avoiding detection by half crawling across fields of wheat, and arrived at the small, decrepit farmhouse. After banging on the splintering wood, an old bearded man cracked open the door. "I've nothing left."

"Your clothes, give them to me. This is German territory, and I can't be seen in a USSR uniform."

"I have no other clothes," the farmer stammered. Pranas saw he only had black stubs instead of teeth, and as Pranas approached nearer, a rank odor emanated from his body.

"I'll give you mine." Pranas could see the farmer got the better of the deal as he put on the farmer's stinking, filthy rags.

"You have a cow," said Pranas, looking over the broken fence to a small field where a brown-and-white cow was grazing.

"Yes, but that cow is all I have left. Everyone has been killed except for my infant granddaughter, who needs milk. The German officer who commanded the last patrol here took pity and left the cow so the infant could live. He told me the child looks like his own little girl in Bremen. Even a Soviet doctor who stopped here left the cow alone. Please, let me give you all my bread instead."

"I'm taking the cow," insisted Pranas.

"But the infant will die," he said as he grabbed Pranas's shoulder. "Do you have less pity than the Germans?"

Pranas took his pistol and shot the farmer in the face as the infant screamed in the background. He tied a rope on the cow's neck, took all the bread, and walked west. He had no remorse since war is state-sanctioned murder and, therefore, not immoral. In war, survival is all.

After a few hours, he stopped, milked the cow, and had the fresh warm milk and some of the bread. He looked at the big brown innocent eyes of the cow and remembered times of peace. He patted the cow's head, and she returned the gesture by licking his hand. They went on their journey side by side, with Pranas holding the rope.

Reaching the medical station, he came upon an abattoir. The rotted body parts were covered by flies and maggots, producing a hideous stench. Scanning the scene, he vomited. Human life had no value to the Soviets or to the Nazis; the war took on aspects of a sadistic contest of murder. Belief in communism for a better life did not materialize in this bloodbath. His revenge on Astrid in Prienai, so satisfying at the time, in retrospect, turned out to be a hollow victory: the triumph of conquest somehow eluded him. Looking around at the results of state-sponsored rage, he saw there was nothing worthy of belief. It was all hell. He swore to save only his own hide. He would not return to the army.

Not finding any medicine, before Pranas left the bombed medical facility, he took the papers of a dead German soldier, lit a fire to a corner, burned one of the edges and smeared the written information with his spit. From a disembodied arm, severed from its owner, he also pocketed a gold watch.

He continued walking west to Vilnius when German soldiers stopped him at a river crossing. They were more interested in the cow than in him, so he gave them the cow and continued walking. He heard a shot and turned to view the soldiers building a fire and cheering at their anticipated meal.

He walked for days, drinking in streams and eating crusts of the dried bread. On the outskirts of Vilnius, he found an encampment in the ruins near a bombed-out building where the recently displaced homeless huddled in desperation. German troops with orders to clean up the rabble patrolled the area. A Lithuanian policeman caught him trying to steal some food. "You, show me your papers," he ordered Pranas.

"Sir," Pranas replied in Polish, "I came from a village burned to the ground. My papers are partially burned and illegible, but I have this." He showed the short, squat policeman the doctored papers and the pilfered gold watch. "Take this watch. I'll do anything for something to eat and a place to sleep."

The policeman examined the watch and put it in his pocket. He returned by the crumbled wall at night, bringing a loaf of bread and a piece of bacon. "The Germans have strict rules for us. We cannot steal or harass women under penalty of death. But the watch is a gift. No?" He came close enough to Pranas that he could smell the policeman's alcoholic breath.

Pranas understood and smiled, nodding yes. "It's a gift."

"You can sleep in my basement and make yourself useful. I'll tell you the addresses of vacated Jewish apartments. At night, you will go there and scavenge any goods left behind. You look healthy and clever, so you can help me."

Sarah, in bed all day, not dressing or eating or sleeping, sank into a deep depression when minutes have the weight of hours. She had lost the will to survive in her despair at the incomprehensible events—her Abraham murdered by Daniel, followed by the surreal news of Daniel's disappearance. Their life savings gone after so many hours of planning their escape. The avalanche of brutal events became a quagmire of agony.

Rachel stopped playing the violin and beheld Sarah's detached, empty stare. Her mother was starting to look like a skeleton. "Mother, we're running out of money for food. I'm hungry all the time," complained Rachel.

Only the survival of her daughter forced Sarah to again appeal to her only hope, Antanas. Her weight loss caused her face to sag in multiple wrinkles, and she no longer cared to make herself attractive. She put on her black dress with the yellow star and stood in the street by the mayor's office. Antanas did not recognize the pale, shrunken old woman who made her way to him and forced a note into his hand. At the last moment, he looked into her eyes. "Sarah," he murmured as she scuttled away.

Dear Mr. Eimontas,
My family is gone, and I am alone with my daughter Rachel. We have no means of support. Rachel is a bright girl and a good worker. I beg you to give her work. I will send her to you as Vida Stropus. Please help me as my only hope.
Sarah Bernstein

Hiring and firing of city personnel fell under the purview of the assistant mayor. After the confinement of the Jews to the ghetto, Jewish employees were no longer able to come to work without travel permission, and since this was rarely granted, most Jews could no longer work. The Gestapo had presented Antanas with a list of employees who, as Jews, were to be dismissed from their positions. He refused to sign the order because firing them for being Jewish was contrary to Lithuanian anti-discrimination laws. He changed the wording so that the cause for termination read, "Failing to appear for work." He enjoyed his victory over Nazi racial policy by maneuvering the legal wording, although the facts remained the same—Jews could not be employed.

Rachel, now eighteen, in a navy-blue suit with a crisp white blouse, walked to the office of the assistant mayor and knocked on the door. Ruta appraised the attractive young woman with raised eyebrows. "Please tell Mr. Eimontas that Vida Stropus is here to see him," said Rachel.

"Let her in," said Antanas. Vida came in, and Ruta closed the door. Antanas sucked in a sharp breath when he beheld her, thinking she was a clone of her mother when they first met.

"Mr. Eimontas, my mother and I are desperate for your help. Please give me work—anything. We need food to survive."

"You put me in a delicate position, Miss Stropus. I know who you are, and this charade is a very dangerous game," Antanas said, appraising her.

"My father has been killed, and my brother Daniel is missing with all the family money. We are paupers. I'll do anything. Please help us." Rachel's tears struck a chord in Antanas, whose weakness was women.

"I do have a position in accounting in the statistical area. You would work independently and report to me to avoid interrogation. I'll make the necessary documents to classify you as Crimean. You must become well versed in statistics and Crimean culture. But if you are found out, I'll deny any knowledge of this subterfuge," Antanas said to an overjoyed Rachel.

Rachel had to leave and enter the ghetto with one identity card and enter the mayor's office with another set of documents. She spent her nights studying the complexities of statistical accounting and finding pictures of Crimea for her desk. She avoided contact with her fellow workers, worked with her head down, and took her finished work to Antanas for review.

Both mother and daughter, now able to buy food, began to recover. Sarah regained energy and wanted to promote Rachel's success. She added bleach to Rachel's shampoo to lighten her hair and made her a fashionable dress. Sarah bought a rosary Rachel could keep on her desk as proof of her Catholicism.

The aroma of the famous German 4711 cologne signaled the arrival of Antanas to the accounting department on contrived pretexts to hover over Rachel. Her heart rate increased at his approach. One day, leaving work, Antanas invited her to follow him and join him for dinner. Entering his apartment in the Eimontas mansion, she observed the masculine atmosphere as he poured wine and served cold chicken. After eating and engaging in some small talk, Rachel said, "I want to thank you, you saved our lives. I would not refuse you anything." Antanas understood her message, and Rachel did not object. The equal physical pleasure hid their differing perspectives. Antanas had a conquest, and she considered giving herself to him a sacred duty. She wallowed in the pleasure Antanas offered and became eager for his signals to follow him home. She was in love.

Rachel's excuses for her late hours were always the horrendous workload, but Antanas's salacious reputation with women and Rachel's dreamy glow led Sarah to suspect an affair. She could not believe Antanas would seduce her daughter, but crushed by loss, she remained oblivious to yet another consequence of evil times and remained silent.

Ruta took some numbers to the accounting department. Her eyes widened with shock and fury to see her boss bending over Vida, the new employee, stroking her shoulder. Ruta reigned as the mistress of Antanas Eimontas in the workplace, despite his reputation with other women in the city. For him to flaunt a liaison in front of her coworkers was to denigrate her publicly and spit in her face. She vowed revenge.

One evening, Antanas attended a late meeting with the mayor. Ruta left the office and followed Vida home to ascertain the existence of a husband. She planned to blackmail Vida into leaving her Antanas alone. To her surprise, she followed her to the entrance of the ghetto where Vida produced documents and entered. Ruta gleefully hurried to the Gestapo office to report her discovery and eliminate her rival.

The next day, the Gestapo apprehended Rachel as she entered the mayor's office. Ruta gleefully informed Antanas, "Your new accountant was arrested by the Gestapo."

Antanas went to Nazi headquarters and talked to the commandant, "I never suspected Vida Stropus had a double identity. You should confine her immediately pending a review of her crime. Information should be extracted from her before she is sent to a concentration camp. She may have been stealing sensitive papers. Leave it to me to get to the truth."

The long days of summer brought Katerina, Vytas, and Antanas together, celebrating the return of Astrid and Dalia from the Erelis estate. The table in the garden, shaded by tall birch trees among a profusion of flowers, was draped in a white tablecloth with glasses of wine and baskets of dark bread. Paulina prepared a summer meal of various cold dishes: a tureen of pink cold beet soup and various salads crowned by trout in aspic. Baby Adam, sleeping in his crib, completed the tableaux.

Taking some fish, Antanas smiled and said, "When I entered my office, I found a large portrait of Hitler on the wall above my desk. I discovered the artist to be a Lithuanian. I ordered the portrait removed and replaced with one of the former president of Lithuania. When questioned about my decision, I answered that it was only permissible to display officially sanctioned German images of Hitler, not substandard art by some unknown artist. In this way, I removed the tyrant from my wall." The whole company laughed.

Katerina turned to Vytas. "Darling, you remember Professor Rubenstein, my mentor in ophthalmology?"

"Yes, very well," said Vytas. "He saved the sight of President Pilsudski, who appointed him an honorary captain in the Polish Army as a reward. He treasures the photograph in his library of him in his captain's uniform with Pilsudski."

"Rubenstein's maid turned him into the German authorities accusing him of being a Jew who did not obey orders to move into the ghetto."

Vytas said, "I have a thought. Tell him to come see me and bring me his photograph with Pilsudski."

Returning to work, Vytas approached the Gestapo Kommissar and showed him the photograph obtained from Professor Rubenstein. "Kommissar, you are mistaking Dr. Rubenstein for a Jew. Here he is wearing a Polish officer's uniform. The Polish Army never, under any circumstances, accepted Jews. He is Chechen."

The Kommissar studied the photograph and nodded. "Yes, there is no way a Jew could wear a Polish colonel's uniform. I believe you. He is not a Jew. I will release him."

Vytas advised Professor Rubenstein to leave Vilnius immediately and flee to a Soviet-occupied zone.

After Antanas accused Rachel—as Vida, his former employee—of having stolen official papers, the Gestapo brought her to him for questioning. He berated her loudly to satisfy Ruta's curiosity and then shouted, "Miss Stropus, you must take me to where you hid the papers and tell me whom you are working for." He told the Gestapo officers in the outer office, "You can go. I will return her to you after I interrogate her thoroughly and retrieve the stolen documents. Then she will be punished."

As they left the mayor's office, Rachel whispered, "I didn't take anything."

"I know, but it is an excuse for us to leave for interrogation," Antanas said, winking. He took her to his car and drove out of the city. "We will have three days alone together. We're going to my estate, Erelis, in the country."

At the estate, they went to the bed in the upstairs bedroom for hours. The frenzy of lovemaking only activated their desire for more. "I love you," Rachel whispered, but her confession was met with silence. She attributed his lack of verbal response by thinking his actions spoke for his love.

They heard a loud noise. Rachel jumped, and Antanas said, "Don't worry, it's only Father Vebra returning from his work in the fields."

Antanas dressed and went to the kitchen where Father Vebra was making lunch. "I have a visitor. Could you please cook us something also?"

"Of course, Mr. Eimontas. This is just some bread with vegetable stew," answered Vebra, accustomed to Antanas and his female friends.

"That will be fine for now, but for dinner, please prepare one of the plump hens."

As Father Vebra went outside to catch the chicken, Rachel looked out the window and saw Jacob. "My god, my brother is alive! Please don't let him know I'm here. I'm so ashamed," pleaded Rachel blushing.

"You have no reason for shame. Love excuses you. Your brother and you are here only because of your mother's pleading." Rachel looked so much like Sarah and his mother, Jadvyga. Lovemaking while contemplating all three women fueled his lust.

At dinner, when Rachel came into contact with Father Vebra, she peered into his changed face and speculated on his tortures. Jacob was too shocked to react to his sister's moral disgrace. Their eyes met with joy at still being alive, but silence reigned. The transformation of innocent Rachel into a woman who was a mistress and Jacob Bernstein into a Catholic priest produced a chasm of change too wide to breach.

Antanas drove back to Vilnius, and he returned Rachel to the Gestapo, saying, "My interrogation was successful. I am finished with her."

Pranas, a Soviet Army deserter, could not sleep in the filthy basement for fear of being discovered. Providing the policeman with stolen goods exhausted him since he always threatened to arrest him. One night, in desperation, he made his way to the old city and the Gates of Dawn. The last rays of the sun reflected the golden icon of the Madonna of Vilnius.

He thought of his father, mother, and Anna. Those bastard communists torturing his brother Jan! He wanted to go to Memel to find Stefan and Valeria for help—they were the powerful ones. In the middle of the cobblestone street, he passed a kneeling, shriveled woman with white hair praying. He turned to look, and she held out her arms. "Pranas! Is it you?"

"Mother!" he whispered with tears as he helped her stand up and embraced her. She was as light as a feather now.

"Thank the Lord. I never thought I would ever see you again. Come home with me." As they entered the familiar apartment, he focused on the bureau where a bouquet of wild roses honored a cross and a picture of his brother: the tableaux formed an altar. "I pray to Jan, who is a saint in heaven, that at least one of my children would return to comfort me," explained Paulina.

The threadbare spotless apartment was empty. "Where is Father? Is Anna in school?" asked Pranas.

Paulina sobbed loudly, and Pranas tried to quiet her with no success, so he put on a pot of water for tea. While the tea steeped, Paulina said, "Let me get you something to eat. I don't have much, but there is bread and farmer's cheese." The homely, familiar serving of food calmed Paulina, and she said, "Your father was arrested and shot for being a communist in the early days of the Nazi invasion. I don't even know where his body lies."

"I know I'm responsible for his death. I talked him into joining the communist party. Those Nazi bastards!" thundered Pranas, somehow deflecting his guilt. "Where is Anna?" he demanded.

Through her tears, Paulina whimpered, "Anna was playing with the Klimas girl when their entire family was arrested, and Anna disappeared with them. The neighbors said they were deported to Siberia."

Pranas's mouth opened, but no sound came out. Visions of little Anna in Siberia grieved him, and he felt his cheeks wet with tears.

In recounting her tragedies, Paulina's head pounded. Pranas was her son, her child, who caused these events with his godless communism. In associating him with guilt, she looked at his missing earlobe, and all his actions against Astrid played out. He was a monster. She should curse him for eternity, but she couldn't. He was her flesh and blood. She was responsible for bringing him into this world and, therefore, must share his guilt. "I had your crimes outlined to me in detail. I know your evil acts in Prienai with my employer's daughter."

Pranas blushed and stammered, "No, I never was in Prienai. What are you talking about?"

"Don't add lying to your sins. I know it was you that raped Astrid in Prienai. You caused enough harm in this life so even the devil could fear you in hell. I raised all my children with love. What happened to you?"

"I'm paying for my actions. I deserted the Red Army and am a hunted man," justified Pranas, cutting a piece of black bread, as if exile were punishment enough for his deeds.

"I should report you or at least banish you from my sight, but you're my son. You are to hide here, out of sight. I'll give you some food, but stay out of my way. Get on your knees and beg God's forgiveness because you will never have my forgiveness for what you have done."

Pranas had never known his mother to be so vehement, but he dismissed her rant. He went to the small room he had shared with his father and Jan and slept soundly for the first time since arriving in Vilnius.

Paulina knelt to pray in front of Jan's picture. "Dear Jan, I know you are a martyr and a saint with God in heaven. Please intercede with the Mother of God that your nephew, little Adam, would not inherit the evil of his father, Pranas. Adam is an innocent little soul, and his conception was not blessed, but his soul will blossom with God's forgiveness. Doctor Katerina will raise him to grow in God's grace. May he never know the truth of his origins." She did not tell Pranas he had a son.

Devoid of appetite, bristling with worry, Sarah picked at a crust of bread with cheese—her first food in days. She heard the door opening and jumped up. The aroma of cigarettes and 4711 cologne confirmed her suspicions. "Where have you been?" she asked. "The ghetto Kommissar was here looking for you. He said you were arrested. What were you arrested for?"

"Mother, I was with Antanas Eimontas at his country estate, working," Rachel stated. "The Gestapo accused me of stealing some documents from work, but it was a mistake. Eimontas promised to void the arrest warrant."

"Are you sure he can do this? Are you sure there will be no punishment?" Sarah asked as her recent lunch seemed to be returning to her throat.

"Mother, don't be naïve. He loves me." Rachel tossed her head in defiance.

Sarah swallowed the acid in her mouth as blood pounded in the veins of her head. "How can you say that? How can you be sure? The Gestapo does not follow Eimontas orders."

"Jacob is there at the estate disguised as a Catholic priest. You would not recognize him. His face has been mutilated. He is doing farm work on the Eimontas estate."

"Oh my god! Did you talk to him?" Sarah asked, grateful to Antanas for saving her son, but before she could get her answer, pounding on the door stopped the discussion and revealed the ghetto kommissar. "Rachel Bernstein, finally, I find you. You are assigned to work cleaning the streets. You start tomorrow," the kommissar bellowed.

Rachel, in her gray uniform with the yellow star on her armband, cleaned the streets on her knees with a small brush for twelve hours a day. The size of the brush made the work longer and excruciating. Torture through order and cleanliness was the motto. Exhaustion voided thoughts of sex and Antanas. The scars on her knees pained her through the night. Her calloused hands no longer played the violin.

Adam was a joy, a good baby, and Katerina considered herself his mother. Paulina loved this child, her grandson, and performed most of the childcare. Astrid studied medicine at the university, ignored the child, and treated him as an unwanted sibling; she had not yet forgiven the child for coming into the world. The war sucked out her youthful enthusiasm and breathed in a depressing reality. She received a letter from Russia, which passed the censors.

Darling Astrid,
Memories of our happy times fill my bitter hours. I am living in
Stalingrad, and when I came home, I discovered my child had died
and my wife had left me for a general in Moscow. So you see, I am
now alone and available. Our child, was it a boy or a girl? When
the war is over, I would like to return to you and our child.
Love,
Georgi

Astrid burned the note with satisfaction. *Bastard.*

Dalia revered her heartfelt meetings with Father Vebra, her spiritual advisor. Father Vebra understood her, forgave her, and released her from the pain of her unforgivable sin. Antanas, pleased at the improvement in his sister's mental state, discussed Nazi prohibited psychiatry with Mayor Heinz. "That Jewish discipline, psychiatry, had not helped my sister, but she is better now. There is a miracle worker at our estate, Erelis, Father Vebra. He freed my sister from depression by his miraculous understanding of human nature. He is a genius, and his ideas should be known to all."

Heinz reported to the Gestapo, "A priest with this much influence with a prominent family should be checked out. He could be secretly practicing psychiatry or by black magic twisting their allegiance to Nazi ideals."

The Gestapo, checking their excellent records, found a Father Viktoras Vebra had been shot by the Germans in 1941 for sermons against the Nazi regime. So who was this Father Vebra at Erelis? On the last day of July, a car pulled up at Erelis. Two Gestapo men got out and found their prey. Vebra was in the field working when they arrested him.

Chapter 20
September 1942

After his arrest at the Eimontas estate, wearing his cassock, chained in Gestapo shackles, Jacob sought to avoid torture by absolute silence. In the truck on the way to the central prison, he passed the autumnal countryside. Birch trees glistened in the sun, and pine trees perfumed the air. In the midst of the beauty of God's creation, Jacob experienced hell in images of Jan Kataski's torture. The heaviness of his guilt crushed him as slithering snakes crawled through his conscience and self-loathing propelled his escape from his former self.

Arriving in the Vilnius central interrogation room, stinking of sweat and fear, the unimpeachable Gestapo records listed him as Jacob Bernstein, a communist Jew. "I am Father Vebra," he stated with conviction, erasing all traces of the ghetto, Bernsteins' fur business, his parents, his brother Daniel, and Rachel. He eliminated memories of his Jewish faith and his enthusiastic work for the communist party.

"Our records indicate a Father Viktoras Vebra was arrested and executed for preaching against Reich's policies in 1941," a Gestapo officer told Jacob, skimming through the files. "Unless you have risen from the dead, you are not Father Vebra."

A rapid change of personnel at the prison, due to requirements at the front, installed a new crew of interrogators. He drew their wrath by not answering questions and reciting prayers in Latin instead. The Gestapo held both his identity documents, as Jacob Bernstein, communist Jew, and Father Viktoras Vebra, Catholic priest, each identity carrying enough penalties for imprisonment. Jacob received the designation for Dachau, a concentration camp near Munich.

"Are priests also sent to concentration camps?" Vebra spoke at last to a fellow prisoner as he was led to a waiting truck.

"Oh yes, they have one hundred sixty thousand prisoners there, and at least two thousand of them are priests," answered the crestfallen man.

Jacob rode for months in cramped trains past Wolfenbutel, Hanover, Kassel, Main, and Nurnberg prisons with parasites and hunger as his constant companions. The victims, one hundred to the cattle car, traveled with locked doors, little air, no water or food. A soldier's gunshot to silence people screaming for a drop of water achieved quiet. Maddening thirst forced people into drinking their own urine. Many died of starvation; others survived by eating those who perished.

The Gestapo specifically imprisoned priests at Dachau. He was the sole Lithuanian and the only priest in a group of thirty-two disembarking at the train station. They rode in silence to the camp through the streets of Munich. A glimpse of normal city life seemed surreal to him.

The gates of Dachau held an inscription: "Arbeit macht frei" (work makes you free). The guards removed his shackles, divided the new arrivals into groups of five, and escorted them into the workhouse. They entered a large square room with highly polished wooden floors glistening in the sunlight through spotless windows.

When Jacob asked why he was under arrest, since he was not a criminal, several SS men jumped on him, hitting and kicking. The impact of a baton hitting his mouth dislodged three incisors which hit the floor in a pool of blood. Jacob watched two prisoners clean the area as if their lives were at stake. After this attack, he sat with the new arrivals, biting on a rag to stop the bleeding and not mar the spotless floor. Prisoners in striped uniforms cut the new inmates' hair, shaved their beards, and photographed them. All personal items were removed—Jacob's prayer book, rosary, and cross. After a disinfectant bath, he received patched worn clothes: gray-and-blue-striped pants, a vest, an unlined jacket, a brimless round hat, gloves and socks made from hemp, and a pair of slippers.

The head of the camp, Lagerführer Manfred, delivered the welcoming speech, "Leave all your dreams of being free one day." Pointing to the crematorium at the western wall of the camp, he added, "You will only leave as smoke through that chimney."

The new prisoners then lined up for their color-coded prisoner identification badges. Political prisoners received a red triangle; criminals, green; work supervisors, black; homosexuals, pink; immigrants, blue; and religious, violet. Most prisoners wore the red triangle, although the political beliefs punished were in question since several hundred children displayed the red badge.

Jacob's jacket received a violet triangle for "religious offender" after the lagerführer concluded, "He only mumbles in Latin, so this is correct." No further investigation into his identity occurred.

Jacob was assigned to one of four large rooms. A central table dominated the space, surrounded by beds at precise angles covered by bedding with knife-sharp-like corners. Lockers lined the walls, and before each locker stood a specifically placed stool. At the far end, a young, muscular man with blond hair and a large nose set in pockmarked skin stood next to a table and introduced himself. "You will get to know me well. I'm Dietrich, your room monitor and king of this space." Silence reigned as Dietrich walked with a limp around the room, squinting at the prisoners as he counted them.

After a pause, Dietrich started his questioning. He asked each new prisoner, "What are you here for?"

"I was arrested for having relations with a Polish girl," the first prisoner, Heinrich, a pale man with red, watery eyes, explained.

Dietrich struck him with his baton, swearing, "You shit, aren't you ashamed of polluting our German blood?" The prisoner crumpled to the floor.

The second to be questioned was an old, shaking German imprisoned for hiding Jewish children. Dietrich beat him as well and said, "How dare you corrupt the German race by harboring scum!"

Jacob waited for his turn at confession, but Dietrich grew tired of beating the previous prisoners and left him in peace. Relief from escaping physical abuse did little to assuage Jacob's gnawing hunger, but no food appeared. Inspecting his locker, he found an aluminum bowl, a plate, knife, fork, spoon, towel, and dishrag—his worldly wealth.

Lagerführer Manfred entered and emphasized the absolute importance of regulations. Bedmaking instructions followed. The making of the beds, made over and over for hours, became the hardest task. The bed had to resemble a box of cigarettes. A stick and boards were used to stuff and shape the straw into the corners and sides to obtain the knife-sharp creases. The inspections with rulers merited a gasp if a corner deviated by one millimeter. Exacting perfect standards in achieving precision, order, and cleanliness and the cruelty to enforce them constituted torture.

Jacob lay down on the straw mattress, but his purgatory of conscience kept him awake. He was being tortured for a fake priesthood that was only a disguise. Jacob, battered about by the chaos of circumstances always out of his control, desired the absolute and unchanging in life.

A morning inspection confirmed Jacob had washed down to his waist outside and dried himself with a thin towel. Returning to the room, he folded the towel into three parts lengthwise, as instructed, the wrinkles smoothed perfectly with his hands.

The first bell rang, and two large urns of coffee were brought into the room. The prisoners stood in line as Dietrich shouted out names and poured one liter into each bowl. After drinking coffee, Jacob hurried to wash and wipe dry the metal bowl. Seasoned prisoners polished their metal bowls to a high gleam with paper before returning them to the lockers.

Dietrich entered the room and, slapping his baton against his hand, gave the command, "Alle raus," to leave the room. Jacob grabbed his stool, placed it in a precise position on top of the locker, and clutching his rough outer clothing and slippers, ran out of the room.

In the yard, Lagerführer Manfred walked with his baton, seeking victims. Some prisoners stood still, while others moved around in an attempt to warm up but accidentally getting too close to their neighbors led to accusations of homosexuality. Energy to exercise did not exist; just to stand was an accomplishment. The prisoners were forced to march with the loud singing of approved propaganda songs praising Hitler.

Roll calls took an average of an hour and a half in the morning, noon, and evening. Mandatory memorization of all SS insignias delineated the level of fear to be felt for the higher echelons. Immediate attention to the commands of guards with an eager, complying attitude helped prisoners avoid problems.

"Form work units!" shouted the lagerführer. The yard became a scurrying ant colony, with everyone running to their assigned units. Escorted by guards with dogs, the prisoners marched to their workstations through the central gates, removing their caps as instructed in respect to the swastika. Jacob mused how the swastika had become the sacred symbol of the Nazi religion. He had experienced the hammer and sickle and now the swastika in turn. Where was the truth? Was it in the cross? Had he completely forgotten the yeshiva? The pain of backbreaking labor erased his thoughts.

Jacob's first assignment was to load and unload contents in the warehouse. One of the workers, an illiterate gypsy, could not tell time. A guard asked the gypsy, "How long have you been at Dachau?"

"Only ten minutes," replied the gypsy. No one understood his answer.

The gypsy explained, "While drinking coffee in my caravan, a Gestapo officer ordered me to go with him at once. 'Wait until I finish my coffee,' I said. He told me to leave my coffee on the table because I would be returning in ten minutes. So you see, the ten minutes have still not passed."

The story resulted in hearty laughter. Later, questioned by Vebra, the gypsy admitted he endured hard labor for fifty months, "The truth brings punishment, so it is better to joke."

Returning from work, Jacob removed, cleaned, and stored his shoes in the assigned space outside to avoid marring the polished floors. In the silence, he found himself saying the prayers of the rosary. Meals consisted of big tureens of soup, mostly water, with cabbage and an occasional potato. Jacob craved even these minimal meals in the face of starvation. A work assignment without food was a common punishment. For greater crimes, an inquest would prescribe beatings, needles under the fingernails, standing for many hours in a tiny cubicle, or twenty-five lashings and a stay in isolation where a piece of bread and a cup of water was provided only once every three days. Another punishment involved being declared insane, taken to the hospital, and injected with gasoline or other poisons.

Jacob observed a guard show a crust of bread to a starving prisoner and throw it, saying, "I can't be seen giving this to you, but go get it." The prisoner would run after the bread, and the guard would shoot him for attempting to escape. Jacob noted that cruelty for pleasure constituted entertainment for some bored guards.

To cure various conditions they inflicted on the prisoners, the prison scientists conducted medical experiments. Jacob was assigned to the malaria experimentation station. A net of mosquitoes with malaria was placed over his body. In twenty-four hours, he was bitten hundreds of times. A doctor recorded his symptoms as he observed Jacob shivering with a high fever. The doctor pronounced the results "very good." He then injected him with a new drug. Jacob survived and observed other experiments where prisoners were being injected with pus from gangrene. A horrendous protocol involved holding naked people in ice water and then reviving them in almost boiling water. Few survived these experiments where hundreds died for German science.

The greatest crimes resulted in frequent public hangings, but Jacob considered the worst torture to be hung from hooks in the ceiling. The victim stood on a chair with his hands tied behind him. A guard kicked away the chair leaving the prisoner hanging by his wrists. Prisoners fainted only to be doused and revived to continue the torture.

Jacob was transferred to the priests' cell block, one of three separate barracks that housed the two thousand priests. Food and lodging in the priests' barracks typified conditions throughout the camp, but the absence of fights, curses, or thievery created a more benign atmosphere.

There he worked the gardens, carting fertilizer, plowing, and planting with a rake and a spade. The hard physical labor and minimal food forced him to forage for roots, grass, green potatoes, or snails found in the ground. Allowed 150 grams of bread per day, it would not take long for Jacob to disappear. Weight loss was rapid, and the weak could hardly walk, rendering the emaciated unfit for any type of work.

Jacob saw invalids separated and herded into isolated blocks before being transported during the night. He was told 250 priests were taken to the crematorium and pushed naked into a room marked "Bathhouse." They received showers, not of water but of carbon monoxide, fatal to all within a few minutes.

This degradation of humanity impressed Jacob as being a force he understood. When in the throes of communist ecstasy, he was capable of the same actions. His torture of the seminarian was not any more innocent than what he was witnessing now. Does committing evil give an aura of good accomplishment if done for your cause while observing others do evil for unknown reasons becomes below the dignity of humanity? Is the morality of torture relative to your beliefs? Jacob's soul screamed NO! It is always evil for all beliefs and for all time. He longed for the absolute and the eternal.

Jacob, returning from the fields, saw Dietrich and another guard beating a priest with swollen eyes and blood streaming from his nose. They held him down in the foot-washing basin until bubbles from the dying man came to the surface. When they lifted his head, the victim drew a breath only to be submerged again. They tortured him until he passed out. They left him half-dead by the wall. Jacob heard him whisper, "Brothers, give me absolution because I am dying." The surrounding priests hesitated, fearing punishment from the guards.

Jacob approached him, sank to one knee, made the sign of the cross, and said, "I forgive you in the name of the Father, the Son, and the Holy Spirit."

Jacob had bestowed false sacraments in his priestly subterfuge, and a desire for truth overwhelmed him. He wanted to throw off the crimes of his previous life and the hypocrisy of his present one. He felt the grace of God and the thankfulness of his fellow sufferers by his priestly act. He wanted to become a real priest and exercise power in the infinite arena of the eternal.

The victim died, and a German priest, Father Miller, impressed by Jacob's courage, came to him and said, "Father Vebra, you must be a holy man."

Jacob joined Father Miller working in the fields and explained to him, "No, Father, I'm not a priest. I disguised myself as a priest to escape arrest as a communist Jew. Now, after all that I experienced, I would like to know how I could truly join the Catholic priesthood."

After the initial shock, Miller questioned him, "Vebra, you've already practiced both Judaism and communism. Is this not just another convenient belief? The taking of the vows of Holy Orders is a most serious matter, and to give you the education and possibility of ordination under these circumstances is impossible."

Jacob explained, "Father, I feel strongly about my destiny to be a priest. This is the final stage of my quest for the meaning of life. Please start to teach me, and if I fail at any point, I will concede and not bother you again."

Father Miller worked by his side and gave him instructions he had been taught in the seminary. In the fields one day, he confessed to Father Miller and asked to be baptized. Two other priests helped Father Miller take his bowl, fill it with water, and baptize Jacob Bernstein while the guard slept. Jacob requested the baptismal name, Jan, for the seminarian he had tortured.

Jacob heard of an arrested bishop who recently arrived at Dachau. The SS tortured Bishop Fouquet for hiding and saving the lives of Jewish children in France. Jacob inquired about the bishop and monitored his movements. An opportunity arose, and Jacob approached the emaciated, crippled bishop as they worked the fields, digging trenches.

"Your Excellency, I stand before you as the greatest of sinners. I'm Jewish by birth and was a communist by force of ambition. I supervised the elimination of religion in Vilnius. In order to fulfill my commitment, I tortured and killed an innocent seminarian," confessed Jacob.

Astounded, the bishop asked, "What are you doing here with the priests?"

Jacob explained, "My mother and good friends hid me from the Germans on an estate in Lithuania. In order to survive, I disguised myself as a priest. This impersonation led many innocent people to believe I possessed the consecrated powers as I forgave sins and officiated at a baptism and death."

The bishop laughed. "You must have been a good actor to pass in that Catholic country."

Jacob shuddered at the bishop's levity, and tears flowed down his cheeks as he whispered, "Now, in this seat of hell, I want absolution, forgiveness, and the love of God to save me. My greatest desire is to become a real priest."

The bishop stepped back and peered into Jacob's face, scrutinizing it for sincerity. The tears and expression of despair reflected a soul in turmoil.

"I've been baptized here at Dachau and have confessed, but I need your blessing and absolution. My greatest desire is to receive Holy Communion."

The bishop reached a decision. "I will give you absolution. In the name of . . ." Jacob had withheld a small sliver of bread from his previous dinner and handed it to the bishop, who said the ancient prayers, turning the bread into the body of Christ. Jacob received Communion.

Over the coming weeks, the priests organized Jacob's investiture into the priesthood. They sewed bedsheets together to make vestments and nailed together a wooden cross. One evening when the guards attended a mandatory training session, all the priests congregated. The dark room had pools of light from the lit candles. The central table, decorated with wild flowers, served as an altar. The priests sang the ancient hymns in soft voices to preserve the secrecy of the occasion.

Over his striped prisoner's uniform, Jacob donned the white vestment. Father Miller blessed and placed a small wooden cross tied with rope around Jacob's neck. The imprisoned bishop performed the ancient rite of ordination into the priesthood.

Many priests cried with visible emotion. For some priests, the juxtaposition of the apex of Christian belief occurring in the hell of inhumanity tore at their minds and hearts, reinforcing their religion.

Jacob felt free and light, as if the world did not weigh him down anymore. He was more spirit than flesh, and deep contentment and happiness enveloped him with loving arms.

After his investiture, his next assignment was as a janitor in the camp hospital, scrubbing floors, washbasins, and latrines. He welcomed his assignment because, in the course of his work, he secretly administered the last sacraments to the sick and dying. His soul was rewarded every time he heard a whispered "Father Jan."

What began as a ruse to avoid arrest had transformed into a calling and a destiny. He prayed daily to the memory of Jan, the seminarian, begging for forgiveness.

This was Jacob's life in the concentration camp, in the house of the dead, where in the midst of the hardest labor, hunger, and torture, some died cursing, some drank the poison cup, and others prayed for God's mercy. At long last, Jacob Bernstein received peace.

Chapter 21
November 1942

A gleaming silver airplane stamped with red swastikas swirled in the brilliant blue sky above Vilnius, rising and falling, buffeted by the high winds. It swooped, swayed, and circled before landing on the airstrip. The propellers still whirred as airport personnel ran to the plane to position the exit ramp. Lower echelon dignitaries arrived by train, so the airplane signaled the presence of important passengers.

The doors opened, and Colonel Helmut Obermeyer, promoted to general in charge of implementing the Final Solution in Ostland, exited giving the Nazi salute. With his tall frame, classic features, and imposing stance, he embodied the ideal of the Aryan race. The silver eagles on his uniform glistened in the morning sun. Three officers, all in impeccable gray uniforms, followed the general down the ramp. Moments later, a platinum-blonde woman in a sable coat stepped out, grasping her hat against the harsh wind. They entered the black limousine with the swastika flags flying.

"Your return home must be conflicting to you. It's been three years, no?" Helmut said, holding Valeria's hand. "Your mother's letter to you contained disturbing news—your father arrested for being a communist, your brother Frank a member of the NKVD. Certainly not a proper Nazi family."

"Yes, these facts torture me," Valeria confided.

"The wife of a general of the Reich should avoid these communist traitors. I've kept your background secret by saying you were from Memel. If anyone finds out the truth, there would be consequences to my career. Don't do anything to arouse suspicion." Helmut turned to see tears in Valeria's eyes. "But I'm sure you long to see your mother."

Valeria looked up, surprised. Helmut avoided being cognizant of her inner life, focusing on her intelligence and appearance. She recalled his fury when he discovered her background, but by then, she was his wife. "Yes, above all, I want to see Mama."

As the car passed the familiar streets of Old Town, she saw the Gates of Dawn, where her brother was arrested. "The murder of my brother Jan fills me with hatred for the enemy. I'll get more details from my mother."

"You'll get your revenge. The Reich will exterminate all the Jew communists," said Helmut, lighting a cigarette.

"My brother, Stefan, and his wife, Monica, are to arrive from Memel in the next few days. The return of her family will make my mother happy."

"Thank God at least Stefan is a good Nazi. Vilnius is starting to become a problem. They value their independence above Nazi aims," Helmut frowned.

"Darling, you and the party mean more to me than my connections to this city." She patted the diamond, ruby, and onyx swastika on her lapel.

The limousine pulled up to the most prestigious hotel in Vilnius, the Astoria. The staff, trained and obsequious, took their luggage and escorted them to the largest suite overlooking a stately church on an ancient cobblestone square. Flowers, fruit, and champagne awaited them. The staff silently unpacked their suitcases. "Darling, I must report to headquarters," said Helmut, giving Valeria a peck on the cheek. "Take this opportunity to visit your mother. Our presence will be reported tomorrow, and then you'll be scrutinized. Do it now anonymously." He took his briefcase and left.

Valeria put on a cloth coat and a scarf and walked toward her old Polish neighborhood. The streets she navigated exploded in a kaleidoscope of memories of her early life. Despite the emotional pull of herself as a poor Polish girl devoted to her home and family, she was now a member of the master race. The Nazi ideology of order and precision was now her home.

She passed the deserted old Jewish area. Helmut had told her all Jews were confined to two ghettos. She reached her house in the Polish area and, after a critical appraisal, found her heart happy at leaving this hovel. She smelled the familiar aroma of overcooked cabbage, and she saw the dirty, crying children and the ragged stinking people. "I escaped," she said.

Climbing the three landings of peeling paint, garbage and graffiti, she knocked. No answer. "It's Valeria, here from Berlin. Open!"

The door cracked a slit, and a bearded face confronted her. "Pranas!"

Instinctively, she hugged him, aware of his bones and bad breath. "What are you doing here? Where's Mother?" asked Valeria, removing her coat and scarf, observing the shabby quarters being more depressing than she remembered.

"Mother still goes to help at the Eimontas household, although she's really too old and weak to work. They have a new baby who needs care. Doctor Katerina has a son, Adam. She'll be back soon."

"That must have been a surprise at her age," Valeria smirked.

Pranas observed her light shiny hair, the fashionable wool dress, and gold jewelry. "You look unbelievably well."

"Don't pay me useless compliments. Tell me, what the hell are you doing here? You were NKVD," Valeria demanded as she sat down by their kitchen table. "You are putting your family in danger by staying here."

"I deserted the Red Army," stated Pranas, looking down at the floor. "Valeria, the war was horrific, and I had to leave."

"You communist pig. So you couldn't be faithful even to your hellish beliefs. Mother wrote Father got arrested because you talked him into joining the communists. How could you fall for that stupid, vile Jewish doctrine? It exalts the weak, subnormal, and insane." Valeria looked at him with blazing eyes filled with anger.

"Father was killed, and guess by whom, by your Nazis!" Pranas spewed into Valeria's face, releasing a smell of sulfurous breath.

"They had to get rid of communists. Too bad it was our ignorant father who never even understood political ideas," Valeria's voice trembled.

"I was responsible, and I'm sorry. I did it so he could get work." Pranas sat down at the table, and his eyes started to glisten with tears.

"Too bad they didn't get you. You'll pay one way or another. If the Germans don't kill you, the Russians will."

"Is cruelty to your family also a Nazi trait? Are you planning to do away with me also?" Pranas pointed a finger at himself and said, "Bang!"

Valeria slumped, took a deep breath, and asked, "Has life changed our family relationships beyond recognition? Our only point of agreement now is our love for Anna. Where is she? I have presents for her from Berlin."

Pranas, after clearing his throat, said, "Valeria, she was taken by the Soviets. She was playing with the daughter of a family on the deportation list and got captured in the sweep. The last we heard, she was bound for Siberia." He saw the look of pain and horror on his sister's face and regretted being the one to tell her.

"God damn them! They tortured and killed my brother, and now they kidnapped my little sister. How I despise them." She tried to summon the same hatred as she had felt upon hearing of the torture and murder of Jan but only registered sorrow. She covered her face with her hands and took deep breaths, but no tears came.

Memories of her little sister appeared, braiding her silky light-brown hair and deciding which color ribbon to attach. She envisioned Anna's soft little hands trying to help her make supper. Valeria then patted the old worn kitchen table and started to cry. She wanted to recapture their family meals with Jan saying a prayer and little Anna whispering "Amen" at the end.

Pranas put water on for tea and said, "You must help me no matter how you despise me. I'm your brother hiding here. I need documents and a way to make a living. I can't live off Mother. She's old and frail and hardly has enough for herself."

"And how am I supposed to do that? You're the enemy."

"So you won't help me? Your own flesh and blood? Your brother?"

"No. I can't jeopardize my position for the likes of you, a degenerate communist deserter. There's not an iota of good in you."

"I've worked as a medical orderly on the front and helped many of the wounded and dying. I've done more for humanity than you!" shouted Pranas. "Do you think the Nazis are above reproach?"

Slow, creaking steps on the wooden stairs announced the arrival of Paulina. A shabby black dress draped a shrunken figure. Her hair, completely white, crowned a wrinkled face, a map of sorrows. Her eyes crinkling in a smile, Paulina gasped, "Valeria, my beautiful daughter, God has answered my prayers."

"Mama!" Valeria ran to her, throwing her arms around her, kissing her.

"Let me look at you," said Paulina. "I wouldn't have recognized you, a platinum blonde, and your clothes must be from Paris."

"Yes, Mama, that is where I married Helmut Obermeyer six months ago. Occupied Paris was at our feet. With the favorable exchange rate, we could buy the best of everything. It's a beautiful city and now a wonderful part of the Reich."

"My dear Valeria, a married woman. Perhaps you could introduce me to your husband. I pray for your happiness every day."

Valeria could not reconcile her mother meeting her husband. She blushed and said, "Perhaps, Mama, when the war ends."

"Dear daughter, here, we've only had tragedy. Our family has diminished by three, Jan, your father, and Anna. You are now rich and powerful. Can't you find little Anna? I don't sleep nights because I see her starving, freezing, and alone. Can't you help find your little sister?"

"I would give half my life to bring back Anna, but it's impossible until we conquer the Soviets. When we win the war, we'll free all the prisoners in Siberia. Heil Hitler."

"You're really indoctrinated, aren't you?" Pranas commented with a smirk. "What's the difference between your beliefs and mine?"

"My beliefs are superior. I still hold them. The inferior communist ideology is losing, and you are holed up here like a rat."

"Children, enough! Valeria, this is your brother, your blood. Our family has lost enough members. You must help him."

"Impossible! It would jeopardize my position. No one in Berlin suspects my Polish background or knows of my deserter communist brother," Valeria said as she took out a wad of reichsmarks from her purse and put the pile on the kitchen table. "Here's enough money for food for at least six months. Mother, I want you to stop working. It's too much for you. You look weak and pale."

"I must go to the Eimontases because the baroness had a baby who provides my only happiness and reason for living these days."

"Live for yourself. Stefan is due here in a few days. Take some of that money to buy a new dress and some food."

"A new dress and food will not erase my heartache. Please stay a little longer. I will make you your favorite dumplings," Paulina pleaded.

Valeria embraced her mother. "I will try to see you again before we leave. There is a dinner this evening honoring my husband, and I must get ready." Valeria threw on her scarf and coat and hurried out.

The dinner at the Astoria Hotel could have been in Berlin. The velvet curtains, mirrored walls, and multiple bouquets of flowers indicated luxury and supremacy. German officers clicked their heels, and the women preened in their fashionable formal gowns cut on the bias to reveal their splendid figures. No rationing was evident. The profusion of roast beef and pheasant served on the buffet table laden with delicacies served as a sign of victory, an appropriate feast for conquerors.

City officials, including Antanas, arrived at this dinner welcoming General Obermeyer. Antanas felt at home among the elite officers and beautiful women. Most officers, representing the upper echelons of German society, were handsome, young, and educated.

One woman caught his eye, the sparkling platinum blonde with Helmut Obermeyer. She seemed an Aryan princess, cold and unapproachable. What a challenge, Antanas thought.

"Stop leering at Madame Obermeyer. She is newly married," cautioned his boss Heinz.

Disappointed, Antanas joined a group of officers in the middle of the room, where the conversation swirled around the latest operas and the wealth of art concentrating in Berlin. Madame Obermeyer, listening, walked to the center of the group and said, "The transformation of the world is in progress, a world of supermen, healthy, moral, intelligent, and cultured. Each following generation will improve on the last."

"General Obermeyer, congratulations on your promotion and your marriage," said Mayor Heinz approaching the group, followed by a waiter with a tray of champagne. The general took a glass and gave one to Valeria, and they all toasted Hitler before their toast to Obermeyer.

Obermeyer said, "I was in Paris to meet with Eichmann, who had plans for a Final Solution. I took the Paris opportunity to get married since Valeria is such a romantic." Another toast for the young couple followed.

Helmut continued, "Of course, my assignment will be difficult: to rid the world of the Jewish plague once and for all. What a relief to coming generations to be free of their influence! These parasites have controlled the populace long enough through finance, the press, and propagation of immorality. Thank God our scientists have devised methods for an efficient system of elimination. They instituted it in Auschwitz."

Valeria drank her champagne and quietly commented, "Difficult but humane: our scientists devised a speedy termination for the race."

After the dinner, returning to their suite, Helmut removed his jacket and sat down on the sofa. He watched Valeria undress and put on her negligee. "How was your family reunion?"

"The surprise of the visit was finding my brother Pranas hiding out with my mother," Valeria said, sitting down next to Helmut.

"I thought you said he was NKVD," Helmut said as he sprang up and lit a cigarette, shocked at the implication of the news.

"He deserted the Red Army in their retreat. He even asked if I could help him."

"Help a communist deserter? Are you out of your mind? We would be charged with treason."

"Pranas said Father was arrested and shot as a communist by the SS. Apparently, as an illiterate, he signed an **X** to join the communists for a job."

"The Nazis obey orders sometimes too efficiently. I am sorry about your father," Helmut whispered and held Valeria as she trembled.

"The biggest tragedy is my missing little sister deported accidentally to Siberia. Anna was playing with a friend when the NKVD stormed the apartment, and she was taken in the sweep."

"Soviet brutality and chaos led to the false arrest of your sister. No wonder the Lithuanians hate them so much," Helmut said, shaking his head.

"My mother, after surviving the shock of losing her son, her little daughter, and her husband, has aged and seems ill. And then to be burdened with a deserter!" Valeria said, crying, "Still, she continues to work for the Eimontas family, apparently caring for a baby."

Later, in bed, Valeria could not sleep, so she turned to Helmut, "He's my brother, no matter what his crimes, and a cross to bear for my mother. Is there nothing we could do?"

"No. And don't speak of helping him in any way. If this criminal story were known, we could be arrested." Valeria accepted Helmut's verdict.

The train from Memel bringing Paulina's son Stefan Kataski and his wife, Monica Foust, chugged through the rain to the Vilnius station. "Monica, take your umbrella and stand here while I transfer our baggage to a taxi." Stefan held Monica by the arm as she hobbled to the car. Stefan had become Monica's caretaker more than her husband. Numerous mysterious health complaints followed her weight gain since he stopped sleeping with her. How could Monica arouse him? Looking at Monica's whale-like body made him limp.

He drew his raincoat closed as the thought of Gretchen produced a physical reaction as strong as when they first had sex without words in the maid's room at Count Doban's party. The virus of lust infected Stefan since their affair began and had continued in secret. They often met when Count Doban traveled to Berlin on Nazi business. Physically, they were a perfect match, and they did not need conversation.

The taxi wound through the ancient streets, passing dozens of architecturally unique churches. Stefan pointed out the sights of his city with pride. Monica's only concern was "Lunch will be ready when we get there, I hope." Reaching the Polish quarter, observing shabby buildings with garbage bins overflowing, she said with a scowl, "You grew up in this slum?"

At their destination, Stefan carried the luggage up the three flights and left them on the landing. He returned to find Monica sitting on the steps. The trip up the steps with Monica heaving and complaining took an eternity. "We can't stay here. We must find rooms on one level. My knees are aching from this torture."

During the ascent, Stefan ignored her only topics of conversation—how hungry she was and her endlessly multiplying ailments. The only variations were her crying jags since she felt deprived of a baby. Any mention of infants, children, toys, or the sight of baby carriages sent her into a paroxysm of tears. She blamed Stefan for her infertility, thinking he was impotent.

Paulina opened the door and embraced Stefan. "My son. I prayed for this moment since the day you left. You are so tall and handsome." She turned to Monica, surprised at her son's choice, but hugged her and said, "Welcome to the family, my daughter. Come, take off your wet coats and sit by the table."

Monica removed her coat and scanned the small space. The kitchen table held only some black bread and farmer's cheese. Paulina sensed Monica's disappointment and said, "This is all I was able to get with my ration cards. Valeria arrived from Berlin yesterday and gave me money to buy food on the black market. I didn't have the time today, but both of you can go shopping for a good dinner."

"Mother, I'll go. Monica has problems walking," Stefan said.

"You're so young. I hope it is nothing serious." Paulina said as Stefan rolled his eyes, shook his head, and looked at his wife with disgust.

The bedroom door opened, and Pranas, scrawny and bearded, peered out. "Stefan, welcome home." He entered the room, and they embraced, notwithstanding Stefan's shock at finding Pranas. "Stefan, I am a deserter hiding, confined to this apartment." He looked at Monica and also embraced her as she smiled for the first time in Vilnius.

Pranas put on the kettle for tea, and they spent the afternoon discussing the circumstances of their lives. Stefan told them about his promotions in Memel, about meeting and marrying Monica, avoiding discussion of what was uppermost on his mind, Gretchen. Pranas reviewed his last three years, avoiding mention of his shame, the rape of Astrid. Paulina, between heaving sobs, described her sorrows and avoided mentioning her secret grandchild.

Monica munched on the bread silently, listening to the conversation. Paulina patted her hand and, glancing at her expanded waistline, so full in the belly, asked with a smile, "Perhaps you will give me my first grandchild?"

A mournful wail came from Monica, "No, I'm not pregnant. My husband is incapable of giving me a child." This unwelcome thought about her infertility screwed up her red face into another burst of crying.

"Come, Monica, we will find a place to stay," Stefan kindly offered.

"I can't make it down those stairs. My knees hurt, and I'm too weak."

Paulina thought quickly. "There's an empty apartment right here. The owners were arrested, but Mrs. Szymanski has the key. I can take some reichsmarks and see if she would let you move in. It is only one floor down and completely furnished."

After Paulina made the arrangements, Monica, leaning on Stefan, descended the stairwell one floor to the apartment. They entered the room, a kitchen with a sofa along the wall. In the adjoining room, a big bed beckoned Monica, who stretched out and fell asleep. Paulina and Stefan went back upstairs to sit with Pranas at the kitchen table. "Your wife is not what I expected," said Paulina.

"She's not what I expected either," Stefan said, thinking of all he found disgusting.

The next day, Stefan spent long hours waiting in line for rationed food. He also scoured the black market where food such as meat, butter, and coffee could be had for an exorbitant price. Valeria's bounty ensured the provisions needed for Monica, who became calm as food tranquilized her emotions.

Stefan, anxious to see his sister, went to the Astoria Hotel. He wanted to confide in her about his marital situation since Valeria knew Monica from their days in Memel. The doorman checked his passport, and his Nazi papers and waved him in. Finding the room, he knocked, and Valeria opened the door in a purple velvet robe. Her appearance amazed Stefan. Once an attractive but plain girl, she was now a raving beauty. He embraced and kissed her. "Where's Monica?" she asked.

"With Mother. You wouldn't recognize her. I'm an unhappy man chained to a miserable woman I don't love. She could not come with me because she has become so obese that walking is painful for her," Stefan said with unaccustomed verbosity.

"So, you have your sorrows. I'm worried about Mother. She has deteriorated with the loss of Jan and Father, but her greatest heartache is little Anna." Valeria clutched her hands until her knuckles were white.

"Did you see Pranas? I was completely shocked to find him with Mother. And he has changed into a bum I could hardly recognize."

"Yes. And now that devil Pranas has invaded her life, making it dangerous for us to even visit her. If someone suspects we met with him, we would be arrested, and Pranas would be shot."

"To put our family in danger. He's crazy!" Stefan walked across to the bar in the room, took out two crystal tumblers, and poured two hefty drinks.

Valeria glanced at her slim, tall, handsome brother and found his description of Monica bizarre. What could have happened to this very placid, uninteresting couple in Memel?

Valeria took one tumbler and, sipping the strong vodka, said, "Pranas asked me to help him escape. Helmut said we couldn't help him under any circumstances. Pranas is an enemy of the Reich. If he were discovered, Mother would be arrested for harboring him. He's one of the vermin that should be eliminated. But I couldn't turn him in."

"I agree—he's our brother," concluded Stefan, downing his drink.

Valeria nodded and said, "Let's go downstairs for lunch and remember our happy days. Wait here while I change."

Valeria went to the bedroom of the suite, closing the door. Stefan heard a knock on the front door and opened it expecting to see the maid. There, in a low-cut tight black dress, stood his desire. "Gretchen!" he said with a dry mouth, inhaling the aroma of her strong Gardenia perfume.

Gretchen looked around and, seeing no one else, whispered, "You told me you would be visiting Vilnius to see your mother. The newspapers wrote that General Obermeyer and your sister are staying at the Astoria. I knew you would also want to see your sister, so I booked a room here and drove from Memel in my new car. I saw you in the lobby and followed you."

Stefan embraced Gretchen and ached with longing. After insinuating her body into Stefan so he had to take a breath to steady himself, he croaked, "Monica is here. She's staying with my mother. Valeria is in the bedroom, changing for lunch."

Gretchen, breathing deeply, said, "You see how we long for each other. This cannot continue. Count Doban is in Berlin at some government meeting. I don't intend to return to him since my marriage is a sham, and I have been writing to my father that he mistreats me. I took money and jewelry and want you to go with me to Dresden, where my family lives and they own a factory. We belong together."

Stefan nodded in consent. He had no words to describe his lust for this woman. Worried about all the complications of Gretchen's request, he only managed to say, "Leave now."

Gretchen exited. "I'll meet you in the restaurant. After lunch, leave the hotel, but after ten minutes, double back and come to my room." Gretchen stood, put a key in his hand, and with a swivel of her hips, was gone.

Returning to the salon after changing into a dark-green dress, Valeria noticed an overwhelming aroma of perfume but did not comment. "Lunch with my handsome brother, what a miracle."

In the crowded restaurant, Gretchen's red hair glimmered as she waved to Valeria and Stefan approaching her table. "Countess, how good to see you," said Valeria with a smile, recognizing the aroma of gardenias. Stefan's reaction to Gretchen explained their relationship.

"Please join me. I'm here alone. The count has business in Berlin, and I came to visit friends." The conversation included the latest gossip from Berlin. The headcheese appetizer and roasted pork made Stefan think of Monica and how she would have devoured this meal. After the apple strudel, Gretchen excused herself and left the table. "I must go lie down in my room to rest. The drive from Memel was tiring."

Alone together, Valeria looked at Stefan and said, "That's your mistress. She came to my room to find you. I know because I could smell her perfume. What are you doing?"

"I don't know what to do," he said, remembering the hours sunk in eternal indecision. "She wants me to leave Monica. She's already left the count. She has a car and wants us to go to Dresden, where her family owns a factory. Gretchen said her father would give me a job there. I want to go with all my heart, but it is the wrong thing." Stefan turned red from the effort at this lengthy dialogue.

"The count is powerful in the party and will be enraged by your actions. He will want revenge. Don't sit there quietly. Answer me!" Valeria's face flushed with anger.

"I don't know. Gretchen is all I live for." Stefan said, hanging his head.

"What will happen with Monica?" Valeria demanded.

"I don't care. I'll send her some money. Let her go back to her parents. I've had enough of her."

Stefan threw down his napkin and, after a farewell to Valeria, left the restaurant. The torment of a life-changing decision ate at his conscience. He had been raised to believe in the sanctity of marriage, so adultery and desertion of his lawful wife would follow him forever.

Was it worth it? He weighed Gretchen and Monica side by side. After a ten-minute walk from the hotel, as if he were a marionette pulled by strings, he turned around and went to Gretchen's room. In their entwined naked bodies, nothing else existed—not mother, not father, not brother, not sister, not husband, not wife, not religion, not career, not the Nazi party.

Stefan never returned to Monica and Paulina. Only Valeria knew he had left for Dresden that day with Gretchen. She never told anyone. Stefan was so quiet and serene, and Valeria had no idea of the passion raging in his heart.

By midnight when Stefan did not return, Monica hauled herself up the stairs and knocked on Paulina's door. Paulina opened the door in her nightgown and, after hearing about Stefan's absence, made Monica some tea. "Do you also have some bacon buns?" asked Monica.

"Of course," answered Paulina, who brought out a dozen she had baked that afternoon. In no time at all, Monica ate all the bacon buns with a desperate hunger Paulina had never observed before. Monica gorged herself to fill a huge insatiable void, to lessen the pain of her life. When she finished the last crumbs, she broke out in loud sobs.

The commotion woke Pranas, who came into the kitchen. Monica told him Stefan left at noon for the Astoria Hotel to see Valeria and had not returned. "He may have decided to stay there. Please call Valeria in the morning. But I can't make it down the stairs. My knees hurt too much."

"Sleep in my bed," said Pranas. "I'll sleep on a blanket on the floor."

"Thank you, Pranas. You are very kind in understanding my pain." She went into the small bathroom area and emerged wrapped in a blanket, holding her clothes. Making sure her body was completely covered, she looked at Pranas and said, "Stefan said I snore, so I hope you can sleep." Tears rolled down her cheeks, and Pranas went back to the kitchen.

When he heard the light sounds of snoring, he went back into the bedroom. As Pranas fixed his makeshift bed, he looked at the sleeping body of Monica, and touched by her misery, he leaned over her and gently stroked her hair.

Monica, feeling his presence, surprised by the compassionate gesture, sobbed, "You are the first man to have touched me tenderly in so long. Thank you."

Pranas, taken aback, asked, "Is that why you are so unhappy with Stefan?"

"Not only does he not touch me, he never talks to me and makes me feel utterly unwanted and alone. I want to die."

Pranas went up to her and kept stroking her hair until she fell asleep.

Arriving at the Eimontas mansion, Paulina asked permission to use their telephone to call the Astoria Hotel. Valeria came to the phone, fearing another plea from her mother to save Pranas. "Stefan left for lunch with you and has not returned. Monica is worried, and I would like to see you."

"Mother, Stefan is not returning. He's been summoned to Germany for war-related work. He told me to say goodbye to Monica, and he'll be in touch with her. I'll come to you but not at your apartment. It would be dangerous for me to be anywhere near Pranas. I'm leaving Vilnius, and I also would like to see you one more time. Where could we meet?"

"I'm at work at the Eimontas residence, so meet me here."

The hotel car drove Valeria to the Eimontas mansion, where Paulina opened the door holding a child. Valeria saw her mother beaming with happiness as the child held her finger. "I hope someday I could see your child," Paulina whispered.

Valeria smiled at the thought of having Helmut's child. Perhaps after the war. "Here, he left this money to take care of Monica." She placed a thick wad of reichsmarks into Paulina's hand.

Paulina put the money on the table and the child back in his crib. "Why didn't he see Monica before leaving? Was the work assignment that much of an emergency? He never even said goodbye to me."

"The war produces many emergencies that take priority over personal matters," said Valeria. "Mother, he told me to say his heart is with you." Then she said with relief, "Helmut and I are going back to Berlin. You need care, Mother. When this war is over, you will come to live with us. I will take care of you and give you the best of everything."

"I know that I am now losing both you and my Stefan again," said Paulina, crying with a breaking heart.

The baby cried, and Paulina said as she picked up the baby, "Look at this perfect child. I wish you would give me a grandchild to love."

Looking at Paulina holding the infant, Valeria said, "It appears that you love this one as your own."

"He is my own. My darling, just take care of yourself."

Valeria turned and said, "Heil Hitler," as she, with tears in her eyes, glided into the black limousine with the swastikas flying and pulled away.

CHAPTER 22
APRIL 1943

Cloudy steel-colored skies hovered over the city, constantly threatening rain until, finally, a severe thunderstorm broke. Vilnius, rudely awakened by German losses on the Russian front, suffered as the Reich squeezed all human effort and goods out of the city. The harsh April sunlight after the storm revealed that the German occupation would never lead to independence and freedom. With permanent German dominion, Lithuania faced a future as a vassal state.

In his office, Vytas read a declaration from Berlin. "The Germans need one hundred thousand skilled Lithuanian workers for jobs in Germany. Also, they require students to devote one year to Germany's Armed Forces to qualify for the university." Vytas shook his head. "This is an outrage! The Germans are losing badly in Russia and need more soldiers. They're making it more palatable by calling it Lithuanian Defense Battalions, hoping to inspire patriotism."

His aide, Simkus, shuffling papers at his desk, said, "Recruitment goals were set at twenty thousand, but only four thousand recruits showed up. Lithuanians don't enlist because it's not under Lithuanian leadership. Our people are patriotic and will fight anyone, but it has to be for Lithuania."

"I agree. Lithuanians are very independent." Vytas nodded.

"Why don't they just conscript the men into service?" Simkus asked, lighting a cigarette as Vytas threw down the report.

"The Germans, unlike the Russians, are very sensitive to legal issues and will not force anyone into their army," Vytas answered with a sarcastic smirk reaching for his pipe.

Katerina, shivering in her light spring coat, entered the hospital, rubbing her hands together. Her face broke into a smile seeing her young friend, Joseph Rudis, filling out a patient's chart. "I've missed you. You were so helpful to tell me of the Soviet danger to my family. I wanted to thank you, but you had disappeared. Come have some hot tea with me," she said, putting her hand on his shoulder as they went to the hospital cafeteria.

Blushing at her touch, Joseph stammered, "I had to leave immediately for our family farm. My mother became very ill, and since my father could not be responsible, I was the only one to care for her."

"How is your mother?" Katerina asked with concern. Having heard that Joseph's father was an alcoholic, she now understood his disappearance.

"She died, and I'm just getting back to my studies. I'm now doing my twenty-four-hour shift. The caseload is brutal. Since orders were given to release Soviet prisoners of war to do farm work, their diseases have spread into the countryside—an epidemic of tuberculosis and venereal disease. By the way," Joseph whispered conspiratorially, "also an astounding number of dog bites."

"Dog bites?" Katerina asked quizzically.

"With the German order banning guns, dogs become the people's only defense. People obtain large aggressive dogs, and the dogs do their duty."

"God bless the hard-working dogs," laughed Katerina.

He whispered to her, "The Germans requisitioned all of our research medical equipment to send to Germany. We have some expensive microscopes that I want to save for our medical students."

Leaving the cafeteria, they went to the pathology laboratory and took six microscopes on a gurney and wheeled it into the anatomy lab. Looking for a good hiding place, they quickly discounted the cabinets and counters. "There is no place that would escape their inspection," concluded Katerina.

"I know a place," Joseph laughed as he took the rubber cover from a formaldehyde-soaked corpse. He took a scalpel and made a long abdominal incision. He removed the organs and squeezed in the microscope. The cavity was not big enough to fully cover the instrument so he placed the intestines on top before covering the body again with the rubber sheet.

"When they come in today to requisition our equipment, we will say the Soviets stole them. I'm sure they will not dig in the stench of the slimy intestines," said Joseph.

Katerina patted him on the back, "You're not only a good physician but a good saboteur." They both hurried to repeat the procedure with five other microscopes.

Later in the week, early one morning, Joseph entered the operating theater and motioned to Katerina as she was finishing a surgery. Stripping off her surgical gloves, she laughingly said, "What now? Are we becoming a team of liberation?"

Joseph melted, looking at Katerina's smiling eyes. "I just heard a news report on the radio. No Lithuanians volunteered to join the SS, and in retaliation, they threatened to close all institutions of higher learning! The Nazis arrested fifty leading intellectuals accused of opposition to Lithuanians joining the SS."

Immediately Katerina lost her smile and said, "When will they learn that our people care only about our country? Vytas told me Latvia and Estonia formed SS units. Our people are more stubborn and would never consider serving under German command." She hurried to discuss the news with Vytas. The loss of their educational institutions would be a horrific blow to the country. She also wanted to know the names of the Lithuanians opposed to having their countrymen join the SS.

Easter, the holiest religious feast in Lithuania, began with a sunrise Mass of Resurrection followed by a celebratory breakfast with brilliantly colored Easter eggs. Paulina drew fine wax patterns of a variety of snowflakes on the eggs before coloring them with the juice of onion skins, beets, or other dyes. The Eimontas family sat at the table and said a prayer.

"An Egg War, an Eimontas family tradition. I will win this year," said Vytas, selecting a brilliant red egg and holding it with the tapered end exposed.

"You always say that, but you always lose," said Katerina. Picking a yellow egg and grasping it firmly, she swooped down to hit Vytas's egg, which cracked. "See? I win."

Vytas then switched to the unbroken end to continue the fight. "Your attack is too ferocious!" laughed Vytas as each family member chose an egg and hit a competitor's egg. At the end, only Antanas's egg remained unbroken.

"Antanas, you win! You are always lucky in everything," said Vytas. Everyone at the table nodded in agreement, knowing if there would be a winner, it would be Antanas.

Only Dalia did not smile. "Antanas has stolen all the luck from the rest of us. Why is life so unfair?" Everyone continued to eat in silence.

In the afternoon, a table of cold foods, including ham, salads, and a variety of tortes, provided a bountiful buffet. Custom dictated alternating years of being a host or a guest for this occasion. This year, the Eimontas family would be hosting the Easter feast for all their friends during an open house.

One of the guests was Colonel Rotheimer of the SS, a bald, rotund man with a pince-nez he kept adjusting. After a glass of champagne, he thanked Vytas, "With all the hardship of war, you still managed to find a pig for your succulent ham."

"Yes, ham is a rare treat these days, but your kindness left us our country estate, and a lone pig managed to escape the requisition," Vytas quipped.

"Tell me," Rotheimer said, "how can we get your countrymen to join our fight against Bolshevism? The Reich is in serious need of your help."

Vytas, shocked at this admission of vulnerability, answered, "Colonel, the tactical plan to call for the recruitment of Lithuanian self-defense units was wise since only patriotism to this country will yield volunteers. But you would do even better to change the wording of their oath. It now states allegiance to Hitler—it should state allegiance to Lithuania."

"Interesting, interesting," mumbled the colonel as he filled his plate with another serving of ham. "I'm glad to have your input."

After eating, Colonel Rotheimer followed Antanas into the library. Sipping a glass of cognac, the colonel said, "I sent a letter to the mayor with a requisition for ten trucks to go to Paneris to pick up the clothing of executed Jews and transport the goods to the Vilnius train station. We need to transport the clothing to Germany to be reworked into uniforms for our soldiers. I have not had a reply."

"Do you mean our official city of Vilnius trucks?" asked Antanas as the colonel nodded yes. "The trucks are no longer under the city's control. When the German army occupied Vilnius, all official means of transportation were confiscated. We were left with only a few horse wagons to take coal to the electrical station."

"Well, use the horse wagons for transporting the clothing," said Rotheimer.

"But Colonel, if we use the wagons for clothing, we cannot get coal for electricity, which is vital to the hospital for treating German soldiers."

"Well, you're right. Our most important duty is the care and welfare of our soldiers. We will have to find another way to transport the clothing."

After all the guests left, Antanas repeated his conversation with the colonel to Vytas, "My argument persuaded the colonel, and he no longer raised the question. In no way did I want the official Lithuanian administration to be involved with the extermination of the Jews."

"You did well, my son. The outcome of this war is now uncertain, and we must remember that our only goal is Lithuanian independence."

Rachel, the big yellow star affixed to her gray clothing, scrubbed the pavement for the next twelve hours in back-breaking labor. While on her knees in the cold April drizzle, she was subjected to the humiliation of insults, spit, and kicks. The liquidation of the ghetto residents played in her mind, but memories of the previous summer with Antanas sustained her.

Antanas must not have any idea of her punishment, or he would have objected. She must see Antanas to report what had been done to her, remind him of his love for her, and ask him to save her. The sheer terror of the death camps overcame her pride.

Sarah heard Rachel's plan to go to Antanas and vehemently opposed it, "Don't beg him for help. Don't prostitute yourself for his pleasure. He doesn't love you. He is using you." Her protestations grew louder and more desperate as Rachel pursued her strategy of proving herself to be beautiful, desirable, and irresistible.

Rachel washed her long black mane with a little precious oil and then brushed and ironed it for a smooth and shiny coiffeur. The homemade cosmetics of beet juice on her lips and cheeks gave her color, and the soot of burnt matches mixed with water darkened her long lashes. She scrubbed her teeth with salt and ate parsley for sweet breath; fresh lilac buds stuffed between her breasts provided the perfume of spring. Her mother's polished high-heeled shoes, although too small, flattered her legs. She put on her red dress, pleased, as her last inspection in a mirror reflected hope.

Sarah watched Rachel's preparations and no longer had the heart to object. In the evening, Rachel left their apartment and walked to the border of the ghetto. To leave without permission was punishable by death. She waited in a doorway next to the guardhouse until she saw a vegetable vendor leave. She jumped into the truck while the driver was in the guardhouse and hid in a dark corner of the truck behind some crates of cabbage. The truck was hardly inspected before it was waved on. At the first stop, Rachel jumped out.

She walked to the Eimontas city mansion, following a small map she had drawn. After a mile, the acute pain from her too-tight high heels made her grimace in pain. A torrential rainstorm started, and she stepped into a puddle, lost her footing, and fell. Her soaked shoes lost a heel, so she removed her shoes and ran barefoot in her muddied dress to the street with many mansions.

Locating the house, she knocked on the back door. The door was locked, and no one answered. The cold downpour added to the hopelessness of her quest. Through the trees, she saw a light flickering in one of the windows. Was this Antanas's room? In desperation, she had nothing to lose, so she picked up a small rock and threw it at the window.

After an eternity of waiting, a middle-aged woman opened the back door. "Who are you?"

"I must see Mr. Antanas Eimontas. It's a matter of life or death."

"I'm his Aunt Dalia, and I will call him, but only in the name of Christian charity. Step inside and wait, please."

Moments later, Antanas appeared with a stricken look. "Rachel, what are you doing here? Come to my apartment." He turned to Dalia and said, "This is an employee with a problem."

Antanas, writing a letter to his current paramour, was irritated at this intrusion from his past.

Entering Antanas's dark-paneled room with a strong aroma of tobacco and 4711 cologne, Rachel felt like an intruder into a stranger's life. Antanas, handsome in a silk dressing gown, took a thick white towel from the bathroom and dried her hair and face. Her naked, dirty feet on his Persian carpet emphasized the incongruity of their status. Her careful coiffure had disintegrated into a mass of frizzy black hair, and her cheeks lost their blush. Antanas took her hand and winced at the ragged nails and grating calluses. She reeked of desperation.

Wet, bedraggled, and crushed—this was not how Rachel wanted to approach him. The scenario of seduction and triumph practiced before the mirror at home metamorphosed into a play of abject supplication.

"You loved me once, did you not?" she asked as she sat down on his sofa. He sat down beside her, holding the red-beet-juice-stained towel.

Observing him, she followed the outlines of his body, his perfect, elegant fingers, the mouth and ears. She studied his expressionless face and melted with shame at his absolute silence. Her heart was beating loudly, and tears formed in her eyes as she remembered their passionate lovemaking.

"What did you come for?" Antanas asked as he stood up.

"You must not be aware that after my arrest, I was sentenced to clean the streets. You would not have allowed such treatment of a woman you love."

"Rachel, be glad you were not sent to a concentration camp. It was the most I could do for you."

Rachel fell to her knees as if hit by a cudgel. "I love you. Please. We need to be together always. Please marry me and save me from my torture now and save my life. I know you love me. I feel it in your whole body." She clasped his legs in her arms and slowly reached up his thighs.

He pulled away. "Rachel, my appetite for you will always exist, but you're talking nonsense. Our connection is only of sex. Think, Rachel, what future could there ever be for us? You are a Jewess."

"You helped my mother, my brother and me. We're all Jews."

"I do what I can out of decency toward my fellow human beings."

"Decency! Is that what you call our affair? An act of charity?" Rachel started to cry. "Don't you realize if you don't help me, I am doomed?"

"We could never have a serious relationship. My future requires a suitable wife of my own race one day. It must be a woman with whom I could have children and perpetuate my family. Rachel, this could never be you. Return to the ghetto before they find you are missing."

Antanas led Rachel to the door and said, "Goodbye, Rachel. I wish you all the best." He shook his head at Rachel's unbelievable impudence in thinking he would marry her: she was delusional.

The knife of rejection cut Rachel and opened her eyes to the cruelty of reality. With no other choice, she limped on her broken shoes back to the ghetto. She had nowhere else to go.

She waited, shivering in the dark street, observing the guards at the gate. If the guards stepped away, it would be her opportunity to sneak back in. The guards rotated so that one was always at the gate, and there were no breaks in surveillance.

After several hours, wet, cold, and abandoned, her future evolved crystal clear from the fog of her emotions. He had never loved her. He only wanted to use her; her mother had warned her. She was a marked woman, a Jew, and after her energy would be drained cleaning the streets, she would be sent to a concentration camp. From there, no one left. The path was so evident. Why even undergo the torture of street cleaning. She gave up and approached the gate. Her life was over in one way or another. Before she could elaborate her contrived excuse, the guard checked her identity papers, compared them to his log, and arrested her.

The hospital corridors were overflowing with casualties. Katerina found it impossible to keep up with the heavy influx of cases requiring her immediate attention. The soldiers appeared younger and younger, almost children, and many wounds had progressed to fatal conditions because of the difficulty of transport from the front.

"Nurse, help me with this injection! This delirious patient is fighting me," Katerina said, holding a syringe as she wrestled with a white-faced man.

"Doctor, you are being paged in Ward Five. There is a patient in room 505 who is asking for you," the nurse reported as Katerina finished the injection.

Entering the room, she stood amazed, "Jonas. My god, is it you?" Jonas, much thinner, with a beard and long hair, lay in the hospital bed.

"I did not get shot to stage a romantic meeting," Jonas joked.

"What happened? Can you ever find a way to stay out of danger?" Katerina smoothed his pillow and sat in a chair by his side. Her heart was beating loudly, and she felt the hot arrival of a blush in her cheeks.

"I enlisted in the self-defense unit and went after the communist partisans. There are thousands of them—snipers, saboteurs, and guerrillas all waging warfare. Some of their actions are understandable, such as trying to shoot the guards at the ghettos. But others are terrorists murdering German soldiers walking down the street or Lithuanian policemen."

"Where are these communist partisans from?" asked Katerina, puzzled.

"Many are escapees from camps or prisons. Some have found their way back from Siberian exile."

"If they are from the camps, where do they get their weapons?"

"They take them from the bodies of their victims, and Soviet airdrops them with equipment. I have seen one such crate dropped from the sky and was lucky enough to confiscate it. What a treasure trove for us!"

"Vytas told me about the guerrilla warfare by the Soviets operating in Lithuania, but we thought these were Red Army soldiers left behind in the retreat," Katerina said, standing up.

"The Jews join them sometimes, although our prisoners say that the Jews themselves are victims of Russian anti-Semitism."

"Will this nightmare never end? I wish for total German victory so that life can return to normal again." She looked at Jonas with tears in her eyes.

"Your hopes rest on thin ice. We have reports that the Germans are retreating in Russia but are planning a major offensive this year. If the Nazis lose and the Soviets win, life in Lithuania will again be under communism."

"What hope is there for us?" mused Katerina, looking out the window at the gray sky and steady rain.

"We are still appealing for the Western Powers to come and save us."

"Vytas knows Lithuanians are desperately trying to get help. He says it is a hopeless cause because America is willing to sacrifice our country in favor of their ally, the USSR."

"How is your husband?" asked Jonas in a low, choking voice.

"He is always prepared to flee. I am trying to get him out of the country before it is too late."

"It's too late for my poor wife, Lina. She was in a sanatorium in Germany when the Nazis took it over. They claimed to be treating insane patients, but Nazi racial policy demands the extermination of the insane. So I can surmise her end. The letter informing me of her death was almost a relief after twenty years."

Katerina stood up, walked over to his bed, and kissed him on the forehead, thinking, *Now he is free when it is too late. Timing is everything.*

She pulled down his sheet to reveal a blood-soaked bandage, "So how did this happen?"

"A farmer in Alytus reported hearing sniper shots and left his farmhouse to investigate. He encountered a band of ragged men who demanded food. He gave what he could, but they robbed him of everything and beat him senseless. The farmer's report to German authorities sent the three of us to investigate. In the dense forest next to the farm, we uncovered a tent where we found only some cowering women and children."

"Escaped Jews," concluded Katerina.

"My fellow soldier, Kestys, reached for his pistol and started to shoot at one of the women, yelling, 'This is for you Jewish communists for taking my whole family to Siberia.' I grabbed his gun, shouting that women and children are not at war. In the struggle, his gun went off, and he shot me."

"What happened to them?"

"The women grabbed the children and ran off into the forest. Kestys wanted to follow them, but I told him to wait since the men would be returning, and then he could shoot the real culprits."

"The tragedy of war is the involvement of non-combatants," Katerina said with deep sadness. "What happened then?"

"We hid in the forest until we saw the men returning. There were four of them, and three were armed. We ambushed the men and killed them all."

"And you did all this with a bullet wound in your shoulder."

"The adrenaline of warfare acts as an anesthetic."

"War acts as an anesthetic to our Christianity and our morals," Katerina said. A force stronger than her rational mind made her bend down and kiss Jonas on the cheek. The look in his eyes chained her and brought her back to her unvarnished love for him.

At work, Mayor Heinz remarked, "I know the German losses are demoralizing for all of us, but don't worry, Hitler is brilliant. He has never lost and is planning a major offensive as we speak."

"I believe in our ultimate victory," said Antanas between sips of tea. "What is to be the disposition of the ghettos? After the war, the city can't maintain all these unemployed parasites."

Heinz lit another cigarette. "Eimontas, by the end of this year, all our Jewish concerns will be gone. We intend to liquidate the entire Vilnius ghetto. The women and children will be sent to the Kaiserwald concentration camp in Riga and the men to the Sobibor camp in Poland. There they will be exterminated by gas, the most efficient means."

"Gas, not shooting as before?" asked an incredulous Antanas.

"Shooting is another method, but it uses up ammunition needed for our war efforts," explained Heinz, rubbing his eyes.

Antanas could not believe the scope of this project. "You mean the killing of one hundred thousand Jews, men, women, and children?"

"That's the only way that we can ensure the success of the Third Reich and fulfill our destiny as a race of supermen. Our aims supersede any sentimental considerations." Heinz hit the table with emphasis.

Returning home, Antanas confronted his father, "We must make plans to leave. They are inveigling us into mass murder. Killing on this scale will taint our whole nation."

Vytas listened with alarm and then said, "Nazi propaganda is laying the blame for the Jewish question on Lithuania. Any opposition and we will be wiped out as readily as the Jews. I've been considering escaping abroad to get help."

"Father, please start to make plans to leave. After an interval, I will follow."

Chapter 23
February 1944

itter cold and icy gale-force winds stung Vytas's face as he rushed home through the deserted Vilnius streets. Frozen oil incapacitated his official car, and he did not wait for his chauffeur to change the oil. Streetlights formed hazy yellow shadows in the early afternoon darkness. Frost-covered windows revealed outlines of Vilnius's inhabitants huddled before space heaters or fireplaces, listening to news of war on their radios.

Vytas confronted Katerina with a blast of Arctic air as he entered the front door. "Katerina, the time has come," he said as he pulled a crumpled paper from his pocket. "This cable confirms the retreat of the Germans and the Red Army's approach to the edge of the Baltics. Soon we will be under USSR occupation again."

Katerina took the frozen piece of paper while Paulina helped him remove his snow-covered coat and fur hat. Hands trembling, Katerina said, "It's over. You must leave immediately. Your name would be first on their execution list. Leave tonight before panic sets in. Your driver can take you to the German border. With your diplomatic status, you could say you were called to a high-level meeting in Berlin."

Vytas wrung his cold, red hands, pondering, "Networks of Lithuanians live in Berlin, and they would help me. What about you? Adam? Astrid? I met Antanas at lunch, and he knows. He gave me the same advice—leave immediately."

"What will Antanas do?"

"He told me not to worry. He said for both Eimontas men to leave would cause suspicion. He would find a way to take care of the rest of the family."

Paulina, overhearing this conversation, realized Baby Adam, her grandchild, would be taken from her care. "Doctor Katerina, I can keep Adam safe," she said.

"Thank you, but now the greatest danger is to Vytas."

Astrid, pale and thin, in a black georgette dress, joined them for dinner, where she learned of their situation. "What do you mean Father is leaving?" she said, her voice rising. "Can't I go with him? I couldn't live through the terror of another Soviet occupation. I would rather kill myself."

Vytas took his daughter's cold hand. "As soon as I find a safe harbor in Germany, I will send for you, your mother, and Adam. Dalia's situation is dire since she's too fragile to endure the hardships of refugee life. Perhaps I can find a good sanatorium that will take her, and she can join us after the war."

"I won't wait for the torturers and rapists to return. Never mind. I'll find a way to get out by myself," Astrid said as she threw down her napkin and left the table. The company continued their dinner in silence.

Turning down the quilt in their bedroom that night, Katerina looked over at Vytas, sitting at his desk, his face lined with concern, chewing on his pipe, studying maps. "Darling, we've been together for so many years. My heart no longer pulses blood but pain at the fear of a permanent separation. Even through the agony I suffered when you were in prison, I knew you would return." She erupted in a spasm of sobs.

"Don't cry, my dear. We've lived through so much, and we'll survive this also." Vytas took her in his arms as he brushed away her tears. "I must pack all my documents," he said, releasing her.

"If the Soviets return, there will be no mercy for us," Katerina said.

"As soon as I'm able, I'll send for you and the family. I still have friends and influence abroad, but all is lost if I stay and get arrested."

At five the next morning, an official car with a Swastika flag flapping in the bitter wind pulled up to the door of the Eimontas mansion. Katerina said farewell and blessed Vytas with the sign of the cross. She was so distraught she did not see Dalia at her side. Vytas, on the way to the car, stopped and turned, hearing his name. The headlights revealed a figure in a fur coat over a nightgown running toward him in bare feet. Dalia threw her arms around Vytas and said, "I couldn't sleep and saw the car waiting outside. I know there is danger, and you are leaving. Brother, I know I will never see you again," she said, clutching him in desperation until Katerina pried her away and took her inside.

Hiding in a farmhouse in the Alytus region, Jonas Saulis planned guerrilla defense against the coming Soviet invasion. His compatriots surrounded him, talking in whispers, concocting violent partisan reprisals. Jonas sat on a horsehair sofa in front of a rough-hewn table covered by a multitude of maps. More maps were posted on the walls. The maps, defaced with a multitude of arrows, the remains of a meal of bread and sausage, and the roaring fire, presented what looked like a parlor game devoid of danger.

"The front seems far away. Are you sure the Soviets are coming?" asked an engineering student who had joined his group of partisans, "The Soviets are inferior to the Nazis as soldiers."

Saulis studied the boy for a moment and said, "They may be inferior soldiers, but they number in the millions. Also, the Nazis are invaders into foreign territory bent only on conquest. Since defense of their homeland gives a psychological edge in war, the Red Army will fight harder."

"God forbid if the Soviets occupy Lithuania once again. My whole family was deported to Siberia, and I never heard from them," the student said.

"What was their crime?" Saulis asked with a smirk of irony.

"My family worked hard and owned a prosperous dairy farm. One night they were rounded up, and all the cows were killed for food. I escaped only because I was in school."

"We must do all we can to save Lithuania. Tomorrow I'm meeting with a government official to discuss how our partisans can deliver the most help." Jonas outlined his plans filled with statistics of armaments, soldiers, and tactics for guerrilla defense. His thoroughness and brilliance gave confidence to his compatriots. Jonas, however, ended on a note of caution: "Of course, all this is a drop of water in the oncoming flood of Soviets. Our biggest strength is our love of country."

The next day, in a warehouse in Vilnius, Jonas and his partisans attended a secret meeting with a representative of Lithuania's government, Antanas Eimontas, who outlined the situation: "The Germans asked us for fifteen thousand soldiers to help fight the Soviets, and only four thousand signed up. Now with an imminent Soviet attack on Lithuania, thirty thousand volunteers signed up. The proviso is they would fight only on Lithuanian soil and only under our own commanders." The news of this massive response to the Soviet threat elicited shouts of "Hurrah!"

"I understand a leading partisan is here at this meeting," continued Antanas. "Jonas Saulis, would you make yourself known?" Jonas stood. Antanas had never met Jonas but remembered his mother's admiration for this man who helped them in Prienai. Antanas asked, "Would you be willing to join us and take the command of our new army? I've heard great things about your leadership abilities and your courage."

Jonas looked down as he said, "I'm honored to be asked. However, I must refuse to lead the Lithuanian Army. In my opinion, even thirty thousand soldiers will not save our country. If the Nazis are defeated, they will retreat to Germany. They will not stay in Lithuania to fight the Soviets, and we will be left on our own. Thirty thousand Lithuanians against the Soviet Army? FUF!" he said, stamping his foot. "Suicidal! Ridiculous!"

"So you will not fight for Lithuania?"

"The best way to thwart Soviet occupation is to engage in guerrilla warfare. By doing nothing, we would be accepting our fate. But our forceful resistance would be a constant reminder to the Western Powers that we are under illegal occupation. Only international recognition of the Soviet crime can save us. We must hope the United States will force the Russians to respect our independence." Disappointed by Saulis's refusal to lead Lithuanian Forces, Antanas, however, understood his logic.

Astrid found herself in a descending spiral of deep depression. She fell into a void of nothingness that occupied the dark corners of her soul. Dana, Astrid's lifelong friend, asked her, "What will you do if the Soviets enter Vilnius?"

Without hesitation, Astrid said, "Kill myself." Thoughts of suicide became a reality. She wanted to be prepared to take her life at her own discretion.

A locked drug cabinet in her mother's office contained drugs with fatal effects taken at high doses. She wanted barbiturates, the gateway to eternal sleep. In her mother's room, she found the extra key. She put on her medical student's uniform and identification tag and set out for the hospital, intending to take enough pills to end her life. She went in the office door, unlocked the cabinet, and took two bottles of barbiturates.

Returning home, Astrid inhaled the aroma of lemon furniture polish emanating from the shiny center table in their foyer. On the table, she picked up a letter in Cyrillic script addressed to her.

Astrid saw Paulina in the next room on her knees, polishing the floors. "Paulina, there is no need for you to do this. Our life is over. Who cares if we die with floors dirty or clean?"

"Dear Miss Eimontas, I have not survived my sorrows by stopping work no matter what the circumstances. It's important to continue as best we can. And if we are killed, it's truly better on a clean and shiny floor."

Astrid broke out into her first smile in a long while and went to help Paulina stand up and said, "Let's have some tea." They enjoyed their conversation about Adam's exploits. When Paulina returned to her chores, Astrid tore the letter open:

My darling Astrid,
I have survived Stalingrad. There is no hell that can be described to equal our sorrows in that battle. Our troops should reach you soon. Our many victorious attacks and the rapid retreat of the Nazi army bring me closer every day. I long to be with you and my child. We will have a wonderful life.

Georgi

Astrid tore the letter in half and threw it in the garbage bin. That man could never redeem himself. But the information of Soviets advancing and thoughts of further torture made her tremble. The scenes in Prienai were still the substance of her nightmares. She must execute her plan before the enemy arrived.

A few days after Vytas left, Katerina, against her better judgment, called Jonas and asked him to come to her office. Her need for seeing the man was answered only with pure instinct, leading to a meeting charged with emotion. She told him of Vytas's patriotic defection to get help. They engaged in a long conversation about the war. However, all these conversations were surface bubbles of a deep inner turmoil felt by both.

"Will the Soviets win?" Katerina asked, thinking, *Will you be mine?*

"The side with the most passion will prevail," answered Jonas with a sly smile.

"Will it be safer to stay or flee?" Katerina asked, although she meant yes or no.

"The difference exists only in your mind."

"Does the face of war change the rules?" Katerina wanted to know.

"Judgment is always external," Jonas answered.

A pretense of higher motives and fear of the future did not disguise their main interest, which was in each other.

Jonas, after some time, bowed his head and said goodbye. He was afraid to shake her hand, afraid of any physical contact that would betray his desire to envelop her in his love. He had no right to love her.

Katerina loved both men. Vytas provided the cocoon of safety, love of home, family, familiarity, and comfort. She saw herself reflected in his eyes as her ideal self—a virtuous, beautiful woman to be protected and cherished. On the other hand, with Jonas, she perceived herself as his equal—a capable woman. Jonas fired her spirit, inflamed her desire, and inspired ideals of patriotism and freedom. The duality of her emotions tortured her moral sense. God's law was one or the other, not both. How could she pray for guidance when either choice would leave her wanting?

After many harrowing close calls, Vytas arrived in Berlin and went to the Under der Linden apartment of Algis Lanskis, a life-long Lithuanian friend. The diminutive gray-haired man led him into a wood-paneled study. Algis's tall blonde German wife brought them tea and sandwiches. "Vytas, my god, you escaped! You will be charged with treason. How could you leave your country? Did matters become too difficult for you?"

"This is not a temporary setback. We are closer and closer to the front, and I tell you, Germany is losing."

"Impossible. Hitler is a genius at warfare," Algis said with a wave of dismissal.

"I've grave doubts about the Thousand-Year Reich. The Soviets have reached the borders of the Baltic states," Vytas said, rising and walking to the window where he observed the lights of Berlin.

"What about your family?" asked Algis.

"As soon as I get settled, they will join me," answered Vytas, but his voice lacked conviction. "I sent a coded message to my wife that I am with you."

"When your abdication is discovered, the Germans will never release your family," Algis said. "You must forget about your family, and I will help you get to Austria with a false passport. Stay with a farmer I know in the outskirts of Vienna, and we will smuggle you into France."

"What will I do in France? The Nazis have a tally of every citizen."

"Dye your hair black, and we will provide you with a Jewish passport. There are a few sympathetic Frenchmen who will hide you. We've taken this route with a few Lithuanians successfully."

"What will become of my family?" Vytas asked.

"The war cannot last forever. You'll be reunited," said Lanskis's wife. Seeing the blanched face of Vytas, she gave them glasses of cognac.

News of the Eimontas defection swirled around Vilnius. A coded message to Katerina from Vytas in Berlin with Algis stated he could not return. Her perceived abandonment increased her dependency on Jonas, and she felt the social ostracism of an unfaithful wife. Between her time at the hospital and her emotional turmoil, Adam's existence imposed little on her life. Paulina cared for the child day and night.

"My love, my little Adam." Paulina's heart beat with joy as she held the smiling toddler. With Astrid at school and Katerina at the hospital, Paulina wanted to show her pride, Adam, to Monica. She dressed the child in a rabbit coat and hat, covered him with blankets, put him in a sled, and walked through the snow-covered streets to the Polish district.

Entering her apartment, Paulina proudly announced, "Here is Adam. There is no love like the love of a two-year-old child."

Paulina smiled as Monica's spirits rose, and while cooing, she hugged Adam, devised a game of hide-and-seek, and sang to him. She recited her favorite bedtime stories until, with tear-filled eyes, she released the sleepy toddler to go home.

Seeing the happiness Adam brought Monica and being tired of Monica's lethargy and moping, Paulina proposed a solution, "I could ask Doctor Katerina if you might be able to come help care for Adam."

"I would do anything to be near that little boy. I love children so much," Monica said. From Paulina's descriptions of Adam's care, Monica believed Paulina bore the sole responsibility for mothering. She thought of herself as a better mother to the child than busy Doctor Katerina or old Paulina. She despised Stefan for his desertion and even more so for leaving her childless.

While serving breakfast in the Eimontas mansion, Paulina broached the subject, "Doctor Katerina, I'm getting too old to care for the house and the child. Adam is mobile, and I'm not able to run after him. My son's wife is staying with me. She's from a good family in Memel. Could she help me with Adam? She could care for him in my apartment during the day while I work here." Since Monica still had some difficulty walking, it seemed a reasonable solution.

"Of course, Paulina," answered Katerina in a distracted manner.

Monica became the surrogate mother of Adam and came to love the child as her own. A letter from Stefan in Dresden asking for a divorce stamped her marriage as a failure. If only Stefan could have made love to her, Adam could have been her child. She could not understand how such a big, healthy, handsome man could not make her pregnant. He avoided her physically. She remembered her few futile attempts at seduction with lacy lingerie and perfume with shame.

Only the child's love negated her misery. Adam should be hers.

In the midst of the hurricane of war, Pranas occupied the dead center, the eye of the storm. He had put his faith in communism, but the Eimontas still lived in their mansion, and his mother still washed their floors. He was useless: a dirty, poverty-stricken bum dependent on his poor mother. Pranas, depressed and bored, focused on Monica. The happiness of caring for Adam gave Monica purpose, transforming her into a more attractive woman. She treated Pranas with kindness, remembering the affection he showed her at the nadir of her despair. She cooked his meals, did his laundry, and cleaned his room.

One day, with Adam napping on the sofa, as she served him lunch, he stroked her thigh and whispered, "I'm sorry, but you're all I think about day and night."

Monica trembled at his touch. "What do you mean? I must take Adam home." She stood up and left. Confusion reigned during her walk, but her heart sang.

Returning, she was alone with Pranas, who took her in his arms, kissed her, and moved his hands over her breasts. She moaned spontaneously. This signaled consent, and he removed her dress. In her delight, she forgot her insecurities about her bloated, shapeless body and welcomed his advances by running her hands over his head and chest. In the throes of passion, she experienced sexual desire and fulfillment.

She wanted to be loved by a man, even a scrawny one with bad breath. "I want you" melted any resistance. "You are beautiful" sounded warm and loving. His rough, hungry approach thrilled her compared to the perfunctory, infrequent sex with Stefan. She surrendered on the small lumpy bed with abandon.

After the initial encounter, their fervor took on some aspects of love. The miasma of sex changed their perceptions. He was no longer so useless and scrawny, and she was no longer so ugly and bloated. They put on the positive qualities of the beloved. Finally, she had a man and a child.

The Eimontas mansion, without Vytas, lost the essence of home, and with no further word from him, Katerina's fear of losing Vytas increased. Many who left for Germany were never heard from again. Jonas and his partisan cause also reeked of danger. For so long, she was tortured by thoughts of which man to choose, and the irony of the possibility of losing both preyed on her thoughts as divine retribution.

Antanas often joined Astrid for a meal, but her lack of appetite, the depressing silence, and conversation limited to the approach of the Soviets gave him no pleasure. His concern for Astrid reached a crisis when one night after dinner, lighting a cigarette, she said, "What do you think of suicide? Is it not the best option sometimes?"

Antanas, expecting to voice his concern at her new habit of smoking, however, was more startled by her conversation and said, "Self-destructive behavior is never a good trajectory, Astrid. What would killing yourself solve? You're a young, beautiful woman. Many men would worship you. Life has been harsh to you, but you must overcome your grief. If you have yet to find happiness, wait—it might be just around the corner." Antanas surprised himself by offering these platitudes.

Astrid viewed him through narrowed eyes. "You've never suffered. You've lived your life in a golden bubble. Your good looks, brains, and charm have given you the best of life. You click your fingers, and women offer their love. You wave a hand, and the best positions in any regime open to you. You were born under a lucky star. I, however, have been cursed."

Astrid started crying, smoothing her black wool skirt oblivious of the ashes falling from her cigarette, and screamed, "What would you know of my reality? You've never been raped or suffered the pain of rejection. You've never given birth to an unwanted child. Now the Soviets are coming back. They will murder and rape. I would rather die than subject myself to humiliation and torture again."

"When they come, we'll escape. We'll go to Germany. I promise to take care of you. You're my sister, and I love you."

"Life as an exile with no means to make a living in a strange land— that's not what I was born for. A life of suffering is a life not worth living," Astrid said as she lit another cigarette.

"Do what I do, Astrid. Find pleasure every day in anything you can because the big picture always ends badly for everyone."

Astrid smirked. "For you, life will always bring pleasure. Only for me does the big picture include horrific pain before it ends badly."

Chain-smoking and pacing the floor, Mayor Heinz read the reports of Soviet victories and called Antanas into his office. "Eimontas, you speak French. A requisition came for an experienced administrator in France to supervise food supplies for the German Army. We need someone trustworthy who speaks French. I wanted the post but was denied because I could not be seen as fleeing the approaching front."

The mayor picked up a piece of paper and continued, "You, Eimontas, would be an ideal candidate, but the problem with you is the abdication of your father. Help us capture him, and the position in France will be yours."

Antanas shuffled his feet and said, "Mayor Heinz, truly, I don't know where he is at present. He believed his position in Lithuania to be untenable. He was powerless to save our country."

"So he defected to save the country from Germany? He is a traitor!" said Heinz as he hit his desk with his fist.

"He did not fear Germany. Rumors of the Red Army approaching caused him to flee."

"Then you should condemn your father as a coward. Doesn't he believe in Hitler's invincibility?" shouted Heinz. "When you tell me where he has been hiding, you can pick up your transfer papers," Heinz said as he dismissed Antanas.

Coming home, Antanas wanted to share the news of Heinz's proposal as the thought of going to France was enticing. Perhaps he could get the whole family out of this hell. However, he could not conceive of any circumstance where he would betray his father.

He sprinted upstairs to Astrid's bedroom, where he found her asleep. Even after he stroked her shoulder and then shook her, she would not wake. He saw a bottle of pills by her side. "Astrid, wake up!" he screamed, shaking her with no response. "Paulina, call Dr. Katerina. There's an emergency."

Katerina immediately arrived from the hospital and examined the half-empty pharmacy bottle. "My god! She was not play-acting. She must have taken these barbiturates from my office." Katerina gave her an emetic to cause vomiting as Paulina prayed loudly. After tense minutes, the treatment worked. Astrid vomited and regained consciousness. Antanas and Katerina exhaled in relief. They took Astrid between them and forced her to walk around the room, stopping to make her drink strong coffee.

Leaving Astrid in Paulina's care to be bathed, dressed in a clean nightgown, and given more coffee, Katerina and Antanas went to the drawing room. Katerina broke down sobbing at her child's despair. Antanas stood by her side, rubbing her shoulders and comforting her.

"This is worse than I thought," said Katerina. "She's serious about ending her life. The possible Soviet approach has placed her in a state of extreme anxiety. We must help her escape."

"Mother, I may have a solution. Mayor Heinz told me of a position in France to help the German occupying army by supervising food shipments. He said I could be a candidate because of my ability to deal with German and French. The price of getting the transfer papers is for me to tell them Father's whereabouts. If the Nazis find Father, they will arrest and kill him since the regime considers a prominent leader defecting equivalent to treason. How could I possibly betray my own father?"

Antanas brushed away his rare tears at the thought of being in a position to harm his father but quickly realized he could not do so since he did not know his whereabouts. Perhaps he could manufacture some story.

Seeing the despair in Katerina's eyes, he continued, "I could take Astrid. I could take all of you to France. But all this is conjecture since I don't know where he is."

Katerina, a patriot loving her husband, became a traitor for the sake of her daughter. Shivering with anxiety, she said, "Antanas, although I swore not to tell anyone, I know Vytas is with Algis Lanskis in Berlin."

"We could give Heinz the information and at the same time warn Father," Antanas said confidently, although the plan was elusive.

"If you reveal that your father is with Algis Lanskis in Berlin, I don't see how we could warn him beforehand," doubted Katerina. "It would be a dangerous and risky business, and it could lead to the murder of your father. Antanas, could you live with that on your conscience?"

"Mother, if only negative consequences are considered in any decision, we would be paralyzed by fear. You forget the hope of success."

"I can see your optimistic version of the outcome since, in your life, luck is always on your side. Perhaps I am too gloomy, and the main thing is that you and Astrid must be saved."

Especially at risk was Astrid, who would not survive another bout with the Soviets. Looking at her beautiful daughter, who had tried to kill herself, Katerina had a rush of acute love for her and confronted her dilemma. Was she sacrificing the life of her husband to save her children?

CHAPTER 24
MAY 1944

Vilnius waited for resolution in the panorama of history. The German occupation had left the ancient city intact, although stripped of most of its goods and services and some of its citizenry. The terror of annihilation surfaced as Soviet forces thundered nearer. In the whirlwind of panic, discussions of means of escape became urgent. Plans for evacuation and the ensuing turmoil occupied the government's concerns. German officers in their impeccable uniforms no longer strutted on the streets, exuding confidence and superiority. The hospitals overflowed with wounded soldiers from the front as the Thousand-Year Reich lost its invincibility.

Antanas hesitated at the door of the mayor's office. To reveal that Vytas was with Algis Lanskis in Berlin would make him a traitor. If the Nazis found and killed his father, he could never forgive himself. But perhaps his father already left Lanskis and acquired passage to a safer place. So what harm would it be to tell Heinz about his destination in Berlin?

The permission to go to France was vital to saving the entire family. Antanas approached Mayor Heinz. "Sir, the information you requested is here." He put down a sheet of paper with Lanskis's name and address.

"Eimontas, I didn't expect you to give up your father so readily. I'm glad your loyalty is to the Reich. I'll telegraph Berlin. As soon as they reach Lanskis and confirm your father arrived there, you'll receive your papers."

The documents for France were on Antanas's desk the next day. Seeing them made him shudder. He went next door to the mayor's office. "Thank you for the visas and passports. Did you find my father?"

"No, he had already gone on. With the allied bombing of Berlin, the city is in chaos, but we will find him. You did complete your part of the bargain, and as you know, we are honorable men who keep our word."

Although Lithuanians celebrated their name days, May 23 was Dalia's birthday and favorite day of the year. The start of her life was in spring, and this connection brought her happiness. Astrid reached out of her self-absorption long enough to acquiesce to Dalia's ephemeral personality by celebrating Dalia's private feast. Katerina brought perfume, Paulina baked a cake, and Astrid bought pink roses. Monica sent a bouquet of daisies.

Antanas, bringing champagne, interrupted their celebration with news, "I spoke with Mayor Heinz and learned that Father has escaped Berlin. We will be leaving soon for France and must take everything of value with us."

Dalia greeted the news with a look of horror. "No, I'm not leaving. I don't feel well now, and I would never leave home in my condition."

"What ails you?" asked Katerina with concern. Dalia had never had physical health issues.

"It's normal not to feel well in my condition. I've prayed to Father Vebra, my personal saint, and I'm expecting a child."

Katerina immediately thought of Dalia becoming psychotic after her recent marked improvement. "What makes you think you are having a baby?" Katerina asked with raised eyebrows as she looked at her gray-haired sister-in-law.

"Look," Dalia said. Stretching her loose-fitting dress over her stomach revealed a huge protuberance. Antanas left the room in disgust, cursing this hindrance to his plans. He believed mental illness to be the result of a lack of discipline or a weak mind.

Katerina examined the growth and, from its solid nature, suspected a tumor. "Dalia, we must take you to the hospital to examine your condition."

"This is not a condition. It is a blessing, a miracle."

"It is for the good of your baby. You need medical care," Katerina insisted.

A biopsy confirmed an aggressive cancer of the omentum that had proliferated throughout the abdominal cavity. The deep invasion precluded surgery and portended a hopeless condition. After three days at the hospital, Katerina said Dalia should be brought home since she did not have much longer to live. "The hospital is overcrowded with moans and screams of wounded soldiers. Dying at home would be more humane."

Dalia, under sedation, slept as the family confronted this complication at home. "We can't wait for Dalia," Antanas declared in panic as he confronted Katerina and Astrid. "My position in France is to be filled at once. Leave Dalia to be cared for by Paulina. Mother, get Adam and Astrid and be ready to leave. This is our only opportunity to save ourselves."

Katerina hugged herself and, with tear-filled eyes, said, "We can't leave Dalia in this condition. She is family and helpless. We are Catholics and have a moral responsibility."

"If you insist on staying at this death watch, it is your decision. But I must go now, or the opportunity will evaporate."

"Antanas, if your position requires you to report at once, go. We can depart in a few weeks. Dalia has so little time left. She cannot be deserted to die alone. We'll join you later."

Dalia smiled as she woke from her drug-induced sleep. "So will it be a boy or a girl?" she whispered to Katerina. To Astrid, she gave a piercing gaze and said very clearly, "Remember, the love of a child cancels many sorrows." Astrid trembled to hear this personal prophecy, and thoughts of Adam flooded her consciousness.

Katerina gave Astrid morphine and instructions, "I must return to the hospital, which resembles an abattoir with the wounded. You know enough medicine to care for her. Just keep her out of pain. Paulina will help you with bathing and changing linens. Give Dalia soft food and liquids but don't force them. Starvation and dehydration at this stage lead to the most painless death. It's best just to keep her mouth moist."

Astrid never left Dalia's side and experienced intimacy with the process of dying. In the last few weeks, her goal was to give Dalia a good death, a peaceful release from this world, to compensate her for all the pain and hardships of her unfulfilled life. By comparing her own troubled life with that of her aunt's, Astrid realized she was not the only tragic victim.

A week later, a letter came from Antanas through the secure diplomatic post:

Dearest Mother,

Please leave as soon as you can. Do not sacrifice the whole family for the last few days of Aunt Dalia's life. She is probably in a coma and does not know she is placing you in great danger.

I am in Paris, and the city is in chaos. The Germans are losing in Europe, so my work in France will probably only be temporary. I plan on keeping a low profile so I may integrate better into whatever the future holds.

I made arrangements to send a truck to the Eimontas mansion. Please fill it with all our best belongings—silver, paintings, and Oriental rugs. Mother, you should take your medical instruments since there will always be a need for physicians. Darius, my driver, will take you to the German border where a man I send, Pierre, will drive you into France. I will meet you. It will be rough living at the beginning, but we will survive.

Antanas

For weeks, Dalia existed in a drugged sleep, a cloudy haze, intercepted at intervals by lethargic awareness. One morning, Astrid woke to see Dalia's white face, terror in her wide-open eyes compounded by increasing sounds of fury from a body resisting death. Astrid had not expected the agony of the last fight with no hope of victory. She gave more drops of morphine and held Dalia's hand so tightly they seemed fused. Dalia choked, gasped for air as a drowning person thrashing about for three hours, and after a spasm, quietly cooled.

Astrid observed that neither the lifetime of religious faith, nor the numbing of psychosis, nor the palliative comfort of morphine earned Dalia a peaceful and painless death. The finality of death signified the most difficult part: the void of nothingness.

Once all was still, Astrid lay down beside the body of Dalia and tried to pray, "Holy Mary, Mother of God, pray . . ." She gazed at the crucifix on the wall. How can God make a helpless innocent suffer like this? God had shown no mercy in releasing Dalia from this sadistic, painful creation called life.

Astrid pondered that evil was born with their monotheistic God. When there were many gods, evil could always be explained by Zeus off chasing women. Even the Manichaean heresy supposed two gods—a good and a bad—to explain the existence of evil. Why these last three hours of torture? However, with one all-powerful God, evil must come from him. Astrid closed Dalia's eyes and knew there were no answers.

After dressing Dalia in her favorite blue dress and combing her hair, Paulina called the undertaker. Surrounded by death, Paulina now knew more people in the other world than she did here on earth. She felt like a balloon whose strings tethering her to this earth were a web of all the people she loved. With death, the strings to Casimir, Jan, and Anna were cut. The strongest remaining ties were to Adam and Pranas. Did Stefan survive the bombings in Dresden? Is Valeria alive in Berlin? If the remaining connecting strings were cut, nothing would moor her to this earth, and she would die, a helium balloon rising to the skies. The lightness of the other world was calling her.

A wartime funeral marked Dalia's exit. Astrid, Katerina, Paulina, and Monica holding Adam stood by the open gravesite as Dalia was lowered into the ground amid incense and prayers. Astrid remembered Dalia's words about the love of a child and looked at Adam sweetly sleeping. Astrid went up to Monica and took Adam into her arms. Adam started wailing and straining to go back to Monica. Astrid quickly returned him to familiar arms.

Back at work in the hospital, Katerina ran from crisis to crisis. Not enough personnel and equipment sufficed to stifle the gore and mutilation of war. She entered a room where a soldier, only a boy, lay on the makeshift operating table with his stomach contents exposed. She gave him morphine, examined his stomach, and covered his wound with a sheet. Nothing could be done to save him.

He opened his eyes. "Doctor, you look like an angel. I know my end is near. I'm dreaming of our farm in Bavaria and my mother, father, and little sister Heidi. I even see my good dog Schnitzel wagging his tail. I can smell the lilacs and taste my mother's strudel."

Katerina was heading for the door when his speech stopped her. His simple affirmation of normal life banished for a moment the gross pornography of war. She returned to his bedside to see his aquamarine eyes alight in his handsome young face, white and waxy due to blood loss. "What is your name?" she asked, stroking his blond hair.

"Adolf Neumann, lieutenant, Fourth Battalion. Could you please write a letter home for me?" he pleaded.

Katerina observed the mad pace of activity around her. She wanted to refuse, but the simple request from a boy who could have been her son forced her to take her pen and a slip of paper and answer, "Of course."

A new patient with a severe head wound exposing brain matter occupied the adjacent bed. His low moans accompanied Adolf's dictation: "Mother, so far, I have survived and am still alive, but I do not know if I will return. I dream of your soft hands stroking my cheek and eating your strudel with milk sitting outside under the apple tree, watching Heidi play with our dog, Schnitzel. I did not know then that I was in paradise. Do not worry about me. Duty demands sacrifice. I send my love to you all. Adolf."

Katerina folded the paper, put it in her pocket, kissed his forehead, and closed his sightless eyes. She entered a stall in the bathroom, sat down, and sobbed.

In early June, after settling in a rented room in Paris, Antanas traveled to his assigned food depot in the outskirts of the city with documents in hand. Locating the facility, he stepped back in horror as he saw swastika flags being pulled down from the sides of the warehouse, folded, and placed in crates. A guard, in German uniform, short in stature, and with enormous ears, halted him at the door and studied his papers.

"What's going on?" asked Antanas in fluent French. "This is treasonous. I've been assigned to work in this facility."

"You are here just in time for the closing of this depot. The Americans have landed in France, in Cherbourg," the guard answered in German.

"So an upstanding bilingual German soldier may lose his position," Antanas said in German, hoping for more information.

"I just want to go home after four years here. I've been lucky not to be deployed to the murderous Eastern front. Now even France is dangerous after the Normandy invasion."

"Who is in charge here?" asked Antanas.

"Commander Werner is in charge, but he is not here. He left for his office in Paris on the Rue de Maupassant."

"I must find him for further instructions," Antanas said as he left and caught a cab back to Paris. He raced to his rooms and burned all evidence of his identity in the ancient fireplace. He organized his belongings, opened the top of his shirt, bought a beret, and went out into the night passing as yet another anonymous Frenchman in Paris.

Desperate for news of his father, Antanas had the address of a Lithuanian diplomat, Stasys Velikis, and found him near Montmartre. A gray-haired woman opened the door. "I'm Antanas Eimontas, and I am looking for my father."

"Welcome, come in. My husband is not in at present, and we don't know the whereabouts of your father. All we know is that the Gestapo searched the Lanskis apartment in Berlin, but Eimontas had already left."

Antanas sighed in relief and was offered a small glass of red wine. "Thank God he managed to escape."

"Yes, he was lucky. Luck was not with Algis and Rita Lanskis, however. Even after extreme torture, they would not reveal Eimontas's destination, so they shot them both." Mrs. Velikis started to cry.

Antanas tried to comfort the woman and felt some weight of guilt. He thanked the woman but left suddenly. He did not want her to see his smile at the joy of his father's escape.

The next morning, he packed a valise with his belongings, including a tuxedo. "Best always to be optimistic and ready for all events" was his motto. He traveled from Paris to Cherbourg, where he rented a room in the home of a French war widow.

Groups of American soldiers filled the streets and cafes. He passed one group of soldiers trying to order food in a local outdoor cafe. The comments grew louder and angrier. Antanas approached and said, "Problem? Perhaps

I help." His English was rusty. The confused look of the young waitress indicated a common problem in translation.

The American looked up at Antanas. "Well, maybe you can. This French gal shore is pretty but so stupid she doesn't even know how to get me a hot dog," complained a husky man with a crew cut. Antanas spoke to the girl in French, and a plate of sausages appeared. He would not only survive; he would thrive. Antanas started flirting with the pretty waitress, who welcomed his advances. He did small jobs for the Americans, who, unused to the exchange rate, overpaid him by ridiculous amounts.

Once the Americans occupied Paris, Antanas took the train there every chance he had and, in his tuxedo, slithered into receptions at the Ritz. His fluent French let him mingle with ease. He later wrote a letter home:

Dear Mother,
Father had left Berlin safely. You must immediately find a way to escape. German collapse is on the horizon, and the Soviets will crush Lithuania. My contacts with the American army in Cherbourg have provided me with identity papers. When they liberate France, they will need a man with my talents.
While in Paris to find information about Father, I met the daughter of the Marquis du Mille. Genevieve is beautiful, rich, and charming and is most suitable to be my wife. She is not Lithuanian, but she has aristocratic blood. We are engaged and will be getting married. Her parents approve since it is her first happiness after her fiancé died in the war. I know this is rapid, but war has increased the pace of life. I am waiting for your arrival.
Antanas

The truck assigned for the Eimontas evacuation arrived. Katerina, on her way to work, said, "Astrid, start packing everything of value." Astrid sorted out items to be taken in rooms filled with paper and boxes. She packed the silver and some clothing, putting aside the crystal and china as too fragile to make the journey. She wanted to leave the portrait of Jadvyga behind, but considering how Antanas valued it, she wrapped the huge portrait in blankets to be stowed in the truck. She needed Paulina's help with rolling up the Persian carpets but couldn't find her anywhere. Paulina had always been in the background, and Astrid had never noticed her except in her absence. Astrid concluded she must have gone home to pick up Adam.

Once she packed, the mild weather encouraged Astrid to go out for a walk. Her strolling took her across the river, and curiosity about where Paulina lived and cared for Adam became a destination. She arrived at the Polish sector and saw the poverty. Hungry, abandoned dogs and cats and garbage were interspersed with bombed buildings. The dirt everywhere explained why Paulina cleaned so much, to scrub out her background.

She asked a woman holding two infants for the Kataski residence. A dirty child of about seven smiled, held his hand out, and said he could take her. She reached into her purse and gave him a few coins. He led her to a building, and she followed him up flights of stairs, wondering how Paulina's aching knees could make this painful climb. The boy knocked on the door.

"Who is it?" asked a voice Astrid recognized as Monica's.

"Company!" yelled the boy as Astrid reached the threshold.

Monica stood at the open door, her face scrunched up in horror. "Why, Miss Eimontas, we were not expecting you."

"I came to find Paulina."

"She is at a Mass for your Aunt Dalia."

"Oh, yes, of course, I forgot." Astrid looked around the spotless room and said, "I have always wanted to see how Paulina lives."

"I'm afraid I'm not prepared to show the apartment," mumbled Monica.

"Please, don't be embarrassed. I want to see where Adam plays." After looking around, Astrid opened the door to an adjoining room.

"No, don't!" screamed Monica.

There stood Pranas. The missing earlobe identified him as the devil. The beard and weight loss did not disguise him enough to erase him from Astrid's nightmares. He was dressed in black, baggy clothes. His hands with their long fingernails recalled her torture. His face was transfixed with disbelief at the sight of Astrid.

"You!" She stopped breathing. "Alive!" She struggled to remain upright, her eyes filled with horror at the sight of all her nightmares. Then she saw Adam sitting in a highchair in the corner. She ran to Adam and grabbed him. Throwing open the door, clutching the little boy, she raced down the stairs.

Pranas stood speechless, frozen by the power of the unexpected event.

Monica ran after her, crying, "Please, Miss Eimontas, you cannot take your little brother from me. I love him more than life itself. What have I done to so disturb you? I'll do anything in reparation. Just let me have him. He is almost my son."

"Your son?" Astrid stopped, turned on the stairs, and shouted with such vehemence that her spittle was evident in the air. "You are living with the devil incarnate, and he has dominion over my son." Shaking with furious rage and fired by violent anger, she screamed, "Yes, my son!" as she exited the building.

Astrid, blinded by tears, walked home, holding the screaming boy, trying to process the outrage of her rapist with her son.

Monica went after Astrid and Adam down the stairs, but because of her breathless slowness, they were gone by the time she reached the bottom. She collapsed in the foyer with a shriek of pain as Pranas ran after her. With difficulty, he lifted Monica to her feet and led her upstairs while trying to devise an explanation.

"What did she mean by saying Adam was her son? Why was her reaction to you so violent?" Monica demanded to know. "What happened between the two of you?"

Pranas quickly devised an answer, "We slept together once, and I left her."

"You slept with Astrid? And she became pregnant? I thought Adam was Doctor Katerina's child," Monica said, processing the information.

"They just made that up to protect the crazy whore. She must have become pregnant by one of the many men she slept with." Pranas wove the lies into the most believable story he could concoct.

"Why was she so angry?" Monica wanted to know.

"She could not get used to being dumped by someone so inferior."

The explanation was not satisfactory to Monica, but she did not want to question and anger Pranas, so vital to her life. Her crying ceased, and her pain eased with the sudden goal that Pranas would father her future child, a child to replace Adam in her heart.

Crying loudly, carrying the struggling little boy, Astrid crossed the river and carried Adam back home.

Paulina stood with mouth open as Astrid walked in the door, holding the squirming toddler. "What happened?" she asked, approaching Astrid to take the boy.

Astrid jumped back as if from a fire, screaming, "Get out of this house, never to return! Traitor!"

Paulina trembled at the outburst. "Why?"

"You've been harboring a criminal in your house. I will report him to the firing squad. If I had a knife, I would have carved up that devil myself. You knew of my torture and let him be with my son! I'll have my revenge, but now I can't bear to be in the same room with you. Get out!"

Astrid went to her room and lay down on her bed with frightened, screaming Adam. Their torrent of tears mingled.

Paulina, in shock, ambled out of the Eimontas mansion and staggered home. She had thought her subterfuge was safe, but now her exposure would change her life. After a stop at the Gates of Dawn, Paulina arrived home and confronted Monica and Pranas. "You must leave immediately," Paulina said. "Astrid, bent on revenge, will report you. You will be arrested and shot."

"Report him for what?" Monica asked. "She's mentally unstable, calling Adam her son."

"She will report Pranas as a deserter of the Red Army to the authorities."

Monica scrunched up her face and said, "But that is not what Astrid was upset about. She was angry about Adam being with Pranas. Why?"

"Not wanting her son to be in the company of a deserter. It could be dangerous. Don't listen to her."

Pranas later whispered to Paulina, "Could Adam really be my son?"

"Of course not. She's crazy." Paulina's secret was eternal.

Monica lost Adam and now also faced the loss of Pranas, her friend and lover who was in danger of execution as a deserter. She came up with a plan. "I know what we must do, Pranas. I still have the documents Stefan left behind when he left me." She took Stefan's passport and examined the picture.

"He's your brother, and there are enough similarities that you could pass for him. We must return to Memel and get my father's help. It's the only way you will survive."

"What about Mother?" Pranas said, but thoughts of his own survival predominated. Monica and Pranas got ready to leave for Memel in the dead of night. "Mother, as soon as we get settled, we'll send for you," Pranas explained.

Paulina, crushed by the desertion of her family, loss of employment, and thoughts of punishment, said, "Don't worry. I'll survive here in Vilnius. Leave, children. I will pray that you have a safe journey, find a home, and have a little one of your own someday. The war cannot last forever. You will return to me someday, and we will be happy."

Monica wrapped Pranas's head with bandages and dressed him in a discarded German uniform. They took a train to Memel, never to return.

CHAPTER 25
JULY 1944

Vilnius writhed in agony, blood and death, destruction and occupation. War now existed not only in concept or conversation but also in reality—in shooting and bombing. Soviet soldiers entered the streets victorious, in tanks, trucks, or on foot. The blue skies on this July morning formed a bubble shielding the eyes of God from the horror below and acting as a sound barrier to pleas and prayers for help from God. Citizens privileged with accurate war information evacuated in droves. Roads leading out of the city to the west were filled with trucks, cars, horses, wagons, and people walking, carrying children, pets and goods.

The hospital could not keep up with the bombing victims brought in: chaos reigned in spite of staff desperately trying to triage patients. Jonas with his band of partisans arrived in Vilnius. Entering the hospital, in the hectic atmosphere, he found out from a nurse that Katerina was in the operating room. Amid sounds of explosions, he startled Katerina, suturing an injured child. He tapped on her shoulder. "Darling, it's time to go."

"I can't leave. There are critical patients here." She looked down on the child whose arm was almost severed from a flying metal cut. "Let me just finish suturing this wound." The lights in the hospital went out as a bomb exploded nearby. "My god, we'll all be killed," Katerina said as she saw a wall implode.

"You must leave. You can't save anyone under these conditions," Jonas pleaded as he shoved Katerina aside from the collapsing wall.

"God forgive me," Katerina said as she looked back at the child in the smoke-filled room.

"Come, follow me," said Jonas as he steered her out through the gurney-filled corridors into the street. The sunset, filtered by a haze of bitter smoke, provided a blood-red backdrop to the confusion and terror. Jonas took her hand, and they raced down the streets to Katerina's favorite church, St. Anne's. They entered the dim, empty church, lit only by flickering candles.

"Katerina, I must say goodbye. I know you're leaving with your family to France to be with Vytas, but I must tell you what is in my heart." They sat in an empty pew in the back as Katerina gazed at the icon of St. Anne smiling from above. Jonas continued, "I'm leaving the city tomorrow night to live in the forests as a partisan. We have arms hidden in an underground bunker as well as supplies of food and medicine. It should last us until we are liberated." Jonas stood up and went to light a candle and leave but returned to Katerina as if drawn by a magnet.

With Jonas by her side, Katerina whispered, "You are optimistic. It may be a long time before we're free again. The Soviets are allies of the West."

"International law can't allow the permanent occupation of a sovereign country," said Jonas with the full force of unshakable belief. He envisioned a future, a free country, and the woman beside him, his only love, living in peace and happiness. He longed to enshrine that moment for all eternity. After contemplation in silence, Jonas turned to Katerina, who was kneeling in the pew and trembled as he whispered, "I have no right to ask, but I beg you to join me as a partisan for the sake of our love and our country. Your sacrifice would make a great difference to our cause."

"You want me to come with you? To be a partisan? To fight? To shoot? To kill? To live underground on handouts from sympathetic farmers?" asked Katerina as she sat upright with a straightened spine.

"You've shown bravery and courage in your profession and have seen death every day. For you being a partisan and providing us with your medical care wouldn't be an insurmountable challenge. You would be doing it for the freedom of Lithuania. Also, you must acknowledge our love, which is strong enough to overcome the impossible."

Tears formed in Katerina's eyes as the pulse in her ear pounded yes, yes, yes. Her entire being pulsed in agreement. Her heart and mind did not have a single objection. A vision of herself helping wounded partisans, living in bunkers, and running from the Soviets played out as a film before her eyes. Jonas appealed to the core of her essence, the desire for great sacrifice for a noble and just cause. Even if she died, it would not have been in vain. She would have given her life for her country.

"If you decide to come with me, meet me here. I will come by here every night to look for you." Jonas stood up and placed his hand on her shoulder and paused, "What am I saying? What am I asking of you?" He shook his head. "This is wrong. It's just my insane dream to have you join me."

Katerina made the sign of the cross and stood up. Jonas took her in his arms and kissed her. Observing the huge gold crucifix and the stained-glass windows and smelling the aroma of incense, she pushed him away, horrified at the venue of their passion.

He led her outside into the secluded grassy courtyard, where their desire for union overwhelmed all their scruples. To the destructive sounds of bombs exploding, no one else on earth existed. His actions seemed the most natural in the world as he gently laid her on the grass, unbuttoned her bodice, and lifted her skirt. Her nipples hardened with the unexpected pleasure of his tongue. His hands slid down on her hips to release her body from its bindings and to reveal the mystery of womanhood. Her hands and body welcomed him in ecstatic rhythm.

Katerina returned home and raced up the stairs to her room. She combed her hair, observed her pink blushing skin, and changed from her grass-stained dress. Removing the yellow linen dress, she examined the embroidered daisies on the bodice. She smiled, remembering in her youth tearing out daisy petals, chanting, "He loves me" and "He loves me not" to solve the puzzle of a youthful beau. She did not need to ask this question now. Their love was not a puzzle but the answer to the meaning of life. Her heart raced with happiness as she basked in the afterglow.

Quickly her feelings shifted into shame. The problem was not one of love but of duty. Should she stay in Lithuania to fight for freedom and be with the man she loved? How could she desert her family and break her sacred vows to God? What takes priority? God and family or Lithuania and love?

Katerina entered the kitchen to see Astrid feeding Adam. "It's wonderful to see you with Adam, but where is Paulina?" Katerina asked. "Is she getting us ready to leave?"

Astrid looked up at Katerina with a face screwed up in hatred and screamed, "She is never to come near us or our house again!"

A nearby bomb exploded, shaking the walls of the mansion and rattling the dishes in the kitchen. The bombing and Astrid's outburst frightened Adam, who started crying. "Thank God they missed us," Katerina said as the bombing had an intermission. "What did Paulina do?" Katerina asked, confused at Astrid's pronouncement.

Astrid, her face filled with venom, said, "That witch harbored the man who raped and tortured me and destroyed my life. She even had the gall to keep Adam in the same place with him. If I could, I would kill them both. If the Soviets were not on our doorstep, I would report him. The Nazis would execute a communist NKVD criminal by firing squad."

Stunned by the news of the betrayal, Katerina walked across the room and hugged Astrid and Adam, both now crying uncontrollably. After a deep breath, she said, "Thank God you're both safe. I never would have expected such treachery from Paulina. She practically raised you. What would cause her to harbor such evil?"

"Since the rapist is living in her home, he must be a close friend or family member, which means she has known the criminal all along. How could she be so two-faced, pretending to care for our family?" Astrid demanded.

Katerina did not have an answer. She sat down at the realization of her ultimate deception. Paulina's betrayal—despicable and unforgivable—was no worse a betrayal than her desire to desert Vytas, Astrid, Antanas, and Adam. Her desire for heroics and sex with her lover would be her true motivation. The eyes of God would see the truth. Calling it love and patriotism was only self-deception. She must follow her principles and conscience and leave this country with her family.

Katerina looked out the window to see billows of smoke from the bombing airplanes flying overhead and woke from her confusion to say, "We must hurry and leave. The next bomb may be on target. The Germans are retreating, and the Soviets are storming the city limits." Katerina packed her boxes of medical instruments, the essence of her profession.

The truck, an old and rusty German military vehicle, its bed covered by a large canvas roof, waited with Darius, the driver assigned by Antanas. The ensuing hours were hectic in packing and loading with the help of the driver. They worked trying to ignore the wails of Adam, and Katerina worked feverishly to blot out her pain at leaving her love and her country.

"Let's go," said Darius. "I have my own family to help later. You're taking almost everything, and the truck is full. If you don't leave immediately, I'm leaving. You'll have to find another driver."

Katerina walked through the empty Eimontas mansion, envisioning her arrival here as a young woman, a stranger, when it seemed so luxurious, so glamorous; she had peeked into an imagined world where she did not belong. Later, as the Baroness Eimontas, she remembered her reception for Count Doban and his young redheaded wife, Gretchen. She thought of her guests, Zygmond and Elena Dielka, God rest their souls, and poor Bishop Venclovas exiled to Siberia. Did that lively, sophisticated dinner party still exist in some happy cloud?

She took one last look through the empty rooms, scarred by years of war and hardship, before she went out the front door. She did not lock the door; the Soviets would destroy whatever remained.

With Adam in her lap, Astrid sat in the cab with the driver, leaving Katerina very little room, so she went in the back and sat on top of the carpets. The huge canvas roof had an open back flap, so Katerina, as they started to wind down the streets, saw the confusion, calamity, and chaos in Vilnius.

People were throwing their possessions out of windows, putting on as much clothing as possible. She saw one heavy woman put on two fur coats on this warm July day. Some people stood in the streets, trying to sell items for cash for their journey. "Silver, silver at a bargain price!" an old man yelled. "My jewelry, my wedding rings, only one hundred reichsmarks!" a young woman offered. A long line queued up at the bank as the shelling drew near. Most people did not have cars or trucks and hitched any available wagon to horses rearing in response to the noise. Children screamed at the pain of being separated from family pets left behind.

Katerina's eyes photographed the widespread terror and suffering as their truck wound its way out of the city onto a road clogged with escaping people. Looking back at the city, she saw firebombs, smoke, and buildings imploding. "My god, my heart, my Vilnius."

Astrid, holding the sleeping little boy, still seethed with the apparition of Pranas before her eyes. The scenes in Prienai were as vivid as life. May the one-eared devil be cursed forever. How could this beautiful blond, blue-eyed child be the result of such a brutal crime? How could she look at him and not remember his origin? Yet he was innocent of his creation. He was here by the will of God. She stroked his silky hair and kissed his head.

The road became clogged with increasing traffic coming in from side roads until the exodus ground to a halt. Katerina came to the cab with water, bread, and cheese. As they were eating, Katerina said, "The driver has been complaining about the time this trip is taking. Darius is worried about his own family." Katerina spotted a group of people walking behind them on the road. "I have an idea. Tell Darius to go back to his family, and I will find a new driver." Katerina walked among the people and found a man carrying a bundle. "Do you know how to drive?"

"I drove a car in Kaunas and know how to fix motors too," answered the slim, pale man with a pug nose. "If you want me to drive, I'll be glad to accept, but there is a problem—I must take my mother with me," he said, pointing to a wrinkled, bent-over woman who also had the same pug nose.

Katerina smiled at the family resemblance as she said, "Of course, your mother can sit in the back with me. What is your name?"

"Kestutis," he answered as he jumped into the driver's seat. Kestutis inched along in the truck, surrounded by a morass of humanity. In the next hour, a woman ran up to the truck with a small girl, "Please, can you take us in the truck? My little girl is too tired to walk, and I am too weak to carry her, please, please." Katerina looked at the eyes of the pleading woman and could not say no. "Yes, get on board."

The problem escalated as those on foot realized that the truck owners were taking people. A little boy holding a kitten was next on board. His mother pleaded for him to ride with Katerina even if there was no room for her. There really was no room for either of them, so Katerina looked around and saw the large portrait of Jadvyga, a thorn in her skin for so many years, and said to Kestutis, "Cut the bindings and throw out this portrait." The portrait, covered in blankets, was cast to the side of the road.

With traffic at almost a standstill, many of those on foot surveyed the truck and cursed, "Look, the bourgeoisie, they are riding, even taking their pots and pans while the tired, sick, and old must walk." Katerina ignored them.

After a few hours with little progress, the traffic temporarily speeded up as Kestutis maneuvered between the human throngs but then stopped. An ambulance from the Red Cross hospital in Vilnius passed them on the grass by the side of the road and motioned for them to stop. The ambulance driver got out and said, "I'm going back to get my children. I have some wounded from the completely demolished Red Cross hospital in Vilnius. Could you take the wounded and transport them further?"

Katerina wanted to refuse but entered the ambulance where she saw three people injured in the bombing of the hospital. Katerina recognized two orderlies and her friend, Joseph Rudis, whose leg, severely wounded, was wrapped in bloody bandages. "Where would we take them?" Katerina surveyed the farms surrounding them.

"There is a small local hospital at Druskininkai, about five miles from here." The ambulance driver started sketching a map on a piece of paper.

"Joseph, it's Katerina. I have a truck, and we will get you to a hospital." The three patients were transferred to their truck with the help of the two drivers. In order to make room, they threw all the portraits and oriental rugs overboard. They continued on to the small town with a hospital. Katerina, the hospital doctor, and a nurse spent the night amputating Joseph's leg and stabilizing the other two patients.

Joseph gazed at Katerina. "You have always been my angel. Thank you. But be on your way. We will survive. Perhaps we shall meet again."

Katerina looked into his pain-filled eyes and shuddered at the thought of Joseph, a perfect young man, now condemned to being an amputee. He had saved Vytas with his information, but she was not able to save his leg.

Returning to the truck, Astrid with Adam and Katerina found the canvas-topped truck bed so packed with people they could not find room for themselves, so all three squeezed in the front with the driver. They squeezed their remaining possessions, the silver and Katerina's instruments, at their feet in the cab.

They again entered the stream of humanity escaping. People clung to the sides of the truck. Adam became restless and needed more room. Katerina said, "Throw out the silver." Looking at the discarded Eimontas silver by the side of the road, Katerina suffered her first pang of sorrow. She was leaving behind everything that was most valuable, the portraits, rugs, and now the silver. But she still had her instruments, symbols of her profession, an extension of herself.

After a few miles, Katerina saw a young woman clutching an infant, trying to grab onto the truck with desperation. Katerina yelled, "Stop!" She got out of the cab, intending to make more room for the new passengers, took the bag of medical instruments, and threw them on the side of the road into the gully.

But at that moment, losing her most valuable possession, she knew in her soul that everything she loved belonged in this ancient land. She could not leave the most vital essence of herself and flee to save herself since, in leaving, she would be forever lost. She ran into the gully and retrieved the instrument bag.

Returning to the cab of the truck, clutching the heavy bag, she said to Astrid, "You go ahead. Antanas's friend is waiting for you by the German border and will take you to Antanas. In France, Antanas will take good care of you. Try to find Father. As for me, I must return." She kissed Adam and Astrid, who tore at her sleeve in trying to restrain her. She motioned to the woman with the infant to enter the cab and started to walk back to Vilnius, lugging the heavy bag, tears streaming down her cheeks.

Two days later, she reached the deserted mansion in the bombed city. The pornography of destruction inflamed her senses, and she could not but ask why. Whose desire did this result satisfy? What good could possibly come of this? Did the lessons of the past never touch anyone's mind?

There was some damage to the roof, but the house stood. Entering, she found the water working and, with a sliver of soap, enjoyed a wash for the first time in almost a week. She slept on some rags left behind.

The next morning, she set out for St. Anne's church. Jonas was not there. She knelt and prayed, "God, this is so wrong according to all our church laws and yet so natural and so right in my heart. Would not the greater sin be not to be true to myself? Please, God, give me a sign that this is my fate."

As Katerina knelt and covered her face with her hands, she felt a hand on the shoulder. Looking up, she saw Jonas, who said, "I knew in my heart you would come, but the last six nights, I was disappointed. My prayers are answered. Here you are. I know what a terrible decision it is for you to come to me. We must be on our way. I prepared some clothing and equipment for you. I will teach you basic shooting and self-defense."

"I managed to save some instruments. I think I'll be more useful with medical care rather than shooting," said Katerina, breaking into her first smile in many days.

Astrid, shocked at Katerina's defection, could not comprehend her action. She always knew her mother obeyed a strict moral code. Katerina must have decided her patients needed her more than her family. But what could be more important than the blood ties of family?

Riding through farmland, Astrid now was alone with Adam, completely in charge of this toddler she barely acknowledged. He put his little hands to her face, and when she lifted him up, he gave her little wet kisses. He smelled of youth and freshness.

The new passenger, a young woman, introduced herself as Milda and her five-month-old infant as Gabriel. "How old is your handsome son?" she inquired.

Astrid, hearing the term "your son," almost replied, "He is my brother," but hesitated. Circumstances had changed. She thought of all the people she knew and loved who were no longer with her. No grandparents, mother, father, or aunt. What if the planned reunion with Antanas never occurred? She would have no one.

God, the destruction of war and the uncertainty of the future were the only facts she could count on. But Adam was not only the seed of the devil but the flesh of her flesh. They were now a family of two.

Astrid answered, "Yes, this is my son, Adam," as she kissed the top of his head and rocked him to sleep.

Milda asked, "Is his father going to meet you at the border?"

"No," replied Astrid. "He was killed in the war."

Paulina, alone, began to pick up debris after the hasty departure of Monica and Pranas. Looking out the window, she saw two German soldiers running as they carried a bleeding comrade. Further down the street, she spotted some bodies. Her helplessness at stopping the carnage irritated her, so she reacted as she always did. She took a brush, soap, and water and started scrubbing the floors of her small apartment. After a thorough dusting and polishing of the furniture, she became aware of her throbbing knees. With nothing more to occupy her time, she lay down on her bed. Only then did her thoughts attack her.

Anna, her little Anna, freezing in some Siberian icy hell. No one to help her or care for her . . . or perhaps the angels had already claimed her. Casimir, her life companion . . . how she suffered without gentleness and understanding. But he was hers, the father of her children. Now he was rotting in some mass grave. Valeria, her successful beauty. With Germany losing, there is no way she could return to help. Stefan, her son . . . betraying his wife and mother to be with a married woman. May God forgive him. May he survive the war in Germany and have time to repent his sins. Pranas, how could that be a child of hers? May the devil be exorcised from his soul and his sins forgiven. And then her greatest heartbreak and her biggest joy, Jan. His suffering and death still gave her nightmares, but she knew he was in heaven, a saint. Only praying to Jan gave her some relief from the miasma of tragedy drowning her.

Paulina heaved herself up from the bed and realized that, after her cleaning frenzy and the draining thoughts of her family, she had fallen asleep with her clothes on.

It was now morning. She washed, dressed, and drank tea with a slice of bread and lard. The sounds of gunshots and an occasional explosion sank into her consciousness. Out of long habit, she began to prepare for work when the horrific scene with Astrid invaded her consciousness. She had been thrown out, cursed. She had become a pariah to the people for whom she had devoted half her life.

As she walked down the stairs, unusual silence signaled that most of her neighbors were gone. The city seemed drained of life. She walked out the front door to confront a dark-brown bloodstain that seeped into the cement stoop. Several dead bodies littered the streets, and only the bombed-out skeleton of a neighboring house remained standing. The interior rooms with their decorations were hideously exposed, all privacy blasted away. She walked toward the bridge at the center of town and to the only consolation left to tie her to this existence, the shrine of the Madonna of Vilnius.

To her amazement, the arch at the end of the Gates of Dawn was intact. In the morning sunlight, the golden apparel of the Queen of Heaven blazed with divine fury. Paulina, the only person on this street, fell to her knees. "Mother of God, have mercy on Vilnius and all her people. Deliver us from evil and repression. Give us our freedom."

In forty-six years, her prayer was answered.

THE END